Kasey Michaels

THE ILLUSIONS OF LOVE

POC

New York   London   Toronto   Sydney   Tokyo   Singapore

This book is a work of fiction. Names, characters, places and incidents are products of the author's imagination or are used fictitiously. Any resemblance to actual events or locales or persons, living or dead, is entirely coincidental.

An *Original* Publication of POCKET BOOKS

 A Pocket Star Book published by
POCKET BOOKS, a division of Simon & Schuster Inc.
1230 Avenue of the Americas, New York, NY 10020

ISBN: 0-671-79340-3

First Pocket Books printing July 1994

10 9 8 7 6 5 4 3 2 1

POCKET STAR BOOKS and colophon are registered trademarks of Simon & Schuster Inc.

Printed in the U.S.A.

To Nora Scheidler . . .
All it takes is a dream!

It is natural for man to indulge
in the illusions of hope.

Patrick Henry

PROLOGUE

HOPES
1814

An illusion which makes me happy is worth a verity which drags me to the ground.

Christoph Martin Wieland

> *What shall be the maiden's fate?*
> *Who shall be the maiden's mate?*
>
> Sir Walter Scott

Everything was overdone.

The towering evergreens lining the gravel drive were too tall, planted too close together, so that it was nearly impossible to see past them and onto the grounds of the smallish, yet definitely ostentatious holding. The massive front doors to Trowbridge Manor itself were twice as high as necessary and half again as wide. A pair of growling lions' heads marked the doors, heavy brass rings jammed through their flat noses.

Inside, it was necessary to negotiate a gargantuan hallway that sported a maze of randomly positioned huge, round tables holding colossal floral displays. Next came an assortment of brightly polished armor standing sentinel along the paneled walls. Lastly, the visitors passed beneath a gaudy gold and crystal chandelier nearly the size of Prinny's coronation coach, then made a sharp left and entered into the purple saloon.

The chamber dramatically lived up to its name, for it was indeed very, very *purple*. Each piece of furniture—and a

3

multitude of extremely large pieces crowded the cavernous room—had been upholstered in varying shades of that royal color. The velvet draperies that hung at each of the dozen or more floor-to-towering-ceiling windows were fashioned of heavy purple velvet. Even the carpets bore garish splashes of overblown purple roses.

And everywhere man-size vases and fluted marble plant stands and carved tables groaned under the weight of collections of amethyst lumps and china orchids and purple blown-glass monstrosities that defied description.

The Chinese wallpapers were rendered nearly invisible behind a plethora of garishly gilded frames adorned with clumps of purple-painted grapes and featuring mirrors or dark portraits of somebody's ancestors, the latter probably bought at auction expressly because the subjects of the paintings were all wearing purple. They had to be strangers, poor dead people that they were, for they definitely weren't representative of any illustrious, long-dead branches of the Trowbridge family tree. That was impossible, for it was doubtful that any Trowbridge born before 1750 even *knew* his sire.

Oh, yes. It was overdone. Laughably overdone, if not in the least funny.

Jessup—the Trowbridge butler who had ushered Curtis Muir, Marquess of Chevley, and his middle son, Lord Dante Muir, through the cluttered hallway and into the purple saloon—now invited the gentlemen to find themselves a seat, then announced that he was retiring to summon his mistress.

The marquess remained standing and looked to his son, who was avidly observing the room through a quizzing glass. "Dante? What are you about, posing like some insufferable prig? Whose is it—Johnny's? Never mind. Just get the damned thing out of your eye!"

Dante allowed the borrowed quizzing glass—for it did indeed belong to his brother and was only worn today as a lark—to fall to his chest, where it hung suspended from a black riband. "What am I about? Why, my good sire, I should have thought that was obvious. I'm searching for the

4

throne, of course. We have been ushered into a royal chamber, haven't we?"

"Don't be any more obnoxious than you can help, Dante. I don't like this any more than you do."

Dante raised one black brow mockingly, rather enjoying his father's discomfiture. "Really, Father? That's exceedingly odd. I should think it would become easier with repetition, this selling of your sons. It can only be hoped that my baby brother brings as high a price as did Tyler. But then, Ty is to be the marquess someday, while Johnny and I are only pockets-to-let courtesy milords. It's a pity you didn't have three daughters as well. I imagine they would have brought handsome amounts of blunt on the open market. I've heard that odiously wealthy coal merchants and fishmongers, as a class, are also hot to marry their sons to titles. Just think of it— you'd be fairly rolling in five-pound notes!"

The marquess collapsed his tall, thin, once athletic but now rather potbellied frame into a corner of one of the purple satin couches and wiped at his brow with a large white handkerchief, for the fireplace was blazing and all the dozen windows were closed. "Dante, for the love of all you hold holy, stifle yourself. The old witch will be swooping in here on her broom any minute, and I don't want you to be mouthing your usual sarcastic jokes when she alights."

"Why? Or are you laboring under the notion that she'd actually understand them?" Dante spread his hands, encompassing the chamber. "A woman who believes this horrible room is the height of fashion? It resembles nothing more than a bordello, Father. A very *inferior* bordello, with our dear hostess cast in the role of madam. But I promise I will do nothing to embarrass you."

The marquess shook his head. "She can't be an abbess, Dante. Remember? According to you, I'm already cast in the role of pimp."

"Again I stand corrected. A thousand apologies, Father." Dante bowed in his sire's direction, then carefully split the coattails of his buff morning coat and took up a straight-backed chair directly across from the older man. "Buying, selling. It still, I fear, seems all of a piece. One son of impeccable lineage and limited income in exchange for one granddaughter worth her weight in gold but with less pedigree than the least of our hunting dogs. Who's to say who is the pimp and who is the madam? Certainly not I."

"Considering the fact that it's not your head I'm bartering with, I should think that you have nothing to say in the business at all. If Johnny hadn't drunk half my cellars last night in fear of today's meeting, then passed out cold on the stairs, you wouldn't be here at all. Now be quiet, I think she's coming. God! I can't believe I've never even met the woman, sending me a letter the way she did, boldly, barefacedly offering to buy one of my sons!"

"A letter to which you raced hotfoot to reply, as I recall. But hark! I believe the moment is at hand! Oh, how my poor heart pounds in trepidation," Dante whispered sotto voce, rolling his eyes. He stood up and looked toward the door politely and entirely without interest, and nearly disgraced both himself and his father by laughing out loud as Mrs. Trowbridge swept into the room. She halted just inside the doorway and struck a dramatic pose, most definitely for emphasis, and most probably because she actually believed she looked regal.

She didn't. If Trowbridge Manor was overdone, Mrs. Trowbridge had accomplished the impossible by succeeding in outdoing her domicile in absurdity. A towering six feet tall or more, she was as large as a fully plumped plum pudding and twice as purple, from her heavy purple gown to the dyed plumes tucked into her thick steel-gray hair.

Dante couldn't be sure, not from this distance, but he believed he could discern more than a few whiskers on the woman's upper lip, and her upper arms spoke more of beefy muscle than aging fat.

Diamonds incongruously dripped from her ears, her neck, both wrists, and six of her ten fingers, although it would take a robber with more avarice than brains to try to wrest any of the baubles from a woman who appeared capable of bowling down a regiment with her mere presence.

In short, Mrs. Trowbridge looked like an unbeatable

opponent, a woman with all the brass of a seasoned infan-
tryman, all the discretion of a loosed cannonball, and all the
taste, grace, and refinement of a Gypsy tinker.

"What? No reaction? I thought so! You don't remember
me, do you, Curtis?" she asked without preamble in a deep,
rumbling voice as the silence in the room was broken only
by the marquess's rather ragged breathing.

The words reverberated in the high-ceilinged room like
rolling thunder, for the woman spoke as if the Muirs were
standing on a different continent and she wished to make
certain she would be heard.

"Remember you, Mrs. Trowbridge?" Curtis Muir repeated, looking to Dante as if for rescue. It was a wasted
motion, for his son, still highly amused and more than
slightly interested in what Mrs. Trowbridge might next say,
had no intention of bailing out the man. "I— Why, I fear
you have the advantage of me, ma'am."

"Ah, a most brilliant, telling riposte. Still the master of
understatement, I see, aren't you, Father?" Dante asked in a
quiet, thoroughly pleased tone. The man might be selling his
youngest son for all the best—which was to say "socially
accepted"—reasons, but that didn't mean his middle son
couldn't cheerfully despise him for his cold-blooded intentions.

Mrs. Trowbridge still, Dante hoped, out of earshot of
anyone like him who spoke in more cultured tones, threw
back her head and gave a sharp bark of laughter—a bellow
worthy of a charging bull.

"The advantage?" she all but chortled. "That I do, Curtis,
that I do. Me and m'fortune have you good and proper. But
I'll help you. It was four or five dog's years ago, maybe more.
Back when I was still Elizabeth *Forrester*. Remember that
name? I was arsy-varsy in love with you, Curtis Muir, pitiful
idiot beanpole that I was back then, and you got wind of it
one day at a picnic—I disremember whose. You laughed
when your friends pointed me out to you and said you might
be inclined to kiss me—if only you could *climb* me first.
Cried for a month, I did, Curtis. Cried till my heart broke,

as I was only ten and six, still too young to overlook my admiration of your fine handsome figure and despise you for your stupidity."

Dante looked at his father, who appeared ready to bolt past Mrs. Trowbridge and run for his life. "Flummoxed, are you? As I may have mentioned earlier, Father," he whispered quietly, "I will be most careful not to embarrass you. Why should I put myself to the trouble, when you've already done such a splendid job of it yourself?"

The marquess squinted, leaning forward slightly as if that would enable him to think, and to see, more clearly. "Can it be . . . Betts?"

"None other, Curtis," Mrs. Trowbridge said as she swept past the two men and plunked herself down in a wide-seated upholstered chair that fit her hips more snugly than its designer could have considered possible. "The fifth daughter of the fifth son of Sir George Forrester. Nary a feather to fly with, my papa, and too many daughters to keep one with an appetite like mine sticking her legs under his table any longer than he had to. Married me off to Sam later that same summer, not that I'm complaining. I never dressed so well or ate better than I did as Sam's wife—or as Sam's widow, now that he went and stuck his spoon in the wall just this past Saint Agnes' Eve, may the good Lord rest his money-making soul."

"Our condolences, madam, although they are woefully belated." Dante had sat down once more, coughing discreetly to hint that his father, who still looked unnaturally pale for a man so sure of the success of this day's mission, should do likewise. He then smiled at Mrs. Trowbridge and added politely, "You have a lovely home, ma'am. Very impressive. I can't think why we haven't visited before now."

"I can," she returned with a good-natured snort. "The nobility hasn't much truck with tradesmen—unless they're looking to marry one of their penniless sons to the butcher's money. Ain't that right, Curtis? You're here to bargain. Your son for my darling granddaughter, Sarah Jane. Just the way you married your heir to little Audrey Webster's daddy's money a half dozen or so years back. A coal merchant then, a butcher now. Money's money, no matter how much it smells of the shop—smells of sweat, of industry and hard work, things you Muirs detest like a cat hates water. What happened? Did you run through Webster's fortune already? Of course you did. You wouldn't have agreed to this meeting otherwise. And it's a good thing, too, for I've spent decades banking on your spendthrift ways."

The marquess spread his hands pleadingly, his customary air of self-assuredness having lost itself somewhere behind his rather red, perspiration-sheened face. "Betts—"

"Elizabeth, Curtis, if you please," she interrupted imperiously, causing Dante to bite the inside of his cheek in amusement for fear he might disgrace himself at witnessing his father's discomfiture. "You may call me Mrs. Trowbridge or Elizabeth. I was Betts as a child and as Sam's wife, but now that Sam's gone and I'm about to climb back up where I belong, it's Elizabeth."

"Of course. Please forgive me. *Elizabeth.*"

"Not that I have any great hankering for society anymore, you understand," she continued as if he hadn't spoken, crossing her legs in a mannish, take-charge sort of way. "I'm years past that, and wallowing in being vulgar now that I'm rich enough to say what I want and do what I want any time I want!"

She threw back her plumed head and laughed at her tongue-twisting witticism, then sobered. "And right now, dear Curtis, I *want* m'granddaughter to get what she deserves. Her mother was a parson's daughter totally unexceptional, I made certain of that. And her great-grandfather was a peer. The butcher blood is well diluted now, Curtis, and I saw to it that she was raised right. She'll not shame you."

"Of course not," the marquess agreed quickly, his voice rather thin, as if he were laboring under a mighty strain and could only open his mouth in order to agree with the encroaching Mrs. Trowbridge.

"But enough of you, Curtis. Now let me talk with this boy of yours. So far he hasn't opened his mouth a peep except to whisper nasty things he thinks I can't hear, and I want to make sure he ain't stupid or something, even if he is a handsome enough sprig of Satan, with those dark eyes and blacker hair. Don't look a thing like you, does he, Curtis?"

Dante raised his eyebrows and looked to his father, waiting for the man to contradict Mrs. Trowbridge's assumption that he, and not Johnny, was to be this year's sacrificial Muir. He might have applied to the Sphinx for all the encouragement he saw in the older man's rapidly blinking eyes.

"Mrs. Trowbridge," Dante said, smiling at the woman, "as my father here seems to be searching in vain for his tongue, I believe it is left to me to explain the particulars of our, um, our *offer*. It is my younger brother, Lord John Muir, who is eager to be your granddaughter's blushing bridegroom. I am Lord Dante, the second son. The *bachelor* son."

"Oh, I know who you are, and what you are," Mrs. Trowbridge pronounced with a wave of one bejeweled hand. "You're the one with the brains, the one with some bottom, or so I've heard—not that I've seen much of either so far. What do I want with the youngest son, and a bloody sot into the bargain? Let's talk with the gloves off, shall we?"

"If you insist," Lord Dante said, sighing. Really, the woman was making him tired.

"As I was saying, with the earl an invalid now and not likely to breed any little coal merchants, you, the second son, will end up as the marquess when Curtis here kicks off. Oh, yes. My Sarah Jane's going to be Countess of Easterly when your brother Tyler goes to his reward, and a marchioness before the decade is out, if Curtis is as sick as he looks right now. My Sam looked more the thing when he was two days dead! So, no, my lord Dante, it's you or no one!"

"Then it is no one, madam!" Any humor Dante had seen in his father's predicament evaporated as he saw himself being drawn into this mad scheme to refloat the fortunes of the Muir family through a marriage to Betts Trowbridge's granddaughter.

Yes, the family fortunes were at low tide.

Yes, the estate, Cliff Walk, was fast falling into ruin.

Yes, the Trowbridge money would be a godsend.

And Johnny, damn it all anyway, had agreed, albeit reluctantly, to the match. It wasn't as if Dante's younger brother had any other prospects, as if any of them had any other prospects.

After all, there wasn't much in the way of opportunity for fortune-hunting gentlemen to meet acceptable, well-dowered debutantes whose fond papas were willing to throw both their daughters and their money away on a wastrel family like the Muirs. Dante knew that well, for he had been shown the door quickly enough five years previously when, caught up in the throes of what he believed at the time to be True Love, he had asked for the hand of the lovely, sinfully wealthy Lady Helena.

He had not even considered the fair Helena's dowry. However, her father had, and Dante had sworn never again to propose marriage to anyone until he had succeeded in rebuilding the Muir fortunes and could pick and choose where he wished when he went bride hunting. *If* he went bride hunting.

But he wasn't bride hunting! And he wasn't even slightly interested in Mrs. Trowbridge's absurd offer.

Dante stood, looking down expectantly at his father, waiting for the man to rise, tell the Trowbridge woman in no uncertain terms precisely what she could do with her fortune, and follow him back through the maze of armor and tables and out the door.

He would have had better luck applying for a box seat to bear witness at the Second Coming.

"Now, Dante," his sire said cajolingly, "don't go cutting up stiff. Betts— I mean, Elizabeth here has a point. Ty, bless the boy, isn't well, and you are the better catch between you and Johnny. Older. More settled. And God knows you have a level head on your shoulders, which is more than Johnny has, much as I adore the scamp. Drinks, you know," he said, shifting in his seat to address Mrs. Trowbridge. "But you already touched on that, didn't you? Made a career of it these past few years—drinking, that is—and it's the one thing he does passably well."

Mrs. Trowbridge hefted her bulk from the chair and crossed to a nearby desk to pick up a closely written sheet of paper. "And you want me to give half my fortune over to the boy to have him drink and piss it away? Not bloody likely! I want some solid return for my money, Curtis, not a spotty liver. Here, I wrote it all down. You—Dante—come read this for me. No sense in keeping a dog and barking myself, as Sam used to say. I'm buying you, so you might as well start yapping."

"What a gracious invitation, and such a delightful picture of my future you have conjured up, madam. Oh, very well," Dante said, shrugging, for he knew full well that he would never marry Sarah Jane Trowbridge. Never. "Father," he ended amiably, glaring at the marquess, "you will pay for this later. You will pay dearly."

He took the paper, squinting at the woman's atrocious handwriting, and scanned the words silently, occasionally casting increasingly amused glances at both Mrs. Trowbridge and his father.

Slowly, as he read, he began to realize that although the woman seemed to have lost all semblance of gentility in both her speech and her tastes, she seemed also to have gained her late husband's acuity in the ways of business. Probably some sort of assimilation, he decided, folding the paper and handing it back to Mrs. Trowbridge.

He felt himself beginning to admire her.

"You are completely serious in this, madam?" he asked at last, knowing, as the smugly smiling woman must also have known, that it would be nearly impossible for him to reject such a proposal, no matter how demeaning he believed a marriage based solely on monetary considerations to be for both participants.

"Like it, do you? I thought you would. Sam taught me to bait my hook well if I wanted to be sure of my catch."

"What catch? What does that paper say?" the marquess demanded, gnawing on his lower lip. "Damn you, Dante, don't just stand there grinning like a bear. What does it say?"

"Mrs. Trowbridge has made a considerable settlement

12

offer, Father. Extremely generous. Almost obscenely generous, actually. In return for wedding her granddaughter and begetting a male heir within five years—I do thank you, madam, for not making me nervous with a necessity to perform conclusive stud service within a twelvemonth—I shall receive one hundred thousand pounds. Fifty thousand on the day of the marriage and the remainder when my heir is born."

"One hundred thousand! My God, it's more than twice what I'd hoped! It's . . . it's— *You* shall receive, Dante?" the marquess blustered as his mind, undoubtedly divided between lovely dreams of full pockets and even lovelier plans for lightening them again, slowly sorted through the information. *"You?"*

Dante smiled, showing his even white teeth to advantage against his tanned skin. Giving him control of the money—that was the well-baited hook, the one the old woman must have known was sure to land her preferred fish.

"Ah, so you heard that? Yes, Father. I shall receive the money. Not you. Not Tyler. Not even poor Johnny. Just me. And this paltry amount of money will of course be separate from the rather intimidating sum Mrs. Trowbridge is giving in order to satisfy the several mortgages against Cliff Walk. Naturally there are a few strings attached in addition to successful procreation, aren't there, Mrs. Trowbridge?"

The woman nodded, the purple plumes bobbing energetically. "You're to put Cliff Walk to rights, open the center chambers instead of living as you do in the family wing, and ready the king's bedchamber for me whenever I take it into my head to visit my Sarah Jane. I've always had a hankering to sleep in a king's bed. I want the whole of it set to rights, as befits a grand estate, you understand. No granddaughter of mine is going to be pinching pennies and burning green wood. No, sir!"

"Which brings us to the disposition of the first fifty thousand pounds, Father," Dante continued when Mrs. Trowbridge subsided once more into her chair and began sorting through a purple glass candy dish, picking out all the pink sugarplums. "You, alas, are not to have a penny of it above whatever quarterly allowance I see fit to give you, and Ty and Johnny. Mrs. Trowbridge must have heard of that depressing loss you took at White's last month, Father."

"Hummph! What's one loss, I ask you?" Mrs. Trowbridge grumbled around a mouthful of sugarplum. "Pity your bloodline is so simon-pure, Curtis. You could have done with an infusion of some of the luck of the Irish. Worst hand at cards ever born, or so I've heard. Cards, women, horses, extravagant parties. And you're the best dressed debtor I've ever clapped eyes on. Oh, no. You'll not spend a bent farthing of my money on your foolishness. This boy here is the only one who gives a tinker's dam about Cliff Walk, about any future farther away than today's sunset. Why, my Sam would be spinning himself dizzy in his grave if I let any of his hard-earned blunt slip through your spread fingers."

"Dante, you're right," the marquess squeaked, jumping up from his seat. "This is totally unacceptable. Come, it's a long drive back to Cliff Walk."

Dante cocked his head to one side, his smile mirroring the pleasure he was beginning to feel deep in his gut. "Oh, let's not be hasty, Father. Mrs. Trowbridge has made a very generous, rather well thought out offer. I think we should consider it, if only intellectually, although I must admit that I had not planned to name my firstborn son Samuel—"

"Dante!"

"No, please, don't interrupt. Fifty thousand pounds, with the chance to double it, *and* the mortgages paid off? That's not to be sneezed at, is it? Audrey brought you only forty thousand, and it took you less than six years to go through it, with nothing to show for any of it. Cliff Walk is still falling apart, our creditors are still nipping at your heels. That is why you and my dear sister-in-law Audrey are rusticating, isn't it, to be shed of nagging creditors? When I returned from the Continent in April, I hoped to see Cliff Walk restored to its former glory, only to discover the place reduced to a skeleton staff and all of us crowded into the family wing, with the rest of the place under dust sheets. And then, when you and Audrey insisted upon keeping the town house open and fully staffed all the summer long for Prinny's peace celebrations—"

"There is no need to catalog family problems in public." The marquess looked from Dante to Mrs. Trowbridge and back to his son, his eyes furtive, his expression faintly embarrassed, faintly chagrined. "We've suffered only a minor temporary setback. Why, next year, when I go off to Newmarket for the races—"

"You'll travel in a hired coach and stay at a bug-ridden inn—unless you plan to try palming off Mother's paste jewels as real to some unsuspecting moneylender, that is—and then you'll drop more money we can't afford to lose betting on flea-bitten plugs that either run backwards or break down in the stretch," Dante finished for him. "No, Father, I think we have to consider Mrs. Trowbridge's offer. As it stands now, we have barely enough money to plant the fields next spring. Though I don't know what we'll do with the crop, with the millrace clogged after that last storm and the last workable wheel nearly broken—"

"See, Curtis? The boy talks sense," Mrs. Trowbridge said just as Dante was convinced his father was going to resort to boxing his middle son's ears. "I've studied up some on him, and I'm well pleased, not to tell you how surprised I was to see that any of your sprouts has a decent brain box. Must resemble his mother in more than his looks, eh, Curtis? Fought with Wellington, has a feel for the land, cares about Cliff Walk, looks more than capable of giving me strapping great-grandsons—why, I couldn't ask for more. So, Curtis, is it settled?"

"Settled? Why ask me? Damn you, Betts, it doesn't matter what I say!" the marquess bit out, shaking his head at yet another defeat. "Dante?"

Dante failed to see that he had any options. "If your granddaughter approves, Mrs. Trowbridge," he answered dully, wondering if he was still hoping to find some way out of this cold arranged marriage.

He didn't believe himself to fit the mold of martyr. He hadn't the humility for it, for one thing, and he disliked intensely the thought of being a paid stud meant to help purify a bloodline. But Betts Trowbridge had planned well. He had no choice. Did he? "After all," he ended almost hopefully, "she might take one look at me and run screaming for her nurse."

"Hardly, son," the marquess stated firmly, already moving toward the hallway. "It's the chit I'm worried about now. Not that she probably isn't sweet as sunshine. Tell me, does she much resemble you, Betts?"

Dante lowered his head and rubbed at the back of his neck, wondering how his father could be considered an asset in social circles when he possessed all the gentle sensibility of a Covent Garden trollop.

"Um, why, um . . ." Mrs. Trowbridge stammered.

Dante was immediately alert, pushing aside all thoughts of selling himself in order to save his beloved Cliff Walk—and, not incidentally, his helpless, self-destructive, but well-loved family—and stared inquiringly at the suddenly nonplussed Mrs. Trowbridge.

"Is there something I should know, madam?" he asked quietly, wondering if Miss Sarah Jane Trowbridge was apt to bay at full moons.

"Sarah Jane is a lovely child!" Mrs. Trowbridge declared, regaining her voice. "Just turned eighteen four months past, sweet, biddable, trained in all the domestic and social graces—a truly lovely child!"

Definitely bays at the full moon, Dante decided, wondering why he should be surprised. Any young woman who had to be sold, sight unseen, for the very hefty amount her grandmother was offering could not be a ravishing beauty. He knew he should consider himself lucky if the chit still had all her hair and teeth! Or perhaps she was a half-wit who not only bayed at the moon but believed she could jump over it?

The marquess shrugged. "Well, there you have it, son. A *lovely* child. What more could you ask? You'll announce the banns, then, Betts? Of course Dante and Sarah Jane could be married from the chapel at Cliff Walk if it weren't such a shambles, but the roof leaks, you understand, and I saw a dove nesting in the rafters last time I ambled by. I imagine there'll be snow on the pews come winter."

"Fix it and have the bills sent to me. And don't think I won't check to be sure you used the best materials and workmanship," Mrs. Trowbridge commanded shortly, once more taking on the air of a field officer barking out orders to the lowliest soldier. "I'm still in half mourning for Sam, so there can't be any big to-do. I may not be in Society, but I still remember how it works! The wedding takes place in three weeks, on the eighth day of November—that's a Tuesday, Curtis—and not a day later. Understood?"

"Of course, Betts—er, Elizabeth—a Tuesday should be fine, I suppose, for a modest ceremony," the marquess assured her in most amiable tones. "We could have a lovely party afterward in the state dining room, an intimate gathering, and . . ."

Knowing his father would talk for at least another half hour, since planning parties was one of the man's few fortes, Dante wandered into the hallway, intent only on stepping outside to blow a cloud and to wonder how he, a usually good but seldom biddable son, had ended up betrothed to a young woman he had not as yet met.

Jessup, obviously taken by surprise by Dante's appearance, hastened to retrieve his lordship's hat, cloak, and gloves from the small reception room to the right of the hallway, leaving Dante alone with nothing to do but look his full at the atrocious collection of expensive, tasteless furnishings.

After tipping back his head to inspect the chandelier and to wonder idly how much it cost to burn the hundred or more candles every evening, his attention was caught by a movement near the top of the wide, curving staircase.

He saw a child kneeling behind the balustrade, a girl child, dressed all in flounced white lace, a wide pink satin sash tied about her slim waist.

Dante looked harder, careful to smile and not scare her off, and noticed a pair of enormous eyes beneath a towering mop of black hair that had been arranged in girlish ringlets as full and as unflattering as an old-fashioned wig.

"Hello there," he called up to the child encouragingly, wondering who she was and why anyone would dress her so horribly.

The girl stood up, one hand pressed to her mouth, her eyes grown even wider, and Dante froze. He had been wrong. This was no child. She wasn't at all tall, but she was also no flat-chested infant.

He swallowed hard and ventured fatalistically, "Miss Sarah Jane Trowbridge?"

She nodded furiously, mutely, the unflattering curls bobbing around her narrow shoulders, then touched her hands to her mushroom of a skirt and dropped into a ludicrously awkward curtsy that ended abruptly as she slipped and nearly toppled down the stairs.

"Oh, good grief!" Dante exploded, turning on his heel to head back toward the purple saloon. *This is beyond belief! Does that harridan believe me to be perverted? A child lover?*

But he checked his anger a moment later and stopped in his tracks, once more looking up to where Miss Sarah Jane Trowbridge still stood, her hand again pressed to her mouth. She was eighteen, hardly a child, even though she looked as if she belonged in the nursery.

He approached the gracefully curved staircase until he stood just below her, close enough to see the color of her ridiculously large, curiously vulnerable eyes as she stared down at him from over the railing.

Those soft cow-brown eyes dominated her small face and were oddly well balanced by rather heavy, nearly straight black brows that turned down sharply as they neared her temples, and by a cleanly defined, vaguely aristocratic jawline that rose above a curiously long, fragile neck. The nose was good, short and straight, and the cheekbones admirably high. If it weren't for the hair . . . and that ludicrous gown . . . and her so obvious *youth* . . .

"Forgive me, Miss Trowbridge," he said, marshaling all his composure while silently wishing Elizabeth Trowbridge at the bottom of some deep, dank well. "I had just realized that we hadn't been formally introduced, and was about to rush off to petition your grandmother to perform that office. But we two shouldn't stand on such ceremony, should we?"

The hand slipped to her ruffled bodice, then fluttered to her side. "I don't know, sir," she offered in, thank the Lord, a soft, well-modulated voice. "I wasn't supposed to leave my rooms, you see. Grandmother Trowbridge was quite explicit on that point. But Jessup told me you were coming this morning, and I thought . . . well, I wondered—"

"You wondered if I was old or fat or had two heads," Dante finished for her when she subsided into confusion, his heart touched by her honesty. "Believe me, Miss Trowbridge, I quite understand. Tell me, now that you've disobeyed, would you care to compound your sin by having your maid fetch your cloak so that you might take a short stroll outside with me? I assure you, I do not bite."

The soft brown eyes filled with apprehension. "I would enjoy that very much, Lord Dante," she answered, her small, delicately formed hands tightly gripping the stair rail, as if that was the only thing keeping her from floating off into the air. What did she weigh? Dante wondered. Seven stone? Only if she were dunked head and ears in the ocean, then rolled in mud! "But Grandmother Trowbridge was dreadfully specific."

Dante's smile faded as his temper rose. This was to be his bride? This timid, spineless little creature rigged out like a Christmas pudding? Was he to be a husband or a governess? Should his bridal gift be pearls or leading strings? And how did Mrs. Trowbridge punish the child for disobeying her orders anyway—by *sitting* on her?

"Very well, Miss Trowbridge. I will not persist in teasing you when you are so obviously torn. My father and I are passing the night at a local inn. Perhaps I might call on you tomorrow afternoon?"

"That—that would be lovely, Lord Dante," she answered quietly, so quietly that he couldn't decide if she was shy or if she was fighting not to show her disappointment—or her anger?—that he had not pressed the matter.

He had the uncomfortable feeling he had not lived up to

her expectations of him, and he immediately resented her, her and her big brown eyes, for making him feel incompetent.

Dante heard voices coming closer, Mrs. Trowbridge's basso tones heralding her appearance long before her entrance into the hallway, and he watched, not at all amused, as Miss Sarah Jane Trowbridge quickly gathered her mountain of skirts and scampered out of sight as if the hounds of hell were after her.

Not that he could blame the child. Betts Trowbridge could intimidate a herd of rampaging elephants, let alone one small, high-strung fawn like Sarah Jane.

He turned to give his farewell to the older woman as politely and quickly as possible and hasten his father out the door, wondering if he might be able to soothe his conscience in this matter of a convenient marriage by telling himself he was effecting the rescue of an innocent from a fire-breathing purple ogre.

Yes, that might work. But how in the name of heaven was he ever going to bed this clearly frightened, naive womanchild without feeling very much the ogre himself?

BOOK ONE

DREAMS

A lady's imagination is very rapid; it jumps from admiration to love, from love to matrimony in a moment.

Jane Austen

CHAPTER 1

*Misses! the tale that I relate
This lesson seems to carry —
Choose not alone a proper mate,
But proper time to marry.*

William Cowper

He will break your heart, you know."

Sarah Jane Trowbridge continued to gaze into the pier glass, intent on arranging her bridal veil so that the heavy lace looked less shroudlike as it hung over her shoulders and dropped to the floor, not to end until its hem trailed behind her by at least eight feet.

Any longer, she had told her maid, Mildred, and the thing could serve double duty as a tablecloth in the state dining room at Cliff Walk. The gown had been altered with some small degree of success, but no one seemed to have considered doing anything about the veil, which had been concocted with an exceedingly taller bride in mind.

But her grandmother had insisted, and Sarah Jane had swallowed down her apprehensions and agreed.

She had agreed to all of it, which was why she did not need to be reminded of the futility of pretending that she was a well-beloved bride.

"Yes, Audrey," she answered her soon-to-be sister-in-law,

doing her best to smile. "I do know. Lord Dante doesn't love me. He didn't love me when he asked me to become his wife, and he doesn't love me now. Grandmother Trowbridge said that in marriages at this rank of society such arrangements are not all that unusual."

"True enough, I suppose," Audrey said. "Yours is to be a marriage of convenience. As, sad to say, was mine to Tyler. But at least Ty and I knew ours was not a love match. And now it is your turn. So here we both are and will remain, trapped at Cliff Walk with those three barbarians—Dante, my poor crippled husband, and that idiot boy, Johnny. What we ladies have to suffer is unconscionable! Ah, but you *do* fancy yourself to be well and truly in love with Dante, don't you, Sarah Jane? You have convinced yourself that you love him desperately while he, caring only for his new fortune, barely realizes that you exist. Oh, you poor sweet child! Life is so unfair! Men are such brutes!"

Sarah Jane lifted her hands to her temples and closed her eyes. Was it the jeweled band holding her veil in place that had served to set up this terrible pounding inside her head? Perhaps that was why she would have liked nothing better than to stuff at least half of the length of bridal veil down Audrey's gullet and then to watch, giggling hysterically, while the woman's lovely peaches-and-cream complexion turned as purple as Grandmother Trowbridge's awful ostrich plumes.

"It's all right. Truly. Please, Audrey, do not be concerned," Sarah Jane said at last in a tightly controlled voice, turning to face the other woman, the silk of the old-fashioned wedding gown whispering accusations of her timidity with her every movement as the faintly sickening smell of camphor rose to her nostrils. "However, if you don't mind, I believe I would appreciate a few moments to gather myself before the marquess arrives to escort me to the chapel."

"Of course, of course! Oh, dear child, forgive me." The Countess of Easterly pressed a kiss on Sarah Jane's cheek, then took hold of her hands, squeezing them through the constricting elbow-high kid. "But only allow me to say again that I will always be here for you. Your dear friend, your new sister. I know Dante, know his moods, his vices, and may be able to help you steer clear of his vile temper."

Sarah Jane carefully removed her hands from the countess's affectionate grasp and firmly folded them together at her waist, pressing them against her worrisome, queasy, potentially embarrassing stomach.

"His temper, Audrey? I have never observed Lord Dante in a temper. He has always seemed very much in control of himself." *Even on our third meeting in as many days, when he proposed to me, down on one knee as is the custom, offering me his worldly goods, such as they are, and telling me quite honestly that he did not—does not—love me.*

Audrey's robin's-egg blue eyes slid away from Sarah Jane's face, and the woman stammered, "Ah, I—that is, never mind my silly natterings, my dear. Dante's temper? Nonsense! He's a lamb, a veritable *lamb,* I assure you. It is only that he has always proclaimed himself to be uninterested in anything but bachelor pursuits, and his fixation with Cliff Walk, of course. To my mind, that makes him barely civilized, but not really *mean.* I can't imagine why I said such a thing! It must be the heat of that enormous fire in the grate. Withering, isn't it! Oh, dear, your lovely coiffure is sagging, and I believe I see a sheen of perspiration on your upper lip. And you're so pale! This will never do! You, woman, tend to your mistress. We can't have Lord Dante upset to see his bride wilting at the altar!"

She kissed Sarah Jane's check a second time, smiling wanly and blinking rapidly—to beat back sympathetic tears? "God bless and keep you, my dear girl. God bless and keep you!"

Then with a swish of silk and petticoats the beautiful countess fled the room, a lace handkerchief held to her lips, as if she could not help but break down at the sight of the naive virgin soon to be led to the altar.

God bless and keep you? What did Audrey Muir know? What was it that this woman who had been living with the Muir family for a half dozen years knew about Dante that Sarah Jane had yet to learn?

Did he have a mad wife locked away somewhere, a woman driven out of her wits by her husband's vile temper?

Or had he killed his first wife outright, thrown her off the cliffs to the rear of the estate, the way Count Somebody-or-Other in one of Grandmother Trowbridge's penny press novels had disposed of his unwanted wife by pushing her from the top of a tower?

But wait! Who said Dante Muir had been married before? Of course he hadn't. Grandmother Trowbridge would most certainly have known, and she'd said the man had not even been affianced, preferring the bachelor life until Grandfather Trowbridge's money served to change his mind.

Sarah Jane shook her head, silently berating herself and her stupid overblown imagination. She had lived such a solitary existence at Trowbridge Manor that her imagination had been her only friend, her single companion in a household not conducive to independent thinking.

But this was carrying things too far, even for her. Perhaps she was only reacting to the vile odor of camphor emanating from her gown. That could be it. The smell was most probably invading her brain, muddling her thought processes!

"Thought she'd never leave, missy," muttered Mildred, Sarah Jane's maid since childhood, breaking into her mistress's thoughts as she approached from a corner of the room. She tipped her head to one side as she looked at her mistress. "Wears perfume thick enough to spread with butter and serve at teatime. Not that you smell much better today. Aired that there gown for three full days, I did, and it still smells of the storage box. What was she runnin' on about anyways? You have no need of powder or the rouge pot. Could do somethin' with that great mess of hair, though, not that anyone can see much of it under this lump of lace—and that's saying somethin'! Would you be wanting a drink of water, missy? Or I can fetch you a chair iffen you wants to sit for a while. I know my knees are knockin' like dry bones in a sack, thinkin' about what's to happen today. Lady Dante! Oh, the marvel of it!"

"Pardon me? Oh, yes, yes. Thank you, Mildred. It is all

rather marvelous, isn't it? But I'd much prefer it if you could find me a glass of wine," Sarah Jane said quietly. She turned back to the dressing table and picked up a small lead-crystal vase, just so that she would have something solid to hold on to, something to keep her from shattering into a thousand small pieces. "I've never had wine before, but I do believe it might be time for the application of some sort of steadying influence."

Mildred clucked her tongue, declared that her mistress would take water and like it, then went off to fetch a cold pitcher. She would have fetched a plate of food for her mistress as well, she grumbled as she quit the chamber, except that in all of the Cliff Walk kitchens there was nothing worth feeding to the hogs.

Sarah Jane stared into the mirror, hating herself for being cowed by the countess, no matter how sincere the woman's intentions.

How could I have let Audrey upset me so? How could I have been so meek and mild? What should I have said? "Now, Audrey, if you have done with this experienced-wife-to-blushing-bride-to-be coze, and of reminding me how woefully inadequate I am to the role I am about to take on, I suggest you take yourself off downstairs before I remember that I am nothing but a butcher's granddaughter dressed in a lady's clothing and not above breaking this lovely piece over your head!" Yes, that would have been rather good. Obnoxious, but with a ring of authority to it. And aeons too late. Why do I always find my courage only after the fact?

She sighed and took one last peek into the mirror, discouraged by what she saw—a small, thin woman-child, all overly large brown eyes and odiously overgrown black hair, the whole of her nearly smothered in heavy silk and heavier lace.

She didn't look anything like the Sarah Jane Trowbridge she was in her heart, the secret, strong-minded, strong-willed Sarah Jane Trowbridge she hid from the world. A woman grown, with a fairly sound mind, and thoughts and opinions of her own. Dreams of her own.

But only dreams.

And now she was to step out from the domineering Elizabeth Trowbridge's image of her granddaughter and take on the role of willing bride. When, if ever, would she finally feel free enough, or threatened enough, to discard the wishful image and become the dream?

"Oh, Mildred," she cried angrily as the maid reentered the chamber, "I look like a nursery brat dressed up in my mother's clothes. How did I ever allow myself to say yes to wearing Grandmother Trowbridge's wedding gown?"

Dante heard the squeak of the Bath chair behind him and turned to see his older brother, Tyler Muir, Earl of Easterly, being wheeled into the small drawing room by his personal servant, Farris. He turned to greet him. "Here to escort me to the scaffold, are you, Ty?"

"With a reminiscent smirk on my lips and a modicum of good-natured malice in my heart, dear brother," the earl answered, waving Farris out of the chamber.

"Thank you, Ty. Your encouragement soothes me no end."

"Think nothing of it. But I have not come to gloat, for I can't enjoy watching you—the best of us—meekly taking your turn bowing to our sire's desire to line his pockets. Johnny is hiding in the green room, torn between elation at his lucky escape and being massively disappointed in this cowardly capitulation of his hero. When last I saw him he was drowning his more personal apprehensions in several bottles of claret, convinced our dear papa is even now eyeing up as his youngest son's future bride a certain member of the distinguished coterie constituting Mrs. Trowbridge's contribution to the guest list."

"The draper?"

"No. I believe the lady in question is second cousin to an extremely deep-in-the-pocket hog butcher. Lovely gentleman. I was being wheeled by him a few minutes ago, and he was most gracious about my sad condition. He never bellowed the word 'cripple' to his companions until I was at least three feet past them."

Dante knew there was no easy way to reply to any of

Tyler's statements. He only smiled his usual one-sided smile and took a sip from his wineglass before saying, "I'm quite convinced that Audrey is holding up her end, playing the hostess?"

"Audrey? Would that be anyone I know? Oh—*Audrey!* My wife, of course. I remember her now, although I am not quite sure I recall her features. But it was good of her to come down to Cliff Walk, tearing herself away from Mayfair's Little Season, to weep over my useless legs and show me her new gowns."

Tyler smiled, shrugging his shoulders. "At least she and our father are enjoying themselves, contemplating spending all your little bride's lovely money. They always were two for eating the calf while it was still in the cow's belly."

Then he sobered and asked, "Why, Dante? Why are you doing this? Why are you sacrificing yourself like this? The chit's barely out of the schoolroom, greener than spring grass, and stupid into the bargain. I haven't heard her say more than a half dozen words since she and that gale of a grandmother of hers blew in here the other night. And she has the most disconcerting habit of staring into space, as if she lives in her own world, perhaps even hears voices. Very strange. So don't keep me in suspense, brother mine. Why?"

Dante took one last sip of the wine he had been drinking, mostly for lack of anything better to do, and turned to look at his obviously concerned brother. "So Father didn't tell you, Ty? I'm not surprised. I imagine he is still attempting to delude himself that I shall be a dutiful son and turn everything over to him. But I won't. You see, it's to be *my* fortune, brother, not our father's. All mine, to dispose of as I like. More than two hundred thousand pounds, once I add it all up—the outright payments, the mortgages, the repairs on Cliff Walk that have already begun. You're looking not at some selfless sacrificial lamb but at a low, money-grubbing bastard, although we will all benefit once the estate is put back on a paying basis. There, now are you less inclined to weep over me?"

Tyler was silent for some moments, his handsome face thoughtful beneath the shock of blond hair, but then he threw back his head and laughed. "That's wonderful, Dante. Absolutely *beautiful!* Papa doesn't get any? Audrey doesn't get any? Oh, quickly, brother Moneybags, where is that lovely great mountain of a Trowbridge woman hiding herself? I must this very moment throw my useless self at her feet and kiss the nethermost hem of her garment!"

Dante felt his lips beginning to twitch as he understood his older brother's reaction. It had been more than six years since Tyler's marriage to Audrey, and more than two since the riding accident that had left him crippled, and none of those years had been easy.

In the early days Tyler had been as eager for the expensive pleasures of life as had the marquess and Audrey. The earl and his new wife had made up for their lack of compatibility by rushing all over Mayfair, attending balls, indulging in romantic liaisons, and, always, discovering new ways to spend money.

The riding accident had put an end to all that for Tyler, but not for Audrey. She and the marquess had continued to pass the majority of their time in London, still spending money although there was none left, and Tyler had been forced to retire to Cliff Walk, alone. Alone enough to know he was not loved by any but his drunken youngest brother and the absent Dante, alone enough to feel sorry for himself, alone enough to remember that he had once been a happy man, alone enough to have turned his once brilliant wit into a caustic humor colored by melancholy and despair.

But the Earl of Easterly still possessed some whimsy and a talent for facetious banter directed at the foibles of his fellow man. Casting his oblivious father and faithless wife in the role of petitioners to his younger brother each time they wished to spend a groat obviously appealed very much to Tyler's skewed sense of the ridiculous.

"I thought you might enjoy my news, Ty," Dante commented at last, when his brother's explosion of hilarity seemed to have run its course, and wondered why it had taken him so long to let his brother in on the whole of it.

Then he shook his head, for he did know: he hadn't wanted to face the unpalatable fact that he was little better

30

than his father, and would marry for money. "But I am entering upon a loveless marriage, Ty, and for all the wrong reasons. Don't you have a moment's pity to spare for me?"

The earl sobered immediately, frowned, then grinned once more. "Nope. Not a jot. Sorry, brother mine. You'll find, as I did, that it's easy enough to buy happiness. Just be careful not to run out of money—or take a fence too low, topple from the saddle, then allow some stupid horse to dance on you. Ah, but your Sarah Jane is no Audrey. That pocket-size mouse won't so much as squeak no matter what you do, will she? All in all, I'd say you have struck a fine bargain. Tell me, dear brother, do you still intend to feed *me?* And Johnny? It costs a pretty penny for our baby brother to maintain his lovely state of inebriation, you know."

Dante knelt beside the earl's chair, looking up at the man intently. "Ty, I won't lie and say that I'm only doing this for you and Johnny. I'm being selfish as well, for I can't stand to see Cliff Walk destroyed and all our people fallen into poverty because the estate is in tatters. I love this house, this land, our people. Someday, when you're back on your feet again, you'll take over the management of the estate, and I'll be more than happy to turn the reins over to you. You'll see."

The earl turned his head away, staring at the weak November sunlight that filtered in through the dusty windows of the family wing drawing room. "How above everything amazing!" he exclaimed, directing his speech to the air. "First he saves Cliff Walk, and now he thinks he can cure the crippled." He looked back to Dante, his sky blue eyes narrowed, the planes of his too-thin face chiseled into pale marble. "What else, dear brother? Please, don't leave me in suspense. Will you raise the dead? Turn water into wine?"

Dante rested an elbow on the arm of the Bath chair and dropped his head onto his hand. He had gone to war, leaving behind a happy, smiling Tyler, and returned to find a beaten, broken, bitter man. And he could not accept that. He *would* not accept that! "Ty, you know what the doctor said—"

"Yes, yes, your damned London quack! I heard him. 'The

31

Kasey Michaels

bones are healed now, my lord, the pelvis, the femurs.' " he quoted in an acerbic singsong voice. " 'It is only your sadly unused muscles and your *will* that remain damaged. If you will but apply yourself, my lord, you will walk again.' Apply myself? The devil I will, Dante! Look at these legs!" he exclaimed, beating on his thin thighs with his fists. "They may pain me like the devil, but they don't move! They'll *never* move!"

Dante had heard all of this before, expressed in varying ways. Tyler had been told that he could walk, if he'd only believe it. He would have a considerable limp, thanks to his more badly broken left leg, but he could walk. If only he would try! If only he had some reason for wanting to get out of that damned chair! Struck by a sudden inspiration, Dante spoke without first examining his words. "Would your legs move for ten thousand pounds, Ty?"

Tyler looked levelly at his brother for a long time, an interval during which Dante cursed himself for being ten thousand times a fool, then said quietly, "You're right, brother mine. You *are* a bastard." He turned his head away and shouted for Farris, who entered the room quickly and wheeled his master from his brother's presence.

Dante, dressed in all his groom's finery, remained on the threadbare carpet, the kneeling penitent, and wondered why he was not feeling the least inclined to pray.

The stone chapel at Cliff Walk, although attached to the main building by a graceful curved corridor, was more than four centuries older than the remainder of the manor house, which had been built in the mid-1700s.

Perhaps it was the chapel's great age, Sarah Jane had thought a day previously when she toured Cliff Walk with the marquess, that explained why it was so very barbaric-looking, with dark, heavy wood and, in one corner, a wolf's head leering down from the rafters.

No matter what the reason, the chapel was most unusual.

But then, there was nothing very usual about the huge, sprawling manor house, beginning with the arrangement of the rooms. The family wing had been constructed first, according to the marquess, so that the Muirs could live in comfort while the remainder of the structure was built in easy stages over the succeeding decades—meaning, as Sarah Jane privately decided, when another marriage was made and the money for further construction became available.

That remainder of Cliff Walk consisted of a large, imposing three-story central brick building housing the state rooms, an enormous separate kitchen pavilion directly across from and designed to outwardly resemble the family wing, and a music room and greenhouse that made up the fourth wing across from the chapel wing, all of these attached to the state rooms by long, curved corridors at each of the four corners.

A large glass dome rested atop the round saloon in the state rooms, an imposing bit of architecture that defied Sarah Jane's ability to understand how it could have been positioned there in the first place.

The rear of the main building was as impressive as its front, each entrance having enormous split staircases leading to ground level, those in the front formed in rigid angles like facing C's, while those leading from the saloon curved in the way of fluid half-moons.

Well, Sarah Jane thought now, a curiously silent marquess at her side as she made her way from the family wing and along the ornately stuccoed corridor leading to the state rooms, perhaps not half-moons precisely.

As a matter of fact, she had decided late last night as she attempted without success to sleep, the curving staircases were more like feelers, or whatever it was that those little outgrowths at the top of an insect's head were called.

If she were a bird and could soar high above Cliff Walk to look down at its sprawling size, she imagined it would be like looking down at a huge, square, backwards bug with feelers on its head and with the front stairs acting as some sort of taillike appendage.

The four wings, attached as they were by the curved corridors—two curving toward the tail, two toward the feelers—would be the feet and legs of the bug. Square feet?

What bug ever had square feet? A squashed bug? Well, perhaps she could improve on her analogy with better acquaintance with the place.

And perhaps not. Especially after she had finally fallen into a fitful sleep last night, only to be awakened by a horrid black bug that had crawled across her hand and frightened her half to death.

No wonder she had likened Cliff Walk to a bug—the place was infested with them! She had seen two in the family dining room and three more in the family drawing room, one of which Grandmother Trowbridge had said looked large enough for Wellington to have sent forth, like Goliath, into battle!

What a shambles Cliff Walk was! Bugs, patches of damp on the walls, curious pale shapes against the darkened wallpapers showing where portraits and mirrors and decorative pieces had once taken pride of place, prodigiously complex and long-lived cobwebs hanging from dusty chandeliers, fireplace grates black with soot, carpets so dirty they sent up clouds of nose-tickling dust with her every step, the dozen or more niches in the enormous marble hallway devoid of the statues that must once have been displayed there.

They came to the end of the corridor, and the marquess ushered her through a wide doorway and into the small red saloon, his hand tightly grasping her arm just above her elbow, so she felt less like a bride being guided and more like a carriage being *steered,* and then into the three-story-high hall, a rather insufficient name for such a grand chamber.

Her footsteps echoed hollowly on the Italian marble floor—the rather dirty Italian marble floor—and she nervously counted the eighteen freestanding, floor-to-very-high-ceiling soaring alabaster columns, nine on either side of the long room, as they continued on their way toward the chapel.

This single chamber, known simply as "the hall," was more than a challenge to her housekeeping abilities. It presented a daunting dare to prove herself worthy of being Lord Dante Muir's bride, for Audrey had already admitted that housekeeping was totally beyond her and had years earlier abdicated any interest in the running of Cliff Walk.

Ah, well, Sarah Jane thought, trying not to giggle nervously, knowing she should strive to be piously serious as she went to her wedding. *At least Grandmother Trowbridge's veil is making a valiant beginning, sweeping the floor as I walk,* she decided.

Dusty sunlight filtered through the four smaller glass rooftop domes that served as the only illumination in the windowless hall, and Sarah Jane wondered idly if there might be some way to have the domes washed without having to rely on the whims of weather to do the job for her.

She wondered about a lot of things, whole volumes of things, as the marquess led her through the round saloon with its painted friezes high on the walls—a fortunate bit of decoration, she knew, as the money mad marquess had long ago rendered most of Cliff Walk devoid of any salable ornamentation.

And it was so cold, even with small, smoky fires burning in one or two of the fireplaces. It would take a forest of logs to warm the rooms once something was done about cleaning the chimneys. Of course, in the meantime they could be roasted in their beds, if all the flues were as choked as those of the two large fireplaces situated in the hall.

She wondered how it would be possible to set Cliff Walk to rights, to replace all the portraits and statuary, to clean the beautiful but filthy circular carpet in the saloon, to find furniture to fill the nearly empty rooms, and to rid the place of dirt and damp and bugs.

But mostly she wondered why she was still thinking of housekeeping when she was now beyond the anteroom and dressing room of the king's bedchamber and on her way down the curved corridor leading to the chapel, to her grandmother, to the wolf's head, and to Lord Dante Muir.

"Will—will there be music, my lord?" she asked, succumbing to a sudden attack of nerves and digging in her heels just before a footman could step forward to open the double doors to the chapel. "I mean, if there is music, perhaps we should wait for it to begin, but if there isn't, how will we know that Lord Dante is already inside and that we are not too early? Or perhaps too late?"

"Dante is within, my dear. At least if he knows what's good for him, he is," the marquess replied, patting her forearm as if, she thought, he were trying to gentle a horse. "Lord Dante, Lord John, the earl and his countess, your dear grandmother and her few distinguished guests. Everyone is waiting for you. Now, I suggest you smile, my dear, as you look none too healthy, your skin as white as that gown you're wearing, your eyes all big and staring. We don't want to have everyone thinking you're a reluctant bride, now, do we?"

"I'm sorry, my lord." Sarah Jane lifted her chin and smiled obediently, although she was sure her features had formed themselves into grimace. She was not a reluctant bride. Far from it. She was overjoyed to be the bride of Lord Dante Muir.

It was becoming the *wife* of Lord Dante Muir that frightened her nearly into insensibility!

How would he appear when she saw him standing in front of the small altar? Resigned? Determined? Disgusted? Would he be standing there of his own free will, or had his father lashed him to that altar with a stout rope?

Maybe it wasn't too late to call a halt to this nonsense, or at least delay it for a while longer. She needed a few moments to herself, a few years to get used to this new arrangement in her life.

She wanted to go back to her room and have Mildred straighten her veil, perhaps have something to eat, or visit the water closet as she had forgotten to do before Mildred laced her into this horrible gown.

She wished she could check under the wide bed, hoping to locate the fleeting courage she'd clung to last night, find the Sarah Jane Trowbridge who had looked forward to playing the role of heroine, the role of wife.

Surely there was something she could do, something she could say, that would delay the inevitable?

But Sarah Jane did nothing. She said nothing. She simply

watched, with ever-widening brown eyes, as the marquess gave the signal to the footman and the doors were opened.

She walked into the antechamber, taking very small steps, and then into the even damper, colder air of the chapel itself, wishing the marquess would stop squeezing her arm, wondering if she would fall if he let her go, searching the dimness caused by the dark stained-glass windows for her grandmother, her bridegroom.

She saw her grandmother first.

It was difficult not to see Grandmother Trowbridge, no matter if she was standing in the midst of a multitude. Sarah Jane decided that she had been fated to spend her life as an insignificant pygmy living amid giants, first her grandmother and now the male Muirs. Thank heaven Audrey was of normal size!

She inspected her grandmother's grandiose ensemble, trying not to smile. The woman's purple plumes rose sharply at attention atop her steel gray head, like sentinels advertising her presence while guarding the fortress that was Elizabeth Forrester Trowbridge: wealthy, powerful, tactless, tasteless schemer extraordinaire.

Perhaps if she herself had been bigger, built more on the lines of her grandmother than on those of her much smaller parents and grandfather, Sarah Jane would have been less intimidated by this woman who had always loomed above her, larger than life, directing her steps along the path Elizabeth Trowbridge had chosen for her.

But how does a person, and a very small person at that, stand in the face of such mountainous purpose? To do so would that person require much more courage than Sarah Jane had thus far discovered in her own small breast?

Or would that person simply have to harbor not a single notion of self-preservation, nary a scintilla of common sense, while at the same time possessing either a large pistol, a stout whip, or a regiment of loyal soldiers willing to tie down this giant purple Gulliver while she slept?

And now Sarah Jane was marrying into the Muir family. Another clutch of giants!

She shivered convulsively and redirected her eyes to the few pews on the right, most especially the one holding the Earl of Easterly, his countess, and Lord John Muir. She smiled slightly as she saw that the earl had been lifted onto the pew, so that his Bath chair was not in evidence.

That seemed a nice gesture, and she thought the earl must feel much more a part of the proceedings this way, rather than having to be shuttled to one side, away from the action. And he was seated beside Audrey, his wife. Audrey, who was so very blond, so very beautiful, so very much the picture of everything Sarah Jane wished to be while she knew she was not.

They looked so well matched, the handsome blond earl and his equally handsome blond wife, so well dressed, so refined, so comfortable with the knowledge that they belonged in this chapel, on this land.

Beside Audrey, yet not so close as to invite comparison with his brother and sister-in-law, sat Lord John, the youngest Muir. The smiling Muir. The most approachable Muir. The—Sarah Jane decided as Lord John gave out a very large, very loud hiccup, then giggled and excused himself in a clear, carrying voice—drunken Muir.

Out of options, unless she wished to turn around and pay homage to the mounted wolf's head, Sarah Jane at last lifted her eyes and stared directly toward the altar, at the robed clergyman waiting for her, and at the tall, dark man who stood just to one side, returning her gaze.

He was wonderfully attractive! Surely none of Miss Austen's gentlemen had ever been half so handsome, or half so formidable. How he must be hating this! How he must be hating her! To have to publicly sell himself, to have to go through this ridiculous ceremony, when all the important papers had already been signed, the ones that began with "I, Elizabeth Forrester Trowbridge, in consideration of my granddaughter's marriage to Lord Dante Muir, do hereby bequeath and bestow the sum of . . ."

She felt such pity for him, for she was certain he was a very proud man.

To marry for money was one thing, but to be forced to

marry so very far beneath him, and to a young woman who, if the smell from the shop had somewhat faded, still reeked most odiously of camphor. To marry such a weak specimen, such an undersized, paltry, insignificant little thing, such a sad disaster of a wife! Afraid of her own shadow, afraid of taking a wrong step, a right step, any step at all. Living courageously inside her mind, slaying dragons and triumphing over evil and dazzling the world with her beauty and wit and being so lovable. But only inside that sad, pathetic mind.

And loving him. Yes, may the dear Lord help her. Loving him.

Loving him because he had been polite to Jessup. Loving him because he wasn't afraid of Elizabeth Forrester Trowbridge. Loving him because he was taking her away from a life of dreams and offering her some semblance of reality. Loving him because his eyes flashed when he smiled, and that smile was so adorably crooked, and his hand, when it had touched hers as he proposed, had been so strong, so dry, and so very, very steady. Loving him because it was inconceivable that she could do anything else and still make sense of all that was happening, was about to happen to her.

She was beside him now, and the marquess was gone, and the vicar was speaking. Daring everything, she looked up into Lord Dante's eyes, those dark, sparkling eyes.

He must have sensed her gaze, for he looked down at her, past the veil and the jeweled band and all her horrible black hair, and smiled at her, one side of his mouth tugging upward. His eyes twinkled with mischief, telling her in silent communion that he knew how silly they both looked, how silly it was to conduct this particular ceremony in front of anyone less than a barrister, and how very much he wished the pair of them someplace else.

Why, if she hadn't known better, she'd have thought he was about to take her hand and hurry her off somewhere on the grounds, to hide them away from all this orchestrated farce, where they could sit, and talk, laugh, and perhaps get to know each other better. They could find a small stream and use her wedding veil as a fishnet and catch themselves some dinner that they could cook over an open fire, and she could tell him that when she finished refurbishing Cliff Walk it wouldn't have so much as a smidgen of purple in it anywhere.

It all would be so lovely, so wonderful. A lovely, wonderful dream. Of course they'd probably both catch a terrible chill and die after daring to sit on the cold ground in November. Oh, dear. Why did reality always have to intrude on such lovely daydreams?

"We are gathered here today, in the sight of God and this company, to join this man and this woman . . ."

Yes? Oh, yes. Yes!

"If there is anyone here present . . ."

"Present? I say! *I'm* present! I think I should say, *someone* should say—Ty, shouldn't one of us *say?* Perhaps we should refine on that question for the nonce. I mean, Dante, you can't *really*—"

"Shut up, Johnny," Lord Dante intoned quietly without turning around, taking Sarah Jane's hand and squeezing it. "Continue, Reverend, if you please. My brother has had a momentary lapse, undoubtedly induced by the slight fever he has been suffering from all week. We can safely ignore him." He smiled at Sarah Jane. "Can't we, my dear?"

Sarah Jane felt herself nodding in agreement, her tongue stuck to the roof of her very dry mouth as her heart pounded in her ears. She would have agreed if Lord Dante had just politely inquired if she wished for him to cut off her left foot and stuff it into the wolf's gaping jaws.

Oh, yes, indeed!

She loved this man.

She was convinced of it.

Or, Sarah Jane thought, shivering, had she found it necessary to her sanity to fall in love, at least with the dream?

CHAPTER 2

Pure and ready to mount to the stars.

Dante Alighieri

I'm sorry, Dante. Horribly, horribly sorry and most dreadfully embarrassed. Or have I already said that?"

Lord Dante stood in front of the dressing table, peering into the mirror and idly wondering if he looked in any way different, now that he was a married man. He didn't think so.

"Yes, Johnny, you've already said that," he answered, turning to smile indulgently at his brother. "You've said it, rhymed it, even put it to music during dinner, much to the delight of the hog butcher and his ample wife. I think we can now safely drop the subject."

Lord John lowered his chin onto his chest as he sat sprawled in a nearby chair, his long legs splayed out in front of him for balance, a nearly empty glass in his right hand. "Protesting the marriage. God, Dante, Papa would have shot me if he'd had a pistol in his waistcoat. Your poor little bride, poor little Sarah Jane. That is her name, isn't it? Sarah Jane? Sarah Jane Trowbridge Muir? Such a long string of names for such a bit of a thing! She forgave me straightaway. Lovely child. Well, not precisely *lovely*, is she? Though

41

I do like her eyes. They're soft, rather like Growler's, don't you think?"

"You're comparing my wife to that hound of yours, Johnny?" Dante slipped his dressing gown over his shoulders. He was minus his jacket, waistcoat, and neckcloth but still clad in his shirt and breeches, for although he never wore any sort of nightclothes, he didn't want to send his bride screaming into the night the moment he entered the bedchamber.

Lord John levered himself out of the chair. He wove his way across the carpet to the drinks table and poured himself another liberal three fingers of brandy. At least he was neat in his habits. Some drunks dispensed with niceties like glasses and drank straight from the decanter.

"I like Growler, Dante. Like him half again as well as I like most people, come to think of it. But I suppose you're right. Shouldn't have said it. Shouldn't have thought it. Apologize to your bride again, will you?"

Dante merely nodded, not bothering to point out that, since he wasn't about to race at top speed to his new bride and repeat his brother's assessment of her looks, he would have no reason to forward the man's apology.

"Don't you think you've made deep enough inroads into the wine cellar for one day, Johnny?" he asked instead, watching as his brother squinted fiercely, trying to locate the chair once more.

"Nope. I'm still standing, you see. Still walking. Still talking. Still thinking, damn it!" He swallowed the brandy in a single gulp, then turned to brace himself against the table and grin owlishly at Dante. "When the thinking stops, *then* I've drunk enough."

Dante shook his head. "Arabella's been married for more than three years, Johnny, and rather happily, or so I'm told. She has a child. Isn't it time you gave it up?"

Lord John pushed himself away from the drinks table and stood at drunken attention as he glared at his brother. "Don't mention her name again, Dante!" he exclaimed heatedly, then giggled. "Did I sound sufficiently outraged, brother? Sufficiently heartsore? No, I suppose not. Shall I tell you a secret? Oh, why not? I can trust you."

He leaned forward and waggled his fingers at Dante. "I don't drink to forget Arabella, Dante. I did once, for perhaps a fortnight, but no longer. Besides, I hear she's grown fat, which cheers me greatly. Fat and most probably shrewish. Married women are, you know. I drink, you see," he began, then stopped, frowning. "Well, never mind. I think I have been drinking too much to remember the reason just now."

Dante frowned, taking his brother's arm and leading him back to the chair, a feat that Lord John was obviously not capable of achieving on his own. The man had been drinking steadily since breakfast, and looked it. His clothing was disheveled, his thick blond hair hung in his red-rimmed blue eyes, his limbs appeared to act independently of his wishes, and now his tongue seemed to have come unhinged.

This was neither the time nor the place for his younger brother to bare his soul. Not while Sarah Jane waited in the next room. While his wife waited in the next room. But Dante knew he had to listen. "You don't have to drink, Johnny," he said, lamely, he knew. But he had to say something.

Lord John sighed as he relaxed into the chair, then grinned up at his brother. "Yes, I do, Dante. It's the one thing I do well. Papa spends money, Ty suffers, Dante saves us, and Johnny drinks. All us Muirs have our roles, Dante. I'm merely holding up my end."

He collapsed his head into his hands. "And sometimes not. Dearest brother, savior mine, do you think you could point me to the door? I know it's over there somewhere, but it will insist upon moving each time I try to search it out."

Dante pulled the bell rope, summoning a servant. He watched while the man assisted Johnny from the room before turning back to the mirror over the dressing table.

He saw a man, not a very young man, but a man of two and thirty, a man who looked very different from his father and brothers and very much like his deceased mother. A man who had fought on the Peninsula. A man who had married for money, telling himself he was doing the right thing while knowing it was the most cowardly thing he could have done.

No.

He didn't look any different.

None of them looked any different.

Not Tyler, sunk in his misery.

Not Audrey, blond and beautiful and totally useless.

Not his father, still trying to conjure up a way to separate Dante from Mrs. Trowbridge's largesse.

Not Johnny, determined to play the role of failure.

No. None of them had changed. Except that there was now another Muir. A very small, bewildered-looking Muir. His wife. Dear God, *his wife!*

Dante crossed to the drinks table and poured himself a generous splash of brandy.

The room was very large and very dark. Larger than the chamber she had dressed in that morning, a lifetime ago. Smaller, though, than the opulent, intimidating suite of rooms she had occupied in her grandmother's house.

And the bed was larger than the room itself. No, it wasn't. Not really. It only seemed that way now that she was lying in the very middle of it, miles from the edges, and shivering.

Mildred, a good woman but at times unbelievably obtuse, decided that her mistress had caught a chill in the damp chapel and had all but buried her beneath a multitude of covers meant to keep her from further discomfort. They weren't working, however. She was still shivering.

But it was a lovely room. Really. Or at least it could be. The damp patches on the wallpaper detracted somewhat from its beauty, as did the sparsity of furniture, which was limited to a few large storage cabinets, a pair of faded brocade chairs in front of the fireplace, and the enormous four-poster bed.

The carpeting was threadbare in spots and the velvet draperies were extremely dusty, as Sarah Jane had learned after Mildred left and she had deliberately pulled them back, hoping for the comforting illumination of moonlight.

The candles, and there were too few of them, cast weird shadows on the walls beside the bed and for the most part hid the faraway door that Sarah Jane knew led to her husband's dressing room.

She had been staring at that door for five minutes, fifteen minutes, a century. But it hadn't opened. Perhaps he had decided to sleep in his dressing room. Gentlemen did that, or so she believed.

They slept in their dressing rooms whenever their wife was indisposed, when childbirth was imminent, or when they simply couldn't stand the sight of the woman who had bought her way into their illustrious family.

Sarah Jane's tour of Cliff Walk had shown her that only the marquess had a suite of rooms that contained two bedchambers, one for him and one for his deceased wife.

Tyler and Audrey didn't share the second largest chamber, but only because Tyler had been placed in a ground-floor room, which had been converted from a small sitting room into an invalid chamber. There were not enough funds to keep open his own small manor house at nearby Easterly.

Johnny's chamber, though roomy, was the smallest of all, not that he was known to sleep in it above twice a week, or so the marquess had warned her.

Lord John usually slept where he landed once the drink had overtaken him, and she had been told not to be surprised to find him and his hound, Growler, curled up together on the half landing or slumped in a chair in the drawing room or, on very warm nights, even collapsed comfortably among the flowers in the tangled gardens.

What a strange, intriguing, and potentially wonderful family she had joined this day! What a marvelous life she would have, armed with the deepest pockets in half of England, refurbishing this beautiful house and bringing it back to all its former glory!

Dante might not know it, but Sarah Jane had her own fortune, one that would make her grandmother's settlement on Dante look like a pittance. For now, for the interim, she would see only the income from that fortune, but when she had produced a male heir, control of the entire amount would come to her. She would give that money to Dante!

She would save them.

She would save them all. Oh, yes. Save them, make them happy, surround them with beauty, bring love and order and comfort into their lives!

That was, after all, what heroines did. It was their stock-in-trade. She had always longed to be a heroine. She couldn't be another Joan of Arc, for she did not quite relish the idea of being burned at the stake, and she did not have the physical presence or the courage to be another Boadicea, or even another Queen Elizabeth.

But she had money. Lots and lots of lovely money. And she had her dreams. More dreams than she could hope to see fulfilled in a dozen lifetimes.

Largest, most important, of these dreams was to make Lord Dante Muir love her. She could not dazzle him with her beauty, as someone like Audrey could, but she had other weapons. Dante loved Cliff Walk; he loved his family. She would put his family to rights. She would save Cliff Walk. That was the way to her husband's heart.

Smiling, and not shivering quite so badly as she had been moments before, Sarah Jane snuggled down beneath the covers and wove colorful daydreams in which everyone at a mistily bucolic and beautiful Cliff Walk loved her, and her husband—her dear, handsome, vaguely frightening husband—worshiped the very ground she walked on.

The lovely picture vanished abruptly at the sound of her grandmother's voice. Did the woman have to invade every moment, every aspect, of her life?

"Was he in here yet? He's downstairs now, you know, in the drawing room, talking with that brother of his. Not the sot, the cripple. Did he do his duty by us? Did he bed you? He won't see a penny till he beds you."

Sarah Jane pushed herself to a sitting position, pressing her back against the carved headboard, and watched quietly as Elizabeth Trowbridge lumbered into the room, resplendent in a purple quilted satin dressing gown.

What was she doing here? Didn't she know Lord Dante could arrive at any moment? Or did she plan to watch as he crawled into bed beside her?

"I—I haven't seen Lord Dante since Mildred brought me upstairs for my bath, Grandmother Trowbridge. You say he's downstairs? Perhaps he's hungry, poor thing. He didn't eat much at our wedding supper."

"Hungry?" Mrs. Trowbridge threw back her head and laughed out loud. "How should I know, much less care? And sit up straight. You look like a child. Should have fed *you* more, and then maybe you wouldn't have ended up so scrawny. Why did Mildred braid your hair? Gives you much more consequence to have it curled—sort of puffs you up."

"Yes, Grandmother Trowbridge," Sarah Jane answered, toying with the thick, brushlike bottom of the single heavy braid that hung over her right shoulder and nearly to her waist. She was a married woman now. Did that mean she could summon a servant and have her grandmother removed from the bedchamber, from Cliff Walk itself?

It was a tantalizing thought. She could have her thrown out into the night, dressed only in that ugly purple dressing gown. That was what heroines did—rid castles of all their ogres. Or was that feat reserved for heroes? And she did love her grandmother. Most of the time. "It's just that my hair becomes so very tangled—"

Mrs. Trowbridge dismissed Sarah Jane's weak explanation with a wave of one beringed hand.

"Never mind, sweetie," she said with what Sarah Jane knew to be sincere, if misguided, affection. She could never really throw her grandmother out of the house. But it *was* an intriguing thought.

"You can't help your size, Lord bless you," Elizabeth Trowbridge said. "You're the female throwback to your grandfather, I suppose. My Sam may have been half my size, but he was *mighty*. You have to be mighty as well, you know, and don't you forget it. You're Lady Dante now, and mistress of this household. Don't count that Audrey chit, even if she is a countess. She's nothing but fluff, a pretty, brainless twit, and couldn't care less if you take on the running of the place. I've trained you well for this day, Sarah Jane, trained you long and proper. You know what's expected of you. And stop playing with your hair."

Sarah Jane, long ago seasoned to obey her grandmother in everything, immediately dropped the braid and leaned forward on the bed, unable to break the habits of a lifetime in a single day.

"Grandmother Trowbridge," she ventured, at last daring to ask the question that had been terrifying her all day every day since Lord Dante Muir had proposed, "what exactly are my wifely duties?"

She watched, amazed, as Elizabeth Trowbridge flushed a deep, unflattering red.

"I've told you a dozen times, sweetie. Planning menus, riding herd on the servants, watching over the household accounts, setting this decrepit pile to rights, seeing to the tenants, playing the hostess—"

"Yes, yes, I know all of that." Sarah Jane pushed back the covers to sit cross-legged in her voluminous white lawn nightgown, looking intently at her grandmother. "I'm talking about my *wifely* duties. About the reason Lord Dante and I must sleep in the same bed. About *children*. Do you understand what I'm asking, Grandmother Trowbridge? Miss Austen alluded to some things in her books, and Mildred told me that there is a great deal more to it than kissing, which was quite agreeable to me when Lord Dante kissed me this afternoon after the ceremony. I didn't wish to shock Mildred, but I do have some fair idea of the rudiments of the thing, the different anatomical arrangements of males and females, and their purposes, their dispositions during attempts to procreate. But shouldn't there be more, some sort of *deep feelings* that enter into the . . ."

Mrs. Trowbridge looked—rather longingly, Sarah Jane decided—toward the door through which she had entered the room, then sighed and approached the bed. Depositing her considerable bulk on the edge of the mattress, she took hold of Sarah Jane's hand and lifted it to her cheek.

"Oh, child, what a fool I am," she said in her gruff voice. "No one told me, either. I hated them for that lapse, and now here I am, guilty of the same crime. You are so well prepared for every contingency; I saw to that. But you are completely ignorant of the most important weapon in any woman's arsenal: her sex. It's just—it's just that you are my little girl, my only grandchild, and I . . . well, let's just say I didn't really want to think about the matter in any great detail, all right?"

Sarah Jane began to shiver once more. It was unusual for her grandmother to show any sign of affection. For her to show any sort of weakness was more than unusual; it had never happened before in Sarah Jane's memory. And it was frightening. She sought to help the woman. "I just think I ought to know a bit more of how to, um, how to go about it, the various mechanics, the step-by-step protocol of the procedure. Mildred said I might even like it, which is very gratifying, I suppose. She said *some* women do."

Her hand was unceremoniously released and allowed to fall onto the covers. "Mildred is an ass," Mrs. Trowbridge responded tightly, then seemed to think better of what she had said. "Look, sweetie, it's getting very late, and I just remembered something I have to do."

She grabbed clumsily at Sarah Jane's shoulders and pulled her into a short, fierce embrace. "Just remember, sweetie, I only wanted you to have what I was denied. I only meant the best for you. You had to marry someday. And, well, drat it all anyway, at least I bought you a *pretty* one!"

Then she was gone, vanished in a cloud of heavy scent and a swish of royal purple, and Sarah Jane was alone once more.

And shivering.

Dante left his brother in the drawing room and headed, slowly, reluctantly, up the winding steps to the hallway leading to his room, his bridal bower.

He and Tyler had sat together quietly for nearly an hour, each lost in his own thoughts as the clock ticked on toward midnight, Tyler disinclined to be wheeled to his lonely bed for another wakeful night while his wife slept alone in her own chamber, and Dante wishing to postpone the inevitable for another moment, another hour.

He had just reached the upstairs landing when Elizabeth Trowbridge stepped out from the shadows. She grabbed his elbow and pulled him into an alcove that had once held a statue of some Greek goddess, long since shuttled off to storage so that it wouldn't be necessary to have extra staff eating their heads off at the Muirs' expense in order to dust the thing and others like it scattered all through Cliff Walk.

"Still up and about, ma'am?" he asked as politely as he could, for he had grown rather weary of this encroaching woman. "I would have thought you'd be sleeping the sleep of the happily triumphant, having seen all your fondest dreams come true. That was you I heard snickering with glee when the vicar at last pronounced the vows, wasn't it?"

"Not now, Muir," she snapped, shutting him off. "Just tell me something. Have you ever bedded a virgin?"

"Have I ever— Oh, that's it! That is well and truly *it!* Madam, I have married your granddaughter. You have what you want, and I have what I want. We are, for the most part, mutually satisfied. But you do not own me, and I refuse to answer your every ridiculous question and obey your every command like some bought-and-paid-for looby. Have I made myself clear?"

She leaned closer in the darkness, so tall that she stood nearly eye to eye with him, and spoke quietly but fiercely. "I never told her. She can sew a seam, paint with water-colors—badly, I admit—and play a tolerable tune. She can run a household, sniff out a slacker or a cheat, do dozens of things no ordinary chit can do—but I never *told her.*"

Dante was now thoroughly confused as well as angry. "Never told her what, madam? I'm afraid you'll have to be more specific. What doesn't my wife know?"

"You know, damn it all, Muir—the *pain!* I'm talking about the pain. One of my sisters—I disremember which one—told me a little, but all she said proved wrong. Sam was a good man, but undemanding and considerably my senior. I think he may have been clumsy, but I can't be sure, having no way to judge, no source for comparison, if you take my meaning. I kept thinking of the title and the consequence and going into Society. I forgot how innocent my granddaughter is, how much of a child. Oh, this isn't coming out right! Lord Dante, son, do you understand what I'm trying to say?"

"Yes. Unfortunately, I believe I understand completely." Dante wished he had drunk more brandy. A lot more brandy. Perhaps an entire decanter of the stuff. "Sarah Jane, my wife, is totally ignorant of what it means to consummate our marriage, completely unprepared for the initial pain that comes along with the demands a husband makes upon his wife. Thank you, Mrs. Trowbridge. Thank you so very, *very* much." He turned to leave the woman standing in the shadows, knowing that if he lingered, he just might want to hit her.

She grabbed at his arm once more. "Look, I'll bargain with you."

Dante stared down at her meaningfully until she released his arm. "I think we've had enough of bargains."

"No. Listen to me. I'll leave in the morning, and I won't return for a month, *two* months, if you'll promise to . . . to be gentle with the child."

Dante considered this for a moment, still longing to strike Betts Trowbridge. Did she think he was some sort of monster? Not only did he not plan to fall on his bride and ravish her, he was having some difficulty believing it would be possible to perform his husbandly duty at all this night, for he wasn't in the least attracted to the child in any remotely romantic sense.

"*Three* months," he said at last, enjoying the thought of a Cliff Walk free of Mrs. Elizabeth Trowbridge.

"Three?" Mrs. Trowbridge frowned. Obviously she had planned to take up residence until the first christening. "Oh, all right. You're twice the man your father ever was when it comes to bargaining. But you have to consummate the

arriage tonight. The longer you wait, the more difficult it
ill be for Sarah Jane. It won't be pretty, but she has to
ecome a woman. Now. Tonight. Or you can go whistle for
ose mortgages. I haven't paid them yet, you know."

"So genteel. So refined. So loving." Dante shook his head.
So very *inspiring*. But it must be closer to *four* months. We
ill be deprived of your scintillating company until the first
ay of March. Agreed?"

"Agreed," Mrs. Trowbridge said with a sigh, lifting her
in and shaking back her shoulders as if she had just
moved something very heavy from them. "I do love her,
ou know. I love her terribly. In my own way."

"As you say, madam," Dante answered, disgusted, and
ft her where she stood.

He approached the bedchamber, resting his hand on the
tch and then directing his gaze toward the stairs until Mrs.
rowbridge retreated down the hallway leading to the guest
ambers on the far side of the landing. Only then did he
pen the door and slip inside.

He needed a few moments to accustom himself to the
mi-darkness, even though this had been his room since
e'd left the third-floor nursery and he was familiar with
very inch of it. He looked first at the chairs and then at the
ed, where he could make out a small figure reclining
gainst the pillows.

She might not know much, Dante decided, but at least she
eemed to know where she belonged.

Taking a half dozen steps in the direction of the bed,
olding his breath and half hoping she'd fallen asleep, he at
ast saw those huge, long-lashed eyes staring at him. Growl-
r's eyes. Big. Brown. Trusting.

And so damned innocent.

"Good evening, Sarah Jane," he said fatalistically, know-
ig that he could no longer avoid the moment he had been
ireading since first he had agreed to this marriage.

Why couldn't he be like other men, and regard this
edding night as a duty to be performed, an exercise in
usbandly rights that, although it might not prove entirely

pleasurable, at least would give him an excuse to rut withou having to worry about gaining himself a dose of the clap ir exchange for a bit of release?

That was what wives were for, wasn't it—safe release anc heirs? Even the Prince Regent had done his duty, only begging his man to bring him some brandy when he first clapped eyes on his own unsuitable bride, complaining, "I am not well."

"Lord—Lord Dante," he heard her say quietly, and he was struck once more with the comforting thought that she had a pleasant voice. Low, faintly husky, almost melodious. Nothing like the grandmother's. Nothing about her was anything like her grandmother.

He supposed he should be grateful for such favors, small as they were.

He smiled involuntarily, one side of his mouth lifting, and replied, "Just Dante, Sarah Jane. I hardly believe we need be so formal."

"Dante," she repeated, and he noticed that she had relaxed somewhat, her fingers no longer clutching the covers in a death grip.

Her eyes were really quite lovely. And they weren't precisely like Growler's. They tilted up at the outer corners, just slightly, just enough to be interesting. Intriguing. And her neck was so long, so strangely graceful, above the straight shoulders. That was rather strange. Up until this moment he hadn't been aware his wife even possessed a neck.

And her face looked somehow different tonight; her fragile jawline was so beautifully, cleanly sculpted, her cheekbones so high and faintly mysterious. He could see her more clearly now that her atrocious mountain of black hair was pulled back from her face and forehead.

Why, for all her great age of ten and eight she was a little fairy child, a delicate wood sprite. And, though thin, she was actually rather pretty. Young, but not too young to marry. Not too young to bed.

Why hadn't he noticed this before? And why hadn't he

noticed how she looked at him, almost as if she worshiped him? Dear Lord, could it be possible? Did the child fancy herself in love with him?

She spoke again. "Are—that is, would you want to come to bed now?"

"Why, yes, Sarah Jane," he said, untying the sash of his dressing gown, his smile widening. Perhaps there were more benefits to be had from this marriage than simply an end to a lifetime of genteel titled poverty. And if she loved him, he had rescued her from Betts Trowbridge. He hadn't done that solely because of the money. He couldn't have. Perhaps he, too, had felt an attraction. Oh, the devil with it! He would analyze his feelings at some other time. He had more important things on his mind now. "As a matter of fact, I just might."

Her eyes widened, then closed when he turned back the covers. He prudently blew out a few of the half-dozen candles on the table beside the bed before quickly slipping out of his breeches and shirt and sliding, quite naked, between the crisp new sheets that had been brought from her grandmother's house.

As moonlight streamed in through the windows, he lay very still for a few moments, allowing her to become accustomed to the fact that he was sharing the bed with her.

At last he turned onto his side and propped up his head with one hand, exposing his bare shoulders and chest.

He saw that she was likewise lying on her side, facing him, those huge eyes open once more and staring at him as if he might pounce on her at any moment. *And I just might.*

"That's right," he began quietly, hoping to gain her confidence. "I'm naked. We're married now, Sarah Jane. Do you know what married people do when they're in bed together?"

"I—I have some idea, yes. I'm not entirely stupid. I've read novels," she answered, still staring at him. She clearly was frightened nearly out of her mind, but she wasn't running. She wasn't crying. She was just staring at him unblinkingly, unflinchingly. Bravely. The way she had the day he had proposed, the way she had in the chapel.

She was very good at staring. It was almost as if she could see through him, brand him the hypocrite that he was, trying to believe he was in love when his primary emotion at the moment could only be described as lust. Dante winced inwardly and dismissed his damning thoughts, preferring to concentrate on the moment at hand. The project at hand.

Ah, this was encouraging! The neck of her gown had slid to one side, revealing a glimpse of beautifully formed collarbone. She had the small, well-defined bone structure of true royalty, and just enough soft flesh covering those aristocratic bones to make it all interesting.

Or was he only trying to convince himself that she was desirable so that he could desire her, at least until the marriage was consummated? Until a male heir was conceived. Until he could make himself believe he wasn't an opportunistic bastard.

It was dark in the chamber, with only the few candles he'd left burning, some stripes of moonlight falling across the foot of the bed, and the dying fire to brighten the room. Perhaps he had been hasty, dousing those bedside candles. He would have liked to see more of Sarah Jane Muir.

A lot more.

At the same time he became extremely aware of his nakedness. His more than slight arousal. Whether due to wishful thinking or a heretofore unsuspected emotional response to his bride, her impact on him was encouraging.

"Novel reading, Sarah Jane?" he answered, realizing he had not spoken in some moments. "So then you do know some things, I suppose. I haven't myself read novels. But that's very good. Do you know how babies are created?" he asked, then immediately wanted to kick himself.

He shouldn't be talking of babies. He should be explaining that what they were about to do was an expression of married love, of mutual caring, and that it could, if done correctly, prove to be a perfectly beautiful experience.

But maybe it was better to stick to this business of procreation. He could most probably deliver on that score. The love and mutual caring and beauty of the experience was another matter, for another time.

And most certainly not a goal to be hoped for this first night, this first time. Not for her, his virgin bride. A virgin! Every man wanted a virgin wife, but no man wanted to deal with the trouble of bedding one! No man, surely, save one who enjoyed inflicting pain.

"Babies, Sarah Jane. You live in the country. Surely you've seen . . . You've witnessed . . ."

She didn't answer him immediately. She only frowned, then shifted her gaze away from him. "I know more than I would wish my grandmother to believe I know, if that's what you mean. I—I had a dog once, when I was little," she explained quietly. "Molly. One day a stray came along, and . . . and— Well, Cook threw a bucket of water on them, and the stray ran off. Later, Molly had four puppies. But you can't mean that it's no more than that. If that's all it is, no wonder Miss Austen didn't go into any detail. I thought it also had to do with kissing, and—and hugging! Surely it can't be . . ."

Splendid comparison, Muir, Dante berated himself silently, *but you're the one who opened the door for it.* He stretched out his arm and began playing with the satin ribbons that held Sarah Jane's nightgown closed at the neck. "Indeed, it does have much to do with kissing. And hugging. Surely."

"That is reassuring, Dante," she told him artlessly. "I don't think Molly much enjoyed the experience. Um . . ." She was still looking straight at him, still trusting him. Loving him? "Would you explain how else it is different?"

Dante wanted to give it up. Give everything up. He could go away. He could go to France. There were monasteries in France, high up in the hills. He could live there quietly, communing with nature, praying, pressing grapes into inferior wine, doing penance for all the exciting, terrible thoughts now running through his brain.

He didn't have to stay here and be trusted by this innocent, intriguing, maddening child. Loved by this impressionable young girl doomed to disappointment.

He dropped the satin ribbon and moved closer, lifting his hand to stroke her cheek. Her smooth, warm cheek. One finger grazed her ear. It was a small ear, shell-like, and tucked close to her head. A perfectly adorable ear.

He longed to run his fingers over it, explore it, tease the lobe, dip inside and watch to see if she shivered in reaction to the intimate invasion.

"Well, as I said, little pet, humans kiss. We kissed this afternoon, in the chapel. Remember? Would you like to begin with a kiss?"

"That—that seems reasonable," she whispered, and he felt his stomach muscles tightening as she moved her head fractionally, gravitating toward his hand, until his palm cupped half her small jaw, one finger pressed in the shallow hollow behind her ear, his thumb lightly stroking her full lower lip.

She was so tiny, so fragile, that he felt suddenly humble, and more than a little afraid he might not only hurt her but break her as well.

Should he warn her about the pain?

No. She'd learn about it soon enough.

Should he get it over quickly?

Did he want it to be over quickly?

"Sarah Jane," he whispered, moving ever closer, so that they were now only inches apart, so close that he could see a small pulse beating frantically at the base of her throat. He felt suddenly powerful, infinitely wise, yet terrifyingly vulnerable. *"Sarah."*

And then he was kissing her.

Her mouth was sweet and tasted vaguely of honeyed tea, soft and moist and thrillingly untutored.

He kissed her mouth, her eyelids, her short, straight nose, her shell-like ears.

He kissed her long throat, quick, butterfly kisses that heightened his desire, whetted his appetite for more . . . more. . . . Then he claimed her mouth again, teaching her, tutoring her, introducing her to the delights of his tongue.

How he had come to be crushed against her he would never know, but he felt her tremble as he slid a hand under her body and employed the other in lifting and caressing one small, firm breast through the soft lawn of her nightgown.

She went rigid with shock. He was sure it was shock.

He was so big, and she was so small. If he eased her onto her back, would the weight of him crush her? If he dared to insinuate his hand beneath the hem of her nightgown, raise the material up and over her head, would she freeze completely into immobility, afraid of him, afraid of her own body, her own nudity pressed against his?

He had thought it might be impossible to bed her. Silly, shortsighted man! It was impossible not to bed her. He didn't love her. He didn't really even know her. But he wanted her.

God, how he wanted her.

"Sarah Jane?" he questioned her quietly, gulping in steadying breaths as he pressed his lips against the hollow behind her ear. "Put your arms around me, little pet. Hold me."

She was nothing if not obedient, immediately clutching his shoulders, clumsily but with an eagerness that did wonders for his plans for the next few minutes.

He wouldn't undress her. Not tonight. There was time enough for that. There were years for that. He would gift her with her own modesty, taking only what he had to take, and leave experimentation, exploration, for another time, another moment, when there would be no worry about pain, and an infinite amount of time for pleasure.

He slid a hand onto her hip, using his fingers to slowly push her gown up past her knees, her thighs.

"I don't want to hurt you, little pet," he said as she held him convulsively, her own breathing ragged, whether with fear or with anticipation he did not wish to speculate. "But there will be some pain this first time. Only this first time, I promise, and never again. It isn't my idea, Sarah Jane, but nature's. Shall we get it over with?"

He felt her head move in the affirmative and wondered if her innocent, trusting eyes were open or closed. He prayed they were closed. He didn't want to see her pain, the pain he would inflict. He knew, at that moment, for at least this moment, he would rather die than watch her as she hurt.

Shifting himself slightly, he used his knee to part her legs,

58

feeling the rigid tension of her muscles, sensing her embarrassment.

Should he stop? Should he spend more time soothing her, hoping to arouse her, easing her slowly toward the disappointment he was sure awaited her?

No. He couldn't wait. He had never bedded a virgin. He had never wanted to bed a virgin. But now the thought excited him beyond measure, beyond reticence, almost beyond rational thought. He *was* a bastard.

He would take her maidenhead, her virginity, her innocence, and God help him, he would glory in the taking. There was something almost primeval in the thought of breaking through that delicate membrane that separated the girl child from the woman. Something infinitely powerful, immeasurably arousing.

He positioned himself between her legs, raising himself slightly so that he hovered over her, looking down into her small face, seeing the growing confusion and fear in those damnable, wonderful, trusting eyes.

Her arms were no longer around him but lay stiff at her sides. The sacrificial virgin offered up on the altar of her grandmother's ambition and her husband's greed. His greed and his burgeoning lust.

Did she have to look at him?

Slipping one hand between them, he sought her, guiding himself toward her, against her, his eyes closed against the shame he felt in his own desire.

Then, at last, he found her. She was wet! Not very, but moist enough to give him hope, encouragement. Enough to make him believe, as he wanted to believe, that she was ready for him.

No. He couldn't lie to himself. She wasn't ready for him. Nothing in her short, sheltered life had prepared her for him. Her body might instinctively know, but her mind, her heart, her soul, did not, could not.

The tension between them rapidly became unbearable, the deafening quiet relieved only by his heavy breathing, her stillness, her silence.

She was so soft, so small, so tight.

He was so very aware of her.

His brain was singing to him, threatening him, reminding him, urging him on, cursing him and exhorting him, challenging him to be less than he should have been, more than he had imagined.

So tight . . . so tight . . . so tight . . . so—*ah. God. Oh God oh God oh God!*

The tension that had been building broke free with the tearing of his young wife's body, and he felt himself falling, to enter, to be surrounded, to impale, to be captured inside the heat, the moisture, the dark secret of nature's plan, nature's most wonderful, most perplexing joke.

He lay very still for a moment, their bodies welded together from chest to knee, his head lying beside hers on the pillow, his breath coming back to him, hot and frantic, from the sheets.

She was quiet, totally unmoving, and he hated himself, knowing she had to be in pain, sure that she was caught between confusion at what had just happened and a deep longing to have his head on a pike for hurting her, for invading her most secret, intimate place.

But he couldn't stop.

He had come too far to stop.

It would be better for her next time. He promised her that, although he did not speak, could not speak.

All he could do was finish what he had started, what her grandmother had started, what his careless spendthrift father had started.

All he could do was lie, and tell himself that this was nothing more than the final seal on a mutually beneficial bargain.

All he could do was feel her terror . . . her softness . . . her warmth.

His lust.

He began to move. Hoping to give her some pleasure, he moved slowly, measuring his thrusts, praying for some sort of response. But all he could feel was his own passion, building rapidly, almost out of control.

So tight. So tight. So tight.

It was over almost before it had begun, and he could only slip his arms around her slim back and hold his breath as his seed pumped into her, branding her, making her his whether he wanted her or not, making her his whether she wanted him or not.

As he lay there, gasping for breath, cursing his lack of control, he felt her small hands come up around him, fluttering to rest on his perspiration-slick back. He felt her lips against his cheek before she turned her head away, before her arms fell back onto the bed once more.

She had forgiven him.

He wanted to kill himself.

Easing off her, he slipped her nightgown back down over her legs and left the bed, quickly pulling on his dressing gown before retrieving a small towel from the washbasin.

The covers were pulled up to her chin once more, and her eyes were wide and unblinking, as if she had just sustained a considerable jolt to her sensibilities. She most probably, most certainly, had. So had he.

"Here, Sarah Jane, you may wish to use this."

That was all he said, all he could think to say. He didn't want to see her blood, the evidence of his invasion.

She took the towel, murmuring her thanks, then turned onto her side, away from him.

He wanted to hold her, to comfort her, but she had rejected him. She probably wanted some time to herself. To think. Perhaps to weep. He had done his duty, and his presence was no longer required. No longer needed.

"It won't hurt the next time, Sarah Jane," he said helplessly, his voice so thick that he barely recognized it. "It won't hurt ever again. I promise."

"So you said, Dante. Thank you. I— Would it be possible for me to be alone now?"

There was nothing left for him to do but gather up his discarded clothing and retire to the small bed in his dressing room, and to the decanter of brandy that awaited him there. He would drink as much as he could as rapidly as he could.

But he would not look in the mirror.

CHAPTER 3

As good to be out of the world as out of the fashion.

Colley Cibber

Cliff Walk was beautiful in the daylight, if one didn't look too closely.

The faded colors on the upholstered pieces in the morning room were lovely, if one didn't insist upon noticing the fraying threads.

The unusually bright November sunshine pouring through the many-paned floor-to-ceiling windows and French doors topped by fanlights made beautiful patterns on the threadbare carpeting, even if that same sun highlighted the cobwebs that hid in the corners and the dust motes that dulled the unwaxed parquet floors.

The morning room, the family wing, all of Cliff Walk, reminded Sarah Jane of an old woman reduced to near penury but still proud, still standing, and still boldly daring the world to say anything disparaging about her.

In short, the place simply cried out to Sarah Jane for rescue, for assistance in regaining its former glory.

Which was a pity, for Sarah Jane Trowbridge Muir had never felt less eager to rescue anything or anybody in her entire life. All her rosy images for the past few weeks, her romantic dreams since coming to Cliff Walk, had disappeared, vanished in the moment when she realized that she really hadn't the faintest notion of what had happened to her and her formerly well-ordered, if dull, life.

She was a woman now, or so Mildred had told her that morning when she came to rouse her from bed and tut-tutted over the small dark stains speckling the sheet, her nightgown, and that horrible, damning towel. She was a wife.

Well, wasn't that above all things wonderful? She was a wife.

Grandmother Trowbridge had been correct: Mildred *was* an ass.

And that was all Sarah Jane Trowbridge Muir had learned with any certainty last night.

But last night was over. This was a new day, the first full day of her new life, and her grandmother had just minutes ago awkwardly kissed her cheek and departed Cliff Walk with hardly a word of farewell and without staying for so much as a bite of breakfast, leaving Sarah Jane alone in a houseful of strangers.

She hadn't a single clue as to what might happen next. She certainly hadn't been prepared for what had already happened, that was for certain. She hadn't been prepared for the humiliation, the violation, the pain—or the sinking feeling that something was terribly wrong with her.

There had to be something awfully wrong with her. After all, she had almost *enjoyed* the experience. Up until the pain, of course. After that, she hadn't really cared about anything except to wonder how much longer it would take before Dante, her husband and therefore her new mentor, her new master, would be done with whatever it was he seemed to find so exhausting, and leave her.

He hadn't enjoyed the experience. That had been painfully evident by his near silence, his quick departure. But Sarah Jane was quite convinced that he should have been pleased.

Considering that the act had everything to do with continuing the species, *somebody* certainly should garner some pleasure from the experience, or else the human race would have died out long ago.

After all, mustn't everyone practice the same method of procreation?

Now, here was a thought worth exploring! She closed her eyes and tried to picture her imposing grandmother and her small, painfully thin, always quiet grandfather indulging in the exertions she and Dante had performed last night. They had to have indulged in it—for her father had been born, hadn't he?

Her shoulders shook slightly as she tried, without noticeable success, to pretend she wasn't amused by the thought of Grandmother Trowbridge bending to a man's will, in bed, or anywhere else.

Oh, what was she thinking! Why should she care about Grandmother Trowbridge when she had her own much more recent experience to think about, to remember, to tease and torture her mind?

She stopped her nervous pacing of the morning room and sat down in a small, delicate rose brocade chair, her deeply ruffled pink skirts spread all around her, and blushed as she pleated one of the lace-edged flounces into a small fan between her fingers.

It hadn't *all* been bad, she decided, remembering the feel of Dante's mouth against hers. The heat of his breath beside her ear. The touch of his hand on her breast, on her bare hip.

The feel of his body pressing into hers, filling her.

He had said there would be pain only the first time. That meant he definitely planned on doing it again. Perhaps, with repetition, she would begin to enjoy the exercise more.

Sarah Jane certainly hoped so.

She dropped the ruffle and raised both hands to wave them at her heated cheeks, the warmth of the rather large fire in the grate combining with her lascivious thoughts, making her slightly uncomfortable.

She lifted the weight of her curled hair and fanned the damp skin at the nape of her neck, wishing for the millionth time that she could always keep her hair in the braid she wore at bedtime rather than endure an hour at the dressing table each morning, Mildred wielding the heated curling stick, pulling and fluffing and torturing until her hair ballooned around her skull, hung over her forehead, and tumbled down past her shoulders.

And her gown. If only it didn't have so many ruffles, so many *layers,* her starched petticoats scraping against the soft skin behind her knees whenever she sat down and making her feel so short and squat whenever she stood up. All her gowns were so very unlike those of the simply but elegantly clad Countess of Easterly, who wore less than half the clothing Sarah Jane did and looked twice as good while she was about it.

Sarah Jane had so many gowns, all of them sewn for her by Grandmother Trowbridge's favorite seamstress. Mrs. Wilcox was prodigiously talented with the needle, and copied all her patterns from the drawings in the dog-eared ladies' magazines she kept stacked in her parlor, so of course Sarah Jane's wardrobe had to be "all the crack," as her grandmother termed it.

Which magazines, Sarah Jane wondered, did Audrey Muir's seamstress consult when fashioning gowns? Maybe it would be worth her while to inquire and then go to the village and order a few gowns from the woman. Gowns without so many ruffles.

But perhaps she shouldn't spend Dante's money on anything so trivial. She had her own income, naturally, but she hadn't really intended to squander any of that money on herself. Would Dante mind if she spent her own money?

She should ask his opinion, although if he proved to be as elusive in future as he had so far this morning, she might have to wait a long time for an answer.

"Out ridin' the fields, like always," one of the footmen had told her earlier when she had summoned the courage to ask after her husband's whereabouts as she prepared to breakfast in solitude in the family dining room. "The marquess has us lug a tray up to his rooms, like we gots nothin' better to do, and the earl takes his in bed too, not that we mind about him, o' course. Can't do enough for Master Tyler, not none of us. His lady is fussed over by that uppity maid she brought with her from Lunnon Town, and Master Johnny doesn't eat breakfast. He drinks it, if ya take my meanin'. So ya might as well dig inta them eggs, ma'am, 'cause ain't nobody comin' ta join ya."

She had indeed breakfasted alone, rather enjoying the experience, for she had always taken her meals with her grandmother, who had used that time together to continue her lessons on the proper running of an estate the size and scope of Cliff Walk.

Grandmother Trowbridge must have been planning on this day for many years, Sarah Jane decided as she picked up her woolen shawl, rose from the chair, and headed toward one pair of French doors, believing a walk in the crisp air in the gardens might help to clear her head.

"There you are, darling child! Babbitt told me I might find you hiding in here. I see you've survived the night. And how beautiful you look this morning! I adore, simply *adore,* that gown! I can't imagine why waist-to-hem flounces have fallen so sadly out of fashion. Why, even *waists* themselves have fallen—or should I say *risen*—out of fashion, haven't they?"

Sarah Jane turned to see Audrey Muir sweeping into the room, a vision of loveliness in her green and white sprigged muslin morning gown, her long blond ringlets tied up artlessly by a thick velvet ribbon.

The long-sleeved gown was low-cut on her generous breasts, but not so low as to be immodest, and high-waisted, its slightly gathered skirt falling nearly straight to her ankles so as to reveal the lovely emerald green kid slippers that so flattered the woman's slim feet.

"Out of fashion, Audrey?" she asked, frowning. Why, her gown was less than a month old, Mrs. Wilcox having sewn it up especially for her trousseau.

Audrey sat down in the chair Sarah Jane had so recently vacated. "La, yes, my dear. This benighted countryside is years behind our London dressmakers. Years and *years.*"

She rolled her eyes and gave a short, trilling laugh. "But of course you know that, don't you, dear? I imagine your grandmother had charge of the dressing of you, supposing that the newer fashions might show your wonderful slenderness to disadvantage. But I can't think why! Small bosoms

66

are nothing to be ashamed of, are they, now? Ah, I see I have my work cut out for me! We'll have such *fun,* Sarah Jane! But we'll leave that for the nonce, for I have something much more important to discuss this morning. Tell me, are you completely devastated?"

The woman spoke so quickly and moved from subject to subject with such alacrity that Sarah Jane almost felt dizzy attempting to follow her. Putting thoughts of a reviving stroll in the gardens from her mind, she dutifully retraced her steps and seated herself on the small couch set at a right angle to the rose brocade chair.

"Devastated, Audrey? I'm afraid I don't understand your question." She leaned forward slightly, a movement that would have sent her grandmother screaming for the backboard if she had glimpsed her granddaughter's sloppy posture. But Grandmother Trowbridge wasn't here, and Sarah Jane would lean if she wanted to. Why, she might even *slouch* if the spirit took her!

Audrey's large blue eyes were eloquent with sympathy. "I shall understand if you don't wish to discuss the matter, Sarah Jane. But please remember that I am your new sister and I am a wife. I have experienced what you have experienced. I, too, have been subjected to a wedding night, and to that most singular, never-to-be-forgotten pain."

Sarah Jane considered Audrey's words for a few moments. It was true enough. Audrey was also a wife. And they were sisters now, at least by marriage. Perhaps it wouldn't hurt to listen to the woman.

"It—it did come rather as something of a shock," she admitted at last, not knowing what else to say. "But I'm fine. Truly I am."

Audrey's pink tongue came out and moistened her even pinker lips. "He came to you, then? I had half thought . . . but he did go through with it? Well, your grandmother must be well pleased. I know my father was in high gig the morning after Tyler's and my marriage, when he found me sobbing in this very room. Sobbing as if my heart would break!"

"Dante said it was necessary," Sarah Jane said quietly,

wishing they had never begun this particular conversation. "He—he said it would get better, over time."

"Better?" Audrey gave a wave of her hand. "Better than what? Better than offering yourself up to be mauled by a bear? Better than being subjected to man's most base perversions night after night, all in the name of begetting an heir? The initial pain men so poetically term 'deflowering' will not be repeated, I grant you, but what of the *mental* anguish? I tell you, Sarah Jane, I nearly wept with joy when Tyler had his accident. Oh, I bled for his tragedy—simply *bled!* But I would not be honest if I did not tell you that I went down on my knees in thanks when I realized that I wouldn't have to be *pawed* and *poked* anymore. Not that he hadn't been going to his mistresses and some low opera dancers for years anyway. Thank heaven for trollops. But Tyler wanted an heir, so he refused to leave me alone."

Sarah Jane was embarrassed for the other woman, hearing such intimate details of her life, of the Earl of Easterly's life. But she was also alarmed. "You—you never liked it? You didn't find it at all pleasant? Not in the least? I mean—"

"Liked it! My dear child, no woman of any gentility and sensibility does more than tolerate such a personal violation." Audrey looked toward the doorway to the hall, as if to be sure they wouldn't be overheard, then motioned for Sarah Jane to lean even closer. "We aren't *meant* to like it, my dear. I believe it is a part of Eve's punishment. Oh, Dante may tell you that you should enjoy his exertions, but that is only a man's way of soothing his own conscience as he ruts on you. *They* like it. Lud, they bloody *adore* it! God is a *man,* remember. Men were designed for pleasure, and it is only we women who must suffer a monthly flux and the agony of childbirth. Would a man suckle a child, I ask you? Would men put up with sagging breasts and swollen, misshapen bodies? Hardly. No, no. We aren't meant to *enjoy* the exercise. Why, I've always personally considered it penance for being able to wear pretty things and not having to go to war or work for my daily bread."

Audrey sat back and lifted her right hand, wiggling her

spread fingers so that the ring on her third finger winked in the sunlight. "Besides, Sarah Jane, if you cry, sometimes they give you diamonds."

"I see." Sarah Jane didn't see, she didn't see at all, but she didn't want to admit it. She had enjoyed Dante's kisses, Dante's touch. It was only at the end that she had wondered if what he was about wasn't some sort of sad, twisted comedy. "Then what you're saying, Audrey, is that no woman of breeding enjoys, um, the *exercise?*"

"Exactly!" Audrey laughed again, tossing her head so that her golden curls danced against the nape of her neck. "Oh, some women do like it," she said arching one perfect eyebrow. "Some *low,* loose women. Birth and breeding aren't everything. Even a coal merchant's daughter or a butcher's granddaughter can be a lady of sensibility. Why, I'm rather pleased that I don't enjoy what the world calls lovemaking. If I did, that would have proved to Tyler once and for all that he had married beneath him. He was happy enough to take his pleasure elsewhere, resting comfortably in the sure knowledge that his *wife* was a lady. I imagine Dante feels the same way. In fact, I am convinced of it! With a modicum of luck, Sarah Jane, once he has gotten you with child he won't bother with you again at all, ever. Then you can concentrate, as I do, on the most important aspects of being a lady—giving successful parties, dressing as befits your station, gossiping, shopping, going to the theater, all those lovely things."

Audrey clapped her hands together a single time. "Which brings us back to the subject dearest to my heart. Sarah Jane, would you like to look at some pattern cards of the latest fashions from London? I brought them here from Mayfair. I am quite convinced that Dante would wish you to order an *entire* new wardrobe, one that is more in line with what is being worn in Society."

"That seems like such a sad waste of money, Audrey," Sarah Jane said, still concentrating on what the woman had told her about what was expected of ladies in the marriage bed. Because she *had* rather liked it, and if she liked it even better the next time Dante came to her, it would prove to him that she wasn't a lady, but only the sad consequence of the fortune he had married.

No wonder he had left her so abruptly last night. She had put her arms around him. She had even *kissed* him. Oh, what must he think of her? Why hadn't Grandmother Trowbridge warned her? Why had Miss Austen spent so much time writing of pride and prejudice when she could have made a far greater contribution to the young ladies of England by penning a treatise or two on *procreation?*

"A waste of money? Ah, Sarah Jane, you are quite simply the most *precious* child I have ever encountered. Dante is worth a king's ransom now, thanks to your grandmother *and* thanks to your own sacrifice, which I happen to believe to be ten thousand times more personal and painful than any contribution your grandmother has made to the Muir coffers."

Sarah Jane bit her lip, looked at Audrey's gown and then at her own, then spoke. "Dante isn't aware of it, but I do have some funds of my own."

"You do? You have pin money? Why, that's above everything perfect! And so wise of you not to say anything about it to Dante, for he'd only fritter it all away on unnecessary silliness like plows and milch cows. You *deserve* a new wardrobe. Lud, how I wish *I* could afford a few new things to replace these rags I now wear. You have earned some pretty gowns. And, bless and keep you, you will continue to earn them almost hourly until you have Dante's child in your belly. I can only pray, for your sake, that it will be soon."

"Grandmother Trowbridge has insisted upon a boy," Sarah Jane said hollowly, wondering why she even mentioned that part of the arrangement. But it only seemed fair, considering that Audrey had shared her secrets.

Audrey's smile was enigmatic. "Oh? Really? Well, wasn't that shrewd of her, especially now that everyone knows Tyler won't be fathering any male heirs. In that case, dear child," she declared firmly, "you definitely deserve a few new gowns. Heaven only knows how many girls you might have *tearing* their way out of your poor little body before

Dante gets himself a son. Anyone would think your own grandmother would have considered your small size before striking such a bargain. Why, when I think of all the women who have perished in childbed . . ."

Sarah Jane's eyes widened as she pressed her hands against her flat stomach. "Perished, Audrey? Really?"

The countess gave another wave of her hand. "Yes, yes. But we'll not repine on such morbid thoughts, as that would serve no purpose. Gowns—that's what we will think about now. You'll need at least six or seven for daytime and a like number for evening. A few spencers, a redingote, a riding habit. You do ride, don't you? A half dozen bonnets, reticules, gloves. Oh, and a fur-lined cape with a muff to match! Sable, I should think. We shall dress you in the highest fashion from the skin out."

Tearing at her body? Hadn't her body been violated sufficiently already? Sarah Jane began to feel that she just might deserve some new gowns.

"If you help me, Audrey, I suppose we could both order some gowns. As thanks for your assistance, you understand. They would be a gift."

Audrey's hands flew to her cheeks, and she batted her long lashes furiously to beat back the tears Sarah Jane saw standing in the woman's lovely sky blue eyes. "Me? You are so *good*, sister of my heart! But I cannot. I simply *can't!*"

Sarah Jane was beginning to feel tired. The woman was friendly enough, but her company could be exhausting. She decided to put an end to Audrey's insincere protestations. "Very well, if you *can't*—"

"But you have *insisted!* I would be a brute to deny you! Oh, dear sister, I will make you look so lovely! Dante will be so proud! Except for your hair, of course. It is unfortunate, but if you are to be gowned in the height of fashion, we simply *must* do something with your hair."

Sarah Jane, who was beginning to feel like some awful oddity of nature, raised a hand to touch her carefully constructed coiffure.

"You don't like it either?" she asked, finally agreeing with her new sister, for it would have been silly to cut up stiff at

Audrey's words when she herself disliked her hair very much indeed. "I always feel as if I must deliberately hold my head very straight, just to carry the weight of all these curls. What do you suggest?"

"Why, to cut it all off, of course! There is a lovely style in London just now; it has been popular for some time, actually. It is called the Titus, and I believe it would be most flattering."

Sarah Jane was intrigued. "The Titus? Um, precisely how does it look?"

"Well," Audrey began, patting her own long, soft curls, which had been pulled back from her face so that they hung down to her shoulders, "it is a rather short style." She giggled. *"Extremely* short, as a matter of fact. But it would be a wonderful change for you, I'm sure. Rather like a soft, fluffy halo, I should say, but curled all over. Lud, you'd look lovely!"

"Oh," Sarah Jane sighed, leaning back on the dusty cushions, her usual ramrod-stiff posture having suffered yet another serious setback in the space of a few minutes. "I'd still have to deal with the curling stick. That's too bad."

Audrey's eyes widened. "My goodness, are you telling me those beautiful curls are not natural? I would *never* have guessed! Really, Sarah Jane, I am quite convinced that once the hair is cut it will curl nicely on its own. Why, *mine* does, and it's much longer than the Titus."

She jumped up from the chair and plopped herself down beside Sarah Jane, pulling her into her scented embrace. "Oh, it will be such *fun* teaching you how to be the perfect Society matron. Why, once Dante is done playing lord of the manor and takes us to London—you must begin now to convince him you desire a Season—you will become the brightest star in all the *ton.* All you have to do, sweet Sarah Jane, is to put your trust in me!"

Sarah Jane allowed the embrace, smiling weakly, and wondered why she couldn't find much to cheer in Audrey's enthusiastic predictions.

* * *

"You've bedded her?"

Dante sliced a look across the drawing room at the marquess. He was still in his riding clothes, having spent the day traveling the fields, mentally preparing a list of projects that could be initiated within the week. He was chilled, tired, and not at all in the mood for questions.

"Always the gentleman, aren't you, Father?" he commented tightly, then poured himself a drink.

"This is no time to badger me, Dante," the marquess answered coldly as he adjusted the lapels of his new jacket. "This is business. Betts Trowbridge is a demanding woman. I wouldn't have put it past her to demand to see the sheets. Where'd she haul herself off to, anyway? I've been avoiding her all day, hiding in my rooms, just to have Babbitt tell me she did a flit before breakfast. I was sure she'd stay to direct the work on the king's chamber. She will sleep there, you know. I can only hope the damp kills her."

"I'll drink to that sentiment," Dante muttered beneath his breath, lifting the glass to his lips. He took a sip of the wine, then answered his father's question. "Mrs. Trowbridge departed before breakfast, expressing her disappointment that she could not bid you farewell before mounting her broom and flying home. It is my understanding that she had some sort of pressing business back at Trowbridge Manor."

The marquess grinned, sitting back in his chair and crossing one well-turned leg over the other. He was crowding seven and sixty, but he was still a handsome man. If anyone doubted it, direct application to Curtis Muir would have elicited the information that he was in the prime of his life and could still turn many a female head when he put his mind to it. Why, he would have married himself a fortune long since, if only he hadn't become so comfortable in his widower status. And so well provided with marriagable sons.

"She's probably meeting with her man of business, to take care of settling our mortgages," he said at last. "Good girl, Betts. She'll keep to her end of the bargain."

Dante set his empty glass on the table and turned to go upstairs, anxious to wash away the smell of horseflesh before dinner.

"As I shall keep to mine, Father," he said, wishing to discommode the man. "I've decided to give each of you an allowance of two hundred pounds a quarter. That should be more than sufficient to your needs."

"Two hundred pounds!" The marquess leaped from his chair with the agility of a much younger man. "Damn you to blazes, boy, that's no more than a pittance! How can I return to London? Do you really believe I wish to stay in this damp house, rotting away?"

"Repairs on this building will commence tomorrow morning," Dante answered tightly, halting near the door, his back to his father.

"All the worse! There'll be hammering and banging and . . . *no!* I refuse! I completely and utterly refuse!"

Dante shrugged. "Very well, Father. Trip on back to London. I'm confident the tradesmen you owe will herald your return with open palms. Will you want me to visit you for Christmas? You'll be in the Fleet, I imagine, but I should be able to locate you."

"Hold there a moment!" The marquess raced across the room to take hold of Dante's arm. "Will Tyler receive the same allowance?"

Dante looked down at his father's hand, reminded that he had been held just this way last evening by Mrs. Trowbridge. He realized that he was becoming rather weary of being pulled on by people. "Why do you ask?"

The marquess shifted his eyes away from his son's intense scrutiny. "No reason," he said, shrugging. "It's only that, if Audrey is to have four hundred pounds—for Ty never spends a groat, does he?—and I am to have two hundred, as is Johnny, well, that should be enough for us to get on with, don't you think? You will not expect us to pay for the running of the town house out of our own pockets, after all. Yes, yes. That should be enough for us."

Dante shook his arm free of the marquess's grasp. "Enough for you and Audrey, you mean," he said, disgusted, "as I doubt you plan to take Ty and Johnny with you to Mayfair. Excuse me, Father. I had thought to rinse off my dirt at the basin, but I suddenly feel myself in need of a head-to-toe bath."

"Don't you cut up stiff with me, son," the marquess blustered, his face reddening. "If it weren't for me you'd not have a feather to fly with. It was I who agreed to meet with Betts Trowbridge, remember!"

Dante chuckled low in his throat. "Yes, Father, I do remember. You were instrumental in making that poor little girl cry, weren't you? I shall give her your regards, if she hasn't locked herself in my bedchamber, fearful that I shall repeat last night's assault on her person. To make my sins the greater, I believe she might have thought herself to be in love with me. Until last night, of course."

"Bungled it, did you, brother? And here I thought you to be superior to the rest of us. I bought Audrey a diamond necklace with her father's money. Calmed her most effectively. You might try it."

Dante turned, surprised that he had not heard the approach of Tyler's chair. "Did Farris grease the wheels on your chariot?" he asked facetiously, wondering how so large a house could sometimes be too small to contain all the Muirs who roamed the rooms.

"I could have my entrance announced with a fanfare of trumpets, I suppose," Tyler said, motioning for Farris to maneuver the Bath chair closer to the fire. "Or would that be too much, do you think? So, is Little Miss Mouse going to present us with some happy news next summer? Perhaps the patter of small feet might cheer you more than the scraping of my wheels."

Dante sighed, feeling nostalgic for the relative peace and quiet of a battlefield. "Go on, Tyler. Surely you must have more to say on the subject? Some ribald joke? A few nasty allusions? Please, have at it. Just get it all said before my wife appears at the dinner table.

"*If* she appears," he added softly, half hoping she would keep to her rooms and away from his inquisitive, faintly barbarous family.

"No, Dante. I'm through," Tyler announced, taking hold of the wheels on either side of his chair and propelling himself toward the drinks table. "As a matter of fact, I've been through for more than two years. Finished. Why, I would have to rack my brain for any slight memory of the joys to be encountered in the marriage bed. Perhaps I'll become a drunkard, like our dearest Johnny. He seems to have found happiness inside his bottles. And you wouldn't have to fear my staggering about or tumbling down the stairs. All you'd have to do is have Farris bind me to this chair, and I could quite safely drink myself into insensibility."

"You won't find courage in a bottle, Ty," Dante said coolly, leaning against the door frame.

Tyler threw his wineglass across the room, where it exploded loudly in the fireplace, the wine causing the fire to hiss and spit. "What was that remark in aid of, Dante?" he bit out angrily. "Or has this become some fashionable new source of pleasure for you these days? Cripple-baiting rather than bearbaiting?"

"Now, boys," the marquess began, stepping in front of his oldest son, "there's no need for fighting. Tyler, your brother is only attempting to help you. You know how stubborn he is. The doctor said you might walk again, and Dante is determined that you shall. Just don't let that Trowbridge woman get wind of what the doctor said, all right? At least not until she's paid the mortgages. And, Dante, why don't you take yourself off upstairs for that bath you mentioned? I hesitate to say it, but you do smell very much of the stable."

Dante looked at Tyler, who was staring into the fire, his jaw firmly set, and then at his father, who was smiling in a most paternal fashion, as if his greatest joy in life was to act as mediator in this dispute between his sons.

"All right," Dante said wearily, running a hand through his dark hair. "It has been a long day. And it will take me forty hours a day for the next few months to set the grounds to rights before I can even think about setting our people to restoring the house in anything more than the most basic ways, unless Sarah Jane is truly capable of taking on the challenge. I imagine I am just feeling somewhat over-whelmed at the moment. I'm sorry, Tyler."

"And I'm sorry I'm no help to you, brother," Tyler answered quietly. "Just do me the favor of concentrating your energies on performing miracles on Cliff Walk, and leave me in peace."

Dante nodded, his hands clenched into fists, for he felt so useless, so helpless, when faced with his brother's refusal to help himself. "We'll talk more after dinner?"

"Of course we shall!" the marquess boomed cheerfully, waving Dante out of the room. As he went, he heard his father say, "Now, Tyler, about this business of an allowance. I've been thinking about how little you need here at Cliff Walk and how grateful dear Audrey would be if . . ."

Dante climbed the stairs two at a time, wondering if it would be possible to drown himself in his tub, and believ-ing, only for a moment, that it might be best for everyone, especially his bride, if he did just that.

CHAPTER 4

Anything awful makes me laugh.
I misbehaved once at a funeral.

Charles Lamb

Sarah Jane shut the heavy door behind her, lifted her skirts, and bolted for the stairs, silently rejoicing that she had been able to quit the bedchamber before Dante could appear from his dressing room. After all, he hadn't sought her out all day. Why should he care if she avoided him now?

As she hastened along, she peeked back over her shoulder to see if Dante had come into the hallway, and abruptly collided with a body that had somehow presented itself in her path.

"Lord John, are you all right?" she asked, attempting to steady the dangerously reeling man who was doing his best to keep the contents of his glass from spilling onto the carpet. "Please forgive me!"

"Oh, hullo there, Sarah Jane," Lord John said, smiling broadly as he peered at her owlishly. "For a moment there I thought I'd walked into another door. What's your rush? Is Dante chasing you for a kiss? But never mind. There goes the dinner gong. I have to find the stairs. Father keeps a prompt table, although I haven't the foggiest notion why,

78

considering our meals are often the worse for being hot. Especially the wine."

Sarah Jane slipped her arm through his, realizing that Lord John was both drunk and somehow sad, a powerful combination of problems that immediately elicited her sympathy. He was so young to be disheartened by the world. Why, he wasn't even married.

"Perhaps you will escort me to the drawing room, Lord John," she suggested, taking his forearm and carefully turning him about to steer him in the correct direction. "Cliff Walk is so large, and I do at times become confused."

He patted her hand, allowing himself to be led, his posture now exaggeratedly straight, as if he could hide his drunken state with a stiff spine. "How wonderful. Dante has married himself a diplomat. But you must call me Johnny, dear sister, as we are informal here at Cliff Walk, you know. Dante, Tyler, Audrey, Johnny, and . . . Papa? No. Not Papa. Father Muir? Egad! Now, *that's* distressing! Not to worry; we'll think of something. Tell me, how do you like life so far at Cliff Walk? Is it everything you'd hoped?"

"Everything I'd hoped? Why, I suppose it is."

Lord John halted at the head of the stairs and addressed the small marble bust of Athena that rested in a wall niche. "Ah! Did you hear that, m'lovely? Lady Dante *supposes,*" he exclaimed, then turned back to Sarah Jane. "I do that myself, dear sister. *Suppose.* I *suppose* that life is real because it is too unbearably silly to be a fiction. I *suppose* that brandy is a gift from the gods, whether those in heaven or in Hades I refuse to inquire. I *suppose* that the dear Lord has a delicious sense of the ridiculous, else why would gentlemen lose the hair on *top* of their heads, where nothing can be done to disguise the sad loss, rather than that on the *back* of those heads, where it could be covered up quite nicely by growing the hair on *top* longer? God had to have thought of that, you know, and decided on the *top* just to vex us. Very funny fellow, God."

He turned to Sarah Jane, squinting as he grinned down at her, his expression half quizzical, half clownish. "Now, sister mine, tell me. How do you suppose all *that?*"

"I'm quite sure I can't suppose most of it at all, Johnny," Sarah Jane answered, laughing in spite of herself. How nice it was to speak with Lord John. She didn't have to measure her words or pretend to be a lady so that no one would remember that she was only the butcher's granddaughter. Besides, by tomorrow morning Lord John would probably not recall a word of what she'd said to him! "I am still trying to *suppose* the reason God created men and women *and* elephants," she told him honestly. "And bugs! Spiders! Do you *suppose* that any of them serve any real purpose?"

Lord John rolled his eyes. "Elephants? Now you've gone and done it, sister dear. You don't expect answers *now,* do you? All life's silly little secrets. All its reasons, it errors, its blunders. Are they mistakes? Poor luck? Terrible timing? Or are they all part of some larger plan? I certainly have to drink on them—I mean, *think* on them for a space."

He looked around questioningly, then tipped his head and asked, "Why are we standing here? Seems a queer place to be, right at the top of the stairs. Someone could slip and fall, you know. And there's no drinks table. Furthermore, my glass"—he lifted it to his mouth, draining the contents in one long gulp, then held it up for her inspection—"is empty."

"We might descend to the drawing room," she suggested, suddenly remembering that Dante could appear in the hallway at any moment. "I believe there is a drinks table there."

"Splendid! We'll have us a little drink before the gong goes again. A little drink, no more than that. Dante has put a lock on the cellars, you know," he said, whispering in Sarah Jane's ear as, together, they all but stumbled down the staircase. "I think he expects me to grow up or something. Damned moral, our Dante. He's married now, you know."

"Why, yes, Johnny, I heard a rumor to that effect."

"Of course you did. I'm drunk, I think." He dropped a kiss on her cheek. "But I do very much like you, Sarah Jane Muir. Truly."

"Thank you, Johnny," she answered, flattered, for even if he was deep in his cups, Lord John was a very affable, very handsome gentleman, and the first, the very first, to ever say that he liked her. All Dante had ever said was that he didn't love her, which certainly wasn't the same.

Still arm in arm, they navigated the hallway and entered the drawing room. The large chamber was empty save for the Earl of Easterly, who was sitting in his Bath chair in front of the fire, his back to them.

Lord John, winking roguishly, pressed a finger to his lips, admonishing Sarah Jane to be silent, then handed her his glass and left her where she stood. She watched, confused, as he crossed the room on tiptoe, not stopping until he stood directly behind his brother.

John twisted his head about, grinning conspiratorially before turning to face Lord Easterly once more and cupping his hands on either side of his mouth.

"Fire!" he shouted at the top of his lungs. "Fire in the kitchens! *Run!* Run for your life!"

Sarah Jane nearly dropped the glass as Lord John's voice reverberated in the room, but Tyler Muir didn't even flinch. He only used his hands on the wheels to turn his chair toward the center of the room and said quietly, "If you didn't announce your arrival with the smell of strong spirits detectable at thirty paces, Johnny, I might be startled. I wouldn't leap to my feet, as you suppose, and race at full tilt from the house, but I *might* be slightly startled."

He pushed the chair past Lord John, who stood back, shaking his head, definitely disappointed. "Well, hello there, Sarah Jane. Don't you look lovely this evening? I hope Johnny didn't upset you with his tired parlor trick. He seems to believe it the height of hilarity, but then, he has always possessed the capability of being easily amused."

Sarah Jane walked farther into the room, searching for a place to put Lord John's empty glass. She had only her experience in her grandmother's company to use as a guide, but she was beginning to believe she had married into a most odd household. "Good—good evening, Lord Easterly."

Lord John pointedly cleared his throat.

"Um, *Tyler,*" she amended quickly, self-consciously.

She hastened to take a seat, her back straight, her hands neatly folded in her lap as she had been taught, for she felt extremely uncomfortable looking down when she spoke to the earl, who was quite handsome in his evening clothes, although his long legs were covered by a thin blanket.

It just seemed so *wrong* for him to be confined to the Bath chair.

She racked her brain for something to say, anything to say, so that she wouldn't be tempted to ask what on earth Lord John had been attempting with his sudden outburst. "It's rather cold this evening, isn't it? For November, that is," she said, knowing she sounded polite, if brick stupid. "Do you believe it might come on to snow?"

"Snow? I think not. But don't play the proper miss on my account, Sarah Jane. We are none of us especially polite. You must be wondering what just occurred here."

He smiled at her, easing her apprehension. "Allow me to explain. Johnny believes that if I am frightened enough, put out of countenance sufficiently, I might rise, Lazarus-like, from this chair and walk again. He's been at it ever since Dante hauled some forward-thinking physician here from London last month to examine me for five minutes and pronounce that I am capable of walking if I only *believe* it. Or if, as Johnny thinks, I am forced into it by some sort of shock that causes me to forget that I *know* I can't walk. So far, and I'm convinced I have forgotten at least half of the occasions, my loving brother has attempted to push my chair into the fireplace, rushed into a room to tell me the Prince Regent was riding up the drive, yelled *'Fire'* in my ear a half dozen times, and hidden my chair while I was abed, then woke me, screaming that a meteor was falling from the sky and heading straight for the house. That is all, isn't it, Johnny?"

Lord John had poured himself another drink and was now sitting at his ease on a chair across from Sarah Jane. "You forgot the pig, Ty," he said, winking mischievously at Sarah Jane. "I set one loose in here last week, just to see what would happen. Nothing did, except that we ate tolerably well for the next few days. It's difficult for a cook to ruin a pig, you know. All she needs to do is poke an apple in its mouth and roast it."

He grinned then, looking so young, so boyish, so innocent, that Sarah Jane knew she liked the man more than anyone else she had met since coming to Cliff Walk. Liked him and wished better for him.

"But my hopes for you, dear brother, remain high," Lord John ended, frowning. "One of these days I'll stumble on something that works. One of these days."

"If I don't shoot you first," the earl said affably. "There is that, Johnny. Ah, is that my wife I see hovering in the doorway, refusing to enter until we stop chattering and dutifully applaud her entrance?"

Sarah Jane shifted in her chair and looked to her left, to see that, indeed, Audrey was standing in the doorway, her blond ringlets piled high on her head and run through with pearls, her creamy shoulders rising gracefully above a simply cut yet elegant gown of dusky rose velvet.

Sarah Jane spared a moment to look down at her own gown, another of Mrs. Wilcox's rustic creations, fashioned in whiter-than-white satin fronted by stiff lace and banded at the waist by a wide yellow sash. The style was nearly the same as that of the gowns she had worn while still in the nursery, while still in leading strings, for heaven's sake! She felt so frumpish, so childish, so *wrong*.

"La, Tyler," Audrey trilled as she swept into the room, her moves so graceful that she could have been floating above the carpet rather than walking on it. "You are going to be a beast again this evening, I suppose? Are you in agony tonight, my poor darling?" she asked as she placed a quick kiss on his hair, then took up a small brocade footstool and sat down close beside him, her hand on his arm.

She was the image of the devoted wife, the two of them the picture of devotion, both of them handsome creatures, both of them blond, both of them well dressed, both of them already knowing who they were and where they were. Only the Bath chair seemed not to belong.

Audrey smiled at Sarah Jane. "It's not Tyler's fault that he's mean. His limbs sometimes pain him, you know," she said, explaining away her husband's boorish behavior. "Poor darling. Men have so little experience tolerating pain, unlike women, who are born to it. Men excel at *inflicting* pain, for they were born for that. Except for dear Johnny here," she ended, indicating her brother-in-law with the wave of one slim hand. "He wouldn't hurt anyone. Would you, Johnny?"

"Audrey, wouldn't you care for a glass of sherry before we are summoned to dinner?" the earl asked, his tone hard, so that Sarah Jane sensed that something was going on that she couldn't understand. An entirely different conversation seemed to be floating somewhere above her head.

Audrey laid her cheek against the earl's leg for a moment. "Not now, Ty, thank you," she answered sweetly, still looking at Lord John, her smile kind, almost motherly. "You are so good, Johnny. Why, like Ty, you even refused to go to war, to follow in the bloody path Sarah Jane's new husband pursued with such ardor. No, no, Johnny. *You* don't have the heart or the mind of a killer."

"I was going to go," Lord John said, his bleak, suddenly sober eyes seeming to appeal to Sarah Jane for understanding. She was only listening with one ear, trying to picture Dante Muir with a saber in his hand and blood in his eye. It was an easy, and disconcerting, image to conjure up.

"You were married, Ty," Lord John continued, "and bore the responsibilities of the heir. Dante bought his own commission with money he had from Mother. But if Father would have agreed to buy me a commission . . ."

"Father didn't need two of his sons at war, perhaps dying," the earl ended when Lord John's voice petered out and he took refuge in his glass. "It was enough that one of his remaining assets had gone off with Wellington. To gamble his last marriageable son on the battlefield would have made the odds too long even for our father. Give over, Johnny. The war is won. Nobody cares anymore."

The room was suddenly thick with tension. Clearly Audrey's inane chattering had opened an old wound. Sarah Jane wished she understood.

Lord John made a second trip to the drinks table. "I could

have enlisted in the ranks. I should have done something. Harry went. Freddie went."

"Harry died, Johnny, and Freddie came home minus his sight and one arm," Tyler said.

"And you ended up in that damnable chair." Johnny held his glass with both hands. "But as you said, it's all ancient history now. My, but I'm thirsty! Sarah Jane? Would you care for some sherry?"

Sarah Jane was confused. What did Lord John's not going to war have to do with the earl ending up crippled? "Sherry? I haven't . . . I mean I've never . . . Why, yes, thank you, I would like some. Only a small amount, please."

Lord John poured himself another drink and provided her with a near-to-brimming glass of the brownish liquid, which she eyed owlishly as he sat down beside her heavily on the couch. She wondered if she would be able to drink such a large amount without becoming as drunk as he was.

That seemed doubtful, as Lord John had downed more than three times as much since entering the room, so she lifted the glass to her lips and took a quantity into her mouth.

Which was where it stayed, for she suddenly couldn't swallow. The taste of the sherry was vile, almost as dreadful as that of the medication Mildred had forced down her throat last year when she'd had that bout of the sniffles.

Sarah Jane felt everyone's eyes on her as she fought the urge to spit the sherry back into the glass, then swallowed convulsively as she heard Dante come into the room, greeting everyone affably as he entered.

Her eyes immediately watered, and her throat stung as if she had just swallowed liquid fire. She took several shallow breaths in rapid succession, her gaze determinedly directed toward the floor until she saw a pair of well-dressed male legs come to a halt in front of her.

"Good evening, Sarah Jane," Dante said, his voice low and incredibly impersonal, just as if they hadn't taken their vows only yesterday, as if he hadn't come to her last night and . . . "I had hoped to speak with you upstairs and perhaps come down to dinner with you, but I seem to have been tardy. Estate business, you understand. Would you like me to take your glass? You really shouldn't drink sherry."

The burning had subsided, and her stomach felt warm. It was a rather pleasant feeling, and she felt more at ease than she thought she would have at seeing her husband again. She was fine, just fine. So, did he have to address her as if she was a naughty child caught out eating comfits before teatime? She was a woman now. Mildred had said so!

Lifting her eyes to look up into his tanned, handsome face, she said, "But I've hardly tasted it, Dante. It's really quite good." She took another sip, a similarly large sip, and smiled tightly as she forced herself to swallow. She held the glass against her breasts so that he couldn't take it. "Why don't you get your own?"

Lord John laughed abruptly, slapping his knee. "Yes, Dante. Get your own! It's not our fault that you're late. Sarah Jane and I are about to discuss elephants and would really rather not be disturbed. Isn't that correct, dear sister?"

"And bugs. Spiders, too," Sarah Jane said, before taking another swallow of sherry. She giggled. "And pigs."

The taste of the sherry was not such a shock anymore, and the effect on her nerves was quite pleasant. She could look at Dante, look at his hands, his mouth, the very *largeness* of him, and not remember last night or think about later tonight. Dear, sweet, *kind* Lord John was beside her, and Audrey and the earl were with her. There was no reason to be afraid. No reason to fear that Dante might pounce on her there and then and repeat the assault of their wedding night.

No, not an assault. A gentle persuasion was more like it. A gentle persuasion with a nasty surprise at the end. If only she could stop thinking about it, wondering about it. If only she could forget that a part of her, an admittedly small part of her, was secretly looking forward to experiencing that gentle persuasion again.

One of her curls slipped forward over her eyes, and she blew at it to get it out of her way. "Audrey believes I should cut my hair," she heard herself blurt out, then immediately wondered why she'd said it. She took another large swallow of sherry before allowing Lord John to fill her glass to the brim once more.

"Indeed?" Dante said, seating himself in the chair across from her, so that he immediately became the center of her attention, crowding out the existence of everyone else in the room. Did he have to be so handsome? So much the intimate stranger? "Audrey, tell me about this, please."

The countess clapped her hands in delight. "Oh, Dante, I knew you'd be pleased! Sarah Jane and I had the loveliest coze today, and I told her about the Titus. You remember, Dante. It is a lovely coiffure. I believe Lady Helena—her grace, that is—preferred just such a style. Or she did until her marriage. His grace keeps his duchess very much at home these days, doesn't he? Not that you'd know, Dante, for you haven't been to London for the Season in so long. What has it been—five years? Dearest Helena. You were so *very* fond of her once, weren't you, Dante?"

"I don't recall, Audrey. I was rather occupied overseas on Wellington's staff for most of those five years, as you might remember. But nevertheless, I am familiar with the Titus. I don't think the style would suit my wife," Lord Dante answered, rather sternly, or so Sarah Jane thought. Maybe even muleheadedly, pigheadedly, as if refusing just because he wanted to refuse.

But then, Audrey had said he had a bit of a temper, and Audrey should know. She would know, but Sarah Jane couldn't say either way, for she barely knew the man. He had bedded her, but she barely knew him. How ridiculous! Ludicrous, actually. *Laughable.* She had believed herself to be in love with the man? How could she ever have thought that? How did one love what one did not really know?

Such a puzzle! She would have to, as Lord John said, "suppose" on it.

But for now she would have to concentrate on precisely what was wrong. Didn't Dante think she would look as good as this Helena person? Not beautiful, perhaps, but at least partway presentable?

Or wasn't a butcher's granddaughter allowed to aspire to the coiffure of a duchess? Was she just supposed to give over her money, give over her body, and then sit quietly in a corner, doing nothing, saying nothing, *feeling* nothing?

That didn't seem quite fair, especially when she remembered her lavish plans for Cliff Walk. For her future as a generous, loving, beloved heroine. How dare he judge her? He didn't even *know* her, not really. And just how "fond" had Dante been of Lady Helena? Sarah Jane took a sip of sherry, then frowned when she saw that the glass was empty again.

She was beginning to feel a headache pressing behind her eyes. Where was the marquess? Hadn't Lord John said that dinner was always prompt? She hadn't eaten much at her solitary luncheon before one of the footmen whisked her plate away, and she was really rather hungry.

Except that perhaps she wasn't. Perhaps she would never eat again. Perhaps some more sherry might serve to settle her stomach. She held out her glass. "Excuse me, but my glass is empty. May I please have more?"

"Certainly!"

"No."

Sarah Jane looked first at Lord John, who had said yes, and then at Dante, who had denied her request. He might be handsome, her husband, but he wasn't very nice. Surely now that she was a married woman she should have more control over her own wishes. She hadn't planned on crawling out from beneath Grandmother Trowbridge's thumb only to have Lord Dante Muir put his foot on her neck!

"Whyever not?" she asked him, amazed to see the hard line of his mouth, the same mouth that had caressed hers, crushed hers, last night. Goodness, but it was warm in the room! "Please, Dante. I'm thirsty."

Sarah Jane watched, fascinated, as a slow tide of color rose on Dante's throat above the crisp white of his shirt points. She bit her lip as she decided that he just might hit her. Yet, when he spoke again, his tone was gentle.

"Sherry is a mild enough drink, Sarah Jane," he explained, "but for anyone who is unaccustomed to wine and spirits it can be extremely potent. It is best, in most cases, to proceed prudently when confronted with new experiences, don't you think?"

Sarah Jane squeezed her eyes shut for a moment, then giggled. She couldn't imagine why, for the thought that had flown into her head wasn't in the least funny. "Perhaps it will only present a problem the *first* time?" she heard herself say cheekily, daringly, and immediately longed to take the words back.

"Uh-oh, Dante," Lord Easterly said. "You might be wise to keep your little mouse out of the sherry. There's a tad more spirit there than I had believed until this moment."

"Shut up, Ty," Dante said succinctly, while Sarah Jane blinked yet again, wondering if she was experiencing what Grandmother Trowbridge had called "an oversetting of the nerves." She most certainly did feel rather queer.

"Shut up, is it? My, my. Toss the man a few thousand pounds and suddenly he is lord high of the manor. He gives allowances, but we all exist on sufferance, and it is best that we remember that fact. Isn't that what you're really saying, Dante?"

"Damn you, Ty, you know very well that I know my place. And if you'd take some responsibility yourself, instead of wallowing in your misery, maybe I wouldn't have had to—"

Lord John's voice was slurred but carrying as he held up his glass and quoted, singsong, from Isaac Watts: "'But, children, you should never let such angry passions rise; your little hands were never made to tear each other's eyes.'"

"Shut up, Johnny," Dante and the earl ordered in unison as Sarah Jane, sure she knew the end of Dante's sentence— "maybe then I wouldn't have had to *marry the butcher's granddaughter*"—turned to Audrey for assistance, for rescue.

She wasn't disappointed. Audrey leaped to her feet and stood defiantly in front of Sarah Jane. "Stop it, all of you! My goodness, anyone would think you'd been raised by wild animals! You should be ashamed of yourselves. Look at what you've done! Little Sarah Jane is *crying!*"

Sarah Jane raised a hand to her cheek, stunned to realize

that it was dry. She wasn't crying. She didn't feel in the least like crying. She felt like laughing. This was a farce, wasn't it?

And the worst of the farce was that she found herself almost wishing that Grandmother Trowbridge hadn't gone home, for she felt certain that the woman would have been stalking about the drawing room in her purple feathers by now, boxing ears and verbally ripping the hide off the three Muir men—an image that set another round of giggles to tickling her throat.

"Audrey, I don't think—" she began breathlessly between eruptions of laughter, attempting to see past the woman to where Dante was sitting.

But it was no good. She had to giggle again. She had to laugh, because she had been dreading this meeting with Dante all day and now that she had seen him she realized that she had nothing to fear from the man. How could she? He didn't even care enough about her to seek her out unless she was surrounded by his family.

But Audrey was already helping Sarah Jane to her feet, saying, "I don't know which of you is the worst, truly I don't. First Johnny plies her with drink, and then the two of you descend into a brawl. This is her true first night at Cliff Walk as a part of the family, and you have ruined it. Totally *ruined* it! It's just as I told her: you Muirs are barely more than well-dressed barbarians! I am so ashamed for all of us. Come, Sarah Jane, let me help you upstairs. Your maid can fetch you a nice dinner on a tray."

Sarah Jane didn't object, for she knew somewhere deep in her brain that, for the moment at least, retreat was her best option. Besides, she wasn't feeling at all well.

The two women had proceeded almost to the doorway when the marquess entered, dressed in the height of fashion, a broad smile lighting his features.

"So sorry I'm late," he said, not sounding the least apologetic. "I was unavoidably detained, penning an answer to dear Lord Hollingsworth, who has written to invite me to join him for the upcoming holiday season—in Scotland, no less. He has a lovely hunting box there, only twenty or so rooms, so we'll be rusticating, but a fine place, a fine place.

And no carpenters! I'll be leaving in the morning. Oh, good evening ladies. I say, Sarah Jane, you don't look well."

"I'm escorting your new daughter-in-law upstairs, Curtis," Audrey said sharply. "And if you wish to know why, I suggest you apply to your sons for an explanation. You should have caned them more often, Curtis, truly you should have. I won't be down again either, as I have no great desire to take my evening meal with such unfeeling monsters, so you animals may feel free to slop your dinner from troughs for all I care!"

Sarah Jane considered this an exemplary speech and smiled at Audrey—her new sister, her protector, the woman who thought she would look very pretty in the Titus—then turned to the marquess.

"Betts will not be best pleased, you know. Good night, *Curtis,"* she trilled happily, daringly, then giggled into her hand all the way up the stairs, remembering the look of astonishment that had raised the marquess's eyebrows nearly to his, she noticed with even more amusement, noticeably *receding* hairline.

CHAPTER 5

Fate chooses our relatives,
we choose our friends.

Jacques Delille

The bedchamber was dark, and quiet now that Mildred had finished with her mother-hen clucking about young ladies knowing their place and the evils of wine and a number of other subjects Sarah Jane wished neither to remember for the moment nor to commit to memory.

What she wanted, simply, was to die. They would all be sorry if she were dead: Grandmother Trowbridge, the marquess, Audrey, perhaps even Lord Dante Muir, her reluctant husband.

How they'd weep and gnash their teeth over their altered fortunes, their unfulfilled dreams of heirs and deep pockets and pretty gowns and mended millstones.

Yes, dying seemed a viable option. A reasonable remedy. A preferable choice. And it would most probably be a lovely funeral, even if she, thank goodness, wouldn't be there to see it.

Oh, she was so embarrassed!

She had made an utter fool of herself tonight, and no one was more aware of that fact than Sarah Jane herself, except perhaps for Mildred, who had brought home the disadvantages of too much wine on high-strung, unsuspecting young females who would be better served to sit up straight, sip lemonade, and otherwise keep their mouths firmly closed.

Thank heaven for Audrey! Why, if that sympathetic lady hadn't rescued her, whisked her away from the scene of her embarrassing unraveling, there was no knowing what would have happened.

Had she truly said *that* to Dante? Had she really addressed the marquess as *Curtis?* What on earth had come over her? She wasn't a hoyden. She was a quiet, biddable, shy, and terribly nervous young woman; Grandmother Trowbridge had told her so, over and over again. Oh, she had dreams and wishes, but she had never been so forward in her life.

And she never would be again! Why hadn't she realized that belatedly marshaling her courage and thinking of wonderful things to say only long hours after the fact was not that bad, for at least she was then alone in her bed and not able to humiliate herself publicly

"Oooh, my *head,*" she moaned as the mantel clock chimed out the hour of twelve, its bell-like sounds reverberating in her head like booming thunder until her teeth rattled.

She turned her face into the pillow and wished for an easier death than this agonizing expiration by sherry. Perhaps she should have eaten something from the tray Mildred had brought to her after that embarrassing interlude with the washbasin, but at the time, the last—the absolute last—thing she had wanted to have shoved beneath her nose was a plate brimming with chicken that appeared to be positively *afloat* in grease.

She lay very still, visions of her shame playing out behind her closed eyes, when suddenly she became aware of another presence in the room, on the bed.

"Mildred? Is that you, Mildred?" she asked. *Oh, please, Lord, if you bear any love for this poor sinner, let it be Mildred!*

"No, Sarah Jane," Lord Dante Muir answered quietly from somewhere not very far away, and she knew, just knew, that he was sitting on the edge of the mattress, looking at her as she lay there, a miserable, pathetic lump. "Do you wish me to ring for her?"

Yes! Good God, yes! Ring for her, run off to the servants' quarters to fetch her, tell her to arm herself with a blunderbuss so that she can warn you to go away or else she'll blast you into little bits! Take your time about it, as well, so that I can be hiding in a cabinet by the time you return.

"No, um, no, that's all right," Sarah Jane answered weakly, then turned onto her back, squinting as she attempted to pierce the darkness and see more than the outline of Lord Dante's body as it was silhouetted against the moonlit windows. "Am I in disgrace?"

His head moved in the negative. "On the contrary, my dear wife. I'm the one who is in particularly bad odor among the members of my family. They are of one opinion in the matter and have, both together and separately, condemned me for a brute, a boor, and a cold-blooded reptile who has succeeded, within the space of a single day, in reducing my bride to a desperation sufficient to necessitate recourse to strong drink. I believe I am to be drawn and quartered at dawn. Tell me, does your head ache horribly?"

"Only when I breathe," Sarah Jane admitted, pushing herself back against the pillows until she was nearly sitting, the satin coverlet slipping down to her knees so that her modest cotton night rail became a visible puddle of white in the moonlight.

The single braid Mildred had woven into her hair fell forward over her shoulder, the shifting of her heavy hair setting off a new round of throbbing inside her skull. "I'm so sorry. I should have listened to you. Grandmother Trowbridge told me that any sort of strong drink is the devil's tool. I can't imagine why I insisted upon drinking the entire glass."

"Two entire glasses, and I can," Lord Dante said, sighing. He reached out a hand to touch hers, and Sarah Jane flinched, then immediately hated herself for reacting like a skittish colt about to be bridled for the first time.

But he didn't remove his hand. He only allowed it to lie

on top of hers, softly, gently, impersonally. She felt her headache beginning to ease. *Was his touch magic? Was she absolutely the silliest, most naive, impressionable goose ever created?*

"Sarah Jane . . . Sarah, I believe that we should talk, don't you?"

"Talk?" She looked about the room, able now to make out the shadows of the two chairs in front of the dying fire, the edges of the tables and other pieces of furniture that lined the walls. But for all intents and purposes, the bedchamber had been reduced to the size of the bed she and Dante now shared. The intimacy was undeniable. Unnerving. Curiously exciting.

"Now?" she croaked at last.

"Last night would have been better, I agree," he said, leaning forward to take up the tinderbox and light the small branch of candles on the bedside table. The candlelight flattered his strong features, and she remembered how he had looked last night just before he kissed her, touched her . . . oh, Lord, was he going to do it all again tonight?

Did she want him to? She couldn't possibly want him to! Could she?

"I have had a fairly vast experience with women, but none with innocents such as you, a statement which, I suppose, alternately condemns and honors me. Last night . . . well, look, we're married now, Sarah. What's done is done. I could, *should,* have handled certain things differently. Better. But I didn't. I bungled it, badly."

"You can't be held responsible, Dante. Audrey explained it to me," Sarah Jane told him quickly, trying to console him, then immediately wondered why it mattered to her one way or the other how he felt.

"Really? Now, there's an explanation I must hear. What did my dear feather-witted sister-in-law tell you?"

Sarah Jane decided that she wouldn't die from the effects of the sherry after all. The cause of her imminent demise was definite now: she would expire of sheer embarrassment.

"She—she told me that you, um, that you like it. That all men like it."

"Is that so? Well, wasn't that helpful of dear Audrey? However, she is nearly correct. Last night's interlude was a generally pleasant experience, with my only regret being that you could not enjoy the interlude as much as I."

It's true. I'm not supposed to enjoy it, Sarah Jane thought sadly, knowing that Dante's statement only confirmed what Audrey had said. He did not expect her to enjoy it. If she did, it would only prove that she was of inferior stock. Peasant stock. *Butcher* stock. She was rapidly becoming prodigiously fatigued by this butcher's-granddaughter business!

"Audrey informed me all about that as well," she told him, wishing the candles didn't burn so bright that she could see his face, that he could see hers.

"She did? Well, that's good. Being a woman, she probably explained everything twice as well as I could. But what I want to say to you now, Sarah Jane, is that I don't want you to be afraid of me. And you are afraid of me, aren't you?"

She withdrew her hand from beneath his and immediately felt his palm against her thigh. The heat of him burned through the fabric of her night rail, searing her. She wet her lips and swallowed hard, deciding that *now* was the time for courage. And perhaps a well-placed fib.

"Afraid? What utter nonsense. I'm not afraid, not in the least."

"You should never lie, Sarah Jane," he told her, shifting his body so that he, too, was propped up against the headboard, his long legs crossed atop the covers. His posture was most companionable, and she would have relaxed if it had been daylight and they had been leaning against a tree near some stream, watching the clouds go by. But they weren't, and she wasn't.

"Lie? Oh, that really is too bad of you. Are you saying that I am lying?"

"Yes, dear creature, I am saying just that. And you do it exceedingly poorly, you know. Not that I blame you for feeling as you do. Your grandmother warned me that you knew very little of what it meant to be a wife. I would have gone more slowly, taking your innocence into consideration, but there are certain rules concerning marriages such as ours. One of them, I'm afraid, is that the union must be consummated on the wedding night. For all our strides in art and literature, and all our heated protests to the contrary, we English are still a rather barbarous race."

"Audrey explained that to me as well," Sarah Jane said, wondering why she felt suddenly optimistic. So he *was* going to kiss her again tonight. Hold her again tonight. She quite liked the kissing, the holding. She was glad she had suffered through cleaning her teeth before climbing into bed. Some of Grandmother Trowbridge's never-to-be-bent rules were commonsensible after all.

The thoughts that had troubled her all day receded as she savored his closeness and knew that, now that she was married, she would never be alone again. It was a comforting feeling, and well worth the inconvenience of what Audrey had termed "Eve's punishment."

"Audrey appears to have been most thorough. It would seem I have underestimated my dear sister-in-law. It had always been my opinion that her mind was filled with nothing weightier than thistledown. I shall have to thank her, won't I?"

Lord Dante turned to look at Sarah Jane. "But we'll forget Audrey for a moment, shall we? Admitting that it is not within my power to take back the happenings of these past weeks, and particularly of last night, I would like for us to begin again. Would that be agreeable to you?"

"Begin again?" Sarah Jane bit her lip, realizing that she had been repeating almost every word Lord Dante said. "I don't understand."

And then, mortifying her beyond belief, her stomach rumbled. Loudly. Hungrily.

"You didn't have any dinner tonight, did you, Sarah Jane?"

So much for the civilized English male! Didn't her new husband know that he should have ignored her grumbling stomach? It was so *personal*.

Sarah Jane felt her lips begin to twitch and wondered momentarily if her earlier fit of the giggles had returned. But really, what did it matter if he alluded to such a personal body part as her belly, when he had been much more intimate with her just last night in this very bed?

"The sherry," she began sheepishly, avoiding his eyes, "and then the chicken was so—"

"Atrocious, inedible, upsetting to look at, and unchewable into the bargain. Yes, Sarah, I agree. Just be thankful you didn't see the fish!" Lord Dante said briskly, taking her hand and all but pulling her from the bed, so that her toes curled as her feet encountered the cold floor. "That's what comes of letting the servants run tame wherever it pleases them. I don't know whether to settle their wages or turn off the lot of them. Come on."

She hastened to pull the hem of her night rail out from beneath the trailing covers with her free hand, feeling the breeze of the night air on her momentarily exposed legs.

"What are you doing?" she asked as he picked up her dressing gown from the foot of the bed and all but shoved her into it, his actions turning them into doting parent and uncomprehending child.

"I would have thought that was obvious. You didn't really believe I came in here this evening hoping for a repetition of last night, did you? I have retained some sense. You're hungry, Sarah. Surprisingly, I'm finding that I am hungry as well. Therefore we're going downstairs to the kitchens. There must be a bone or two there worth gnawing on. Now, where are your slippers?"

He was taking her to the kitchens? At this hour? Goodness, at *any* hour? The kitchens were the domain of the cook and the other servants, who did not appreciate their employer's presence. Why, she didn't believe her grandmother had been in the kitchens at Trowbridge Manor above twice, and one of those times was because the place had caught fire! Would she never understand these Muirs?

"Somewhere beneath the bed, I suppose," Sarah Jane answered at last, realizing her husband was waiting for an answer, then watched wide-eyed as Lord Dante dropped to his knees and began searching the dark floor. "Why don't we simply ring for Mildred?"

He pushed her back onto the edge of the bed, then lifted each leg in turn, cradling each calf, and slid the slippers onto her feet before yanking her upright once more.

Grinning boyishly—he did look rather boyish, for a husband—he said, "And what fun would that be, I ask you, Lady Dante? Are you ready? We'll have to be quiet. Lord knows if Johnny is still up and about. I locked up the cellars, rationing the amount of wine and spirits I'll allow served in a day, and he has nothing with which to bribe Babbitt for the key. Not that Babbitt would indulge him. For tonight, Johnny has taken to prowling about, searching the cupboards for any errant bottle I might have missed. By tomorrow night he'll probably be reduced to roaming the halls like some lost soul, howling to bring down the house."

"Poor Johnny," Sarah Jane said, her kind heart touched by the image of Lord John in such despair.

"Not really. I could have locked him in his rooms without a drop, you know. But I plan to wean him slowly, for everyone's sake. Now come with me."

Lord Dante took her hand and led her to the door, turning to wink at her as he pressed a finger to his lips, cautioning her to be silent.

"You wouldn't be about to yell 'Fire' at the top of your lungs, would you?" she whispered daringly, thinking he looked very much like his fun-loving younger brother at the moment.

"Johnny's been at it again, I imagine," he answered, one corner of his mouth lifting in that lopsided smile she found so appealing. "As I said, we have a lot to talk about, Sarah Jane. We'll take the servants' stairs at the end of the hallway, all right? They lead directly to the family wing kitchens. We rarely use the main kitchens anymore, which might be a good thing, for we'd both freeze to death if we had to travel that far. Now, be very quiet, Sarah Jane. Here we go!"

Feeling like a truant infant escaped from the nursery, and not a little pleased by the prospect of an adventure, Sarah Jane exaggeratedly pressed her lips together and allowed herself to be led out into the dimly glowing hallway, her hand still held tight in her husband's.

The servants' stairs were quite narrow, with a wicked twist in them halfway down, so that she laid her free hand on Lord Dante's back as they navigated the poorly lit passageway, finally exiting directly into the kitchens, where a softly glowing fire was banked against the back of the soot-encrusted inner hearth of the wall-length fireplace.

This area appeared more spacious in the daylight. And it's none too clean, either. I shall have to have a word with the servants, for a clean kitchen is absolutely necessary to good food preparation, she thought nervously as she padded toward the sturdy wooden table in the center of the room, watching as Lord Dante took up a three-pronged candleholder and began investigating the thick-walled cold larder that occupied a room separate from the main kitchen, leaving her in the near-dark.

"Have you found anything?" she asked a moment later, just to hear his voice.

He reappeared shortly, the candleholder in one hand and a large platter in the other. The platter was wrapped in layers of cloth, but she was sure he had located the remains of Lord John's performing pig. He plunked the platter down on the table and unwrapped it.

"Voilà! A thing of rare beauty, isn't it, and a joy until we demolish it! There should be some cheese in that heavy cabinet over there, Sarah," he said, using one of the candles to light several more around the room.

Then he set off again, this time in the direction of the pantry where the breads, flour, and other such items were kept; she knew this because of her quick introductory tour of the kitchens prior to her marriage.

Sarah Jane found a small wheel of cheese and then crossed to an open-fronted cabinet to collect two chipped earthenware plates, obviously used by the servants, and a knife that was one of an impressive array of cutlery stuck into a wooden block beside the dry sink.

"I don't suppose there is any milk?" she asked as Lord Dante returned with a crusty loaf.

He placed a chair in front of the table and, with an elegant sweep of his arm, requested that she take her seat.

"I thought there might be a pitcher in with the cheese," she explained, "but there wasn't. I shall make a list of necessary items for the larder in the morning. I can do that, you know. Grandmother Trowbridge taught me." Then she lowered her head, immediately embarrassed. How could she have put herself forward like that? What was it about this man that made her believe he might actually be interested in her opinions, her thoughts, even her small domestic talents?

"So Betts has been of some use after all. Good. And may I say, Sarah Jane, that I quite enjoy hearing that ring of authority in your voice. My wife, it would appear, is about to become the terror of the kitchens." Lord Dante then procured another small caned chair for himself and sat down close beside her at the foot of the table, motioning to the pitcher and two earthenware mugs that she now saw sitting beside the ham. "Water is the order of the evening, milady," he declared sadly, then smiled. "Although I am sure I can locate some sherry, if you so desire."

"Thank you, no," Sarah Jane replied quickly, laughing nervously as she cut two thick slices from the round loaf of bread and placed one on each plate, forgetting that she was sitting beside her husband, forgetting that she was clad only in her night rail and dressing gown, forgetting that it was after midnight and she was *alone* with that husband, forgetting everything save that she was enjoying herself very much. "Water will suit just fine, although," she added daringly, looking straight at him, "I do believe I should mention that it is *vastly* ill-mannered of you to remind me of my poor choice of liquid refreshment earlier this evening."

"Really?" Lord Dante's left eyebrow crept upward. "Well, good for you! I was out of line, wasn't I? You should say what you think more often, Sarah. Honesty becomes you."

Sarah Jane could feel her cheeks coloring and was grateful for the dimness of the kitchen. "Perhaps you're right. But I believe I will begin slowly, for my nerves would probably not support a full disclosure of all that is in my mind."

"Now you have me shaking in my boots, little pet." His

one-sided smile was devastating, nearly causing her to slip from her chair and become a puddle of insensibility on the cold stone floor.

She looked away from his all too penetrating gaze. "Yes, well . . ." she said quietly, longing for a change of subject. "Perhaps I should find forks?" she suggested at last, taking refuge in matters domestic.

"There's no need." Lord Dante retrieved the knife and made quick work of slicing into the pink flesh of the ham, placing equal amounts on each plate before doing much the same with the cheese. He then pulled Sarah Jane's plate in front of him and layered one side of the bread with cheese and ham before folding the bread in half and holding it up to her as if presenting her with a gift.

"There you go, Sarah. It's a little trick we Englishmen learned from John Montagu, Earl of Sandwich. He found it easier to take a meal at the gaming table this way, leaving one hand free for the cards."

"How very ingenious, I suppose." Sarah Jane took the folded bread and peered at its thickness owlishly. "Um, what am I to do now?"

"Watch me," Lord Dante suggested, for he had already repeated his motions with the ham, cheese, and bread on his own plate. Opening his mouth wide, he dipped his head and took a large bite, grinning closemouthed as he began to chew.

"Ah, ambrosia of the gods!" he declared encouragingly once he had swallowed. "Go on, Sarah. I promise, Betts will never know."

"I suppose that's for the best, considering all her lectures on proper manners at table," Sarah Jane mumbled, then took hold of the food with both hands, placed her elbows firmly on the table for balance, and bit into the thick folded bread, tearing off ham, cheese, and bread in a single healthy attack.

"This is delicious!" she exclaimed around a mouthful of the forbidden delicacy. She laid down the bread and wiped her mouth free of crumbs with the back of her hand. "Absolutely *delicious!* Shame on your servants, Dante! How dare they serve us greasy chicken and save all this lovely ham for themselves?"

Dante took a drink of the cold water, then slammed the mug heavily on the table. "It's criminal, that's what it is. But remember, Sarah, they are now your servants as well. What shall we do with them? I say we draw and quarter them at dawn!"

"Rather than just you? Or will we dispose of them first and then have at you?" Sarah Jane was emboldened to say. Then she giggled, knowing that she was no longer pot-valiant with sherry. She had become drunk on Lord Dante's kind words, his sweet companionship. And she had dared, just for these few delicious moments, to be the woman she wished to be.

But Lord Dante was looking at her curiously, as if he had never truly seen her before. Had she gone too far? Dared too much, too soon? Her new joy evaporated, to be replaced by the nagging notion that she had opened her mouth only to make a fool of herself.

Lord Dante propped his elbows on the table and dropped his chin into his hands, his dark eyes now twinkling mischievously. "Then you haven't forgiven me, Sarah? I had hoped that feeding you might serve to put me back into your graces. I hold out no hope for my family, who see me as part savior, part persecutor."

Sarah Jane frowned, then sobered even more. It had occurred to her only briefly that Lord Dante might be as much the sacrificial lamb as she in this arranged marriage. But of course it was true. If she had been offered up in exchange for social advancement, her husband had been sold outright for his family's benefit.

Impulsively she laid her hand on his. "Has it been very bad for you?"

Lord Dante lifted her hand to his mouth, gently kissed it, then pressed the back of her hand against his cheek. Sarah Jane felt her stomach turn over once more, but this time the sensation was pleasant, and her toes curled delightedly inside her silken slippers.

"No worse than it has been for you, I'd wager," he said, at

last releasing her hand. "Which is why, Sarah Jane, I believe we must have a talk."

"I like it better when you call me Sarah," she blurted, immediately sensing she had once more gone too far. "That is," she continued rapidly, her tongue tripping over her words, "if you *want* to call me Sarah. You could just as easily call me Sarah Jane, I suppose, which is how I have always been addressed, even if it is the most ridiculous, *juvenile* appellation ever created, but—"

Her stomach growled once more, and she was immediately tongue-tied.

"Sarah," he said softly, his tone soothing, his one-sided smile turning her knees to butter. "I agree, it is prodigiously better. Now, why don't you make further inroads on your meal while I see if we can't settle a few things between us?"

Sarah Jane nodded wordlessly, knowing she would climb to the top of the tallest mountain and leap off it, if only Dante would ask. She was back to worshiping him and didn't care if it was wrong-headed of her, even stupid. He was someone completely outside her experience, and she found him to be simply too magnificent for words!

Lord Dante took a drink of the water, then held the cup between his hands, rolling it against his palms, as if taking a moment to marshal his thoughts. "Where do I begin?"

She offered a suggestion. "I know very little about you and your family."

"Well, then, Sarah, I shall begin there." He smiled at her and she took a large bite of her makeshift meal, feeling she had accomplished something wonderful, and the ham and cheese and crusty bread were her reward.

"I love my family very much, Sarah," he began quietly. "I'm telling you this because what I am about to say may make you believe that I don't, which is not true. We are an odd lot, we Muirs, and rather rough-and-tumble, thanks to being without a woman's softening, civilizing influence since my mother died some twenty years ago—you'll notice I don't count the fair, fairly brainless Audrey anywhere— but we all are quite fond of one another, in our own way."

"My parents perished in a carriage accident when I was

seven," Sarah Jane told him, feeling she should say something. "Not that I remember them very well. Grandmother Trowbridge has always loomed largest in my life, as she kept me by her side almost exclusively, preparing me for a proper life, as she termed it. I think everyone, Grandfather Trowbridge included, was somewhat in awe of her."

"I can't imagine why," Lord Dante responded, his dark eyes twinkling mischievously, so that Sarah Jane had to suppress yet another giggle.

"She is rather imposing, isn't she?"

"I see my dear bride has the gift of understatement. Why, Sarah, if Wellington had been able to field but a thousand like Betts Trowbridge, Bonaparte would have been reduced to tears within a week, *begging* for the chance to be sent packing to Elba. But to get back to my family . . ."

He took another sip of water, then set the mug on the table. "The family fortunes have taken a large dip since my father ascended to the title at the tender age of one and twenty. He inherited the Muir failing of gambling, you see, and is incurably detached from the day-to-day running of Cliff Walk. Tyler and I did our best to hold things together, as did Johnny, once he was done with his schooling. Audrey's money helped, for a while, but then Tyler took to following Audrey's lead in London, living from Season to Season, party to party. Tyler never was one to wax nostalgic over draining fields and the latest advances in agriculture, I'm afraid, but he did enjoy dancing and visiting his tailor. The constant round of parties helped him to forget a woman he'd once . . . Well, that is another story, isn't it?"

Sarah Jane formed a mental picture of the Earl of Easterly, a man forced to give up what most certainly had been a true love in order to marry for money. He became at once a romantic figure in her mind, unloved, confined to his Bath chair, a bitter, broken shell of the handsome young fellow he most certainly had been. It was a romantic, if sad, vision.

But Lord Dante was speaking again. "At last I bought myself a commission, believing it the duty of the second son to either go to war or join the clergy, a notion that was and is totally alien to me, and hoping that Ty, and Johnny, who had joined the rest of the family in London, would come to their senses and return to Cliff Walk before they bankrupted us."

He propped one elbow on the table and rested his chin in his hand. "To be truthful, I was feeling rather put upon, Sarah, trying to run Cliff Walk by myself, and with precious little money to be getting on with."

"The house does need some repair," Sarah Jane said, for she felt she should make some sort of comment. Were heroes allowed to feel put upon? Were husbands allowed to be human?

"Again the mistress of understatement. You haven't toured the grounds and gardens, have you? They're ragtag, scraggly, but the working estate is a shambles. Several of our farmers have gone, and those who remain know that without a large infusion of funds there will be no salvaging anything. Which is why your grandmother's offer was impossible to refuse. There is so much to do—in the mill, the forestry, the fields, the village. But I digress."

"You care very deeply about the land and the people," Sarah Jane stated, knowing it was the truth. Lord Dante Muir was a good man, and she was proud to be his wife, even if she was still slightly in awe of him and still, she acknowledged silently, not much more than a girl herself and prone to melodramatic conclusions. "I'm so glad I could be of help, even in only some small way."

Lord Dante gave a low, pleasant chuckle. "Fifty thousand pounds and all the mortgages settled is hardly helping in a small way, Sarah. You have saved Cliff Walk. Now it is up to me to turn the estate into a moneymaker again. Which, I'm afraid, brings us back to my family."

"Your father is leaving tomorrow, isn't he?" Sarah Jane asked, blushing as she remembered calling the marquess by his Christian name. Now Lord Dante was speaking in the way of a hero again, and his wife had just behaved like an ill-bred hoyden in front of the whole family. Having the marquess gone would certainly simplify matters and perhaps even give her some breathing space in which to recover her composure and begin the chore of playing heroine to her husband's hero. "Will he leave early in the day, do you think, or late?"

Lord Dante smiled, his cheek crinkling against his hand and giving him the appearance of a little boy up to mischief. "If you breakfast in our rooms, you should be able to avoid him, pet," he said, then sobered. "I should have known better than to believe he'd stay here and help me. He didn't come back to Cliff Walk when I left to serve with Wellington's staff. None of them came home. Which was a pity, considering what happened."

Sarah Jane lifted the bread to her lips, then hesitated, sensing some sort of intrigue. "What did happen, Dante?"

"After I'd been gone about two years Johnny decided to follow me to war, a plan Father thoroughly scotched by refusing to buy him a commission. Or Ty, who also wished to volunteer, as we needed all the men we could muster by then. Johnny and Tyler, unable to purchase their own commissions, remained in London, both of them at loose ends, for yet another year. I suppose that's how the idea of a horse race came to them—as something to do."

He sat back and drained his mug, as if forgetting that it contained no wine but only water.

"And Tyler was injured," Sarah Jane ended for him, quickly coming to her own conclusion. "I gathered earlier tonight that Johnny feels responsible for the earl's reduced state. But," she added hopefully, "Johnny feels sure that Tyler could walk again, if he'd only try."

"Hence the cries of 'Fire!'" Lord Dante said, grinning once more, endearing himself to Sarah Jane, who believed her husband to be prodigiously handsome when he smiled, and aeons more approachable.

"That, and this lovely ham, if it is indeed the same one and your—*our*—servants aren't living high, butchering the livestock willy-nilly while the rest of us starve," Sarah Jane said, frowning. "Is it true? Does the doctor really believe that Tyler can walk?"

"We all do, for all the good it does us, for Ty refuses to believe it. It's just that his muscles, and his will, have all but disappeared thanks to his enforced inaction while his bones mended. Poor Ty. I wish you had known him before. Before Audrey, before his accident. He was so full of life, so carefree!" Dante sighed. "He came to me early this morning, asking me to pen a letter to our solicitor to inquire as to how he might be able to secure a bill of divorcement for Audrey, so that she might, in Ty's words, 'have a chance to live again, this time with a whole man.'"

"Oh, dear," Sarah Jane said, her soft heart touched by the earl's generosity. "He must love her very much."

Lord Dante rose from his chair and then leaned his hands on it, looking at Sarah Jane. "I don't think so. As a matter of fact, I believe they cheerfully detest each other. It's pity for himself that drives Ty in this, even if he won't admit it. Audrey's presence at Cliff Walk reminds him of his former life in London, and her absence brings home to him the fact that she is continuing to live an existence replete with fun and freedom in Mayfair while he is stuck here at Cliff Walk. And," he added, not looking at Sarah Jane, "I believe he rues their lack of children."

Sarah Jane was tempted to tell her husband that Audrey merely detested submitting to her wifely duties, but she was not so at ease with Lord Dante that she felt she could broach such a delicate subject without blushing and stammering herself into insensibility. So she answered quickly, and not at all prudently, "Yes, Grandmother Trowbridge explained that to me. I believe she harbors the notion that her great-grandson will one day be the Marquess of Chevley. Oh! I shouldn't have said that, should I?"

"Why not, pet? It's true enough. Betts is certainly out to get her money's worth. Which is another reason I wanted us to have this talk."

Sarah Jane relaxed. "You hate her, don't you?"

"Not at all. She is a commonsensible, pragmatic woman. It is her tactics that I cannot like. Her willingness to use other people to gain her ends. Sarah"—he came around the table and took hold of her hand—"what's done is done, but that doesn't mean we have to play entirely by your grandmother's rules."

Sarah Jane withdrew her hand. Was he about to send her away? She raced into speech. "But I want to help you. I am prepared, really. I can run a household, visit the sick, even understand the accounts. You may not believe it to look at me, but I do know how to handle servants, and I am not afraid to issue orders. I've even learned the rudiments—much more than the rudiments—of overseeing the day-to-day problems that must be confronted on a working estate. I may not read Greek, or recognize fine art, but I am a sort of domestic bluestocking. My mind is just crammed full of useful information."

She frowned as he smiled rather indulgently and shook his head. "But if you don't—"

"That's not what I mean, pet."

"No?" She relaxed a trifle. "What—what do you mean?"

"I mean, Sarah, that I think we must take some time to get to know each other before we repeat the actions of last night. We married as strangers, but the time has come for us to learn to be friends. Then and only then should we continue with this business of possible heirs."

"Oh, I see." Sarah Jane said, so quietly she barely heard herself speak. Why was she so disappointed? What on earth was wrong with her? She dared another question. "Will you be sleeping in your dressing room, then?"

His smile was rueful. "I don't think anything that dramatic is necessary. Besides, we wouldn't wish the servants to talk, would we? Betts is probably paying at least two of them to report our every move to her. Don't worry, Sarah. I believe I can share the same bed with you without pouncing on you like some wild animal. Later, some weeks or months from now, when we have become more familiar with each other, more used to this marriage of ours, we can rethink the arrangement. I just don't look for a repeat of tonight's fiasco, with my wife so nervous about the coming of evening that she feels the need to take recourse in sherry. All right?"

He sat down once more. "Now, why don't you finish off your meal, and I can lead you back upstairs to bed. You have to be exhausted."

"All right." Sarah Jane dutifully took another bite and

then another, finishing her meal not because she was still hungry but because her husband had asked it of her. If only he had not asked her to understand what he had just said, for she was certain his request had nothing to do with her nervousness or her sensibilities or even her foray into strong spirits.

He simply wasn't attracted to her. Why, he could even sleep in the same bed with her and not feel the slightest urge to bed her. Married only two days, she was a failure as a wife!

"I—I rather like Audrey," she said at last, tumbling into speech when Lord Dante remained silent and that silence grew uncomfortable, picking a subject that popped into her mind without warning, "even though she can be rather silly. She has been most helpful to me. Are you quite convinced that I shouldn't cut my hair? I do hate it most prodigiously, you know. Grandmother Trowbridge chose the style, saying it would give me more height, and *consequence,* but I believe I look as if I am in imminent danger of being smothered by its sheer mass. And I do *so* hate that curling stick!"

Lord Dante laughed aloud and held out his hand to her once more, bidding her to rise. "Well, that tears it, doesn't it, Sarah? If Betts Trowbridge chose the style it simply *has* to go! I command it! We'll have to see about getting someone responsible to wield the scissors. Not the Titus, I think, but a less drastic change. Now, come on, it's past your bedtime. We'll leave this mess for the servants, who deserve the extra work."

Sarah Jane took his hand, looking at him nervously. He had that gleam in his eye, the one she had seen last night, just before he slid his hand beneath her gown. Perhaps, just perhaps, he had changed his mind. Now that he had fed her, was he about to bed her again? Would he give in to man's basest instinct, as Audrey would doubtless term it?

That would, she thought, be a terrible pity, especially when she considered how well they had been dealing with each other this past hour, for he would surely hate himself, and her, when he came to his senses.

"Yes," she said softly, "I would like to go to bed now. I am *exceedingly* tired. Why, I don't believe I can keep my eyes open above another minute. Truly!"

She stumbled then, whether over the hem of her dressing gown or her latest terrible lie she did not know, and Lord Dante immediately swept her off her feet and held her high against his chest, like a child.

"You weigh less than Growler, I'd wager," he said cheerfully enough, "although I believe your eyes are bigger." He bent his knees, motioning with his head for her to pick up the small branch of candles. "Here we go now, little pet," he said once she was holding the candles high. "Hold on tight. I wouldn't wish to drop you."

Sarah Jane did as he bid, gripping him tightly about the shoulders and laying her head against his chest, to help him balance her, and because she felt so comfortable with her cheek pressed against the fine lawn of his shirt, against the taut muscles beneath the material.

He did not attempt to navigate the narrow servants' stairs but went straight for the baize door and the hallway beyond, heading for the main staircase.

Sarah Jane caught a glimpse of their two bodies as he passed a large mirror in the hallway and saw herself being held high off the floor, her braid hanging free, her slippered feet visible beneath the trailing hem of her dressing gown, one hand clutching the candleholder and the other tightly gripping her husband's shoulder.

She looked, or so she decided, like the heroine in a penny press novel, a fair damsel being carried off by her lover. It was a startling, wonderful, and rather intimidating thought, and she quickly closed her eyes and buried her face once more against his chest. She felt so safe, so vulnerable, so cherished, so apprehensive.

Surely he could feel her trembling.

Lord Dante had just mounted the first step when the slightly slurred voice of Lord John brought him to a halt. "Caught her out trying to escape her fate, did you, Dante? Good for you!"

"Go to bed, Johnny," Lord Dante ordered, his voice rumbling deep in his chest, so that it tickled Sarah Jane's ear. "All the bottles are locked up for the night."

"Go to hell, Dante," Lord John replied amicably. "Not that you'd feel at home there. You're such a bloody saint, ain't you?"

"Good night, Johnny," Lord Dante said quietly, and continued up the staircase.

Sarah Jane kept her eyes closed as Lord Dante fumbled with the latch to the bedchamber door, her arm beginning to ache with the weight of the candleholder, so that she was relieved when he took it from her, then laid her on the bed.

She shifted quickly to the far side of the mattress, sliding out of her slippers and burying her legs under the covers, then belatedly remembered that she was still wearing her dressing gown.

He'll remove it for me, she thought, then shivered. No. No, he wouldn't. He had said he wouldn't. Very well, then, she'd simply sleep in the thing, for she wasn't about to come out from beneath the blankets again!

The covers pulled up to her chin, her eyes wide with mingled apprehension and curiosity, she watched as Lord Dante cupped his hand behind each of the candles in turn, blowing them out, casting the bedchamber into darkness.

Her eyes snapped shut, but then she peeked out from under her lashes as, silhouetted in the moonlight, he began opening the buttons on his shirt, the length of his throat visible to her, then the breadth of his chest, and finally his strong, well-muscled arms.

When he reached for the buttons at his waist she prudently turned away, lying on her side, staring at nothing.

A moment later she felt his weight on the mattress, and the covers lifted fractionally, then fell back into place once more.

"Sarah?"

She could have pretended to be asleep, but she didn't. She turned, slowly, and found herself staring straight into his dark eyes. She blinked once, twice, and carefully yawned. "Yes, Dante?"

He was smiling that one-sided smile again. "Are you really all that tired?"

Her heart was pounding in her ears, and her mouth had gone dry. Bone-dry, as if she had just crossed a wide desert on her hands and knees. Her breathing was somehow shallow, as if she had run up and down the stairs as fast as she could go—twice.

"No. Not really. I—I'm actually quite awake now."

"That's nice, Sarah. There seems to be a problem, an argument taking place at this moment between my mind and my body. How can I say this? About what we spoke of earlier, downstairs? About the two of us taking our time? . . . getting to know each other better . . . and to like each other? Well, Sarah, although it seemed a good idea at the time . . ."

She couldn't breathe at all now, so that her words came out on a sigh, a hope, a prayer. "Yes, Dante?"

"Yes, Sarah? Then you do understand what I'm trying—cow-handedly, I think you'd agree—to say?"

She bit her lip for a moment, then, believing herself to be behaving in the truest tradition of a heroine who would give anything, dare anything, for the man she loved, whispered, "Yes, Dante."

His smile was slow and well pleased as he reached for her. "Ah, pet, I was so hoping you'd say that."

CHAPTER 6

Women are like tricks by sleight of hand,
Which, to admire, we should not understand.

William Congreve

Audrey? Might I have a word with you?" Lord Dante had been waiting in the family drawing room for what seemed like hours for his sister-in-law to appear. He rose impatiently as she entered, obviously after having spent most of the morning on her toilette.

She looked her usual self, beautiful, pampered, and totally useless. Not at all like Sarah, who was so eager to please, to help him set Cliff Walk to rights.

"A word, Dante? To what end? Or are you about to explain this pittance you are doling out to Tyler and me? Oh, yes, I have heard of your closefisted largesse. Two hundred pounds? Why, the lowest paupers on the street must need at least twice that amount to exist!"

"Hardly, Audrey," Dante answered, motioning to a chair, then seating himself once she had daintily spread her pink taffeta skirts and sat down, her bottom lip thrust forward petulantly in the way of a thwarted child about to throw a tantrum.

"And your father is absolutely no help at all," she continued, as if he hadn't spoken. "I never saw the man

114

move half so quickly as he did in getting himself shed of this place of torture. He'll be well served, living off the largesse of his wealthy friends as has been his custom these past years, but as for myself—well, I simply cannot *conceive* of how I shall be able to go on. If only my dear papa were still alive. He wouldn't stand for such ill treatment of his only child!"

"You could always apply to your dear *mother* for assistance," Lord Dante inserted, knowing full well that Audrey's mother had married a much younger man, two years previously, and did not seem to care a snap about her beautiful daughter, whom she may have seen as a threat to her marriage.

"Oh, pish tosh!" Audrey said with the wave of her hand. "Mama and I have never rubbed along together very well. We won't speak of her, or of her husband, who is still, I imagine, doing his utmost to shed his leading strings. I don't know, I simply cannot fathom, *how* I shall survive in this dank backwater until the Season, Dante. We *are* traveling to London for the Season, aren't we? I am quite convinced you will wish to show off your dear bride to the *ton.*"

Lord Dante knew any such sojourn to be an impossibility. He would not be willing to spend the funds necessary for a Season in Mayfair at this time, and his presence at Cliff Walk would be necessary for the spring planting, the completion of repairs just begun, and many other pressing issues that Audrey would find unbearably dull if he were to catalog them for her.

"We'll see," he answered noncommittally, as if he were soothing a fractious child who had asked for a slice of the moon.

"But," he continued, "that is not why I wish to speak with you, Audrey."

"Really?" she asked, raising one eyebrow inquiringly. "Then I cannot imagine why I am here, for you never wish to speak with me unless it is to berate me for spending a few pennies on the barest of necessities. Why, only last month, when that beastly Mademoiselle Tullard was so unbelievably rude as to forward you the bills for those few gowns I purchased this summer for the Peace Celebrations, you cut up so stiff I thought sure you were about to beat me. Physically *beat* me! As if you were lord and master of us all, and not just a younger son, waiting for his poor crippled brother to die. I told dearest Sarah Jane about your vile temper, Dante, although the sweet child did not believe me. Just wait until she attempts to properly outfit herself for spring! Oh, she'll see the truth then, won't she?"

"A few gowns? I could have purchased a small country for the money you— *What* did you say?"

Audrey took refuge behind a small white lace handkerchief, pressing it against her eyes. "No, no, Dante, don't yell so! I didn't mean it. I didn't mean any of it, truly, and Sarah Jane defended you most rigorously. Please, you're frightening me. You know how I ramble, the way I did last night about Lady Helena. I never should have mentioned her name! You always say that I ramble, saying any silly thing that pops into my head. You've been most kind, and I know how deep your affection is for Tyler. It's just that I do so want to go to London for the Season, especially now that I've heard how that horrid Emma Franklin woman has returned to the village! And with her *son*. Oh, that she has borne a son, and I have not!"

She began sobbing daintily into the handkerchief.

"God's teeth!" Lord Dante exclaimed, then took a deep breath and willed himself to be calm. He had been right in his assessment of his brother's wife: she did have a skull stuffed with feathers. But that didn't mean she couldn't do considerable damage with that flapping tongue of hers, both to Sarah Jane and to Tyler.

"Audrey," he began again, careful to keep his voice low and calm, "I'm sorry. I didn't mean to explode. In fact, I wished to speak to you about another matter entirely. I wanted to thank you, actually, for speaking to Sarah about . . . about married life."

"Thank me? Really?" She brightened immediately, wiping her eyes one last time before shoving the handkerchief into the pocket of her gown. "Oh, Dante, that isn't necessary. I only said what any loving sister would say."

"Yes," Lord Dante went on encouragingly. "And precisely what is it that any loving sister would say?"

"Do you truly wish to know? How diverting!" Audrey leaned toward him, her shoulders slightly hunched, her hands clasped together tightly in her lap, her eyes searching left and right as if she didn't wish to be overheard. "I told her of the beauty, the absolute *marvel,* of married love," she whispered, then giggled, rolling her eyes. "Oh, I shouldn't be so forward, Dante, truly I shouldn't, but when I remember the rapport, the absolute *ecstasy,* that I shared with dearest Tyler—before his sad accident, of course—I knew I simply *had* to allay Sarah Jane's fears."

"I see," Lord Dante said, frowning. Tyler had more than once alluded to the more private side of his marriage to Audrey, but Dante could not remember the word "ecstasy" being mentioned. "Frustrating" seemed more apt. Even "dashed boring, actually, with her screeching about mussing her hair and all that."

"Oh, yes," Audrey continued breathlessly, sitting back once more. "I found Sarah Jane yesterday morning, white-faced and frightened, and immediately *knew* that she had not fared well on her wedding night. You men are such *impatient* beasts, aren't you? Well, naturally I hastened to assure her that everything would be fine now that the marriage had been consummated, knowing I must be loyal to you, even though women like poor Sarah Jane . . . Lud, Dante, you wouldn't wish to put me to the blush, would you?"

"Yes, Audrey, I believe I would. Please continue. What were you going to say about Sarah?"

Audrey tipped her head to one side, so that the sunlight coming in through the windows set small golden fires in her hair, rather like a halo, Lord Dante thought, then dismissed any such notion as ludicrous. The Countess of Easterly wasn't an angel; she was a brainless chit whose inane chattering and blatant ignorance could prove dangerous.

"Oh, dear. How do I begin? Very well. Men are much the same, Dante. You all enjoy bedroom antics, with everyone from wives to low doxies. Isn't that correct?"

"I suppose," Dante answered, wondering if *he* was the one who was about to be put to the blush.

She leaned forward once more. "Women aren't like men, Dante," she whispered importantly. "Some of us, sadly, are not constituted for—oh, Dante, how can I say this?—for ever enjoying that sort of *pleasure*. From what Sarah Jane confided to me yesterday, and from what I'd already guessed on my own, I fear that she is just such a woman."

She sighed deeply, reaching out to take his hand in both of hers, as if to console him over a death in the family. "Ah, you poor, poor dear."

Lord Dante shook off her hands and rose, beginning to pace. "That's utter nonsense, Audrey," he declared, wishing he could believe his own words. But he was a man, and Audrey was a woman. Perhaps there were things he didn't know.

He stopped pacing and wheeled about to confront her as another thought occurred to him. "Dear God, you didn't say any of this to Sarah, did you?"

The white lace handkerchief was once more in evidence. "Say anything? How you wound me, Dante! Of course I didn't *say* anything. But it is a known fact, if only to women, and not to you men who believe your prowess enough to have any woman *melt* at your touch. Sarah Jane is so small, Dante, so very *delicately* constructed, that lovemaking, for her, is *impossible* without pain, *ever*. I suppose that is nature's way of protecting such women from a potentially deadly encounter with childbirth, and with men as tall and, um, *large* as you. You are much like Tyler, aren't you? Perhaps I'm wrong. I certainly would like to be wrong. But no matter what the reason, Sarah Jane is terrified of your touch, Dante, nearly as much as she is terrified of disappointing you, for the dear infant believes she loves you. She would rather die than admit how your intrusion on her person pains her. Of that much I am quite convinced!"

Lord Dante said nothing, for there was nothing to say. Nothing he could say.

"You went to her last night, didn't you, Dante? You imposed on her again. It's true, I can see it on your face. And

118

you hurt her again, didn't you? Oh, you men *are* beasts! Lud, I can only pray you have gotten her with child, so that you don't have to go to her again. Then we will all have to live with the fear of seeing her in childbed."

Audrey sniffed, then wiped at her tears. "Yet, even with her pain, her very real fear, I believe Sarah Jane will always fancy herself to be in love with you, until the *end*. Such a sweet, *caring* child, so pathetically eager to please. Dante, it's not her fault she cannot ever enjoy the marriage bed. You will try not to hurt her again, won't you?"

So eager to please. Just as Lord Dante had described Sarah Jane to himself earlier. He looked at Audrey for a long time. He had the evidence of his wedding night, of last night, to lend damning proof to his sister-in-law's words.

And Sarah was so small, just as he already knew. *So tight.* Why hadn't he considered the danger she would be in during childbirth?

"No, Audrey," he said quietly before quitting the room. "I won't hurt her again."

Sarah Jane had thrown a cloak over her shoulders shortly after luncheon and disappeared into the gardens, where she could think without Audrey chattering into her ear nineteen to the dozen about ribbons and materials and lengths of lace.

None of the three remaining Muir gentlemen had joined them at table, which had pleased Sarah Jane, for she hadn't wanted to see Lord Dante again until she could get herself back under control.

For she was out of control. That was definite. She was terribly out of control. Why hadn't she realized that the leap from timid mouse to brave lioness was too great to make in only a few days?

She found a small stone bench and sat down, sure that the overgrown hedges would hide her from anyone in the house who might decide to pass the time staring out one of the windows, and closed her eyes, reliving the debacle that had constituted her second night in Lord Dante Muir's bed, in Lord Dante Muir's arms.

How could she have wanted to give herself so shamelessly, and to a man she scarcely knew? But his mouth had been so warm on hers, so insistent, and his hands had brought her body alive with pleasure, with an unknown longing for something she could not see yet longed to touch.

Even now, in the cold light of day, she could remember clearly how her blood had sung through her veins as he divested her of her dressing gown and night rail, how she had wished to hold his dark head against her breast when he took her nipple in his mouth and suckled there, gently, insistently, how she had ached to shower him with kisses as he used his fingers to stroke the soft skin between her legs. . . .

She was so wanton!

Sarah Jane buried her head in her hands, feeling the heat of her flushed cheeks even in the dampness of the gray November afternoon that had dawned so bright that she had been able to clearly see the taut line of her husband's lips as he had left their bed early that morning after a night they had both spent lying very still, pretending to sleep.

Audrey had to be wrong. She had to be. There was nothing else for it, Sarah Jane decided in a moment of insight that she knew was probably born of her own most fond wish. Lord Dante had been disappointed in her lack of response, even as she knew that holding herself aloof from his lovemaking was not only wrong but somehow obscene.

Perhaps even ungrateful of her.

But once again, at the very end, he had hurt her. She hadn't expected the pain again, although she had felt slightly sore all day. Audrey had said it wouldn't hurt after the first time. So that made twice that her new sister had been proved wrong.

Yet, Sarah Jane *supposed*—as she remembered Lord John terming any bout of thinking—what if she hadn't held herself so tight, doing her best not to shame herself by responding like some low woman of the streets?

Well, then perhaps it wouldn't have hurt so much when Lord Dante spread her rigid, trembling legs with his knee, exposing her, and pressed himself between her thighs . . .

finding her, entering her, filling her, and then moving, moving, plunging into her over and over and over again before collapsing on her, breathing heavily, holding her to him as she felt his seed hot against her womb.

"Oh, Lord, oh, Lord, oh, *Lord,*" Sarah Jane whispered fiercely as she remembered how Lord Dante had felt inside her, feeling the strange tightening, the tingling, the slight burning ache between her thighs again now, as she had so fleetingly last night.

He had found that something that she could sense but could not feel. *He* had enjoyed the moment. But only for the moment. For afterward, when he raised himself up on his elbows and looked down at her, and saw the tears in her eyes, he had sworn briefly, quietly, and rolled off her, returning to his own side of the bed, then moments later pretended to fall asleep. He had feigned sleep, leaving her to lie there, rigid with a tension she could not understand, and a longing for something she had never experienced.

What had he looked for in her eyes and not seen? Was Audrey wrong? Had he wanted her to hold him, to return his kisses, even to cling to him mindlessly as he took his pleasure, hoping for some of her own in return?

Again the notion seemed reasonable. And most certainly preferable to biting the inside of her cheek until it bled to keep from showing her enjoyment of what Audrey said *real* ladies merely tolerated.

Sarah Jane stood up, looking around her as if for outside guidance, then straightened her shoulders, knowing that she would have to look inside herself for the answers to all her questions. Grandmother Trowbridge was far away. Audrey was a silly goose whose advice she should never have trusted. And Lady Helena, whoever she was, whatever affection Dante might have felt for her in the past, was far away and married.

It was up to *her.*

Sarah Jane began walking toward the house, suddenly anxious for evening. The time had come for action and for her to have the courage of her newfound convictions!

Tonight, when her husband came to her bed, she would let

her heart guide her, let her own body guide her, and good riddance to this business of true gentlewomen enduring lovemaking but never enjoying the "exercise."

She would do what she had to do, daring anything, daring everything, for she knew in her heart that this was the only way she would ever find any happiness, any real peace inside herself.

Lord Dante would simply have to take her as she was, the butcher's granddaughter who believed she just might find lovemaking to be the most beautiful, wonderful, exciting experience on earth. She had already broken one of Society's rules by marrying above her station. It was time she broke another, and the devil take the hindmost!

So pleased was Sarah Jane by this daring decision that, halfway down the path to the small patio outside the family drawing room, when she noticed another path branching to the left, toward the family wing kitchens, she immediately recognized it as an avenue to another venue for her new feelings of independence and perhaps even power.

Remembering the sad condition of those kitchens, and the watery soup and stringy mutton that was supposed to be lamb that had been presented for luncheon—not to mention Dante's seeming delight in the notion that she might assert herself—she narrowed her huge brown eyes, steeled her small, faintly square jaw, straightened her slim shoulders, lifted her ridiculously full ruffled skirts above her ankles, and set off to do battle with the staff.

She was Lady Dante Muir, by God, she was the new mistress of Cliff Walk, *by God,* and from this moment on, nobody, least of all Sarah Jane herself, was going to forget it.

And then, once she had set the servants straight, she was going to go upstairs and cut her hair!

"Hullo, Dante. Somebody die? That's a mighty thundercloud you've got hanging over your head."

Lord Dante lifted his gaze from the ledger he was reading, trying to make some sense of the household accounts, which interested him far less than they should have when compared to the estate accounts, and deliberately unfurrowed his brow as he looked at Lord John.

"Do you have any idea how far in arrears the servants' wages are, Johnny?" he asked, his head still awash in figures that he was foolish enough to apply to his younger brother for an answer to a question that would never have occurred to the man. Or mattered to him, more was the pity.

Lord John sank his long, thin frame into a chair and crossed his legs, the shiny wet-dark finish of his Hessians glinting in the sunlight that came into the study through the French doors.

"Wrong question, Dante," he said, taking a sip from the glass that seemed to be permanently attached to his right hand. "Do I *care* how long it has been since the wages were paid? Now, *that's* the proper question. The answer, of course, is no, not a whacking great lot, I don't. Especially now that not a man-jack of them will slip me a key to the cellars. I'd have packed up and gone by now, following the lead set by our scapegrace father's none too elegant flit, if only I had two pennies to rub together. Perhaps I could cudgel my brain into thinking up a free bolt-hole that would come equipped with an ample wine cellar. Who do we know nearby? Do you think the Randolphs might have me? Lucy Randolph is a good sort, if I recall correctly. Too tall, none too pretty, a trifle horse-mad, but not one to badger a man either, always sniffing around for compliments—although I once thought she fancied me a bit. Yes, Sir Thomas Randolph might give Growler and me a spot by the hearth."

Lord Dante closed the ledger with a snap. "Am I that much the penny-pinching ogre, Johnny?" he asked, remembering his earlier conversation with Audrey. At the rate he was going, his family would soon be hanging him in effigy from the highest tree on the estate and then doing an impromptu jig around it.

Lord John stuck his little finger in his ear and gave it a shake. "Did I hear you aright, Dante? Are you asking my opinion on your actions? Zounds, there's a breakthrough. The man believes himself in need of advice. Anyone would have thought he'd just clamber up the mountain and bring back another couple of clay tablets. You know, from God's mouth to Dante's ear. Or would that be the other way 'round? Doesn't matter. You're always right, ain't you, brother mine? You say the right thing, do the right thing, offer to sacrifice your life and limb for your country, and now give over the rest of your body, and your freedom as well, to save your family from ruin. Tell me, is it very painful being so depressingly wonderful?"

He took another drink from his glass, then smiled at his brother. "Sorry. I'm just a trifle in my cups, that's all. I love you, Dante. Truly. Even if you have lately become a bloody boring saint."

Lord Dante rested his elbows on the desk and dropped his head in his hands, his fingers digging into his hair. Was no one at Cliff Walk happy? His father had already run from him, Tyler was sulking in his rooms, Audrey was pouting, and now Johnny had joined in the chorus of disapproval.

What had he done that was so awful? He'd married Sarah Jane Trowbridge. He'd saved Cliff Walk. Didn't his brothers have it in them to give him a little credit for the sacrifice he'd made? The sacrifice Sarah had made?

He lifted his head and stared at Lord John. "What do you think of Sarah?" he asked, not sure why he would apply to a drunken Johnny for information on anything weightier than his opinion on the possibility that grass was green.

"Little Sarah Jane? A creature intelligent enough to wonder about elephants? She's too good for you, Dante, too good by half," Lord John pronounced, his expression unusually serious. "If I hadn't run scared into a bottle that day instead of tripping off to meet her, I might have married her myself. She's too timid for you, Dante, you know. Too young, too innocent—and rigged out worse than the vicar's wife on Christmas morning. I would have dressed her, taken her to London, made her smile. But you won't. You'll use every cent on Cliff Walk and let the poor girl smother in those wretched ruffles, suffocate in this backwater. Yes, I should have married her. *I* wouldn't have made her cry."

Lord Dante was becoming weary of his new position of

family ogre. "That's true enough, Johnny. You wouldn't have made her cry. You'd just have fed her sherry until she became either dog-sick or used to it, while running through the money she brought us as fast as you could manage. Until Betts Trowbridge beat you into flinders, that is."

Lord John took another drink, then shivered. "Don't remind me of that woman! Best thing I ever saw was her broad back as she swept out of here the other morning. She comes back anytime soon, I'll shoot you before I let you keep the cellars locked. I'm warning you, Dante. The only way I'll face that battle-ax again is with a glass in either hand and one balanced on my nose, ready to tip over and spill straight down my gullet!"

He stood up, swaying only slightly as he turned for the door. "Which reminds me, I have an appointment in an hour in the village. A very important appointment you might say. Not that you would. It has nothing at all to do with crops or field drainage. You will excuse me, won't you, Dante?"

"Go on, Johnny," Lord Dante said with a dismissive wave as he reopened the ledger. "I'll see you at dinner."

"Ah, yes," Lord John said, pausing in the doorway. "Another delightful evening at Cliff Walk. Do you suppose we'll recognize the meat?"

Lord Dante grinned weakly at his brother's joke, then decided to soothe his pounding headache with a bit of brandy before remembering that he had ordered all the bottles locked up until the dinner hour.

He began scanning the pages of the ledger once more, idly wondering how Lord John stayed so well supplied, even two days after the cellars had been locked, deciding that his brother had yet to drain his various caches of strong spirits secreted around the family wing.

But Lord John's supply would run dry soon, and then perhaps Dante would be able to convince him not only that he did not wish to bear the full responsibility for maintaining the estate but also that he could not possibly run it without some help from his two brothers.

And his wife, he thought, slamming the ledger closed once

more. Betts Trowbridge said she had trained Sarah Jane to run a household, and his wife did seem eager to lend her assistance. Perhaps she would know what they should be paying for candles and for green peas.

It was just that she was so young. It seemed impossible that the servants would heed her if she chose to assert her position as wife of the second son.

The second son. He had no business being in charge. It was his father's place, and Tyler's after him. The household was Audrey's responsibility, one she had not abdicated, for she had never assumed it in the first place. There was nothing else for it. The success or failure of Cliff Walk was up to Sarah Jane and Dante himself.

He had to put aside this business that Audrey had brought up, this ridiculousness, and please, Lord, let it be ridiculousness. Even a gentle wooing of his bride had to be shelved for the moment. All that mattered right now was Cliff Walk.

Besides, he found it far easier, and more comforting, to think about crops and draining fields and the rest than to dwell on Sarah Jane's unhappiness, her tears—and even his growing desire for her.

For now they would have to be friends, the way they had been last night in the kitchens. He smiled at the memory of her astonished expression after taking her first bite of his impromptu creation of ham, cheese, and bread.

Yes, that was the way to go. Slow and steady, gaining her confidence, learning about each other—that was the path to success, with any other sort of triumph to come later, slowly, gradually, naturally, if at all.

And that meant he would be spending his nights in his dressing room after all.

"What a long face, brother mine. Your chin is nearly to your knees. Did someone die?"

Lord Dante looked up, smiling wanly to hear the same sentiment coming from both his brothers, and watched as Farris wheeled the earl into the room. Tyler looked fit today, more lively than yesterday, and Lord Dante wondered if Audrey's presence at Cliff Walk was finally serving to cheer the man, although that seemed unlikely.

He waited to speak until the servant had retired to the hallway, although Farris showed little interest in anything beyond pushing the Bath chair without mishap, thus avoiding being sent back to his previous job of mucking out the stables.

"No one has died, Ty," he said affably, rising to walk around to the front of the desk and lean back against it. "I was just thinking about my marriage."

"Ah, so that explains your gloom," the earl said, laughing. "Such a cheery subject, marriage. You know, it really hadn't struck home before that we are both old married men now, aren't we? Comrades in misery—I believe that to be a fitting description—you with your timid sugarplum of a bride and I with my bored and boring wife, and neither of us with bedding privileges. Or am I wrong in assuming you spent last night in your dressing room?"

But Lord Dante had had enough of talking about his success, or failure, in that category, and refused to answer. That did not, however, keep him from seeking some advice.

"Was it very difficult, Ty, to begin your married life with Audrey?"

"You mean, did Audrey ever warm my bed with anything more than a lukewarm 'Again, Tyler?' when I reached for her?" The earl shook his head. "Seek your pleasure elsewhere, Dante. That's my advice, and that's what I did. Until the accident. Now, of course, it doesn't matter anymore, which probably explains why Audrey is so kind to me. She knows I can't make any demands on her. Is it any wonder I want that bill of divorcement?"

Now Lord Dante was thoroughly confused. Audrey had hinted—more than hinted—that she and Tyler had enjoyed lovemaking, but his brother's words contradicted what she had said. Totally.

And this woman was giving his bride advice? Giving *him* advice? What was Audrey's definition of "ecstasy"— anything short of "horrible"?

"What is it, Dante?" the earl asked, pushing his chair close beside the desk. "Don't tell me you're falling in love with the little mouse? Good Lord, of course you are! It would be just like you. Otherwise you wouldn't care a fig whether she *liked* it or not. You'd just do your duty, fill her belly the way the Trowbridge bitch wants, and then find yourself an eager female in the village. God, Dante, don't you have enough? You've got Cliff Walk, all that money, all the power. Do you want love as well? Why? Why should you have it all, when the rest of us have nothing? You make me sick! Farris? *Farris!* Get me out of here. I've better things to do than watch my brother sobbing into his deep gravy boat."

"Ty, wait." Lord Dante took hold of one arm of the Bath chair. "I wasn't complaining. It—it's just that I'm worried about Sarah. Audrey said—"

"Audrey? Go away, Farris," the earl said quietly, looking at his brother. "All right, Dante. I'm sorry I flew into the treetops. Something's beginning to smell very bad in here. What did Audrey say?"

Lord Dante looked over at the empty drinks table. He really did want some wine. "Your wife hinted that Sarah Jane, being so small, so delicate, might be unsuited for lovemaking, and for childbirth," he said quietly. "Of course, she also said that she had enjoyed making love with you."

"Oh, really?" the earl shot back, shaking his head. "It must take much less to please her than I thought. I've seen her five times more excited by the prospect of a new bonnet than she ever was when I came to her bed. Ever try to make love to an unmoving stick, brother? Yes, I suppose you have. Audrey is a strange creature, Dante, and even less bright than I gave her credit for, not that I've ever believed she was overly stuffed in the brain box. But this business about Sarah Jane? Well, to tell you the truth, I have no idea whether Audrey is right or wrong. Sarah *is* small, isn't she?"

"Yes, Ty, she is. Do you believe she could safely give birth?"

The earl slapped his palms against the arms of the Bath chair. "Bloody hell, Dante, now I see it! If she dies in childbed you'll never get the second half of the money. That would serve to squash your plans for Cliff Walk, wouldn't it? I misjudged you. You're not falling in love with the chit. You can't. You've already tumbled top over tail in lust with her money."

"Farris!" It was Lord Dante's turn to call for the servant, who lumbered into the room, blank-faced, and took hold of the protruding wooden handles behind the Bath chair. "Take your master the hell out of here," he ordered coldly, turning his back on his brother.

"See you at dinner, Dante," the earl called over his shoulder as he was wheeled away. "You know, I do so enjoy having the family here at Cliff Walk. Such a merry group. So close, so loving. It's only a pity that Father couldn't have stayed. He'd have given you odds on whether or not the girl would die and the child survive."

Lord Dante knew he would have hit Tyler, if only the man hadn't been confined to that damnable chair. If only his brother would transfer some of his dogged determination away from being miserable and toward regaining the use of his legs, his life, his former good humor, his *humanness*.

But the men in the Muir family seemed incapable of doing more than perfecting the roles they had chosen for themselves. Self-pitying, self-serving, and just plain selfish —that described the Muirs in a nutshell.

No wonder Sarah Jane seemed like a breath of fresh air to him. And no wonder he would rather have cut off his right arm than hurt her or put her in jeopardy, no matter how much money the loss of a new heir might end up costing Cliff Walk.

How much walking away from Sarah Jane might cost him personally.

Lord Dante waited until the sound of the Bath chair's wheels had died away down the hall, then closed the door to the study. He eyed the ledger in frustration before he picked it up, weighing its heaviness in one hand, then launched it across the room, where it hit the French doors to the courtyard and shattered the glass into a thousand pieces.

CHAPTER 7

*Oh, how many torments lie in the small circle of a
wedding ring!*

Colley Cibber

The dinner gong sounded once, then again a few minutes
later, demanding her appearance downstairs in the family
drawing room, which was just too bad, for Sarah Jane had
no intention of responding to the imperious, impersonal
summons.

She was going to stay precisely where she was, alone after
Mildred's desertion, and remain there until she died. Or
until her hair grew out once more.

How could she have been so foolish? A pox upon Lady
Helena and her lovely Titus! And a pox on Audrey as well. A
halo of curls, indeed.

It had all seemed so simple, so logical, when Sarah Jane
had tied her hair tightly at the nape of her neck with a thin
ribbon, screwed up her courage to the sticking point, then
sawed off the fist-thick length just above the knot.

But it hadn't been that simple, for she had been left with
nothing but ragged ends, too long on one side, too short in
the back. A solid hour spent snipping, clipping, biting her
lip, closing her eyes, and praying silently as Mildred moaned
and groaned and took her own turn with the scissors had

ended in nothing less than disaster, causing the maid to quit the room in tears.

And no wonder, Sarah Jane thought, for she knew she looked very much like a newly shorn sheep or a young boy just fallen out of a haystack, and not at all like a fashionable Society matron such as the faceless but undoubtedly gloriously beautiful and feminine Lady Helena.

It was remarkable, really, how quickly a person could plummet from the heights of confidence to the depths of despair and desperation.

She had been feeling so sure of herself, so powerful, after her midday visit to the kitchens. She hadn't scolded or even complained. She had not done as her grandmother had instructed her, blustering and threatening and ruling through intimidation, which would have been above everything silly, since the cook stood a good foot taller than she and twice as wide. Instead, she had entered the room with a smile and a greeting and then had tsk-tsked over the sad plight of persons having so little idea of the proper methods of running a marquess's kitchens.

Such a sad lack, she'd commented, but understandable if the staff was unhappy. Perhaps the cook, the scullery maid, the servant of all work, and every last one of the others would be better pleased to work elsewhere? In the dairy, perhaps? Tending the fishpond? Wielding the churn in the cow yard?

Difficult tasks, surely, but doubtless preferable to working and sleeping within the confines of the house, peeling vegetables rather than enjoying the invigorating exercise of hoeing the fields on a fine, hot summer's day?

No? Oh, but how could that be so? Surely happy workers would be capable of much better than the disappointing fare that now reached the Muir dinner table? Please, could they tell her what was wrong, so that she could help? For she only wished to help.

She had sat back then, having been led to a chair near the fire and presented with a steaming cup of sweet tea and three fresh scones topped with strawberries from the succession house. She had listened while the servants cataloged their grievances, all the while wringing their hands and promising that they could do better, *would* do better, once they could depend on the firm hand of a mistress who knew what she was about. And could they be paid, ma'am? Please?

Sarah Jane wished she could be at table tonight when the roasted joint of beef was carried into the family dining room. She longed to see the looks of disbelief on the faces of all the Muirs as course after course of the meal she had planned, then nursed through the early stages of preparation, was set before them.

And it had been so easy. All one had to do was care about other people, listen to their grievances, and then common-sensibly go about setting things to rights. A compliment on the cook's talent for creating sauces. A kind word to the scullery maid on her expertise with a paring knife. An exclamation of praise for the servant who suggested that the new mistress have a personal word with Babbitt over the proper seating order in the servants' dining room. A heart-felt promise to the cheeky tweeny who dared to suggest that Lady Dante might whisper in her husband's ear about the servants' sad lack of wages for the past two quarters.

No longer did Sarah Jane feel out of her depth, tolerated but for the most part unaccepted at Cliff Walk.

Audrey might profess to being her new sister, but Sarah Jane was not such a gudgeon as to believe the woman would be half so kind if she were not hoping for a few new gowns as a reward for her kindness.

The marquess had fled rather than stay and get to know his new daughter.

The earl looked upon her as a necessary evil, pitying her, she thought, but not really liking her, for he liked no one, least of all himself.

Lord John had been kind, but as he had been three parts cast away each time they'd met, she couldn't count on his friendship, only on his drunken good humor.

And as for her new husband?

Well, Lord Dante had been kind, remarkably kind, but he had his reasons, and his guilt. If it had been possible to save

Cliff Walk another way he would have run after it fast as he could and left her at Trowbridge Manor, still under her grandmother's thumb. She might be grateful to him, she might love him—if she could recognize love—but she knew he had not sought her out. He hadn't wanted her.

Not really.

But now the servants were hers. She had listened to them, and they had responded by pledging their loyalty, not in so many words, but the slice of pie still warm from the oven that had arrived in her rooms an hour previously, placed lovingly on a silver tray and accompanied by a tall glass of fresh milk, had said more than thank you. It had said that she was accepted.

She was the mistress of Cliff Walk.

Now if only she could grow back some of her hair overnight, so that she could continue as she had begun, rally the remainder of the servants to her side, and go about setting the rest of the massive house to rights.

She knew how she would do that, too—the cleaning of Cliff Walk, not the growing back of her hair. She would lead by example, setting to with mop and pail and dust rag, beginning in the family wing and not stopping until every last inch of Cliff Walk had been scrubbed until it shone. Where she led, the servants would follow.

And then, once all the bugs and the spiders and the mustiness had been banished, she would search the attics and outbuildings for the furnishings and statues the cook had told her were stored there and begin making Cliff Walk not only livable but beautiful as well.

If only, that was, she could grow back her hair.

"Oh, dear," she said, sighing. Everything was so muddled! All her dreams, all her plans, her one small success, had been overshadowed by this latest great foolishness. And Lord Dante would absolutely abhor what she had done to her hair.

Where she had once looked like a squat pudding, her mass of stiffly curled hair weighing her down and her ruffled skirts ballooning about her, she now resembled nothing more than

133

a shaved peach sticking out of an enormous bolt of unraveling tulle. A pyramid. An apple riding atop a pumpkin. A . . . oh, what did it matter? She was a *mess!*

As she scrambled off the bed to take another look at herself in the long mirror, one of the ruffles on her ivory gown snagged on a nail sticking out of the bottom of the bedpost and was ripped away for the length of a foot or more.

She turned back in frustration, gave her skirt a vicious tug, and tore the flounce further. "Oh, drat!" she exclaimed, ready to dissolve into tears once more. Then she suddenly stilled, barely into her first sob, and tipped her shorn head to one side in thought, and sudden inspiration.

Realizing that the gown was ruined in any case, she reached behind her and tugged at the buttons, ripping at them in her haste to strip down to her underclothes and head for the cabinet holding her wide assortment of equally ugly gowns.

Buttons popped and seams tore as she worked, until she was finally able to step out of the gown, which she left lying on the floor, discarded, despised, and unlamented.

Racing to the cabinet, she threw the doors open wide and surveyed its contents through narrowed eyes, at last choosing the least ornate gown, a butter-yellow watered silk with a modestly squared and fortunately ruffle-free neckline and small capped sleeves. The skirt was full and covered with three rows of foot-long gathered lace-edged flounces, two of which she was already mentally discarding.

The gown, although new, was woefully out of date, according to Audrey, whose own London-fashioned wardrobe added credibility to her protestations that longer sleeves, higher waistlines, and slimmer, nearly unadorned skirts with single small hemline ruffles were all the crack now and would be even more so for the spring Season.

But Sarah Jane couldn't be bothered with raised waistlines and longer sleeves now. She would simply have to make do with what she had.

The gown thrown over her arm, she snatched up her

sewing basket and hopped back onto the bed, letting the gown spill over her crossed legs.

It took some minutes, applying herself carefully, her tongue caught between her teeth as she concentrated, but at last all the small, carefully placed stitches holding the two highest flounces had been dispatched, leaving only one foot-wide flounce at the hem.

Next to go was the wide white satin sash that had been tacked to the waist of the gown, meant to be tied into an enormous bow at her back. Standing up once more, she divested herself of two of her full petticoats, then wriggled into the gown, turning it backwards in order to secure most of the buttons before taking a deep breath and maneuvering the garment around her slim waist, sliding her arms into the short sleeves, and by way of contortions she knew to be most unladylike, fastening the remaining buttons.

She could have rung for Mildred, but she held the maid in too much affection to send her into what was sure to be another round of high hysterics.

Another trip across the room, to the cabinet holding her footwear, resulted in the location of a pair of soft yellow kid heeled slippers, which she stepped into before taking a steadying breath meant to lend her courage before she approached the full-length mirror once more.

"Well, my goodness!" she exclaimed in mingled shock and surprise.

The first thing she noticed was that her exertions had served to wreak a sort of miracle on her hair, for it looked vastly different now than when Mildred had combed it back from her face severely, proving to her mistress that she looked more boyish than feminine.

Her hair was slightly mussed now, but not completely unruly, some of it falling forward onto her brow as it parted naturally just above the arch of her left eye, some of it lying close against her cheeks, and some of it, that which was behind her ears—her still, alas, *visible* ears—clinging to the nape of her neck in a fashion that was not halolike but more like a close-fitting, not entirely unattractive cap.

All in all, her hair no longer looked atrocious. It merely looked short. Very short. Extremely straight. But presentable, if just barely.

And her eyes! Had they ever before appeared quite so large? So brown? And her eyelashes! Heavens, had they grown longer?

Sarah Jane stepped forward, raising one hand to her face as she noticed her cheekbones. They appeared higher than she remembered, with rather flattering hollows beneath them, and her fair complexion was slightly flushed from her exertions, so that she looked pleasingly healthy.

Had her chin always been this delicate, placed so gracefully above her long neck, the sharply angled lines of her rather square jawbone visible just to the front of her ears? Not at all like Grandmother Trowbridge's jaw, which served mostly as a stepping off point for her three chins, or even like Audrey's rounded chin, which was softer and fuller, as were her cheeks.

And her nose was actually rather appealing, short and straight, with a bit of an upward tilt. And her mouth, always too wide, now appeared to be balanced nicely by her rather straight brows and her enormous eyes.

Was this really her? Was this person in the mirror truly the mousy little Sarah Jane Trowbridge? Sarah Jane Muir? *Lady* Dante?

"Goodness," Sarah Jane breathed quietly, very much in awe of the vision looking back at her from the mirror. "I believe I am almost pretty. I've just been *buried,* that's all."

Tearing her amazed gaze away from her nearly unrecognizable face for a moment, she knew it was time to see what sort of damage she had wrought upon Mrs. Wilcox's creation.

And then she smiled, something she hadn't done when she examined the changes her impromptu haircut had wrought in her physical appearance. The gown was lovely! It fit her snugly at bodice and waist, then widened gracefully over her underslips, rather like an upside-down tulip, ending in that single flounce, her yellow kid slippers barely visible beneath the now lower hemline.

If she looked closely, which she refused to do, she knew she would see small holes in the material where the threads had once pierced it, but she couldn't be bothered with such trifles now.

She was much too happy to dwell on trifles. She only gathered up her skirts as the dinner gong rang again, calling to her, and she raced out of her bedchamber before her usual good sense could persuade her to do otherwise.

Lord Dante glanced at the mantel clock for the third time in as many minutes, wondering if he should go upstairs and see what was keeping his wife or stay where he was, propping up the ornately carved chimneypiece, and pretend that he expected her to be tardy.

After all, Audrey often arrived late for meals, sweeping into the room in the fashion of invading royalty just before Babbitt announced that dinner was served, her cheeks flushed, her apologies a little breathless, her eyes alive, searching everyone's face for approval of her toilette. A silly, vain creature with all the feminine failings Lord Dante so thoroughly despised.

God's teeth, was his wife to become a replica of Audrey? He took another sip of wine. Now *that* was a distressing thought! And a rather ridiculous one, too, now that he considered it, for Sarah Jane did not have the makings of an Audrey.

She was too small, for one thing, and too shy. And Lord knew she didn't possess the wardrobe, the confidence, or the arrogance to carry off the role of a Society miss.

One side of his mouth lifted in a small smile when he remembered her as he had last seen her this morning, upon leaving her bed, her night rail a vision of maidenly modesty, and that ridiculous braid hanging down nearly to her waist.

Aside from her vaguely intriguing, obviously intelligent eyes, the most he could say in praise of his bride's appearance was that she had fine unblemished skin and was always scrupulously clean. Not a very romantic thought, or a sure way toward becoming the toast of Mayfair.

Lord John sidled up to him, whispering out of the corner

of his mouth, "I can't believe I'm saying this, Dante, considering the disaster that undoubtedly awaits us in the dining room, but I'm hungry. Do you think we should tell Babbitt to get on with it, or is Sarah Jane soon to make her appearance?"

Audrey, who was sitting nearby, making a shambles out of whatever she was attempting to stitch on a small tambour frame, looked up, smiling. "Gentlemen must learn the virtues of patience, Johnny," she said. "I'm confident Sarah Jane will be with us shortly. Obviously she is taking great pains with her toilette this evening. Do be a gentleman and see that you compliment her when she finally appears, poor dear. She is so young, you know. So lamentably young."

"She's past her eighteenth birthday, Audrey," Lord Dante snapped, disliking the role of nursery robber. "You were married to Ty at much the same age."

"Audrey was never that age, Dante," the earl put in from his seat in the Bath chair. "Were you, darling?"

"And precisely what do you mean by that, *darling?*"

"Stand clear, Dante," Lord John advised quickly. "The fur is about to fly."

Audrey nearly blinded both her brothers-in-law with her bright smile. "Don't be ridiculous, Johnny. I would never argue with Tyler in his weakened condition."

"How noble of you, my dear," the earl said from between clenched teeth. "Just don't spend any of Dante's blunt on an array of widow's weeds. Such an expenditure would be premature, as I fully intend to remain above ground for several years yet, living long, if not well."

"Great God, Ty, *look!*" Lord John exclaimed suddenly, pointing toward the doorway. "It's a polecat! Quick, everybody, run before it sprays us!"

The black and white cat, out of bounds and clearly bewildered to find itself outside the kitchens, paused in the doorway, meowed a single time, and passed on, the latest failed prop in Lord John's continuing theatrical productions meant to startle his brother into mobility.

Lord Dante, who was standing close to Lord John, gifted the young man with an affectionate clout on the head, thankful for the interruption, as Tyler was becoming agitated. "You never change, do you, Johnny?" he commented, grinning. "As if a skunk could wish to lower itself in society by breaking in here."

Lord John shrugged, rubbing at his head. "Well, *something* was beginning to smell remarkably bad in here, Dante," he said by way of explanation, then grinned. "Perhaps it is the main course, even though the odoriferous emanations from the kitchens have never before made their way as far as the drawing room. Great God, *look!*"

"Give it up, Johnny. That trick is wearing thin," Lord Dante said. Then, as he realized that his brother's eyes were rather wide with what seemed to be genuine surprise, he turned to look toward the doorway.

"Great God," he murmured, unconsciously echoing Lord John's sentiments as he saw Sarah Jane standing just inside the drawing room.

He couldn't move, couldn't take a single step or say another word. All he could do was stand there, like a brainless looby, and stare.

What had she done? Was this really his wife—this slim, elegant creature with the regal bearing and the bewitching figure and the most beautiful, exotic, appealing face? Could this be Sarah Jane? *His* Sarah?

"Lud, Sarah Jane, whatever have you *done* to yourself?" Audrey shrieked before anyone else could speak, hopping to her feet and running toward her, stopping just in front of Sarah Jane and shaking her head as if she were staring into the inescapable jaws of death. "Your hair, Sarah Jane! Oh, dear me, your *hair!* I know I mentioned cutting it, but . . . but . . . lud, child, your woman should be *flogged!*"

"Stop her, Dante. If Audrey convinces Sarah Jane that she has ruined herself, I'll throttle her personally," Lord John whispered into Lord Dante's ear. "It's just like Audrey, you know. Has to be queen of the walk or else she gets her nose all out of joint. And Sarah Jane's a good half dozen years younger into the bargain. I'll wager tonight's ration of brandy that Audrey didn't count on creating a swan when she told Sarah Jane to cut her hair. Her gown ain't quite so bad either, come to think on it. You lucky devil. Now go rescue your beautiful bride, Dante, before Audrey tells her she's passed beyond the pale."

"She *is* beautiful, isn't she, Johnny?" Lord Dante asked, taking a single step forward, not realizing that his grin was wide with appreciation, with possession, with pride. "I can't believe it."

"Believe it, Dante," the earl said, having laboriously turned his chair to face the doorway. "Christ on a crutch, you do have all the luck, don't you? But Johnny's right. Audrey is over there clucking like a mother hen over a chick that has just fallen into a mud puddle. She'll have the child in tears in a moment if you don't do something."

The earl's warning was enough to push Lord Dante from stunned astonishment into action. He crossed the width of the drawing room slowly but with purpose, stepping in front of Audrey to take Sarah Jane's rather cold, slightly trembling hand.

Bowing, he pressed a kiss on the very tips of her fingers, then held her hand tightly as he straightened, saying, "You are a true vision of loveliness tonight, my dear, and well worth any wait."

"Really, Dante?" Sarah Jane asked, her lovely brown eyes wide with apprehension, giving the lie to her show of bravado when she first entered the drawing room.

"Yes, my dear pet, *really*. You are lovely. However, Johnny has told me that his stomach is complaining that his throat must have been sliced, and Babbitt, who has been waiting without most impatiently, is eager to call us to table. May I take your arm?"

"No, you most definitely may not," Lord John piped up, appearing beside Sarah Jane as if Merlin himself had just conjured him up out of thin air. "You're too stuffy by half, brother mine, and I am much more the expert in giving compliments." He took hold of Sarah Jane's other arm and slipped it through his, smiling down at her. "You are the most gorgeous creature that I, drunk or sober, have ever seen. A vision of perfection that dazzles the eyes. A creature fashioned by the gods! Come, my little nymph. Ambrosia awaits us! Excuse us, Audrey," he said, his voice turning rather hard. "And do close your mouth. It's deuced unattractive, gaping like that."

"Tyler!" Audrey exclaimed, lifting her skirts as she ran to her husband's side, tears welling up in her lovely blue eyes. "How can you just *sit* there? Are you going to let that drunken lout insult me?"

"Yes, Ty," Lord John said as he guided Sarah Jane toward the dining room, "are you just going to *sit* there? Why not rise and beat this drunken lout unmercifully about the head and ears for his horrid insult? Come, come, now, Ty. Two miracles in one day shouldn't be impossible."

Audrey sniffed, rolling her eyes at the thought of such lunacy, and stepped behind the Bath chair, fully prepared to play the martyr as she wheeled her husband forward.

"Don't tease, Johnny," Lord Dante heard Sarah Jane scold, although she was smiling now and her eyes were dancing mischievously. "Another miracle awaits us in the dining room, if we're lucky."

Lord Dante, feeling more than a little neglected and wondering why he should envy his younger brother, was left to follow along in his wife's wake, leaning forward slightly to ask, "What sort of miracle, Sarah?"

She turned, her smile dazzling him, nearly stopping him in his tracks, filling him with a sudden, almost debilitating desire to take her in his arms, rush up the stairs with her, and love her until she whimpered for mercy. But then he remembered that she had whimpered on their wedding night and again last night, and his ardor, born so suddenly, died a quick death.

"I don't want to spoil the surprise, Dante," she said, her low, rather husky, always appealing voice now somehow sultry—if anyone so small, so fragile, so very young, could be considered alluring.

Not just sweet, not just innocent. But sweetly, innocently alluring. Even exciting. God's teeth! What was happening to her? To him?

Babbitt, who had been waiting by the dining room entrance, a rather enigmatic smile on his face, came forward and threw open the double doors with a flourish, then stepped back to offer a sweeping bow, encouraging the Muirs to enter.

"Now I know who's got the key to the cellars, Dante," Lord John said, looking suspiciously at the grinning butler. "The man's half-seas over from sipping at the stock, or I'm a Chinaman. Zounds, Dante, give a look!"

Lord Dante peered around his brother and felt his own jaw drop to half-cock as the brilliance of the dining room shocked him into reacting as if he'd never seen the chamber before this evening.

Candles glowed in every silver holder on walls and side tables, and the chandelier, usually so dusty and minus half its candles, like an old crone with half of her teeth gone missing, was once more the brilliant object of beauty that had so awed him when he was at last considered old enough to leave the nursery and take his dinner with Ty and his parents.

The walls were still nearly bare of paintings, and the carpet was threadbare and faintly dusty, but the rest of the room had been transformed. The long, highly polished table was now adorned with glittering cutlery and china, the enormous silver epergne, which he had last seen tarnished and stuffed in a cabinet, now occupied the place of honor in the center of the table. If his father had been present, he would have sold the thing tomorrow.

"Move along, Dante," the earl prompted from behind him. "I have to see the rest of this." Lord Dante stepped aside as Audrey pushed the Bath chair to the place assigned to her husband, to the right of the marquess's empty chair at the head of the table, then watched as his older brother placed his palms on the table, arching his back as he craned his neck this way and that, surveying the room. "Audrey, you slacker," he pronounced at last, winking at Sarah Jane.

Lord John, in the process of sliding in Sarah Jane's chair, threw back his head and laughed. "Don't berate your wife, brother," he said mockingly. "Dear Audrey can work on only one beautification project at a time, unlike Sarah Jane, who is capable of accomplishing not only great personal beauty but aesthetic comfort as well. Now, if only the mutton isn't stringy!"

"I think you're perfectly *horrid,* Johnny Muir!" Audrey exclaimed, taking recourse in her lace-edged handkerchief. "You know I am not in the least domestic."

Then she brightened, smiling at Sarah Jane. "But I must compliment you, dear sister, on this transformation, although I cannot fathom how you brought it about. Perhaps your background has made you better suited for domestic chores. Did you polish the epergne yourself?"

"Her background, Audrey?" the earl questioned her caustically, reaching for the wineglass Babbitt had just filled. "Is that where I erred? Opting for the coal merchant's daughter rather than Sir George Forrester's great-granddaughter? Or were you referring to the butcher stock? Surely not. You would never be so déclassé!"

Dante found himself forcibly stifling a smile as he helped the tight lipped Audrey to her seat across from the earl's, then quickly took up his own chair at the foot of the table, his bride already seated to his right, with Lord John across from her.

"Oh, Ty, don't be crude," Audrey responded at last, taking up her own wineglass. "I only referred to Sarah Jane's past because Mrs. Trowbridge made such a point of trumpeting the child's domestic abilities. Really, Sarah Jane, I applaud your success and envy you your prowess. However did you accomplish so much with these recalcitrant servants? I am in awe, totally in awe!"

"I—I," Sarah Jane began, her cheeks coloring and then paling. "Thank you so much, but no wine, Babbitt," she said politely as the butler moved to fill her glass. "Would it be possible, please, for you to fetch me some lemonade? I know Betsy prepared some this afternoon."

"At once, Lady Dante!" Babbitt responded, clicking his heels together smartly before exiting the room, leaving John and Dante with empty wineglasses.

"I say, Sarah Jane, that ain't fair," Lord John protested. "I've been waiting all day for a glass of wine. Never saw Babbitt jump half so fast to do *my* bidding."

"Probably because you'd choke to death on the words 'please,' and 'thank you,'" Lord Dante said, looking at his wife's flushed cheeks and catching a glimpse of her wide brown eyes before she looked away nervously, beginning to pleat her serviette in her lap.

"Audrey," he began, knowing that he had to compliment his sister-in-law soon or else Sarah Jane, despite her temporary triumph, would never survive Audrey's revenge, "I must thank you yet again for being so astute. If it hadn't been for you, Sarah would never have dared to cut her hair. The Titus, isn't it, or even an improvement on that style? Yes, Audrey, the notion was inspired. I believe you ladies, our two beautiful ladies, should be rewarded, don't you, Ty? Perhaps three new gowns apiece?"

"Three?" Audrey gave a toss of her golden curls. "Always the miser, aren't you, Dante? Why, Sarah Jane has already promised us each a half dozen. Haven't you, dearest sister? From her own very generous allowance—whoops!" She clapped a hand over her mouth for a moment, looking at Lord Dante, then squeaked, "Oh, dear. I shouldn't have said that, should I? When will I ever learn to curb my foolish tongue? I've upset you, Dante, haven't I?"

Lord Dante's pleasure in the evening, in his wife, evaporated in an instant. An allowance? He had heard nothing of an allowance. Did Betts Trowbridge think he was going to force her granddaughter into penury while he set Cliff Walk to rights? Did she think he'd ration Sarah's food, keep her on bread and water? He had never been so affronted, so insulted, in his life! He looked at Sarah Jane piercingly, willing her to raise her eyes, willing her to tell him Audrey was wrong. "You have an allowance?"

"I—I," Sarah Jane began again, looking up at Lord Dante guiltily through her ridiculously long black lashes. "Well, yes, actually—um, Grandmother Trowbridge termed it pin money, I believe."

"Pin money," Lord Dante repeated dully as Babbitt placed a frosted glass of lemonade in front of Sarah Jane. He had found ice? The icehouse, thanks to its rotting roof, had been flooded in the last rain, its contents ruined, or so Lord Dante had been told. But his wife had ice in her lemonade?

My God, had he married a sorceress, a witch who had cast a spell over the servants, making them her slaves? "Precisely what is the amount Mrs. Trowbridge terms pin money, Sarah Jane?"

"The amount?" She smiled at him weakly, as if she knew what she was about to say would not serve to shower him with joy. "It is made up of the interest on the capital that will be mine when I, um, that is to say, that will be mine at the same time you receive a second settlement. The amount of my allowance varies, but it is approximately two thousand five hundred a quarter, I believe," she said quietly, so quietly that he had to lean forward to hear her.

"But I would never be frivolous in spending it, Dante," she vowed with mounting courage. "Why, just this afternoon I paid all the household servants their back wages and next quarter's as well. It seemed a reasonable solution at the time. I thought—"

"You thought?" Lord Dante gritted out from between clenched teeth. No wonder Babbitt was all but kissing her feet! No wonder the dining room had been set to rights. His wife, his innocent bride, was *buying* his servants! Just as Betts Trowbridge had bought him. "You *thought?*"

"Two thousand five hundred? Ten thousand a year? As *pin money?*" Lord John interrupted just as Lord Dante knew he was about to lose his temper, which he had not done since his teens, when he had learned that anger was usually useless when attempting to deal with the impossible. "Christ, Dante, that's rich! Dearest Sarah Jane, will you marry me? Don't worry about Dante, as I think you've just killed him. Babbitt!" he commanded, holding up his wineglass. "Fill it to the brim and don't walk away with the bottle. This calls for a celebration. *Please,* Babbitt?" he ended, winking at Lord Dante.

His glass filled, and either oblivious to the tension around him or reacting to it, Lord John raised it high and quoted from Richard Sheridan: "'Here's to the maiden of bashful fifteen; here's to the widow of fifty; here's to the flaunting, extravagant quean, and here's to the housewife that's thrifty. Let the toast pass—drink to the lass; I'll warrant she'll prove an excuse for the glass.'"

He tossed off the wine in a single gulp, then launched the glass toward the fireplace. It missed, as Lord John was not seeing too clearly, and shattered against the wall, causing the earl to laugh in genuine enjoyment, Audrey to roll her eyes, muttering something about being forced to live with barbarians, and Sarah Jane once more to lower her gaze to her lap, her cheeks pale, her slim shoulders slumped in misery.

Later, very much later, Lord Dante learned that dinner had been a huge success, with the roasted beef the center of attraction, the succulent pink-centered meat eliciting praise for both the kitchen staff and the very modest Lady Dante, who refused to take credit for anything above having asked the servants to do their best.

The reason Lord Dante's information was delayed was simple. He had thrown down his serviette and quit the dining room immediately after Lord John's amused outburst and had left Cliff Walk itself a few moments later, walking all the way into the village for a plate of mediocre roasted pigeon and several mugs of ale before forcing himself to return to the scene of his anger, his disappointment, his confusion.

And to his wife. His beautiful, alluring, childlike, innocent yet not innocent, naive yet curiously brilliant, impossible-to-understand wife. He knew she was his wife, for he was her husband, bought and paid for.

Still, he concluded—Lord John's laughter as he waxed poetic over their luscious dinner echoing in his ears as he bedded down for the night in his dressing room, his bare feet hanging uncomfortably over the foot of the lumpy cot— some things simply could not be bought.

And his manhood was one of them!

At least now he didn't have to worry about Audrey's assertion that Sarah Jane could not accommodate lovemaking without pain and would be threatened by childbirth. He'd done his duty, but that didn't mean he had to provide stud service now that the butcher's granddaughter had become Lady Dante, by God! He'd be damned if he would go near his wife again for a long, long time, not until he proved what he could do with Cliff Walk, until he proved he was master of the estate, master of his own household, master of his own heart. And in the meantime, Betts Trowbridge could just go hang for a great-grandson!

CHAPTER 8

What if this present were the world's last night?

John Donne

Sarah Jane did her best not to criticize as Cloris, one of the half dozen new maids she had employed on Babbitt's recommendation, dipped her rag into a bucket of filthy water and prepared to wipe the floor tiles in front of one of the large fireplaces in the hall.

She had hired Cloris and the others from the village because Dante had turned over the entire running of Cliff Walk to her, from managing the household accounts, to planning the menus, to overseeing the small army of workmen patching roofs and painting or papering walls, to arranging the existing furniture and purchasing more— everything and anything that had to do with the day-to-day running and refurbishing of the gigantic estate house.

Which was a good thing, for Sarah Jane certainly needed something with which to occupy her mind or else she might have spent all of her time crying, rather than whimpering silently into her pillow only at night while her husband of almost two months slept in his dressing room.

"Cloris dear, I believe both you and the tiles might be better served to seek fresh water for that bucket," she said evenly, then smiled her thanks as the maid curtsied crudely and rushed off to do her bidding. Sarah Jane turned to look at the massive hall, which had shown great signs of improvement over the last week.

The family wing was already completed, for it had been the least ravaged by the years of neglect that had served to turn the remainder of Cliff Walk into such a sad shambles. For this past month, while they had been locked inside, thanks to rain and generally damp, cold December weather, Sarah Jane had shifted her army of servants and workmen to the state rooms in the large center of what she still mentally termed "the squashed bug."

The red saloon now wore new Chinese paper on its walls, and the stucco ceiling had been painted a creamy white, as had the ornate moldings surrounding the windows and the arched doorways and bordering the walls at floor and ceiling.

A mercifully clear and balmy stretch of three days early in the month had been seized upon by the industrious Sarah Jane, and the servants had worked from dawn to dusk, rolling up all the enormous carpets in the center wing, including the ones in the red saloon—those she had deemed worth the effort—and carrying them outside for a thorough beating. Some of the furniture she had found in the attics now served as seating for the family, who often chose to take their leisure in the red saloon after dinner, except for Dante, of course.

The cavernous drawing room adjacent to the smaller red saloon was also entirely refurbished, although it was too large and too scarce of furniture to be suitable for anything less than the most elaborate entertainments. Its walls, too, seemed woefully bare, thanks to the marquess's free hand with selling off anything he thought would afford him another few weeks of grandeur in London.

But the library was Sarah Jane's personal pride, its four walls lined from floor to high ceiling with freshly wiped books that dated from the seventeenth century and covered every subject beneath the sun.

Although large, as were all the state rooms, the dark paneling, now polished, glowed softly in the candlelight. The deep burgundy-and-blue-patterned carpets, combined with an array of comfortable leather chairs, heavy Tudor-style desks, and a single midnight blue leather sofa, made the library a haven on rainy days, a cheery fire crackling in the hearth.

She had sat there many afternoons once the servants understood their chores for the day, her feet tucked up beneath her skirts, reading any book that captured her fancy, while pretending that Lord Dante sat in one of the chairs across from her, also reading, the two of them looking up occasionally to exchange loving smiles before returning to their books.

But that, of course, was only a dream, as were all Sarah Jane's thoughts concerning her husband, the man who had been so kind, then turned so cold.

"You have made Cliff Walk yours, madam," he had told her the morning after that disastrous dinner, the dinner she had planned as such a pleasant surprise and which had turned into the most embarrassing evening in her life, when she had sat at table attempting to smile, though her husband's chair stood empty, her husband having gone off in a huff.

"This is your home, not mine, Dante. I was only trying to help," she had answered, she remembered now, wincing yet again as she knew she had not said the words so much as whined them, like a child who had broken a cherished vase while attempting to set it straight on a table, knowing full well she never should have touched it in the first place, at least not without permission.

"Nonsense, Sarah Jane," he had answered almost kindly. He had called her Sarah Jane; he still called her that, never Sarah, when he addressed her now. "You were only doing what you were trained to do, following the path your grandmother laid out before you, the path to social acceptance, while totally usurping my authority. Ah, well. I asked for this, didn't I? Very well. Order the servants about any way you wish. Pay them from your pin money. They're yours now; the house is yours. You may have an additional five thousand pounds to use for furnishings, draperies, and the like. Consider it another bridal gift from your grandmother. As for me, I shall confine myself to the running of the estate."

"You wanted some assistance. You wanted the freedom to run the estate. Didn't you?" she had dared to ask, for she was daring much with so little to lose, having already shorn her head and been fairly satisfied with the results of her initial forays into independence.

He had looked at her strangely then, almost sadly, saying, "Yes, that was what I wanted, wasn't it? I'm a fool, pet. A proud fool. Perhaps even an idiot. Please give me time. Give us both time." And then he'd smiled wanly. "Just promise you will leave the king's bedchamber to last as you go about working your domestic miracles. Betts has promised not to reappear until March, and I wouldn't want her to renege in her desire to rest her carcass on the king's bed."

And that, Sarah Jane remembered, was the last time her husband had spoken to her at all intimately or called her his pet. Their conversations now took place only in the company of the rest of the Muir family, excluding the marquess, who had written to say he'd been invited to remain in Scotland with his friends until the Season.

But if Dante was sulking, he was not doing it in his rooms, as Tyler did, or from behind a bottle, as Johnny still did, even though all the wine and spirits were kept locked up until the dinner hour.

No, not Dante. Not the industrious, hardworking, almost obsessed Lord Dante Muir.

He was up and gone each day before dawn, riding the fields, deciding which were to be planted early and which were to be spared another poor crop until they could be reclaimed after years of neglect.

He spent his days at the forestry, at the mill, or in the meadows where newly purchased horses and cows and goats and sheep were being introduced to the land.

He came home after dark each night, dusty or muddy or both, his clothing caked with dirt, his hands roughened and red from the cold, soil packed under his nails, cuts on his face, the returning hero who had fought the good fight putting in a fence or mending a farmer's leaking roof or pulling a stupid sheep out of a bog.

He had even, much to her dismay, spent several days away from Cliff Walk, sailing with their own fishermen out in the Channel, braving the high winter seas and the very real chance of storms in order to check the seaworthiness of their small fleet of boats.

She loved him so much. She was so proud of him. She wished he would go away and never come back.

"Would this be good enough for me to be gettin' on with, milady?" Cloris asked, rousing Sarah Jane from her sad reverie as she held up the heavy wooden bucket, now filled with fresh, clean water liberally laced with vinegar. "Albert says I'm ta tell ye, milady, that he needs to see ye in the saloon—the round one, milady."

"Albert?" Sarah Jane repeated, confused, and then her brow cleared. Cloris had become quite fond of the strange little man Sarah Jane had retained to clean and repair the statues that had been stored in an outbuilding and were soon to be returned to the niches waiting for them in the hall and elsewhere. "Oh, you mean Mr. Yarrow. Of course, Cloris. Thank you."

Her steps dragging, Sarah Jane headed down the length of the hall toward the massive doors to the round saloon, wondering not for the first time why she had thought putting Cliff Walk to rights would be such fun, such a tempting challenge.

It was work, hard work, and she doubted that anyone appreciated her efforts. There were actually days when she longed to be back at Trowbridge Manor, merely passing time, waiting for the day when she would have to put to use all the domestic skills her grandmother had insisted she learn.

"What is it, Mr. Yarrow?" she called out as she stepped

into the round saloon, threading her way through the forest of crates either containing or lying stacked beside statues of Greek and Roman gods and goddesses in varying stages of repair.

Mr. Yarrow appeared from behind a large statue of Aphrodite, his narrow face a study in frustration, a large apron tied around his frayed suit of clothes. He reminded Sarah Jane of a nervous, underfed hare, his long, thin nose almost constantly twitching as he attempted to keep his spectacles from slipping off his face.

His nose was twitching furiously, almost frantically, now. Obviously something was wrong.

"Have you come upon a problem?" Sarah Jane asked fatalistically.

"Indeed I have, milady. It—it's *him!*"

"Hullo there, Sarah Jane!" Lord John trilled, appearing from behind a rather vulgar statue of Bacchus, the god of merriment, she believed—merriment and, perhaps, wine? "Tell the cadaver to be on his way, will you? He's threatening my friend, and I won't have it!"

Sarah Jane rolled her eyes when she saw that Johnny held in his hand a glass that contained a goodly quantity of brandy. "Johnny, what on earth are you about?"

"His lordship is *about* to topple that statue, ma'am," Mr. Yarrow said, wringing his hands, his expression so missishly tragic that Sarah Jane wondered what on earth Cloris could possibly find attractive in the thin, bandy-legged man.

"I have tried and tried to convince his lordship that the Bacchus is past saving—you will notice the rather ominous cracks in the base—but he will not hear of discarding it." Mr. Yarrow made a face and cleared his throat, avoiding Sarah Jane's eyes. "He—he says it's his brother, ma'am."

"My brother! Exactly! The brother of my soul, my bosom chum; the one man who understands me." Lord John kept hold of the statue with one arm as he leaned around it to gaze up into its face. "Ain't that right, Bacchus, old friend?"

He held his glass up to the statue's marble lips. "Here you go, brother. Have yourself a little nip."

"Oh, Johnny," Sarah Jane said, watching nervously as the statue began to list slightly to one side, putting her brother-in-law in danger, "you've had too much to drink."

"Too much? Pish tosh, sister mine, to quote dearest Audrey, who has thrown me out of the red saloon, where she is murdering a sampler extolling the virtues of spring. She says I'm disgusting. I'm not disgusting, am I, Sarah Jane?"

He let go of the statue, much to Sarah Jane's relief, and stumbled across the room to stand directly in front of her, swaying from side to side as he looked down at her, his blue eyes almost feverish, his neckcloth twisted to one side. He looked so young, so very sad.

"Want to hear something, Sarah Jane? Want to hear the most brilliant thing any one man has ever said?" he asked, turning back to the statue. "Sorry, old man, but it wasn't you," he told the statue, then turned once more to Sarah Jane, his movements so exaggerated that she knew from sad experience that he would soon pass out where he stood.

"What was I saying?" he asked, frowning. "Oh, yes! I was going to tell you the most brilliant thing—*brilliant* thing—anyone has ever said. It was Lessing what said it. Gotthold Eph-*Ephraim* Lessing. Gad! Was there ever such a name! German, I think. Anyway, he said, Lessing said, 'One can drink too much, but one never drinks enough.' Now confess, Sarah Jane, ain't that *brilliant?*"

"You'll have to remove him, ma'am." Mr. Yarrow's weak whine had become most unpleasant. "I cannot vouch for the safety of my statues else."

"I quite understand," Sarah Jane said, slipping her arm around Lord John's waist and leading him toward the library, where she hoped she could persuade him to lie down on the sofa before he fell down.

"You may continue with your work now, Mr. Yarrow. Johnny, listen to me, please," she pleaded as his lordship's weight threatened to send them both crashing to the floor. "You have to help me. Put your arm around me. Only for balance, you understand."

"O'course, little Sarah Jane," Lord John responded, his words beginning to slur. His glass, she noticed, was now empty, and it could not have been the first, or even the sixth, glass of the day, though it had just gone noon. "You'll save Bacchus for me, won't you? He's my best friend, my bosom chum, my brother.

"Little Sarah," he continued as they made their way slowly toward the doors leading from the round saloon to the library, his voice echoing hollowly beneath the glass large dome. "Dear sweet wonderful little Sarah. Our own busy bee. You want me to declaim again, dear sister? Exercise my voice, demonstrate my marvelous elocution even when half-seas over? It's my one talent, you know. My only talent," he ended sorrowfully.

Lord John was leaning very heavily against her, and Sarah Jane wished he would concentrate on walking rather than speaking, but she would have agreed to anything if he would only keep moving. "Of course, Johnny. Go on, recite for me."

He pressed a kiss against her temple, thanked her, and then quoted: " 'How doth the little busy bee improve each shining hour, and gather honey all the day from every opening flower!' That was Isaac somebody-or-other, I disremember at the moment. But that's what you are, little Sarah, our own sweet busy bee improving each shining hour. I love you, Sarah Jane Muir," he ended, dropping another kiss somewhere beside her right ear. "I really, *really* love you."

There was a slight sound, perhaps even a laugh, from inside the library. "Is that so, Johnny? Well, now, how should I feel about that, I wonder?"

"Dante!" Sarah Jane exclaimed, immediately aware that she was dressed in one of her oldest gowns, its flounces covered by a none too clean apron, her hair likewise covered so that it wouldn't get stuck all over with cobwebs as she joined the housemaids at their work. Why couldn't she have been wearing one of her new gowns?

And she probably had no fewer than three smudges on her face, for she couldn't seem even to observe the servants at work without becoming grubby from head to toe.

It did not occur to her that Dante might be angry with her,

155

or with Johnny, for that would have been the height of ridiculousness. Johnny was drunk, for one thing, and for another, her husband couldn't have cared less who loved her. How could he, seeing that he didn't care a fig for her himself?

Why, she never even saw him anymore except at the dinner table. Cliff Walk was a very large house, and with any care two people could have resided there for years without ever seeing each other. As if by unspoken agreement, she and Dante had been extremely *careful* for some time.

"Dante!" Lord John echoed comically, peering across the room to where his brother stood holding what appeared to be a letter. "What are you doing here in the middle of the day? Shouldn't you be out and about somewhere, birthing a calf or mucking out a stable? Never mind," he said with a wave of his hand—the one holding the glass, unfortunately —and losing his grip, so that it crashed to the floor. "Just go away, please. I'm telling your wife how much I love her. Adore her, actually. Only good thing to happen at Cliff Walk in years, that's what Sarah Jane is."

"Is that right, Johnny?" Dante folded the letter and slipped it into his jacket. "What did you do, Sarah Jane, open your deep purse to purchase another supply of brandy for my brother? That *is* where he's getting it, isn't it? From his generous, naive little sister-in-law. Nobody in the village taverns will sell him any. I've seen to that. So I can only conclude that you have bought yourself another adoring subject. First the household servants, then Audrey—whose affection did not come cheap, judging by the gowns she's been sporting these days—and now my younger brother. Even I have been purchased, although I cannot complain, can I? After all, I had a price."

"Uh-oh," Lord John said, placing himself directly in front of Sarah Jane, "methinks our lord and master is angry about something, little bee. Careful now, lest he charges like the thickheaded bull he is. But not to worry. I'll protect you."

"Step away from her, you fool, before you fall on her," Dante ordered, crossing the room quickly and taking hold of his brother's arm, giving him a none too gentle shove toward the midnight blue leather sofa. "Even drunk, you must know it would do you no good to kill the golden goose."

Lord John staggered a few steps, then caught himself and turned to glare angrily, hatefully, at his older brother. "You're an ass, Dante. Do you know that? I may be a drunk, but you're an ass!" Having said all he seemed to have wanted to say, Lord John drew himself up very straight and walked with exaggerated steadiness toward the drawing room, where he would doubtless collapse into one of the few chairs and sleep until dinner was served.

Sarah Jane would have to remember to have someone fetch a blanket for him, else he would take a chill.

She fought the desire to follow Lord John, but stood her ground, surreptitiously sliding the kerchief from her head and running her fingers through her short hair to smooth it back into its customary dark, sleek cap as Dante watched his brother's progress.

"I must speak with you," Dante said once Lord John had disappeared, the remnants of some bawdy ditty filtering back into the library. "I have to leave Cliff Walk. Tomorrow."

Sarah Jane felt stunned, as if he had just slapped her. "You're going away?" She didn't want him to leave. She never wanted him to leave. Oh, she might have *thought* it when he was being particularly obnoxious in his neglect of her, but she had never *meant* it. Not really. "Where? Why?"

Dante perched on one corner of the desk, his right foot dangling just above the floor so that Sarah Jane noticed, not really caring, that mud still clung to his boots, as if he had just ridden in from the fields.

She knew he had received no mail in the morning post, so the letter he had in his jacket must have been delivered by someone who had taken the time to locate him on the estate.

Her heart began to pound, as she sensed danger for her husband.

"Castlereagh is running amok at the conferences and

Wellington has summoned me to Vienna to help him sort everything out. Talleyrand and Murat are at each other's throats one minute and scheming together the next. King Louis and the rest of the Bourbons are no more than a sad joke! If we're not extremely careful, Sarah Jane, Napoleon may decide we've bungled things and attempt to sail to France's rescue, as he would term such a move, God help us. Seven frigates and a thousand men are at the deposed emperor's disposal if he chooses to follow such a course! How could the victors have rewarded the vanquished with such dangerous presents?"

Sarah Jane took three steps into the room, then stopped, knowing that she could not go to him, would not be thanked if she did go to him. "But—but the war is over. We've had all those victory celebrations with Blücher and the czar, parades of peace, and even a temple of concord erected in Green Park. I've read all about them and . . ." She trailed off into an embarrassed silence, aware that she was rambling, aware that Dante would not leave his beloved Cliff Walk unless the duke was quite serious in his concerns. "How—how long will you be gone?"

Dante stood, walking around the desk to open one drawer after another, piling the desktop high with papers she hadn't realized were there, for she hadn't known he'd been making use of the library.

When did he come here? It had to be late at night, when the household was abed. Did he ever sleep? No wonder he always looked so tired, so strained. Why was he working so hard? What did he feel he needed to prove? She knew so little about her husband, less than nothing.

"I don't know, Sarah Jane. Months, probably. These papers detail my plans for Cliff Walk, for the plantings, the livestock, the mill—everything. The names of my most trusted tenants are here as well as notes concerning those who need to be watched. We have gathered more than our share of lazy men over the years. We'll have Hunsberger, the estate manager I hired last week, as soon as he arrives, which should be in the next two weeks, but for now, Sarah Jane, I have no choice but to entrust Cliff Walk to you. Ty and Johnny are useless. Betts—um, your grandmother said you'd been trained in all aspects of running an estate the size of Cliff Walk."

Sarah Jane approached the desk and the papers as if both might burst into flame without warning, scorching her.

"Yes, that's true enough. I have been taught, but I have never been forced to implement any of my lessons." She picked up one of the papers and saw Dante's bold, masculine handwriting crowding it from top to bottom, side to side. He was so meticulous, so knowledgeable, so obviously reluctant to trust her. "You—you say the man's name is Hunsberger?"

"I interviewed him last week in Folkestone, and he seemed competent enough. But he does not live there, more's the pity, for Folkestone is fairly close by. He is currently situated near Wimbledon," Dante told her, moving away from the desk to stand at the window, his hands clasped behind his back, slowly opening and closing his fists.

"His wife—" Dante hesitated for a moment, then continued. "His wife is due to present him with their first child at any time, so their arrival at Cliff Walk will be delayed. I've arranged for him and his family to occupy a cottage in the village, the last one at the end of the lane leading to the estate. Perhaps you can have it cleaned, now that the thatchers are through with it? And it will need all new furnishings, I'm afraid."

"Of course," Sarah Jane promised automatically, fighting back sudden tears. Why did she feel as if she was about to be deserted when she had, for all intents and purposes, been alone at Cliff Walk ever since her grandmother's departure the day after the wedding? "Will you need anything else? Some assistance in selecting and packing your things for the voyage, er, the trip?"

"My man Lowell, who accompanied me to the Peninsula, already has everything well in train, thank you," Dante told her, turning away from the window just as raindrops began splashing against the pane, nature crying her tears for Sarah

Jane as the day turned as sodden as her mood. His expression was bleak. "Please allow me to make my own announcement tonight at table, after which I shall retire early, as I must beat the tide at Folkestone in the morning. Wellington's note was penned three weeks ago, so I cannot afford to waste any more time."

And then, without another word, and without looking at her again, Dante quit the room, leaving her to wonder what might have been if she had ever summoned up all her courage and lived out her late night dreams in his presence, daring to show him the Sarah Jane Muir she had always wished, and hoped, she could be.

And wondering when she would forgive herself if she didn't show that Sarah Jane Muir to him soon. Very soon.

He heard her stirring in the next room. The thickness of the heavy door was not enough to muffle her restless pacing, just as it had never been enough to keep him from hearing the occasional sniffle or slight sob in all the nights he had passed in his dressing room these past weeks, tossing and turning and hating himself, hating Betts Trowbridge, hating the fates, hating everything and everyone except Sarah Jane Muir.

His Sarah. His Sarah of the large brown eyes. His Sarah with a smudge on her face as she rolled up her sleeves and showed the servants what she wanted them to do. His Sarah, the courageous little sprite he had once believed to be nothing more than a cipher.

Much as he wanted to believe that she was a calculating miniature of her grandmother, he knew differently, had always known differently. She acted out of concern in everything she did, out of her wish to be what she had been trained to be, married to be—a fitting mistress of Cliff Walk.

Her success with the servants had galled Dante at first, even though he knew she had done just as she ought, and her further successes with the house itself were more than surprising, they were spectacular, nearly overwhelming, in their completeness, their display of good taste combined with an astute recognition of the costs involved.

In short, Sarah Jane was just what he wanted in a wife, just what he needed in a wife.

But she wasn't his wife. Not really. She hadn't been his wife since the second night of their marriage when they had spent a few idyllic hours together in the kitchens before he allowed his baser instincts to overcome him, and he had made love to her a second time, hurt her a second time.

If only they had met by chance, he and Sarah Jane, and fallen in love, then married. If only he hadn't bowed down to Betts Trowbridge's ambitions. If only he had not allowed himself to be bought, allowed Sarah Jane to be sold. It had been two months, and still he could not reconcile himself to what he had done in the name of saving Cliff Walk. He still could not look into Sarah Jane's trusting, questioning, innocent eyes without feeling the guilt of their strange beginning, the fear that Audrey was right, and that Sarah Jane could end up paying for Betts Trowbridge's longed-for great-grandchild with her life.

Sarah Jane was not breeding, or at least it didn't appear so. That was something, some small solace, especially now that he was going away, perhaps to fight in yet another war if Wellington was to be considered a good judge of the way the wind was blowing from Napoleon's Elba.

Not that Dante entirely believed Audrey's warnings about Sarah Jane's slight frame and her chance of having difficulty bearing a child. Audrey, he had discovered by watching the smiling, chattering woman closely during their time together, was deeper than anyone, including himself, had ever suspected.

Not intelligent, perhaps, but smart, and crafty, sly as a fox. By dint of playing the brainless society miss, she could say anything, do anything, sow seeds of distrust, plant unanswerable questions, and twist and turn her words to suit her audience, her own purpose.

He had seen her do it with his brother Tyler, professing to love him while carefully inserting her velvet-tipped darts into any conversation, referring to his crippled state and to his—to hear her tell it—imminent further decline and certain death.

Audrey worked her wiles on Johnny, too, teasing him as was the custom of his older siblings, but always with a small, sharp hook at the end of her taunt, a stinging jab meant to remind him that he was right to drink, for he had ruined his brother's life.

And then there was Sarah Jane. She seemed to like Audrey well enough, but she couldn't be so young, so naive, that she did not realize that Audrey would flatter her only as long as it suited her to do so. Audrey had thus far flattered her way to a new wardrobe and a halfhearted promise to be allowed to travel to the town house in Grosvenor Square in March, supposedly for the purpose of directing refurbishing there in the event Sarah Jane ever wished to travel to Mayfair.

Once the woman got herself to London, Dante knew, Sarah Jane could wait a long time to see her again which, he realized now with a small smile, might just prove that Sarah Jane was *not* as innocent or naive as Audrey supposed. Maybe she was smarter than all of them!

Dante threw back the covers and rose from the uncomfortable cot to go to the window and stare out at the overgrown gardens, wishing for the thousandth time that he was not such a proud man, and such a stubborn one.

If he were less stiff-backed, he would not still be spending his nights in his dressing room or working in the library, then bending his long frame uncomfortably to sleep on the leather couch.

If he could only unbend a little, admit what his eyes, mind, and heart told him, he would go to Sarah Jane on his knees, if necessary, and beg her forgiveness for being, as Johnny had termed him, such an ass. What did it matter now if he had married Sarah Jane for all the wrong reasons? They *were* married.

No, he didn't love his wife. But he did admire her, greatly. And he did desire her, very greatly. Setting Audrey's warnings to one side, and keeping very much in mind her motives in not wanting Sarah Jane, instead of her, to provide an heir to Cliff Walk, it didn't seem implausible to suppose that a patient man, a man who bent his mind to the task, could persuade Sarah Jane to relax in his arms and perhaps even to become an active participant in, rather than a reluctant recipient of, the act of lovemaking.

For he wasn't a total monster; he did know how to pleasure a woman. Why, more than one of his mistresses during his salad days in London had told him he was the best, the most inventive lover they'd ever had. But should a man perform with his wife as he did with a mistress, a member of the unshockable demimonde who would lie back and allow anything up to and including a mauling in return for the gift of a few diamonds?

And what did it matter, now that he was about to leave Cliff Walk? Before he'd received the letter from Wellington, he could console himself that he had time to plan his approach to Sarah.

But now that time, these past squandered weeks, was behind him. He couldn't go to her now. He couldn't risk impregnating her now. Even less could he risk making her cry again as he rode her, feeling himself move deep inside her, losing control of his better instincts when confronted with her small body, her tightness, her miniature perfection, even her slight whimpers. Were those whimpers of pain or of pleasure? How he wished he could be sure.

God! He *was* a monster! How could he think he had been pleasuring her when he knew she had no idea why he was so excited; she, who could only lie there, impaled by him, experiencing none of the ecstasy he wished for her but only the fear that he would never stop, never go away.

Go away. Yes, he would go away. He had almost rejoiced when the summons from Wellington arrived, for each day spent at Cliff Walk had grown longer, and the nights had become interminable. He labored beside his men from dawn to beyond dusk, working himself close to exhaustion, at first to prove he could, but now in the hope that he would then sleep, and not dream.

But it hadn't worked. It wasn't working now, with Sarah Jane moving about in the next room, doing God only knew what, keeping him from his rest, keeping his mind moving around and around in damning, confusing, guilty circles.

"Dante? May I speak with you for a moment?"

He whirled about at the sound of his wife's voice, thankful he had thrown his dressing gown over his nakedness.

"Sarah," he said, peering through the near darkness to see her standing silhouetted in the open doorway, the outline of her slim body visible, thanks to the candles that burned in the chamber behind her. He had been so lost in his thoughts of her, his misery, that he had not heard her enter. "What is it? Is something wrong?"

She shook her head, and he could see the clean, sculpted perfection of her jaw, the graceful sweeping lines of her throat from chin to shoulder. "No, Dante," she answered quietly. "It's just . . . Well, I just wanted to tell you that I've had nothing to do with Johnny's brandy. Where he obtains his supply is as much a mystery to me as it is to you. I wouldn't wish for you to go away thinking that I would be so terrible as to try to win his friendship by such a destructive means."

He let out his pent-up breath on a sigh. "I was wrong to accuse you, Sarah Jane." He smiled wanly, one side of his mouth lifting in what could almost have been a rueful grimace. "I was striking out at you, at both of you, and it was a stupid, selfish thing to do. But"—he hesitated, then pushed on truthfully—"he was kissing you, Sarah Jane, and I . . ."

That was all he could say, especially since she insisted upon standing there in front of the candles, where he could see the outline of her slim waist, the sweet flare of her hips, the length of her straight legs.

"Johnny was in his cups, Dante," she said quietly, her voice steadier, slightly more confident, in the way it had been that long ago night in the kitchens. He knew she was frightened, and her display of courage elicited his admiration, and his desire. Such a brave little fairy princess, bearding the ogre in his den.

"He was only teasing, I'm sure," she continued, "and in the morning probably won't recall a word he said. I can only hope he likewise forgets his strange affection for that statue of Bacchus that Mr. Yarrow has ordered patched and banished to the gardens." She lifted her chin. "But enough of Johnny. To be perfectly truthful, he served only as my excuse for speaking with you. I have come here for another reason." She lowered her voice to a near whisper. "Quite another reason entirely."

Dante shook his head slightly, not quite understanding her words, and not really caring, if she were to appeal to him for his opinion in the matter. His mind was busily concentrating on more important matters. Her dressing gown seemed so sheer, for instance, so revealing.

Was she wearing her night rail beneath the dressing gown? Somehow he didn't think so.

"Can't you sleep?" he asked at last, unable to think of anything else to say. It was as if he had been reduced to the rawest youth, tongue-tied at the prospect of his first conversation with a lady.

"Can you, Dante? Tonight of all nights?" she countered, her voice steady, even more confident, and perhaps a tad suggestive. Again she amazed him. Was this truly his Sarah, his little pet? His once shy, innocent wife? How far she had progressed in the past weeks, having had only two choices open to her: to grow, or to wither and die under the burden she had been forced to carry.

Yet she was still somewhat shy, still slightly tentative, and that simple knowledge cheered him greatly. His innocent seductress.

There was a world of questions hiding in her last inquiry, and a galaxy of hopes, of dreams long wished for but never truly believed possible of coming to fruition danced through his brain in return. Did his bride also dream? Did she also want? Need? He had seen sparks of independence these past weeks, but could he really dream that she had come to him, come to offer herself to him . . . ?

No, he decided sorrowfully, cutting off his hopeful

thoughts. Not now, and perhaps not ever, thanks to his bullheadedness, his stupidity, his clumsy fumbling in the marriage bed.

He took a single step in her direction, the small dressing room seeming as wide and impassable as a mountain range. But he had to try. Just this one time, this last time. He had to try.

"No, Sarah Jane. I cannot sleep," he said quietly at last, for the time had come for truth, and the devil fly away with pride. He had been reduced to begging, and he didn't care.

"I can lie down," he said slowly. "I can even, by a strong application of will, close my eyes. But I can't find my way to sleep. As a matter of fact, dear Sarah, I am very certain that unless I can hold you once more before I leave tomorrow I will never sleep again."

"Truly, Dante?" And then she spoke quickly, her words tumbling over themselves, so that he had to concentrate to understand her.

"You've been so *angry* with me, Dante, so disappointed. I had decided to be brave, which was above all things silly, for I am not at *all* brave, not really, except in my own mind, and then I paid the servants, and you left the dinner table and didn't speak to me except to be odiously *civil,* and you stayed in here each night, so that being brave did me not a penny's worth of good, did it? I was quite afraid to come in here even now, not wishing to make a fool of myself as I am so prone to do, but at the same time—for these past nearly two months, actually—I have been convinced that it would do me absolutely no good at *all* to sit back and play the lady when I . . . But now you're leaving, and I think about you *leaving,* and I know that I could not live with myself if I thought of just what to do only *after* you'd gone! It was time, more than time, I thought, for me to take a forward step, burning my bridges behind me. Do you really wish to hold me? Oh, *thank you,* Dante! That was what I hoped you might say, *prayed* you would say. And I must tell you, Dante," she ended rather furiously, "considering how very good I have been, that it is *about time!"*

Lord Dante could not suppress a smile at this garbled

speech that seemed half rambling confession, half accusation, but then he sobered. "And now that it *is* time, pet? What now? Perhaps you should tell me, as I wouldn't wish to take a wrong step toward that burning bridge, although your temper is proving to be decidedly delicious."

He watched, transfixed, as Sarah Jane took a deep breath, then raised her hands to the bow at the waist of her dressing gown, untied it, and allowed the garment to slip from her shoulders and puddle at her feet.

She stood there before his amazed eyes, entirely naked, her fair skin glowing silkily in the candlelight, her arms at her sides, her facial features all but obscured in shadow.

And then, slowly, she lifted her arms, beckoning him to her. All her bridges burned. All their past behind them. All their future before them.

Another man might have gloried in what could only be seen as a victory, but Dante did not feel in the least victorious. He felt humbled, blessed, and as near to tears as he had been since his childhood.

"Ah, God, Sarah, when you make up your mind, you don't do things by half measures, do you?" he groaned, bridging the gap between them and lifting her high against his chest. He carried her back into the bedchamber and laid her gently on the wide bed before quickly stripping off his dressing gown and joining her.

He hesitated only a moment, looking deep into her eyes, before asking, "Are you sure, Sarah? Quite sure?"

"I have been for weeks, Dante," she said, lifting a hand to caress his cheek, the action sending a shiver down his spine. "If you had looked, you might have noticed. Please, Dante, kiss me. Help me understand why I feel this way whenever you're near."

He needed no further urging. His mouth found hers hungrily, greedily, moistly clinging to her as he fed on her innocent seduction, his teeth and tongue engaging her in an erotic battle that, if they were lucky, would have two winners and no loser.

"So sweet, so sweet," he said as he showered her face and throat with kisses, his tongue tracing the outline of her jaw, the enticing hollows behind her ears, the throbbing pulse at the base of her throat.

Her skin was so soft, so warm, so very alive, and he knew that she was offering herself to him as she had on their wedding night.

But this time it was different, for she was holding his shoulders in her small hands, her fingers digging into his muscles, her own mouth busy as she kissed his neck, his chest, even his arms, showering him with her consent, her inexperience mingling with her eagerness to please until he thought he would explode with the ecstasy of her untutored ardor.

He found her lips once more, easing them open and sliding his tongue inside, grazing the roof of her mouth, plunging into her again and again in a simulation of his coming possession of her body, and his heart sang when she did not stiffen but met him thrust for thrust, even biting at his tongue as he dared to withdraw.

This was heaven, this was more than heaven, to have his wife in his arms, to have her willing, even eager.

His hands moved to her shoulders, her small breasts, as he lay half on, half off her, his fingers finding her hard nipples and urging them into fuller flower before he slid down her body and replaced his hands with his mouth, tending to each of her breasts in turn, glorying in the small triumph of hearing Sarah Jane's low moan of response, feeling her move toward him, not away from him, granting him even better access to her body.

What had happened to change her he did not bother to investigate, did not care to know at the moment. All he could do was take what she was offering, and give to her in return.

He slid one hand down to her waist, molding her hip with his fingers, then dared to slide those fingers low across her belly, just above the curls that hid the treasure he was seeking.

Her belly was so flat, almost concave, and he could feel her pelvic bones, could nearly span the space between them with his spread fingertips, for she was that small.

168

The realization gave him pause, reminding him of Audrey's warnings. But he banished that disquieting memory when Sarah Jane pushed her heels into the mattress, an action that raised her hips against his hand, inviting him to further advances.

He dared the intimate touch, and her legs fell open as she sighed against his ear, then sighed again as he slid his fingers into the nest of curls and beyond, to the sweet, secret center of her.

And she was ready for him. Incredibly, unbelievably, she was ready for him, wet and warm and open.

Although his heart was pounding and his body was on fire, he willed himself to go slowly, taking his cue from Sarah Jane's responses, not attempting to mount her until he could hear her moaning low in her throat, feel the slickness against his fingers as he brought her to the point of mindlessness.

"So sweet, so sweet. I won't hurt you, Sarah," he whispered to her then, slowly slipping between her legs. "I'll never hurt you," he swore as he sank into her, filling her, all the while gentling her with his hands, kissing her face, her eyes, her hair. "Never hurt you . . . never hurt you . . . *ah, Sarah!*"

The age-old rhythms caught at him then, so that his hips moved without conscious thought . . . as she lifted her legs to clasp him about the waist . . . as he raised himself on his hands in order to stare down at her . . . to see the place where their bodies were joined . . . to watch the wonder, the awe, dawning in her lovely brown eyes as she gripped his forearms tightly, her head now thrown back, her bottom lip caught between her teeth, her small, perfect breasts visible to him in the glow of the bedside candles . . . as he felt his body preparing for the final release . . . as her breathing grew rapid, shallow . . . as together they soared upward, toward the far-off moon and beyond, to where the stars all burned brighter than the sun.

He held her then, soothing her with silly, meaningless sounds and tender kisses as he waited for her trembling to cease, willed his own heart back to a normal steady rhythm.

He didn't speak, didn't wish to break the spell of the past

minutes with anything as mundane, as possibly injurious, as mere words, but only covered their bodies with the blankets and continued to hold her, cherish her—and silently curse himself for a fool for having spent these past interminable weeks away from her.

"Dante?" she said at last, raising her head from his shoulder.

"Shhh, pet," he cautioned, slipping his fingers into her hair, pressing her to him once more. "We have so much to talk about, to learn about each other. I have so much to explain. But let's not spoil this perfection with words. Just lie still and let me hold you. Let me take this sweet memory of my wife away with me in the morning. It will make my journey easier and the rapid success of my mission all that more important, for I want nothing more than to be here again, with you."

He felt her nod in the affirmative, and then she sighed, curling her body closer against his side, and almost immediately fell asleep, like a child exhausted after a long day of adventuring.

One side of his mouth lifted in a wry smile as he decided that she had been adventuring, as had he, exploring the realm of glorious lovemaking. He was a lucky man, he knew, and the future was bright. Betts Trowbridge had done him a favor. Pride meant nothing now. He had Cliff Walk, he had a courageous, willing wife, and one day he would have a son.

An ice-cold shiver ran down his spine then, and his smile stiffened. It was almost too perfect, after their imperfect beginning. But perfection was impossible, and he knew it. Life always intruded; reality always intruded.

He wrapped his arm tighter around Sarah Jane's body, wishing he could wake her, love her again, and then give in to her pleas when she begged him not to leave her.

She was a woman, and it would be in her nature to want to keep him with her now, now that they were so close. Just as it seemed natural for him to want to forget his summons from Wellington, and stay. Not confident that he could hear her plea and still deny her, he allowed her to sleep.

Dante did not sleep himself, for he was not willing to miss

a single moment of his remaining time with Sarah Jane. He lay there, achingly awake, listening to her soft breathing until dawn began to creep over the horizon.

Then, knowing that Lowell would be waiting below with their mounts in a few minutes, he kissed his sleeping wife gently before laying her back against the pillows and quietly slipping from the bed, from the room, from Cliff Walk . . . and from the woman he could love.

INTERLUDE

WISHES
1815

Go where glory waits thee!
But while fame elates thee,
Oh, still remember me!

Thomas Moore

CHAPTER 9

❦

I am the cause of France's unhappiness. I must effect a cure.

Napoleon Bonaparte, in exile on Elba

I still fail to see why you insist upon refusing my every invitation to dinner," Sarah Jane said as she and Emma Franklin, a young widow she had met on one of her infrequent visits to the village, walked through the hall on their way to the round saloon, Sarah Jane's second favorite spot now that most of the state rooms had been refurbished.

She gave a single tug to the bellpull near the door, sure that Babbitt would respond shortly by bringing tea and some of Cook's lovely warm scones. "I have spent the months since my marriage convincing myself that there is, as was written by Edmund Burke, 'a limit at which forbearance ceases to be a virtue.' You should remember that, Emma."

Emma smiled indulgently, for she was more than a dozen years Sarah Jane's senior and had taken on the role of older sister without much prompting. "Been reading more dusty books, Sarah? Be careful, else Dante will return home to find himself wed to a bluestocking. Imagine his dismay!"

"Nonsense! Dante would never be dismayed; he wouldn't

allow it. But don't interrupt, please. There comes a time, Emma, when the hopes and dreams we hold close to us must either be taken out of hiding or left to wither and die. Dante taught me that, although he doesn't yet know the whole of it, poor dear. I may not be able to physically outgrow the appearance of the little mouse Grandmother Trowbridge sold to the Muirs, but I have learned to unleash my roar. It is quite fun, actually, and extremely enlightening. Now it is time for you to take hold of *your* dream and give it a mighty shake!"

Sarah Jane's smile was less than teasing, more than simply interested. "Surely you can't still be afraid to see Tyler?"

Emma, a tall, rather thin woman with soft hazel eyes and light brown hair, twisted her hands together at her waist, lowering her head. "And I thought you promised me that you would not mention Lord Easterly's name in my presence, Sarah Jane," she rebuked her friend quietly, her cheeks flushing.

"Don't spoil everything now by becoming self-effacing, Emma. It is so unlike you." Sarah Jane motioned her friend to a chair and sat down across from her, taking a moment to look up and admire the way the early March sun lit the massive glass dome, turning the huge round room into a softly glowing orb, a self-contained planet, an intimate if formally furnished and extremely large chamber.

The state rooms were very nearly complete, all except the king's bedchamber, which was why Grandmother Trowbridge was still at Trowbridge Manor, undoubtedly grinding her teeth in consternation. Sarah Jane was now, quite happily, the only woman at Cliff Walk. She believed herself, like the flowers in the solarium, to have finally come into bloom after a very long winter, an eighteen-year span of dormancy.

"I did tell you that Audrey left for London these three days past, didn't I?" she said after a moment. "The first of March, to be precise about the thing, in order to prepare for the Season," she ended mischievously, carefully watching for Emma's reaction.

"No, you did not, as you very well know," Emma

responded shortly, her spirit once more in evidence. "Honestly, Sarah, I cannot believe your cheek. As if I would go to Ty because his wife is away. And don't you dare mention that business of Dante speaking to you about Ty's unhappy marriage, because I won't allow myself to find any sort of hope in any such nonsense. I may have disgraced myself ten years ago, but I am not totally without scruples. I know my place."

Sarah Jane laughed. "Your *place,* Emma? If that isn't above everything silly. Why, if I had known my place do you think I would be here—Lady Dante, mistress of Cliff Walk and overseer of this entire rambling estate?"

"I still think it is unconscionable of Dante to be rambling all over Europe and the good Lord only knows where else as if he were a young bachelor taking the tour, leaving his wife behind to sweep up after him."

"He'll be back soon, if his infrequent letters are to be believed. The Congress will eventually come to an amicable conclusion. Poor lamb, racing around Europe at the duke's bidding, attempting to keep the various negotiations on the correct path. In any event, Dante believes Mr. Hunsberger to be in charge," Sarah Jane reminded Emma, not about to tell her that, although the state of her marriage to Dante might be aeons better than it had been on their wedding day, it was still far from perfect.

It was, actually, in a sort of limbo, and she had not been terribly saddened to be on her own for a while, unobserved by her husband as she exercised her fledgling wings undisturbed, and reviewed the extremely gratifying conclusion that she had been correct to go to Dante that last night. Besides, he would be home any day. Any day now at all! In the meantime, Sarah Jane was content to allow Emma to believe the marriage was totally successful.

"Ah, yes, the *late* Mr. Hunsberger."

"Don't laugh, Emma! He wrote just last week to say that it may be another month before his wife is capable of enduring a week's travel on our terrible, muddy spring roads. Just think, Emma—triplets, and all boys! I cannot conceive of the prospect. But the cottage is ready for them now, more thanks to you and Robbie than to me. I don't know how I could have found the time to set it to rights *and* oversee the addition of another room if you hadn't volunteered your services that first day I came to inspect it."

"I had no choice, if *you* recall," Emma said, smiling. "My naughty son had done everything but take up residence in the place, believing it to be his private castle, as it had stood there empty since the last estate manager left. But Robbie has been good, hasn't he?"

"He doesn't drag his pet goat inside the cottage anymore whenever rain threatens, if that's what you mean," Sarah Jane agreed as Babbitt appeared, a large silver tray in his hands, and began setting out the tea service on a low table between the two chairs.

The two women fell silent until the butler had positioned every plate and cup precisely to his satisfaction and had withdrawn with a formal bow to Sarah Jane, not saying a word to either mistress or guest.

"Did you feel the chill just now, Sarah? He hates me, you know," Emma declared, reaching for the teapot, as it was an extremely heavy piece and she always did her best to keep her new friend from doing any extra work.

"Who? Babbitt or Ty?"

Emma shrugged. "Both of them, I suppose. Babbitt because I disgraced myself by eloping to Gretna Green ten years ago, then returned to my dying mother's house from Hastings last autumn, a near penniless widow, my fatherless son in tow. We are distantly related, Babbitt and I, and he was always faintly starchy, even before he snared his butler's keys."

"And Tyler? You can't really believe *he* hates you," Sarah Jane prompted, mentally deciding to have a brief talk on the virtue of forgiveness with the Muir butler.

"No? Oh, perhaps he doesn't *hate* me, precisely, although I know I disappointed him. But what else could I do, Sarah? It's no great secret how money-mad the marquess is. Tyler's father forbade the match, which he should have done, for I was only a schoolteacher's daughter, and without a groat to bring to any marriage by way of a dowry. I couldn't bear to stay here once I knew it was fruitless to hope—so close to Ty but unable to be with him. I was, and am, no fit wife for an earl, a future marquess. If Jack hadn't agreed to take me away I don't know what I would have done. And yet, as it worked out, I've ended living in the shadow of Cliff Walk anyway, once more close to Tyler but never seeing him, never speaking with him. My life has gone for a full, rather pathetic circle."

"You could see him, Emma," Sarah Jane pointed out, as she had done a dozen times before. It hadn't been easy for her to take her courage in her own two hands and go to Dante that last night, but she had done it. Surely Emma, so much stronger than she, could do no less. "He's not on the far side of the moon. He's where he always is this time of day—in the family wing drawing room. *Alone* in the drawing room. With no one about. Not Johnny, and not Audrey, who is, as I said, in London."

"That's not what I meant, Sarah, and you know it." Emma sighed, then smiled sadly. "But enough of this fustian. I positively refuse to be maudlin on such a fine day. And I *utterly* refuse to allow you to bait me. Tell me, how are you feeling? Are you still so ill in the mornings?"

Sarah Jane's eyes twinkled with mischief. However, she knew she had dared as much as possible and must now abandon the field. But she also knew that Dante had told her Tyler was considering a bill of divorcement. It didn't seem completely terrible to think of her new friend in the role of sister-in-law.

Tyler desperately needed someone to love him. Audrey might pretend affection, but a blind man could see that she had no feelings for him whatsoever, not even pity. If anything, she was hurting him.

"Have I been ill? Not these past three days, no," she said, going along with the change of subject. "But do not mention such things here at Cliff Walk, where I vow the walls have ears! No one save you even knows of my condition—and Mildred, of course. I do hope my moods improve. Poor Mildred. I upset her almost hourly as I vary between giggling at nothing and bursting into sobs over the least little thing. Why, just yesterday, when I said I was going to take a stroll to the pond, Mildred told me she wouldn't be surprised if I came back to the house crying because the ducks were forced to walk around barefoot! Unfortunately, she is not exaggerating my silliness."

Emma laughed. "That, too, will pass. *Eventually.*"

"I hope so. I cannot thank you enough for explaining childbirth to me, Emma, after Audrey frightened me so. I'll never forgive her for that, no matter how scatterbrained she might be, for I am quite convinced her advice was not well intentioned! Oh, Emma, if only I could be sure Dante would receive my letter, I would write him about our coming child. I can tell from the questions he raises in his own letters that he rarely receives my news from Cliff Walk. But he will be home soon; I am convinced of it."

Emma raised her eyebrows, shaking her head sadly. "I can understand why you would rather wait until he is home to break the happy news about the baby. But I remember Dante in his youth, and I do not think he will be best pleased to learn that his wife has not told him about the difficulty with Mr. Hunsberger. However, if you cannot rely upon the post to the Continent, you can surely trust it as far as London. It is more than time the marquess came home and took up his responsibilities. Or, failing that, you could appeal to Johnny."

Sarah Jane sat back in her chair, realizing that she had eaten all the scones by herself, leaving none for Emma. Honestly, if she wasn't hiding from the breakfast Mildred now brought her each morning on a tray, she was devouring everything in sight.

Soon she would not be able to keep her pregnancy secret from the other members of the household. Why, at this rate, by the time Dante returned home she would be positively huge!

"Johnny?" she repeated, laughing ruefully. "Although you may have a good point, Emma. If Johnny were half as industrious about managing Cliff Walk as he is in obtaining fresh stores of French brandy, I would not be needed. Dante should never have given him an allowance."

"French brandy, you say? I thought he had simply found a way to raid the Cliff Walk cellars. But *French brandy?* Why didn't I realize it before now? No wonder I see him so often in the village."

"But Dante assured me that he had spoken with all the innkeepers. Johnny can't be buying brandy from them."

"Not from the innkeepers, silly." Emma placed her cup on the tray with a small thump and rose, placing her fists on her hips. "He's using his allowance to buy brandy from the *smugglers!* There has been a flourishing trade between our fishermen and Calais for generations, even during the war, sad to say. Ah, Sarah, we have him now. All we have to do is have someone whisper a word to Ronson. He is the local leader of the free traders, and a cousin of mine, and of Babbitt's into the bargain. That will serve to put a cork firmly in Lord John Muir's bottle! Come on. This is too important to simply ring for Babbitt. We'll beard him in his own den, and the devil take his starchy spine!"

Sarah Jane rose as well, suddenly excited. "Do you really think that's it? That this man is the one? Dante would be so pleased if Johnny were to stop drinking. But what does Babbitt have to do with it? I don't know Mr. Ronson, but if you will take me to him—"

"You? I think not, Sarah. It wouldn't be fitting for Lady Dante to be seen with a free trader, not that he'd talk to either you or me about the subject in any case," Emma interrupted just as Sarah Jane was mentally summoning her bonnet and one of the grooms, who would drive her to the village. "How much do you suppose Johnny is spending with Ronson?"

Sarah Jane frowned, feeling herself being robbed of a great adventure, which a meeting with a smuggler would certainly have been. Surely Mr. Ronson must a very singular-looking person, perhaps with an eye patch or even a wooden leg and a parrot perched on his shoulder. It was a pity that the free trader was destined to remain a figment of her imagination. Unless, of course, Ronson turned out to be depressingly ordinary, which was also quite possible.

In that case, it would be better for her to never see him.

After all, to date only Dante had been able to live up to Sarah Jane's imaginings. Up to them and beyond anything she had ever dreamed! She banished her daydreams and returned her mind to the subject at hand.

"Why must you know the amount?"

"Because Ronson won't give up his profit out of love for either of us, silly," Emma responded as they made their way out of the saloon and into the hall on their way to seek out the butler. "But if we pay him *not* to sell Johnny the contraband, it will give him twice the profit, as he will be able to sell the brandy to someone else."

Sarah Jane grinned in admiration of this brilliance. "I knew I liked you, Emma Franklin. It must be above all things wonderful to possess a devious mind. Mine has always been limited to the fanciful, when I am not ordering up the freshening of mattresses or making certain the fences are strong enough to keep the cattle from wandering."

Still excitedly discussing the strategy they would use to enlist Babbitt into their scheme to deprive Lord John of his single solace, Sarah Jane and Emma made their way along the curved corridor leading to the family wing and into the smaller, more informal hall, where Sarah Jane was secretly amused, and Emma visibly dismayed, to see the Earl of Easterly just being pushed from the drawing room.

"Emma!" the earl exclaimed in obvious surprise and alarm, looking first to the love of his youth, then to his useless legs, and at last to Sarah Jane, his eyelids narrowing in almost naked hatred, as if deciding that she was behind this accidental meeting. "Farris! Take me to my rooms!"

Sarah Jane didn't know if it was the sharp intake of breath from the woman beside her, the stricken look on Tyler Muir's face, or her own newly discovered stubbornness that made her take hold of Emma's elbow as she turned to make her escape and say, "Tyler, is that any way to treat our guest? I had thought better of you. Farris, you are dismissed."

"Sarah Jane, leave it," Emma pleaded quietly, her voice trembling. "Please."

"No, I won't leave it," Sarah Jane said heatedly as Farris,

whom she had gifted with a dozen juicy plums from the succession house just last week when she saw him eyeing a plate of fruit longingly, gave a quick bow and headed for the baize door to the kitchens.

"Tyler, Emma is my friend and my guest. I will not be so horrible as to take a page from Johnny's book and suggest that if you don't wish to see my friend you should simply rouse yourself from that chair you cling to with such dogged resignation and walk away, but I will ask that you be civil."

"Dante should have held out for a rich draper's whelp," the earl declared bitterly, his hands clenched in his blanket-shrouded lap. "Butchers' granddaughters, it would appear, are too crass by half."

That statement served to rouse Emma from her embarrassment. Shaking her arm free of Sarah Jane's grip, she marched directly up in front of the Bath chair and stared down at the earl's bent head through narrowed lids.

"I'd box Robbie's ears for such rudeness," she said in what could only have been a fine duplicate of her schoolteacher father's strictest tones, "save that my son is all of nine now, and past such juvenile, spiteful speech. How dare you? *How dare you* speak that way to Sarah? And to think that I harbored such fond memories of you. Well, thank you, 'Ty, for you have made my future that much lighter, for now I know that marrying Jack saved me from making the most disastrous mistake of my life!"

She whirled, ready to leave, this time halted by the earl's hand as he reached out and grabbed hers. "Emma, wait," he said, looking up at her as she turned back to him, his blue eyes, Sarah Jane noticed with a stab of pain in her heart, nearly brimming over with tears. "Ah, Emma, you're still my same lovely prickly pear. Don't leave me again. *Please.*"

They remained that way for some moments, staring into each other's eyes, frozen in a tableau very like the one Sarah Jane's vivid, fanciful imagination had pictured several times.

And then, slowly, Emma sank to her knees on the tiles, her dark green skirts blooming around her, and held up her other hand for the earl to lift to his lips. "Leave? I'll never leave you, my dearest Ty," Emma finally said quietly. "In truth, I never have."

Sarah Jane quietly backed out of the hall, retracing her steps to the corridor and heading for the quiet of the library, wiping at her own tear-filled eyes with the back of her hand, happy for Emma, happy for Ty, but suddenly terribly, crushingly lonely for Dante.

"When did we hear of this?" Dante asked, sitting in his Brussels headquarters, where he was attending to Wellington's business.

"Just a few days past, sir," the travel-stained subaltern said, barely able to hide his excitement at the news.

But then, the young subaltern had never seen war, never witnessed what it could do to fine young specimens such as him.

"Here, sir, is a copy of the dispatch as it came to Metternich from the General Consulate in Genoa," the subaltern continued. "It arrived during the night, but he did not read it until the following morning, if you can believe such a thing! The dispatch is dated twenty-eight February. The duke thought you should know, and he desires your presence back in Vienna at once, sir."

Dante unfolded the single page and read quickly and silently: "Campbell, the English commissioner, has just called to enquire whether Napoleon has been seen in Genoa. He has vanished from the island of Elba."

He laid the copy of the dispatch on the desk and ran a hand through his dark hair as he leaned back in his chair and looked at the calendar that sat in a silver frame: 9 March 1815.

"Christ on a crutch! He must already be in France, and halfway to Paris, just as we feared. Damn Talleyrand and Murat for their scheming, their wild talk of kidnapping the man. We knew Napoleon wouldn't sit still once he'd heard of their plot. The Congress leaks like a sieve, spilling information everywhere! Hell and damnation!"

The following day, just as the taciturn Lowell had finished

packing his master's things, two other officers entered the small Brussels hotel room that had become Dante's private study. They were full of news and rumors.

They spoke quickly, interrupting each other as they related tales of the emperor's movements.

Napoleon and one thousand men had landed at Cannes on the first day of March, they told Dante, then made their way through one small Alpine village after another, surrounded by cheering crowds. He then rode forward freely for more than one hundred miles without incident, leaving his cannon behind in the snowy mountains in his haste to reach Dauphiné.

Only outside Grenoble, near La Mure, rumor continued in the voice of the officer, did Bonaparte encounter royal troops of the Fifth Army Corps, but he rode out to meet them, spurring his once loyal troops with an impassioned speech, daring any one of them to come forward and kill his emperor.

"Vive l'empereur!" the thousand had answered as one in what must have been a truly stirring moment, and an hour later two thousand soldiers marched behind their leader as he moved on toward Paris.

Toward Paris . . .

"Seven thousand men now follow him as he marches to Lyons, or so I've heard it said," one of the officers informed Lord Dante, shaking his head. "A paltry few, but then our information is several days old; he could have fifty thousand by now, perhaps even one hundred thousand—plus the Old Guard, those seasoned veterans! Curse that fat Bourbon for a miserable king! Those soldiers would never have joined with the emperor if the royals knew what they were about."

"Royals very rarely know what they are about," Dante said offhandedly, his thoughts having turned to Sarah and the sure knowledge that it could be long months before he would see her again. *If* he saw her again. *If* he survived the battle that was certain to come. "What else have you heard, gentlemen? What happens now?"

The second officer shook his head. "We wait, I suppose. Baron vom Stein is already screaming for the Congress to outlaw him, but Napoleon still has the loyalty of the Hapsburgs. How do you outlaw a son-in-law, the husband of your daughter, the father of your grandson?"

"A better question, sir," Dante responded, already imagining his first conversation with the strong-willed Wellington. "How can he fly in the face of the allies?"

By the time Dante had reached Vienna the question of the Hapsburgs' loyalty had been answered by the Austrian emperor's daughter, Marie Louise herself, the wife of Napoleon who now lived openly with an Austrian officer and insisted that her four-year-old son, once proudly named Napoleon Francis, must now be addressed as Francis.

She had penned a formal declaration to the Congress, vowing that she would have nothing to do with the banished emperor, and she had begged to be placed under the protection of the allies along with her son. So much for the fealty of love-struck women!

But Napoleon still had his loyal Frenchmen, and they had fought well in the past. Napoleon's ambition had never been confined to France. No one believed that he had changed his plans to conquer the world.

On March thirteenth it became official. The Congress acted: "The powers declare that Napoleon Bonaparte has placed himself outside the bounds of civil and social relationships, and that as an enemy and disturber of the peace of the world he is consigned to public prosecution."

Napoleon Bonaparte, emperor, was now an outlaw. No longer would he be referred to by any formal title. The allies would refer to him once more only as Bonaparte. Usurper. Outlaw.

And war was now inevitable.

"Hell and damnation!" Lord Dante Muir exploded in the privacy of his rooms overlooking the Danube, cursing the Congress, Marie Louise, the pathetic Bonaparte, cursing everyone and everything that kept him from Cliff Walk, from Sarah.

" 'My dearest Sarah . . .' " Sarah Jane blushed prettily as she read the words aloud to Tyler, Johnny, and Emma as they sat together in the family drawing room early in May. She felt a small fluttering in her gently rounded stomach and knew that Dante's child was stirring, also intent on listening to every word of his father's letter.

She took a deep breath and continued: " 'I take up my pen to worry you with news both old and new, for I do not know how much you have learned or how long it will be before I can find time to put pen to paper again. It will come soon now, my little pet, this battle we all fear, now that Ney has joined Bonaparte along with the others.

" 'We have heard it rumored that Madame de Staël, who often spoke of her hatred for Bonaparte, has promised to devote her literary gifts to the cause of France if only Bonaparte will pay her the two million francs she says France owes her father. Bonaparte, it is said, replied that he is not wealthy enough to grant her request!

" 'I admire the man's humor even as I detest the trials he places before us. Even so, we've heard for certain that Benjamin Constant, Madame de Staël's brilliant, politically ambitious friend, has rallied to Bonaparte's side.

" 'In return for his own sentence from the Congress, Bonaparte has outlawed Marmont, Augereau, and—at long last—Talleyrand himself. I believe each is sorry for that, as they despised each other through eighteen years of friendship and admired each other by way of their jealousies. The world is in turmoil, and friendships and loyalties become scrambled in the ever-changing wind.

" 'Bonaparte promises much to the French: freedom of speech, free elections . . . and much to the rest of us: a ban on all war, his willingness to confine his ambition to France. He promises and promises. No one believes him, or his sudden lack of ambition, which brings me, little pet, to my saddest tale.

" 'The Vienna decree precludes peace, and Bonaparte readies himself for battle. We have left him no choice. If he is ever to win the hearts and minds of the French he must have himself a victory, just as we must deal him his last defeat. We cannot count on another such as Marmont, who handed Paris to the allies in Bonaparte's absence.

"'As I write this we are already on our way back to Brussels, dreading the battle, but knowing it must be joined before Bonaparte gathers more supporters. And so the world once again hovers on the edge of war. Bonaparte needs a victory to show his power; we need a victory to avert even more bloodshed. Either way, as it always falls out, many will die in the name of peace.

"'I ride with the duke, Lowell as always by my side, and Cliff Walk and my family always in my every thought. Pray for me, little Sarah, pray for England, pray we do not fail!'"

Sarah Jane's eyes filled with tears as she spoke the closing lines through trembling lips. "'With all my good wishes and affection, now and forever, I remain your husband, Dante Edward Muir.'"

"Sarah? Are you all right?"

She looked up to see Emma standing in front of her, and smiled weakly, nodding. "I'm fine, Emma. Truly. Nothing will happen to Dante. God wouldn't allow it." Her voice cracked, and she could not stifle a small sob. "Would he?"

15 May 1815
Grosvenor Square

Greetings to all!

Is this not the most Exciting, Delicious time! Curtis Frowns and Grumbles and goes back to Scotland, vowing London is dull as ditch water, but to me it is a Heaven on Earth! For tomorrow I am off for Brussels, the Center of the World, of the entire Universe. Everyone is going, simply Everyone. Do not fear for me, for I will be traveling with the Viscount Blackstone and his dear wife, who have promised to take their Utmost Care of me. I have so many Lovely Friends.

Perhaps I shall see dearest Dante when I am there. Will he be in uniform, do you suppose? He was always so handsome in his uniform! Ah, Ty, that you are too crippled to go a-warring, and poor Johnny, that you are too deep in your cups to feel the thrill of battle! I weep for you, and I will explain to All why you are not in Brussels with the Rest of the World.

I have written a draft on your bank, Ty, which it would please me if you would honor, as I Simply had to have a new gown. The Countess of Richmond has promised us a Ball!

With all my love to everyone—you, too, little Sarah Jane, little housewife—I remain, in haste,

Audrey

"Ignorant, selfish bitch," the earl grumbled as he crushed his wife's letter, then reached for Emma's hand as Sarah Jane rose quietly and quit the drawing room, determined not to cry.

Lord John, who had endured no more than a fortnight of enforced sobriety before discovering yet another source of brandy, one that even Emma's determination could not ferret out, staggered from the room, intent upon refilling his glass.

20 May 1815
Brussels

Tyler, dear brother,

So much of what we are, what we aspire to be, depends upon our own spirit, our own will. At the moment, at every moment, I will myself at Cliff Walk. But this is a foolish wish, a selfish dream at such a time in history, at the crossroad of the world, which Brussels has become.

The city is insanity itself, full of giggling women and posturing peers, none of whom possess the faintest notion of the carnage that is sure to come. Is it an unwritten rule that Society must be brainless?

Enough complaints! Enclosed you shall discover the key to a small drawer in my desk in the library. In that drawer you'll find the will I wrote out, with Lowell and Babbitt serving as my witnesses, before leaving for Vienna. I would have consulted with you and Johnny, but I did not wish to seem morbid. Now I am grateful I have one less thing to worry about as I prepare for battle.

I beg you to follow my instructions should I not return from Brussels. Do not show this letter to Sarah, for I do not wish her to know that I am feeling somewhat maudlin as I await the inevitable. I flinch from the thought of leaving her now, with so much between us still to be resolved. I believe we can have a good life together if we are blessed with that opportunity. There are times, many times, when I wish we could erase everything that has passed between us and begin once more from the beginning, at the day we first met, without my bunglings and missteps to stand between us. I could love her, I think, if we were to be granted that precious time. My little pet . . .

But enough sad stories! Let me tell you what is transpiring here, none of it encouraging.

Bonaparte has taken up the offensive we have thrust upon him. He moves more quickly than we supposed, marching to meet us rather than fortifying Paris while we gather our forces here in Brussels. He is eager for a victory before the Russians and the Austrians arrive in July—near the end of July, unless our information is wrong. I pray to God that we are wrong and they arrive sooner. Blücher is a good soldier, a firm ally, but he is not divine, no matter what the ladies think. We are none of us divine. We are none of us immortal. And our numbers are limited.

I consider Hunsberger a good man, a competent manager, and Sarah's infrequent letters—I believe many have missed me—report that all is well at Cliff Walk and that you and Johnny have been of great assistance to her. I beg you, Ty, to protect Sarah from our father, from that harridan Betts Trowbridge, from her own softheartedness. We need you, Ty, all of us. I put my dependence on you, and Johnny as well. I need my brothers to be strong for Sarah, for Cliff Walk, for themselves.

Pray God we shall all be together again soon.

Dante

Lord John handed the letter back to the earl and then threw himself into a nearby chair, his arms and legs flung wide, his chin on his chest. "Well, that tears it! As if it wasn't enough for your dear wife to all but call us out-and-out cowards! Lead me to a pistol, brother mine. I feel a distinct need to blow out my addled brains."

The earl moved his Bath chair forward slightly, placing himself directly in front of his youngest brother. "Are you as weary of being a millstone around Dante's neck as I am, Johnny?" he asked quietly, seeing the pain in Lord John's normally laughing, if always somewhat bleary, blue eyes.

Lord John raised his head. "What do you suggest?"

"I suggest, Johnny," the earl said solemnly as he carefully folded Dante's letter, "that, much as I appreciate dearest Sarah Jane's desire to make us look good in our brother's eyes, we have been derelict long enough. I *suggest*, Johnny, that we make a pact between ourselves. For every drink you don't pour down your throat, I shall allow you to help me with these miserable legs, employing the techniques Dante's quack outlined, if I can remember them. In short, Johnny, I suggest that it's high time we two grew up. It's more than time. I only hope we haven't left it too late."

7 June 1815
Brussels

Greetings to my dear family!

Oh, the Thrill of it all, the Excitement that permeates the very air we Breathe! All Brussels is Alive, throbbing with Expectation of the coming battle, the Grand Retribution when we will grind the French Frog into the dust with our Mighty British Heel. My, don't I sound Fierce! We plan to go out in carriages to observe the tumult from the hillsides. Can you Imagine the spectacle?

I saw Dante last night, but he would only tire me with questions about Cliff Walk, so that I, knowing little and caring less, did not linger. He looks very well, Sarah Jane, dear sister, and he remains a Masterful Figure in uniform, and on the dance floor as well. All the ladies are Agog at his Dark Brilliance! I do hope you have taken my advice and let your hair grow out, as curls are much more the fashion. Of your gowns we need not speak, as you have made great strides to rid yourself of those antiquated styles your silly grandmother fancies. Dante, you know, is a great devotee of the feminine figure, but of course you cannot help your thinness.

Sad to say, the Duchess of Richmond has limited her guest list to little more than two hundred—all the Best People, of course, and so my gown will be admired by far fewer than I had imagined! The ball, less ball and more party, is set for the night of June fifteenth, so, dear husband, by the time you read this, I shall, as one of the fortunate few, have gone down the line with the Iron Duke himself! Such a Coup for your little wife!

But I must Dash! We are a-picnicking today in the country, a lovely Interlude in flower-strewn fields that in another month or more, if Dame Rumor is to be believed, will be the Stirring Scene of the Iron Duke's greatest triumph. Waterloo! La Belle-Alliance! Such strange names! Blücher is coming to the city soon as well, that lovely drunken man! We needs must hide all the strong drink, as we try so fruitlessly to do with dear Johnny. Is this not above all things Exciting? Oh, to be alive in such a Wondrous Time!

My love to all!
Audrey

"Here, read this drivel and then destroy it." The earl, sitting in the sunlit gardens with Emma, handed her the letter.

The earl was in his Bath chair, Emma beside him on a blanket spread on the grass. The two of them had contentedly passed the time painting the west aspect of Cliff Walk in watercolors until Babbitt brought him the latest post. Emma's son, Robbie, bored by such tame amusement, had gone off with one of the gardeners who was on the lookout for a mole that had been making inroads on the flower beds.

"And as you read, my love," the earl added, "please remember that I married the woman for her father's money and that I did so only after I had learned that you were lost to me. It is not much of a defense, I know, but it's the only one I can muster."

"I knew that sooner or later you would find some way to lay at least part of the blame at my feet, dear heart," Emma said, shaking her head. But by the time she had finished deciphering the crossed and re-crossed lines of Audrey's atrocious handwriting, her amusement had disappeared.

"And soon Audrey will be home," she said sadly, "and peaceful days like this will be behind us. I shall miss being a fallen woman, and I know Robbie will miss you and the silly stories you tell him. I can only hope that Dante returns soon as well, so that Sarah will smile again. I worry so for her and for the child. And Mrs. Trowbridge has recovered from her injuries, Sarah tells me, and will arrive here within a few days. After hearing Johnny speak of her, I dread meeting the woman. According to your brother, the only other creature in history to have had such success in filling the hearts of others with fear and dread at their impending arrival was Attila the Hun. If only she could have broken *both* her legs in that fall from her dogcart!"

The earl touched Emma's cheek. "All will work out, my love. I promise."

Emma smiled, pressing a kiss against his palm, then squeezing his hand firmly. "I shall hold you to that, Tyler Muir. I *will* hold you to that!"

On the sixteenth of June, striking with just half his army, the outlaw Bonaparte secured victory over Blücher at Ligny.

Two days later, after a shaky beginning as men ran straight from the Duchess of Richmond's party to the battlefield, and with a miracle of luck, the Duke of Wellington's battle was all but won.

The lessons the allies had learned while fighting the strategically brilliant young Bonaparte for twenty years led to his doom, for the allies remembered these lessons while the former emperor, who had devised them, seemed to have become worn out. He had grown tired and had lost the swiftness of movement that marked his campaigns before this pathetic, preordained meeting outside Brussels.

No one could believe that Bonaparte, this master of the battlefield who had attacked so early in the morning all those years ago at Jena that his cannon roused his foes from their sleep, could allow the sun to rise at four and not move his troops until twelve.

The relentless Prussians marched as soon as it was light, but the former emperor, recoiling from the rain-soft ground like a woman refusing to soil the hem of her gown by crossing a muddy street, remained in his tent until noon.

That was a blessing which Blücher received and used to best effect.

Charleroi fell to Bonaparte but he delayed too long, precious hours too long, to follow this small victory with a mass onslaught against Blücher. He actually sent Ney and half the army along the Brussels road to meet the English, leaving himself open to attack by the entire Prussian army!

It was, of course, impossible to recall Ney once Bonaparte saw the folly of this move, for Ney was already committed to the fight with Wellington at Quatre Bras. Ney sent only one army corps to Bonaparte's aid, and he ordered that contingent to the wrong place. For France. For the allies, that error was like a gift from the gods.

The fatal, final day of battle—for surely retreat was by now the only option—dawned with Blücher having barely recovered from a fall from his wounded horse at Ligny, and Bonaparte still sluggish, still underestimating his opponent, and still making his moves too late. The Iron Duke, for all his bravery and brilliance, was not winning this battle; Bonaparte was losing it.

Dante first saw Bonaparte late in the afternoon at La Belle-Alliance. Through the smoke and mist that had all but blotted out the sun, the unbelievable gore, and the seething crush of men, he raised his eyes and espied the former emperor clad in his bottle-green campaign coat, seated astride a great horse, looking down on the battle.

Napoleon had held the Old Guard in reserve even though

the only clear avenue to any semblance of victory was to commit them to the battle, and now it was possible only to sacrifice them. The Scourge of Europe must have known he was a beaten man, for Blücher had arrived on the scene with all speed, heeding Wellington's urgent message: "Unless your corps keeps marching, and attacks without respite, the battle will be lost."

Dante, staggering with fatigue, climbed a slight rise and observed the scene from amid the tall grass that beat against his thighs in the stiff wind. Two horses had already been shot out from beneath him, but he could not resist standing there, alone, slightly above the field and watching, mesmerized, as the Old Guard was at last committed, eons too late, their cries of *Vive l'empereur* stirring the blood, perhaps, but not moving the English or the Prussians, who could smell victory now, even as they could smell the blood that had turned the grass slippery beneath their feet.

As Dante watched, unbelieving, Bonaparte rode down the hill and into the open, daringly exposing himself to the British guns, exhorting his men to fight on. He was a glorious sight, fearless in his fear of not dying in battle, of ending his days in yet another British prison, and Dante felt a moment of sadness as he witnessed the final defeat of a once great enemy.

It was true. The struggle was over at last. Napoleon had lost, completely and utterly and at a terrible cost to both sides.

Only two squares of French infantry remained, two small citadels of French power, and their emperor rode into the center of one of them, still refusing to give up the fight. But the heart of Napoleon was no longer the heart of France, and the squares dissolved, leaving Bonaparte unprotected except for a few mounted grenadiers who surrounded him as he galloped toward the grassy rise, toward safety.

Dante, filthy and bleeding from several small cuts but otherwise sound, stood with his spent pistol in one hand, his blood-encrusted saber in the other, and watched the vanquished emperor ride by, passing within twenty yards of him, the thunder of the horses' hooves shaking the ground beneath his feet. Even if he'd held a loaded pistol, Dante would have stood thus, his heart in his throat, watching.

He could not have given Napoleon Bonaparte what he must have craved, the healing benediction of a soldier's death. The world of laws would have to decide the man's fate.

Dante turned away at last, only vaguely hearing the terrified screams of belly-shot horses, the cries of the wounded, the pitiful whimpers of the dying. It was over, and he felt nothing.

He was numb with fatigue, with relief, with an overwhelming sorrow that the world had come to this point, to this place in history, to this moment where the honor and glory of battle was replaced by the reality of suffering and death.

He did not hear the frenzied hoofbeats behind him, nor did he see the fear-bright eyes of the young French grenadier chasing after his fleeing emperor.

He did not feel the bullet, fired more in panic than in fury, that brought him down.

CHAPTER 10

*In the middle of the journey of our life
I came to myself within a dark wood
where the straight way was lost.*

Dante Alighieri

"Mildred," Sarah Jane pronounced ruefully as she stared at her body in profile while she stood before the pier glass in her bedchamber, "I should seek Lord John out at once, for I at last know why there are elephants in this world. Elephants are here to prove there does exist on earth something larger than themselves. That *thing*, Mildred, is *me*."

The maid, who had remarked to Mrs. Emma Franklin only a day earlier that Lady Dante would soon have to be pushed about the estate in a gardener's wheelbarrow, shook her head, saying, "Nonsense, missy. Why, it is only the first day of July and the babe is not due to appear until almost the last day of August. You have still days and days, and miles and miles of room for growin'."

Sarah Jane placed one hand where her slim waist used to be and another beneath her belly, sighing as she measured herself by eye and decided that she had grown for enough "miles" and did not wish to proceed an inch more. If she did, she would risk having to dress herself in bed sheets rather than the constantly altered gowns Mildred slaved over, letting out seams and adding skirt panels until any sense of fashion had been distorted beyond recognition.

"Thank you, Mildred, for cheering me so. It is so comforting to hear your estimate of my potential growth, truly it is. Grandmother Trowbridge has compared me to a house—a very large house—and Lord John believes I have taken it into my head to become a duplicate of the dome over the saloon. If anyone else offers an opinion I may just scream."

The maid mumbled something about breeding ladies always being too touchy for words and stood back to allow her mistress to pass, for the dinner gong had rung and Mildred knew better than to stand in the way when Lady Dante was called to table.

"Eating for two?" Sarah Jane heard the woman grumble as she closed the door behind her. "Could feed a regiment on what that little girl puts away three times each day!"

Once out in the hallway Sarah Jane noticed, not for the first time, that there were entirely too many mirrors in Cliff Walk. She passed by no fewer than four of them as she made her way to the top of the stairs, the sight of herself as she passed by reminding her constantly of her misshapen body.

It wasn't as if she had grown fat, for she hadn't. Her face and arms, even her legs, were nearly as thin as ever. It was only her stomach, her *enormous* stomach, that seemed to enter any room a good five seconds before the rest of her, immediately becoming the center of attention, and comment, from the rest of the family.

Grandmother Trowbridge, who had taken up residence in the king's bedchamber as threatened, seemed to find her granddaughter's delicate condition a constant source of delight, which Sarah Jane could have accepted with more grace if the woman hadn't constantly touched her distended stomach as if it were somehow separate from Sarah Jane herself, an action she considered an embarrassing intrusion of privacy.

The earl didn't say much about the impending birth, but he did mutter at least once a day that he wished Dante would bring himself home soon, because it wasn't right that his brother should become a father before he knew he was to be one.

Sarah Jane echoed this sentiment heartily, wishing for the millionth time that she had written to him about the baby even as she was gratified that he hadn't had to go into battle with the worry of a pregnant wife at home.

But now the anticipated look of astonished surprise she longed to see on his face when she sat him down and told him of the pregnancy had re-formed itself in her mind to what would surely be Dante's wide-eyed glare of dismay, or perhaps even disgust, when he saw the grotesque figure that his wife, his "little pet," had become in his absence.

If only he hadn't referred to her that way in his letters, his infrequent letters.

If only she had not conceived in the first week of her marriage.

If only he hadn't had to go to Vienna.

If only they could have been together these past months, becoming friends, as Dante had hoped they would be, learning about each other, daring at last to say out loud, "I love you."

If only he were home. If only she'd received a single letter from him since Waterloo.

But, no. She wouldn't think about that. His name had not appeared on any newspaper listing of the dead. Audrey had not written, either, although she was probably back in London, knowing more than any of them.

Dante was fine. Completely fine. He was simply busy working with Wellington, totally engrossed in this business of rounding up Napoleon and finding a secure place to put the man, a place with dozens of sturdy locks and high fences and no avenue for a second escape.

That was why he hadn't written. He had been on the move, tied to his duties, too busy to pen a letter to his wife, who should know there was nothing he could tell her that she could not learn from the newspapers which were driven down from London.

She would concentrate on worrying about her altered appearance and thinking about Dante's shock and, perhaps, his elation when he first saw her and realized that she was soon to present him with a son.

She would concentrate on ordering the finishing touches for the music room, the kitchen wing, the still barely tamed gardens, the chapel.

She would devote her time to amusing her grandmother, whose movements were still limited by her injured leg.

She had a million things to think about. Dante's kiss. His touch. The thrilling intensity in his dark eyes when he reached for her. His crooked half smile. His promise of friendship. His loving.

She would concentrate on those million things.

Or else she would go mad.

Dante awoke in the same room he remembered from his last awakening, a large airy chamber containing a four-poster canopy bed and a small bedside table holding a single candle and a jumble of dark bottles.

This time he ordered himself completely awake, refusing to allow the pain in his head to overwhelm him so that he would be tempted once again to gratefully embrace the gray mist that descended to block the agony that had assaulted him then as it did now when he opened his eyes.

Only by a strong application of willpower did he push his tortured brain to remember where he was and why he was in this place. But, although he had succeeded in banishing his longing for the gray mist, he could not recall anything beyond that mist, beyond the pain.

Wetting his dry, cracked lips, he tried to speak, but only managed a groan, a wordless appeal for assistance.

It was enough.

He heard a shuffling from somewhere in the room, the quick tattoo of wooden clogs against the floor, a door opening, and then, a few minutes later, a voice coming from somewhere above his head. He squinted, silently commanding the muzzy shapes to form themselves into something stable, something solid, until he thought he saw the smiling face of a young woman.

An angel? Was he in heaven? No. Angels didn't have two

heads. Besides, his head wouldn't hurt if he were in heaven. Only if he were in hell.

"You're awake again! How above everything wonderful. I cannot tell you how tedious it has been, rushing to your side time after time, only to be told you had gone back to sleep. I am thoroughly out of patience with you, Dante, and I won't fib and say that I'm not. Everyone else has gone back to London, leaving me here to nurse you back to health, as if I know a thing about such matters. Or care a snap about them, either. It was just like Lowell to die of his wounds and not be a thimble's worth of help to me! Of course I could not *say* any of that, for everyone would think me horrid, for which I blame you entirely. I am not horrid at all. You know how perfectly *dreadful* I am in a sickroom! You must remember how I could not abide being with Ty after his accident."

The two-headed woman's jabbering was killing him, crushing his head in a vise. "Where—where is here?" he asked, hoping she would keep her answer brief and to the point.

"Where? What a silly question! Why, in Brussels, of course. You were lying in a farm wagon, right outside in the street, when the viscount found you, piled up like cordwood with a dozen other wounded soldiers. You cannot *imagine* such a horrific scene! The viscount recognized you at once, although I vow I don't know how, as you were nothing but blood, and ordered you brought inside. That's where you are now, in the viscount's rented house. But now the viscount and his wife are gone. *Everyone* is gone except for me and that crow-faced nurse, and all *you* do is sleep. I still can't fathom why I couldn't simply have allowed the nurse to tend you and gone on with the viscount. But no, *family* must stay! I cannot tell you how bored I am! It has been weeks, positively *weeks!*"

His head hurt so much. He hated to ask any more questions, for he knew they would most probably bring forth another lengthy string of complaints, but he had to know. "Weeks? Weeks since what?"

The mussy-featured blond widgeon looked shocked, her

four blue eyes widening almost comically as they swam in his sight. "Why, since the battle, of course. Perhaps not really weeks and *weeks,* for it is now only the second day of July. What a madhouse the city was, with everyone scrambling for each last coach and carriage, trying to flee back to London! They are calling the battle Waterloo, although that is above everything silly, for it didn't really take place just there, or so I'm told. War isn't anywhere so glamorous as I thought, but only very messy. Thank heaven we won, or I cannot imagine what would have happened to me."

Her eyes narrowed. "Shouldn't you be asking to eat or something? You've been wasting away in that bed, and will have to gather some sort of strength if we're ever to be shed of this dreary city. Really, anyone would think you'd have more consideration for the person who stood by you in your time of trial."

He wasn't at all hungry. He was just tired, so very tired. And his head was pounding. He felt the gray fog descending again and knew that this time he couldn't fight it. There was only time for one more question.

He looked up at the woman as her two heads at last re-formed themselves into a single rather beautiful face. "You say we are family. Are—are you my wife?"

"Sarah Jane? Come in here, sweetie, and sit down. Don't force me to fling this damnable cane at your feet to block your escape! You've been avoiding me for days, but I insist upon an end to such silliness right now. It is time we had us a little talk. About this Franklin woman . . ."

Sarah Jane took a deep breath and turned, leaving the hallway behind and walking resolutely into the red saloon, where her grandmother was firmly ensconced, reclining lengthwise on one of the couches. She was dressed in her usual purple and, in the heat, reminded Sarah Jane of an overripe plum about to burst.

"What about Emma, Grandmother Trowbridge?" she asked as she gingerly lowered herself into a straight-backed wooden chair. She had given up attempting to rise from soft chairs and couches weeks ago, for she almost always had to resort to calling for assistance, which could be terribly embarrassing, especially when Lord John was the only one about, and always very free with jokes at her expense. The man had actually become more amusing in sobriety than he ever was when deep in his cups.

"What *about* her?" Elizabeth Trowbridge snorted. She didn't sniff. She snorted, rather like a bull. "The woman has all but taken up residence in this household, that's what *about* her. And don't tell me she's your friend, for I didn't cut my wisdoms yesterday. She is up to something hugger-mugger with the earl. Pushing him out for walks in that chair of his, painting silly pictures with him in the gardens, laughing with him in the music room, allowing her son to run tame through the house—such a forward creature! Babbitt tells me she's widowed, but I wonder. Why'd she leave here ten years ago, if she had a husband for herself, a father for that boy of hers? And what's she doing holding hands with a married man, even if he is an invalid and most probably unable to get up to much mischief? Although I am sure there are ways. I know I've sheltered you, sweetie, but does the word 'doxy' mean anything at all to you? There's nothing else for it, Sarah Jane. As mistress of this household, it is up to you to order her away. Her and that whelp of hers."

Be calm, Sarah, Sarah Jane warned herself silently. *Be calm, and for pity's sake don't cry. Don't be a little mouse. Ty needs your help. Ty needs Emma. It is up to you to do what is right. You are a heroine, remember?*

"No, Grandmother Trowbridge. I will not do that." Sarah Jane's grandmother had been in residence for nearly two months, and Sarah Jane had done her best to keep her teeth tightly clamped each time the woman ordered her about or commented disparagingly on the sad lack of ornamentation incorporated in the refurbishing of Cliff Walk.

Sarah Jane had kept her silence, no longer cowed by her grandmother, but unwilling to cause a scene when that woman had, in her own way, been so very good to her.

But enough was enough! And now at last she had taken a stand.

Elizabeth Trowbridge leaned forward on the couch, her eyes narrowed, her purple-turbaned head cocked to one side. *"What* did you say, Sarah Jane? I don't believe I could have heard you aright."

"I said no, Grandmother Trowbridge," Sarah Jane answered quietly after clearing her constricted throat, twisting her hands in what remained of her lap. "Emma Hamilton is welcome at Cliff Walk at any time. I cannot imagine how any of us would have managed these past months without her quiet strength."

"Hummph! *Snakes* are quiet, Sarah Jane, as they slither about, insinuating themselves, causing all sorts of damage. What will happen when the countess returns? *Then* the fur is going to fly! And what of the marquess? What will Curtis do? He'll be finding his way back here sooner or later, sniffing out for more of my money unless I miss my guess. What will he say? What will your *husband* say?"

Sarah Jane looked at her grandmother levelly. This wasn't so bad, really. Bravery wasn't difficult to achieve, if one was being brave to help others. Now perhaps she might even help herself! "I don't particularly care what anybody says, actually. However, as you and I have already had a lovely long visit, if Mrs. Franklin's presence distresses you, perhaps you should consider an immediate return to Trowbridge Manor."

Elizabeth Trowbridge sat back sharply, as if she had been dealt an unexpected slap. And then, much to Sarah Jane's surprise, she smiled, a wide toothy grin.

"Well, well, well. Look who's gone and become the lady of the manor! Wonderfully done, sweetie. You spiked my guns good and proper, didn't you? I'm down, and with not a shot fired! You may not look a whit like me, thank the Lord, but you've got some of my spleen. About time it showed up! Yes, yes, I've noticed quite a change in you since last I saw you. Can't say as how I like the hair, but you're coming along. Coming along. Maybe it *is* time I was on my way."

This development was almost incomprehensible! All those years of timidity, and was this all it would have taken to assert herself? A single no, uttered with quiet conviction?

Sarah Jane bit her bottom lip, partly so that she would not smile as she rejoiced in this last victory, this final shift from well-behaved child to independent woman, and partly so that she would not cry.

"You'd leave me now, Grandmother Trowbridge? Now, with Dante still gone, when I am with child?"

The older woman raised a hand to her throat, literally puffing up in front of her vaguely astonished granddaughter, preening at this invitation. "Well, sweetie, if you really want me to stay . . ."

Sarah Jane smiled, inwardly wondering if she had just nullified her first victory as the Heroine of Cliff Walk.

"Dante?"

He turned away from the window, to look at his sister-in-law as she swept into the small sitting room, already clad in her emerald green traveling cloak, a large bandbox clutched in her left hand. "Yes, Audrey?"

"Oh, nothing, Dante. I only wished to observe you as you reacted to hearing your name. You don't seem to be having the least trouble remembering it, do you?"

Dante shook his head, touching a hand to the small bandage, which was all that was needed now to cover the wound just above his left ear where a ball had opened his scalp to the bone for the length of three inches.

"No, Audrey, I don't have the least trouble remembering my name or your name, both of which you've told me. It's only everything else that remains a damnable blur."

"Yes, and may very likely remain so forever, according to that doctor," Audrey replied, smiling tenderly. "Poor, darling Dante. And you've remembered nothing else since yesterday? Nothing more than what I've told you?"

"No, Audrey," Dante said, longing to hit her, for his lack of memory was more than simply frightening; it was maddening. Did she have to seem to be enjoying his predicament, asking him ten times a day if he remembered anything? "Will the traveling coach be here soon?"

"Not soon enough," Audrey answered pettishly, sweeping a towering pile of newspapers from one of the chairs before sitting down, sighing in the July heat that had penetrated the small Brussels house.

"Honestly, Dante, don't you think you are in danger of a relapse, reading all these dreary newspapers? I would most assuredly suffer a brain fever if I even *attempted* to read such depressing information. All that is in them is more news of that boring Bonaparte. He is on his way to Plymouth harbor on an English ship. Such grand treatment for a deposed emperor! If only *we* could already be aboard ship. But we shall be tonight! I can scarcely contain my joy!"

Dante took up a chair across from his sister-in-law and looked at her closely. Even after having been with her for nearly ten days, he could not decide if she was the silliest creature in nature or if he—the Dante Muir he was *before* Waterloo—was the most blockheaded man since Adam took Eve's advice on eating that apple. "Tell me more about Cliff Walk, Audrey—about my brothers, my wife."

"Must I, Dante? They are all so dreadfully *boring.*" She took up a lace-edged fan and began waving it in front of her face, setting the delicate curls at her ears to fluttering like small flags in the breeze. "Oh, very well. I've already told you about Tyler, my husband and your older brother. You must be kind to him, Dante, for he is a bitter, bitter man, although I doubt he will live much longer. Invalids invariably die, don't they?"

Dante's head was beginning to pound. "You said he disliked me. Something about my having usurped his place since the riding accident that crippled his legs."

Audrey snapped the fan closed. "Now, Dante, don't go twisting my words! I only pointed out that you have taken over the running of Cliff Walk *and* the family coffers. I can't imagine why Ty is so outraged, for you have allowed him to continue living on the estate—our own being in such sad repair—although we both know why you *really* did that, don't we? And it isn't as if he will survive to rise to your father's title. I, for one, am endlessly grateful for your largesse and your kind permission for my continued sojourn in London. Of course I shan't go to the town house now, for I cannot think to leave you alone at Cliff Walk with your ungrateful family, even though you've always told me it would be best for us to remain apart for the nonce, to avoid raising suspicion in that harridan, Betts Trowbridge."

Dante shook his head, then quickly regretted the action as the pain behind his eyes redoubled. He had been pushing himself to recover his strength, and he had paid the price. The pounding headaches grew worse with each hour he stayed out of bed. "And Johnny?"

Audrey rose and went to the window, her back to Dante. "Ah, dearest Johnny! You do remember my telling you that he drinks? Poor boy. He was to have wed Sarah Jane, until you came along with your delicious scheme. All that lovely money, and now it's all yours—all ours. Yet I feel confident that Johnny is still fond of you, as is your father, whom you have put in the position of pensioner, doling out an allowance to him as if he were nothing more than a poor relation, and not the marquess. But not to worry! As I told you, Curtis has many good friends who allow him to be their guest, and Johnny and little Sarah Jane seem to have become *extremely* good friends."

"And I accomplished all of this through my arranged marriage to a butcher's granddaughter, a meek, barely-out-of-the-schoolroom infant whose face I cannot even remember? What am I, Audrey—money-mad, a heartless bastard, or both?"

She turned her back to the window and smiled at him, although her face was in shadow so that he could not read the expression in her eyes. "Why, Dante, now you are putting me to the blush! I've told you and told you. You are my own true love!"

BOOK TWO

REALITIES

What is life? A madness.
What is life? An illusion, a shadow, a story.

Pedro Calderón de la Barca

CHAPTER 11

No mask like open truth to cover lies,
As to go naked is the best disguise.

William Congreve

The small party had taken up positions beneath the stand of trees near the formal gardens, the earl and Emma with their watercolors set on easels as they cheerfully tried to outdo each other in capturing the facade of Cliff Walk's west aspect, young Robbie frolicking on the grass with Growler, and Sarah Jane and Lord John sitting quietly on a blanket, sipping lemonade and trying not to speak about Dante's lengthening, worrying absence.

Even Elizabeth Trowbridge, now an accepted if not universally adored member of the family, was present, sitting off by herself in a drawing room chair she'd ordered dragged from the house, her feet propped up on a low stool as she lazily fanned herself in the July heat after stuffing herself full at the noon meal.

"Ah, a well-deserved day of rest for the weary, a week of hard work behind us and another in the offing. We are all looking most indolently bucolic, don't you think?" Lord John said quietly to Sarah Jane as she shifted slightly on the blanket, attempting to make herself more comfortable. *"The Country Family at Their Sunday Rest*—that's what I call it.

211

Or I would, if this damned lemonade wasn't making me queasy."

Sarah Jane tilted her head in his direction, smiling. "Don't spoil it, Johnny. Although you do look most natural to me with a glass in your hand, I am only grateful it no longer resides there for twelve or more hours a day."

He sighed and downed the last of the lemonade. "So am I, actually," he said, returning her smile. "I spend my days marveling at how much more valuable I feel riding the fields than I ever did wallowing in my own misery. The only thing still amazing me is why none of you shot me. Have I thanked you for that small mercy, little Sarah?"

"We did consider it, you know," she told him cheekily, watching in delight as his blue eyes widened in feigned shock. "Shooting you in the foot, tying you to a bedpost, bricking you up behind a wall—anything to keep you in one place long enough for us to banish brandy from all of England. But you surprised us all by your actions. That ceremony we held in the gardens was most moving, when you spilled out all the bottles from your secret cache into the lily pond, then swore never to touch strong drink again. Of course, I fear the pond will never be quite the same."

"Nor the frogs, I suppose," Lord John answered, busily fashioning a daisy chain from the flowers Sarah Jane had gathered earlier. "Have you heard them croaking outside your window at night? For the first time in my memory, they seem to be in tune."

Sarah Jane patted his hand, for some reason unknown to her feeling herself close to tears. Not that she was surprised, for she was often weepy, no matter whether she imagined herself to be happy or sad. Perhaps it was the way Lord John's lips had lifted in a one-sided smile that had set her off this time, reminding her yet again of Dante.

Or at least she thought it did. So many months had passed that she was beginning to forget Dante's features, another reason for her jangled emotions. Would she even remember him when he came home? Would reality live up to her dreams, her hopes for their shared future? The wild fancies she had indulged in, not really lying, but foolishly, hopefully, allowing everyone to believe that she and Dante were happily married, very happily married indeed?

Or was the midnight dream all that she would ever have? Would Dante's return bring a horrible truth with it and put a period to all her hopes? This endless waiting, this not knowing whether Dante's return would signal a new beginning or an end, was driving her to distraction!

Lucy Randolph's oldest brother had been at Waterloo, and he was home. He was lacking his left arm below the elbow, but he was home. The Randolphs had been kind enough to send Lucy to Cliff Walk with the message that her brother had seen Dante during the second day of the battle and that he had been as fit as a fiddle, spending most of his time on horseback, ferrying orders back and forth between the Iron Duke and the various commanders in the field.

But Lucy's good news was not enough to keep the demons of fear from Sarah Jane's mind in the hours after midnight, when she lay alone in her bed, the babe stirring beneath her heart, reminding her that Dante was not near and did not even know of his child's existence.

Blinking back tears, for she did not wish to dampen Lord John's bright spirits with her melancholy mood, she asked, "Have you seen Lucy lately, Johnny? I watched her watching you the last time she rode over on that great stallion of hers, and I believe she might fancy you."

"Lucy?" Lord John shook his head. "Maybe once, Sarah Jane, but no more. She's a good girl, Lucy is, but horse-mad. The only way she'd really pay me any attention would be if I could grow a mane and a tail, and even then only if I could produce a tolerable whinny. Pity. She's grown rather beautiful, in her own way, and was always a jolly good sport. But enough about Lucy. Here," he said, holding out the completed daisy circle and dropping it lightly on her head, "allow me to crown you, dear ma'am, Queen of the July."

Sarah raised her hands to adjust the circlet of flowers as it threatened to tip forward over her eyes. "I believe that should be Queen of the May, Johnny."

"May, July, what difference does it make? You are queen of all you survey and the best thing that ever happened to this sorry estate—and would have been even if you'd succeeded only in setting the kitchens to rights. We Muirs haven't eaten so well in years! And now, just to put the Muir seal of approval on the matter, I shall bestow upon you the kiss of kinship, reserved for special occasions when we are sitting together, sipping lemonade, and generally behaving like solid citizens."

So saying, Lord John leaned forward and pressed a great smacking kiss on Sarah Jane's cheek. Laughing, Sarah Jane prepared to return the favor, her lips pursed comically, holding on to his shoulders as she leaned forward, for her increased bulk made her clumsy and she didn't wish to plummet forward in a heap.

And then she stiffened, her blood hot and frigid at the same time, unable to believe what her eyes could see, unable to move, forgetting to breathe, suddenly lacking the ability to do anything more than stare at the two people who stood not fifty yards away, on the steps leading up to the house.

How did I ever think I could forget him?

"Dante." Her voice came out in a fierce whisper, her throat so tight she could scarcely speak. "Oh, dear, sweet heaven, Johnny, it's Dante!"

"What? Dante? Where?" Lord John spun about abruptly, nearly causing Sarah Jane to topple over as she grabbed at his arm to retain her balance. *"Dante!* Ty, look! It's Dante! Good God, man, don't just *sit* there! It's Dante!"

"You never give up, do you, Johnny? As I keep telling you, all good things in their own time," the earl responded evenly, still wielding his paintbrush against the heavy sheet of paper tacked to the easel in front of him. "Emma, be a love, won't you? Put down your brush, go on over there, and cuff m'brother a good one on his ear?"

Sarah Jane heard the earl speaking, but she couldn't really understand him, as her ears were ringing and her head seemed to be stuffed with cotton wool.

All she could do—as Lord John jumped to his feet and ran toward the steps, as the earl belatedly turned around and shouted a delighted greeting, as Emma murmured, "Oh, dear," and began looking about for Robbie and, most probably, a convenient exit from the gardens, as Elizabeth Trowbridge slapped her knee and began to laugh—was sit there on the blanket, her full skirts spread around her, praying she would not disgrace herself by swooning dead away. Feeling suddenly young and gauche and very, very fat, she lifted a hand to her head and pulled off the whimsical daisy circlet, crushing Lord John's creation between her fingers.

He was so thin. Had he always been so tall? So remote? So much the lord of the manor?

A bandage was visible on the side of his head as he reached the foot of the steps and slowly began walking toward them through the glare of sunlight. He *had* been injured, just as she had feared. And he wasn't smiling, wasn't waving back at Ty and Johnny, wasn't calling out greetings to them all, wasn't looking at her with anything more than mild curiosity as a brightly smiling Audrey clung almost possessively to his arm.

As the babe pushed a foot up and under her ribs, Sarah Jane realized that Dante appeared now as he had in her worst waking nightmares—as almost a stranger to her. The man she had married. The man she had barely known before he went off to join Wellington. The man who had kissed her, held her, and then left her. Without a word of love. But not without the promise of love.

Had he changed his mind? Had the long months that separated them served to make him look back on his short marriage with disgust, remembering the reason for the marriage and discounting the brief happiness they had shared as an aberration of the moment, a frantic reaching out for happiness by a man who might well be going off to die in battle? Had she refined too much on a single shared meal, a single glorious night, and from them created a fantasy of a perfect marriage that never was, never could be transformed into a reality?

She had waited so long for this reunion, but now he was here, and he wasn't running to her, his arms spread wide. He wasn't calling her name, calling for his "little pet." His face was unsmiling, austere, almost uncomprehending.

215

Quite nearly forbidding.

His dark eyes, usually so brilliant, so alive, seemed blank, almost cold. She pressed her hands to her mouth, fearing she might cry out in her sudden unexplainable pain. Dear Lord, what imp of mischief had allowed her foolish imagination to tease her that Dante's return would immediately bring them both undiluted happiness?

"Dante, you miserable cur, how could you have not written?" Lord John shouted as he reached Dante's side, laughing and slapping his brother heartily on the back.

"Audrey? I thought you said you penned a note to the family," Sarah Jane heard Dante say as he shook hands with Lord John, the action impersonal and, again, almost cold.

The family? Sarah Jane winced at the formal term, the detached tone. Something was wrong. Terribly, dreadfully wrong!

"I did, Dante, I swear it," Audrey responded, taking a lace-edged handkerchief from her pocket and fanning her cheek with it. "You know how miserably unreliable the posts are these days. Johnny, do stop pulling at your brother. Can't you see that he has been injured? You always were irresponsible. Why, I have worn myself to a frazzle these last weeks, nursing dear Dante day and night, and I do not need you to undo all my good works. Who is that with Ty? Have you hired him a nurse? Honestly, Dante, the extravagance of this household, when I am kept to a few miserly pounds in allowance!"

"Oh, stifle yourself, Audrey," Lord John said affably, pulling on Dante's arm, bringing him steadily in Sarah Jane's direction. "That's Emma taking off as if the hounds of hell were after her. Surely you remember Emma, dear sister-in-law, although I don't think you two have ever met. Done old Ty a world of good, having her here, though I'm not surprised she isn't about to stay around waiting for your thanks. You can do the pretty with Mrs. Trowbridge in a minute, Dante, as I'm sure she'll keep, picklepuss that she is. Now, come on. Sarah Jane's got a surprise for you!"

Out of the corner of her eye Sarah Jane watched Emma and a reluctant Robbie rapidly walking toward the garden gate and wished she could call her back, even though she knew Emma was right to leave. The earl also watched her go, his expression sad and somewhat lost before he turned once more to Dante and called out yet another greeting.

"Yes, thank you, um, Tyler," Dante replied as he nodded in his older brother's direction. "It is good to be . . . to be home."

Sarah Jane exchanged startled looks with the earl, whose knuckles were white as he gripped the wheels of his Bath chair. Unable to maneuver it himself on the soft grass, he was forced to stay where he was, alone, his brother making no move to approach him.

"And this, dear Dante, is little Sarah Jane," Audrey said a moment later as the two of them came to a halt directly in front of the spread blanket. "Your wife. The one"—she giggled, then went on "the one who was kissing Johnny as we arrived on the scene. Poor dear child, still persisting with that unique hairstyle, aren't you? But it's not to worry, for I am here now to help my little sister."

"He knows she's his wife, you twit. And she wasn't kissing me. I was kissing her," Lord John piped up from behind her. "And Sarah Jane looks just fine! What in the devil is going on here? Anyone would think we were strangers being introduced at some garden party. Dante, kiss your wife hello! And where's Babbitt? We'll have him break out something from the cellars to celebrate. But not for me, Dante. That's another surprise!"

"Sarah Jane?"

Sarah Jane looked up as Dante said her name in an odd, questioning way, as if he wasn't sufficiently sure that he'd gotten it quite right. "Dante," she said quietly, feeling a single tear slide down her cheek. "Welcome home."

And then, to her mingled embarrassment and relief, she fainted.

"Sarah Jane? Sarah Jane! Come on now, sweetie, open those eyes. It's good to show how much the delicate female you are, but enough is enough. Do you hear me? Open your eyes!"

"Really, Mrs. Trowbridge, I believe a little more sympathy and a little less shouting might better turn the trick. And for pity's sake, stop waving those burned feathers under her nose." So saying, the handsome blond man Dante now knew to be his younger brother stepped in front of the purple-clad dowager and knelt down beside the divan in the drawing room.

"Sarah Jane?" he questioned softly, taking up her hand and pressing it to his cheek. "I don't blame you in the least, m'dear, for this hasn't been the most pleasant shock any of us has ever had, but I think it's time you came back to us. Everything will be all right, I promise. Come on now, darling girl. Open those lovely Growler eyes and give us a smile."

"His *darling?*" Audrey whispered as she stood beside Dante in a far corner of the room. "How terribly quaint and touching, don't you think?"

Dante didn't know what to think. He felt as out of place, and as guilty, as a housebreaker caught with the family silver in his hands. He had spent most of the trip from Brussels in an agony of mental anguish, hating himself for his infirmity while anticipating his homecoming, convinced that, with the sight of his home, his family, his memory would return.

But it hadn't. He was in a household of strangers, people who looked at him with varying degrees of affection, pity, and frustration, and he didn't know whether to hate them or himself. Then his wife had fainted. His pregnant wife. Dear Christ, his pregnant wife!

It was Lord John, not Dante, who had lifted the unconscious Sarah Jane in his arms and carried her into the house. Dante had been able only to stand there, aware that he had handled his homecoming in all the wrong ways, unable even to pretend he knew who these strange people were until he could find a way to tell them that he did not.

"What?" he asked blankly at last, realizing that Audrey had spoken again.

"As I've already said, *twice,*" Audrey told him in obvious exasperation, "Johnny called Sarah Jane his *darling.* Now, don't you find that amusing? He never was much of a dissembler, which is why he was such a pitiful drunk. And you have noticed your wife's delicate condition, have you not, Dante? Strange. I have heard nothing about a pregnancy. She must be due to whelp soon, judging by the enormity of her, poor thing. Let's see . . . if we could just put our heads together and count backwards on our fingers . . ."

Dante looked quickly to the divan where his wife lay, now awake and softly weeping, and then turned to glare at Audrey. "Haven't you made enough trouble for one afternoon? These people are obviously upset."

"Trouble? Why, whatever do you mean?"

"I mean, Audrey, that you didn't write to them of my condition. I may have misplaced my memory, but I believe I can spot a lie at twenty paces. Why didn't you warn them that my homecoming wouldn't be all they'd hoped? That girl could have taken an injury from the shock."

"That *girl,*" Audrey responded tightly, her fine aristocratic features pinched, "was kissing your brother when we first saw her. Or perhaps you have forgotten that as well? Have you also forgotten that your brother Tyler despises you for usurping his position here at Cliff Walk after he himself refused to accept the responsibility, and that your own father would rather live on the charity of strangers than bow to your efforts to save him, and that Johnny, a totally useless drunkard, is at this very moment all but slobbering over the *girl* who married you for your title? Honestly, Dante, if you can't tell by now that I am your only friend here at Cliff Walk, then your brains are more addled than that fool of a doctor in Brussels believed!"

"Yet they all seemed happy to have me home." Dante tipped his head to one side, still watching Lord John as the younger man ministered to Sarah Jane. "Not that they fell over themselves in greeting *you,* Audrey."

As soon as the words were out of his mouth he regretted them, for Audrey immediately took recourse to her lace-edged handkerchief and began weeping quietly as she moved to a chair and sat down. How could he have been so rude to the woman he loved? *The woman he loved?* He didn't even remember Audrey. He remembered no one.

Nothing. He was a stranger in a strange world, a man alone, unsure of anything save his aloneness.

"So, a knock on the head did this to you? That *is* what Audrey said when we first settled down here in the drawing room, waiting for Sarah Jane to wake? Sounds fairly queer to me. You sure you're not running some rig, you and this bubble-headed girlie-girl?"

Audrey, tipping up her chin as she obviously took offense at Mrs. Trowbridge's words, rose and retired from the drawing room. Dante felt himself torn between wanting to see the back of her and realizing that she was, in point of fact, his only bridge to his family, the only familiar face.

Dante turned back to see that Mrs. Trowbridge was now standing uncomfortably close beside him, her arms akimbo. She was a singularly strange-looking woman, taller than most men, who reminded him more of a washerwoman dressed in her mistress's clothing than a lady of fortune. Except for her jewelry. The woman was wearing a king's ransom around her neck, in her ears, stuck to her fat fingers. "No, madam, there is no deception. And it *was* a bullet that did the deed, or so I am told. Will the girl . . . will my wife be all right? I imagine her delicate condition is to blame for the swoon, at least in part."

"And *you're* to blame for m'granddaughter's delicate condition, my boy, and don't let anyone tell you otherwise," Mrs. Trowbridge responded flatly. "Now hie yourself across the room and kiss your bride hello. Even addled in the brain box, you must know what is correct, else you'd not be looking so guilty."

He stared at the older woman, idly noticing the slight mustache that darkened her upper lip. "I don't have the faintest notion of what I should say to her," he admitted, feeling more uncomfortable, more physically exhausted, by the minute.

He hadn't realized how much of his limited strength he'd invested in the hope that the return to Cliff Walk would jog his memory, providing a lifeline to which he could cling, for he was heartily sick of feeling that he was adrift in an unknown sea of places and things with no recognizable realities. No memories. No feelings. No attachments.

And the worst of it was his wife, this Sarah Jane, this small, wide-eyed creature who had looked at him with such hope, such fear, such eloquent despair. Audrey had told him theirs was a marriage of convenience, an arranged marriage, a union fostered by economic and social needs mutually fulfilled by the exchange of vows.

So Audrey had told him.

But this child, this little Sarah Jane, hadn't looked at him as if he were nothing more than a purchased husband, a means to an end. Why, if he hadn't known differently, he would have said that the girl loved him.

But if she loved him, why had she been kissing his brother? *Johnny, who has kissed her before.* Dante shook his head, dislodging the voice that had just whispered the damning words inside his head. It was impossible to know that; he had no memory. Not that he cared, for his wife was a stranger to him, as all of these people were strangers to him. He could only pity the man who was once Dante Muir. Lord Dante, cuckolded by his own brother?

He took two steps in Sarah Jane's direction, halting abruptly as the earl pushed his Bath chair in front of him. "No, you don't, Dante. Not yet. We need to talk," Tyler Muir said solemnly, quickly looking toward Audrey, who had returned to the drawing room. *"Now.* Mrs. Trowbridge, if you will excuse us?"

"Oh, go on, if you must," Mrs. Trowbridge grumbled, turning one of the two rings that resided on the index finger of her left hand. "I don't suppose another few minutes will matter either way. But you bring him back, you hear me? Deep purses can be closed as well as opened, remember, and I'm none too happy at the moment."

The earl inclined his head slightly. "Thank you, dear lady. You are the epitome of graciousness, I suppose. Now, Dante, push me out of here and turn to the right. We'll go to the library."

"But my wife—"

"If we're lucky, no permanent damage will have been done. If we're not, it will be impossible for us to do anything but more harm. Sarah Jane will be better served if you stay away from her, at least until you and I have discussed a few things. Now come on, before Audrey takes it into her head to join us."

Secretly happy to have been rescued from having to approach his wife, Dante took hold of the handles of the Bath chair and pushed his brother from the drawing room. As they made their way through the foyer and along the curving corridor that led to the central structure of the house, Dante was struck by the simple elegance of Cliff Walk, though he was disappointed that nothing looked familiar to him.

"This is a lovely estate," he said as the earl directed him through a room furnished almost entirely in red, then another large chamber, and finally into the darkly paneled library. "Has it been in the family long?"

"Long enough for us to have run it nearly into the ground. Until you and Sarah Jane married, that is. Pour us each a drink, will you?"

Dante looked around, then located the drinks table which was laden with cut-glass decanters. He frowned, something about the table bothering him. "I don't think I like spirits," he said, pouring only a single glass of wine.

"Hah! You mean you don't like seeing them at Cliff Walk. You ordered all the bottles locked up except at the dinner hour because of Johnny's tippling. Remember?"

Dante handed the glass to his brother, then retreated to the dark blue leather couch, sat down wearily, and rubbed his temples. "That's right. Audrey said Lord John drinks."

"*Lord* John, as you call him, *drank*. He no longer drinks, in part because of you, but mostly, I believe, because of Sarah Jane."

"I don't understand." Dante felt a momentary tightening of his stomach muscles, a reaction to the earl's words that, if he could believe the sensation, felt akin to jealousy. How could he be jealous of Lord John? He had no feelings for his wife one way or the other. She was simply another person with a face but no recognizable features, another part of the life he could not remember.

The earl took a drink of wine, then cupped the glass between his hands. "I'm not surprised, and wouldn't be, even if you hadn't taken that wound to your head. Sarah Jane has astonished us all. We thought you had wed a little mouse, but she has a way about her, a quiet strength and quite the most engaging manner. She brought happiness into my orbit, daring to beard me in my own den and shake me back into life, into living. It is difficult to be in her presence without wishing to do something for her, make her smile. You've met Elizabeth Trowbridge, Dante. Even with no memory of her, you must have seen that she is an encroaching, smothering sort of female. It took some time for Sarah Jane to begin breathing, once she came into her role as mistress of Cliff Walk, but her good heart and cheerful manner have won out, in turn, winning us all."

"Especially Lord John?" Dante asked, his left temple beginning to throb.

"*Including* Johnny, Dante. There's a difference. They're like children together, and Emma and I have encouraged their friendship during your absence. They've been good for each other. Nothing more."

"Emma?" Dante repeated, rising and beginning to pace the unfamiliar room. He stopped in front of the heavily carved wooden desk, sensing without knowing why that he had sat there many times. The image of papers, many, many complicated papers, came to him. Papers. And problems. Suddenly, without warning, he felt the weight of the world descend upon his shoulders, the responsibility for that world nearly sending him to his knees while at the same time making him long to run for his life, his freedom. But why did he feel that way? Why?

"Yes, *Emma*. My very good friend. The woman, the *one* woman, I have ever loved. Look, Dante, I know this has been a lot for you to endure today, meeting all of us as if for the first time, Sarah Jane's lengthy swoon, Mrs. Trowbridge —all of it. I probably should leave this for another time, but I have to ask. What has Audrey told you about us?"

Dante turned toward his brother, leaning back against the desk, his hands stroking the warm wood. "She has told me who you all are," he said carefully. "Who I am." *You are my own true love.* He could hear Audrey's words inside his head, knowing he would have to leave them there. It wasn't the sort of thing one said to one's brother, especially when that brother was a cripple, tied forever to a Bath chair, unable to be a husband. Even if that brother had just admitted to being in love with another woman. "That's all. The doctor said not to rush things. Too many facts being pushed upon me might trigger a brain fever, I believe he said. He is not sure that my memory will ever return."

"That's a pity, Dante. I wanted to tell you everything. Audrey has never got the straight of anything in her life. She sees things only as they relate to her. There's a gleam visible today in her usually vacant eyes that I cannot like, although she hasn't the brains for any sort of intrigue. Or a motive either, now that I think of it. But I imagine a longer talk will have to wait until you are further recovered physically, and for now we shall have to deal with what Audrey has already disclosed. I suppose she told you that we all cheerfully despise one another?"

Dante picked up a glass paperweight shaped like Pegasus and balanced it in his hand. "And do we?" he asked, looking straight into the earl's clear blue eyes. Both of his brothers had blue eyes and light hair. It was difficult to believe that he, who was so dark, could be related to either of them. "Do we cheerfully despise one another?"

"Occasionally," Tyler Muir answered, grinning. "Mostly, we've made a career of despising ourselves, although both Johnny and I have made positive inroads on our failings of late, amending our sorry lives. But that story, too, will wait for another day. You must be exhausted from your journey. For now I wish only to assure myself that you understand your feelings for your wife, for that poor child you recently shattered with your overly polite greeting after an absence of seven months. I think—I believe—that you loved her. That she loves you."

Dante replaced the Pegasus on the desktop. The earl was

right. He was very weary. And his head was near to splitting. "You *believe* so? You're not certain?"

The earl motioned for Dante to take the handles to the Bath chair in preparation for their return to the family drawing room. "Is anyone certain about anything, dear brother? Was that doctor in Brussels positive that your memory would never return? Was Audrey, dear Audrey, accurate in her descriptions of your family, of your life? If you are truly without any memory, if you can be sure of nothing, how can you believe my wife? Or will you put your trust in the evidence before your own eyes? For myself, I am certain of only one thing. That thing, Dante, brother or no brother, injured or whole, is that I will most definitely punish you if you hurt Sarah Jane."

"Welcome home, Dante," Dante said on a sigh as he pushed the earl's chair back along the route they had taken from the family wing. "Welcome home."

CHAPTER 12

*Were it not better to forget
Than but remember and regret?*

Letitia Elizabeth Landon

I haven't seen him since I fainted and spent the remainder of the day with Mildred fussing over me. He passed the night in one of the guest bedchambers," Sarah Jane said, accepting tea from her friend Emma as they sat in the fully refurbished round saloon early the next morning, away from the rest of the family. Babbitt had brought them refreshments, then prudently closed the doors as he left them alone.

The saloon had a pinkish glow in the morning sun. The freshly reupholstered custom-designed rounded-backed chairs that hugged the curved walls added a sense of coziness to the large room, as did the freshly cleaned round carpet. Clutches of bleached wood tables and chairs were arranged tastefully for conversation, and a half dozen statues gleamed in their niches among the wall paintings. The room reflected taste, charm, relaxed formality, and Sarah Jane's eye for understated beauty.

Emma was dressed today in somber gray, in direct contrast to the sunny saloon, clad as if in mourning for her relationship with the earl, her hair tied back severely, her expression solemn. "That may have been for the best,

Sarah," she said, sitting back against the cushions. "You've both suffered a major shock. It took some time for Ty and me to bridge the years that had separated us. You and Dante will doubtless have to go through a similar, if more extensive, readjustment."

Sarah Jane pressed a hand to her mouth, once more forcing back tears. "Oh, Emma, whatever am I to do? He doesn't know me. He doesn't remember me. He has no memory, yet he has a wife, a child. It's all so impossible, so tragic."

"Yes, rather like something out of a Gothic novel," Emma agreed, smiling encouragingly. "Just the sort of thing you delighted in imagining. Until now, I suppose. But you will get past this, Sarah, I assure you. Dante loved you once. He will love you again. How could he not?"

In the silence that followed Emma's question, Sarah Jane believed she could hear her own heart breaking. "He—he didn't . . . He doesn't—" She sighed. "Oh, what is the use? There is nothing left now but the truth. Emma, Dante has never loved me."

Emma abruptly sat forward once more, Sarah Jane's declaration bringing a frown to her usually placid features. "What are you saying?"

Sarah Jane was so embarrassed, near to collapsing under the weight of her despair. "Oh, Emma, it was all wishful thinking on my part. *Supposing,* as Johnny might term it. I've been living a dream, spinning fantasies of happiness from a few encouraging actions, gleaning hope from Dante's infrequent letters. But now that dream is over."

"You're overset, Sarah," Emma said, going to the younger woman and sitting down beside her, placing her arm comfortingly around her shoulder. "I know Dante cares for you. Ty told me about a letter he received from his brother, detailing how he wished you to be cared for in the event he died in battle. That is not the action of an uncaring man."

"No, but it is the action of a gentleman," Sarah Jane pointed out. "I never said that Dante was cruel or unfeeling. Just that he doesn't love me. He was simply trying to make the best of a situation he could not change. But now—now he *can* change it. He may even have forgotten me on purpose. Heaven knows he hasn't had much in his life save the trials and tribulations of riding herd on his family, attempting to save Cliff Walk, and learning to deal with the butcher's naive, socially unacceptable granddaughter who was forced upon him. Why would he want to remember any of that? Who would expect him to remain married to a woman he cannot even remember?"

"Hummph! I never heard of such foolishness. The man's swimming in nearly the deepest gravy boat in all England. He would have to be mad to want to forget *that* fact!"

Both Sarah Jane and Emma turned toward Elizabeth Trowbridge's booming voice, to see the woman stalking toward them, her words still echoing up under the large dome.

"Grandmother?" Sarah Jane saw that, after a week of navigating on her own, her grandmother had once more taken to using her cane, a sign that she, too, had suffered a setback thanks to yesterday's excitement. "I didn't know you were up and about." *Or eavesdropping,* she concluded mentally.

"Up, about, and thinking nineteen to the dozen, sweetie," Mrs. Trowbridge pronounced, easing her bulk into the chair so lately vacated by Emma. "Got quite a fortune riding on that addled husband of yours, you know. Now, this is how I see it. We give him a week or two—oh, all right, a month, for I'm not a heartless woman—and then we have Curtis lock him away someplace, with the other lunatics. For the right figure, Curtis will do anything I say."

"Dante is *not* insane!" Sarah Jane pulled herself free of Emma's restraining hands and pushed herself to her feet. "He has suffered a wound to the head that has robbed him of his memory. Nothing more!"

"Nothing more? God's teeth, sweetie, isn't that enough? You'd think he'd twisted an ankle, to hear you tell it. Or wasn't that you I heard whimpering when I came in here?" Mrs. Trowbridge questioned her with a quick toss of her purple-turbaned head. "This is business, little girl, and my bailiwick, not yours. He can still be earl once Tyler has stuck his spoon in the wall—and don't you look at me that way, Mrs. Franklin, for between you and that featherheaded wife of his pulling both ways on him it's a marvel he ain't already underground. Now, we English are not so blockheaded as to allow a little dottiness to strip a man of his title, but Dante will never succeed to Curtis's position. That will be left to your son, sweetie. In the meantime, I want Dante locked up where he can't hurt anybody."

"Get out," Sarah Jane commanded coldly, although she was trembling so violently she was sure she would soon have to sit down once more before she fell down. "Get out of this room, get out of this house, *get out of our lives!*"

"Hush, dear, you'll injure the babe," Emma warned, rising to slip an arm around Sarah Jane's waist. "Mrs. Trowbridge? You are a woman who obviously loves her only grandchild, and I believe you're convinced you are acting in her best interests. However, I suggest you do as your granddaughter says, or else I won't be responsible for the consequences. Those consequences, if you should wonder what they are, have a great deal to do with my beating you severely about the head and shoulders with your own cane. Like you, I make no pretense of being a lady, and thus fainthearted, and I harbor no qualms about saying precisely what is on my mind. May I feel confident that I have made myself understood?"

Ignoring Emma, Mrs. Trowbridge used the cane to boost herself to her full imposing height. Sarah Jane could not look at her. "Sweetie, listen to me. We have to think with our heads now, not our hearts. I didn't raise you to be a romantic fiddle-faddler. You're a practical soul. There are legal matters to be considered now, papers to be drawn up, arrangements to be made—"

"The cane, Mrs. Trowbridge," Emma reminded the woman, taking a single step forward. "I'm smaller than you, I admit, but younger and stronger, and not one to make idle threats. Rest assured that your granddaughter will be in good hands as long as I have breath in my body. Now go, please."

Sarah Jane collapsed onto the couch once more as her

grandmother, still blustering, at last left the room, and began weeping quietly against Emma's breast, wishing she could be as strong as her friend, wishing she could be a heroine in more than domestic matters, wishing she were the sort to act rather than merely to dream, wishing she could wave a magic wand and be everything Dante needed to make him whole again.

"And that's the tree I tumbled out of after you chased me up it, swearing to have my liver and lights if I ever again took out your horse without asking. You said I was lucky not to have snapped my neck riding that ripping great stallion, but instead I ended up breaking my arm when I fell. Father caned the two of us with a will, as I recall, then gave Ty a few good whacks as well, saying he must have done something to deserve it at one time or another. Don't you remember?"

Dante shook his head. He and Lord John had been walking about the estate for over an hour, his younger brother stopping every few paces to recall moments out of their shared past. None of them seemed in the least familiar to Dante.

Dante had not passed an easy night, unable to lose the image of Sarah Jane's haunted eyes, the vision of her tragic expression as last he had seen her yesterday afternoon in the family drawing room. Of all the hurt his loss of memory had caused him, this knowledge that he was bringing pain to that innocent woman was the worst.

"Why don't I look more like you and Tyler?" he asked after another uncomfortable silence had brought them back inside the family wing. He found it impossible to believe that these people were only pretending that he was a member of their family, for there was, after all, no reason for such a subterfuge, but it was an idea that refused to die.

He had no memory of them, no feeling for them save a small pity. Audrey had already shown herself to be shallow and, if he could believe his own instincts, somewhat of a liar. How was he to know what was true and what was fabrication? The fact that he supposedly was quite wealthy and the only one with control of the Muir purse strings, did not serve to soothe his mind. How could he know who was out to tell him the truth and who might see a way to advance his own fortunes by inventing a past in which that one person was the only one Dante supposedly had ever truly cared for?

"Why don't you look like Ty and me? That's easy enough to answer, Dante. Come with me to the family drawing room. There are portraits of both our parents there. Ty and I look like our father, poor us, and you resemble Mama. Don't worry if you can't remember much about her. She died years ago, before the worst of it."

"The worst of what?" Dante looked about as they progressed to the drawing room, some of the furnishings giving him a vague, eerie feeling of recognition but the whole, the entirety of Cliff Walk still seeming alien to him, unrecognizable.

"Why, the decline and fall of the Muirs, of course. Rome had nothing on us, even if Gibbon didn't live long enough to catalog our moral and financial dismembering," Lord John answered amicably. "We lived in the most elegant hovel in all the British Isles—until you married Sarah Jane, of course. Ah, Dante, the miracle that little angel has wrought, she and all that lovely money! You wouldn't have recognized Cliff Walk even if you had returned from Brussels without your brains scrambled by that Frenchie bullet. A pure domestic goddess, that's our Sarah Jane. I wonder, were you a hero at Waterloo? Hardly worth it if you weren't, don't you think, especially with your man, Lowell, dying and all? Gad, how I wish I could have been with you, but I was still living in a bottle then, and couldn't go. Now, here, see the portraits? That's our mother. Lovely, wasn't she?"

Dante stared into the eyes of the two complete strangers in the large portraits placed side by side on the freshly painted ivory walls. The man, his father, looked very like Tyler, his grin boyish, his eyes alive with the joy of living. "Is that me?" he asked, pointing to the dark-haired child of no more than three who sat on a small stool at the woman's knees. She was a beautiful woman, more handsome than pretty, actually, whose hair and eyes were as dark as his own.

"Yes. You're on the left, and Ty is standing beside her. I was there, I believe, just not yet visible, if you take my meaning. There was no money for another portrait once I was born, but I am told I was a beautiful child."

Lord John turned away from the portraits as Babbitt entered the drawing room carrying a tray containing two glasses and a pitcher of iced lemonade. "Ah, here is some refreshment. Sarah Jane cunningly keeps me from growing too thirsty, and thus away from temptation. If it were possible for men to give birth, I should think I would soon be presenting the world with a litter of lemons. Would you care for any? Lemonade, that is, not the pick of the litter."

Dante followed his brother to the tray that the butler had placed on a low table and sat across from Lord John. His fanciful thoughts of not really being Dante Muir had been satisfied at last with the sight of that portrait. He was Dante Muir, even if he didn't remember it, and he had no choice but to accept that fact. It was good to know *something*.

"Will the child be coming soon?" he asked, Lord John's banter reminding him of his wife's delicate condition. He asked the question merely so that he would know something more about Sarah Jane. He refused, or so he told himself, to believe he was, like Audrey, planning to count on his fingers.

"Sometime near the end of August, or so I've heard," Lord John told him, sitting back at his ease, crossing one long leg over the other, and raising the glass of lemonade to his lips. "Plenty of time for the two of you to get to know each other again. Plaguey awkward, ain't it, having a pregnant wife and not remembering her? And you really don't remember, do you? There were times, when I was drinking everything but the ink from the pots on the desk, that I found myself unable to remember things I'd done. Frightening," he said, exaggeratedly shuddering. "Damned frightening. I used to drink twice as much, just to forget how frightened I was. Do you suppose that would work? Could we give you another little nick on the head, just to see if a second brain-ringing would jog you into remembering?"

Dante raised a hand to the bandage that still covered his wound. "I'd rather not risk it, thank you, Johnny," he said, smiling, and beginning to like Lord John very much. "The doctor said I may never remember. Much as I'd like to prove him wrong, I am not yet so desperate as to open myself to another injury. Sorry."

Lord John gave a dismissive wave of his hand. "Not to worry. I've given up trying to solve other people's problems. And blaming myself for them, come to that. Nearly drove poor Ty mad, you know, attempting to startle him into getting up from that damned chair after his riding accident. But now . . . Well, we'll leave that for the moment, for it's Ty's story, and not mine. Are you fatigued? Or shall we continue on with our little tour?"

"Actually, Johnny, I should like to see my wife now," Dante answered, knowing he had put off this second bound-to-be-traumatic meeting longer than he should have, considering the disastrous effect he'd had on her at their initial encounter. "Do you suppose you might know where she might be found at this time of day?"

"I used to suppose a lot of things, Dante, but then you wouldn't remember that, either, would you?" Lord John rose, pressing a finger to his lips as he eyed the mantel clock. "Let's see. Little Sarah is fairly regular in her habits. As it's just gone two, I should say she is still at work on her latest project. Yes, that's it. You'll find her in the chapel. You do remember where it is, don't you? I pointed it out to you when we walked around the house. Most exercise I've had without a horse under me in weeks!"

"I'll find it," Dante replied, already heading out of the drawing room. "Thanks, Johnny. I appreciate all your help."

"Think nothing of it, brother mine," Lord John replied, pointing Dante in the correct direction as he followed him into the hallway. "Be good to her. You're a lucky devil, Dante," he added, clapping him on the shoulder, his eyes suddenly sad. "It's a pity you don't remember why."

Lord John's parting words echoed in Dante's head as, after a series of wrong turns, he at last made his way down the curved corridor that led to the chapel. Was his wife the heavenly creature his brothers had portrayed? She certainly looked the part of an angel. But how could he explain away his first sight of her, kissing his brother? How could he explain Audrey's declaration that he and she were lovers, had been lovers for years? The earl certainly had no interest in his wife, even associated publicly with another woman. Who could he believe? The two men he had just met or the woman who, in the past few weeks, had become his only memory?

He stood back as three maids exited the chapel, buckets of dirty water in their hands, giggling conspiratorially as they saw him, dropping awkward curtsies, then rushing away. He couldn't blame them. He and his strange condition had probably become quite the most exciting topic of conversation at Cliff Walk in a decade, and as he had already learned, this was not a quiet household. Taking a deep, steadying breath, he entered the small vestibule, pausing until his eyes became accustomed to a dimness broken only by the faint prisms of light filtering in through the stained-glass windows.

And then he saw her.

She was standing with her back to him on the raised altar, a mere dab of a girl with an enormous apron tied beneath her breasts and a white cloth swathing her head. There was a bucket beside her on the floor and she was leaning forward, busily scrubbing the intricately carved wooden altarpiece. He could see her slim, well-turned ankles as she struggled to reach across the marble altar, one leg bent at the knee, as if to help her balance.

"Should you be doing that?" he asked after a moment, having silently made his way to the front of the chapel, knowing he had to announce himself in some way. "I mean, I just saw three maids leaving here. Why didn't they clean the altar?"

She turned so swiftly that he had to step forward to catch her before she fell, the feel of her soft, small, slim upper arms against his palms decidedly unnerving. Almost as unnerving as seeing again the swelling of her belly beneath her huge apron, the sign of an advanced pregnancy that he had caused. Almost as unnerving as the startled expression in her large brown eyes as she looked up at him before quickly disengaging herself and averting her gaze as if she were afraid of him.

"Cloris and the others are competent," she explained at last in a small voice, "but they will always miss a spot or two. Grandmother Trowbridge always said that a good mistress cannot be afraid of a little hard work, not if she expects the best from her servants. But I suppose you're correct, Dante. I should have called them back. How—how are you feeling today? You look very well."

"I am reasonably sound, I suppose," he answered, picking up the cloth she had let fall and dropping it into the bucket, "for a man who wakes every morning not knowing who he is. At least this morning I know where I am. I'm home." He looked at Sarah Jane's bowed head, wondering if she could feel the tension between them. Tension caused by the evidence of the child they had made together. Tension due to the knowledge that one of them could not even remember the night of conception. "Are you happy I'm home again, Sarah Jane?"

"Sarah," she corrected softly, raising her expressive eyes to his, as if apologizing for having to tell him something he should know. "You—you had agreed to call me Sarah. And yes, Dante," she ended in the formal words of an obedient child parroting a lesson, "I am prodigiously glad that you have come home."

Dante smiled, a knot that he had not realized had taken up residence in his chest slowly easing, so that, for the first time in a long time, he felt nearly human. "Thank you, *Sarah.*" He looked around the chapel, frowning as he spied out the wolf's head hanging on the back wall. "This isn't the most cheery spot at Cliff Walk, is it?"

Sarah Jane walked down the two small steps and sat in the first pew. "We were married here," she said simply, folding her hands over her expanded stomach. Then, just as he was about to apologize for his faux pas, she smiled, adding, "And you're right. It isn't remarkably cheerful. But the roof no longer gives the worshipers a clear view of the sky, which is something, I suppose."

He joined her on the unyielding wooden pew, the two of them looking forward to the altar as if a clergyman were there, about to deliver his sermon, the tension between them now nearly a visible thing. "Was it a fine ceremony?"

"Our wedding?" He sensed her shaking her head. "It was dreadful. I'm almost glad you can't remember it. I wore Grandmother Trowbridge's gown, which reeked of camphor, and her veil, which was longer twice over than I am tall. Actually, I'm still amazed you didn't take one look at me and run screaming from the estate, which certainly couldn't be important enough for you to sacrifice yourself by marrying such a dreary, dowdy creature."

"Not a sacrifice, surely. I married you for your grandmother's money, or so I've gleaned. That knowledge does not serve to make me admire the man I was."

She shifted on the pew, placing a small hand on his forearm. "Oh, no, Dante," she said fervently, looking up at him. "Don't ever think that. You are the best of men—kind, caring, and endlessly generous, remarkably charitable and unselfish—but Grandmother Trowbridge is a clever, astute businesswoman who always gets what she wants. She wanted you, and left you no choice, knowing how dearly you loved your family and Cliff Walk. You do know that she made you a very rich man, don't you? Rich enough to set Cliff Walk to rights, rich enough to keep your family in the manner in which they should be kept."

"If you're trying to comfort me, Sarah, I suggest you find another avenue of attack. No man of honor, no man of conscience, would marry for money. I may not know who I am, but I have a reasonable sense of what it means to be a gentleman."

She was silent for some moments, her hands once more in her lap, her posture rigid. "You made me happy," she said at last, her voice so quiet he had to lean toward her to hear her words. She turned to him once more, so that he could see tears standing in her eyes. Her huge soft brown eyes. Her hurt, trusting eyes. The most eloquent eyes he had ever seen. "Does that count for anything, Dante?"

He dropped his head into his hands. "I don't know,

Sarah," he admitted, hating to hurt her but unable to begin his new life with a lie. "I suppose it does. Yes, yes, of course it does. It means I'm not a complete monster, doesn't it?"

He sliced a look at her out of the corner of his eye and was gratified to see her smile. "And we're soon to have a baby," he added, quietly marveling at this miracle. "That also means something. A new life. A new beginning."

"You—you spoke of a new beginning between us. Once you were home again."

"Did I?" Dante felt vaguely uncomfortable. The niggling thought that he had somehow hurt this small creature turned his blood cold. "What had I done wrong in the marriage, to be speaking of new beginnings?"

"Nothing!" she exclaimed, and he knew she was lying. *She was never very good at lying* He blinked, hearing the voice inside his head telling him something about this woman he did not know, could not remember knowing, loving. But surely he'd had some feelings for her. A man would have to be deaf and blind not to recognize her goodness, her purity, her innocent seduction even as she was swollen with child.

Seductive? She was almost painfully pregnant. How could he consider her seductive? Yet even with the apron, the scarf hiding her hair, the single smudge of dirt on her cheek, she was the most heartbreakingly beautiful creature he could ever hope to see. So small. So fragile. Huge eyes, a most intriguing, cleanly sculpted jawline, an incredibly long, enticingly slender throat. A full, inviting mouth. A softly swelling bosom.

He had married for money? He had allowed this lovely, innocent girl to become a sacrifice to greed, to an old woman's desire for social advantage, and to his own wish for a fortune? That was difficult to accept, but he had to accept it. But if he had then gone on to hurt the woman he had married? That would be insupportable, unforgivable!

He took her hands in his, anxious for her to say more. "Tell me, Sarah," he said, his voice husky with a passion for the truth, a dread of that truth. "What did I do that I don't want to remember? Has it anything to do with Audrey?"

"Audrey?" She tried to pull her hands free, but he wouldn't let her. "I don't understand. What has Audrey to do with anything?"

"I don't know," he lied quickly, refusing to tell her what might not be the truth and thus cause her even more pain. He needed to speak with Audrey again, beat the truth out of her if he had to, because he couldn't believe that he would have been such a cad as to have an affair with his crippled brother's wife. "I just suspect that nobody at Cliff Walk likes Audrey very much. Even Tyler. Especially Tyler."

"Audrey is . . ." She hesitated, sighing, then continued. "Oh, dear. I hadn't thought how difficult it would be to tell you all you have forgotten. After all, most of what I could say is only my own opinion, which may or may not be correct. Audrey . . . I believe she means well. It's just that she usually means well for Audrey."

Dante felt his mouth lifting in an amused one-sided smile. "That's very diplomatically said, Sarah. And I believe I understand. She wasn't a very sympathetic nurse in Brussels, constantly bemoaning the fact that my man, this person called Lowell, had 'gotten himself killed' so that he couldn't minister to me and allow her to return to London. In the beginning, as I recall it, she had no intention of accompanying me to Cliff Walk. It was only . . ." he hesitated, realizing exactly when it was that Audrey's treatment of him had changed, becoming almost loverlike. It was the same day the doctor informed them that Dante's memory would most probably never return.

He shook his head. "But enough of Audrey. I'm home now, home with my wife, my brothers. I should be thinking of the future. *Our* future. Ours and our child's."

"Thank you, Dante. I have so hoped, these past months, and then—Oh dear, look at me," she said in a rapid flurry of speech, "sitting here as if I had nothing better to do, leaving Cloris and the others to their own devices, which is the same as saying Cloris and the others are doing *nothing*. I must go!"

Sarah Jane's blush was a delight to watch as he helped her to her feet, even if her suddenly hopeful expression told him he might be promising more than he could deliver. He didn't know this woman, no matter how well she might know him, and he wasn't in love with her. He might never be in love with her.

He would have to get to know her, learn everything about her, forget that theirs had been an arranged marriage, and concentrate on making her happy. He owed her that. He didn't know much, but he was confident that he owed this small woman-child something that had very little to do with the money she had brought to Cliff Walk. Why he believed this wasn't yet firm in his mind, but his brothers had made it clear that Sarah was important to all of them and to their happiness, that her advent into their lives had changed them all for the better. His brothers certainly didn't appear to be the bitter, dispirited men Audrey had described.

"I will see you at the dinner table, won't I?" he asked as he took up the bucket, not wanting Sarah Jane to carry it in her delicate condition

He followed her back down the short aisle of the chapel and into the curved corridor leading to the state chambers. "Yes, of course, Dante," she answered, touching her face just where that most intriguing smut of dirt smudged her cheek. "And I promise to look more presentable by then, truly."

"You are eminently presentable now, Sarah," he told her honestly.

A maidservant met them halfway down the hall, quickly taking the bucket from him and clucking her tongue at her mistress as if to say that it was a good thing someone was looking after her or there'd be no knowing what sort of mischief she'd get herself into, and in her condition, too!

"And by the way, Sarah," he added, hanging back as Sarah Jane made to follow after the maid, a hand pressed to the center of her spine as if she had a backache, "I am convinced you were a most beautiful bride."

CHAPTER 13

What I have been taught I have forgotten; what I know I have guessed.

Charles Maurice de Talleyrand-Périgord

Dante, at loose ends after watching Sarah Jane go off with the maid and unable to find either of his brothers, made his way to the library, the one place at Cliff Walk where he felt somewhat less alien, more at home.

Feeling uncomfortingly like a common thief rummaging through another person's belongings, he sat behind the desk and began going through the drawers, not knowing what he was looking for, but urged on by some nagging suspicion that he might discover some recognizable part of himself there.

He found dozens of papers, closely written notes concerning the estate, and several large journals listing expenses and income. Putting the papers to one side, he began paging through the journals, taking note of a succession of varying styles of handwriting until the previous year, when the same bold, dark hand he had seen earlier in the journal and that was evident on the notes appeared to have taken over completely.

But the entries for the current year were done in an

unmistakably feminine hand. Surely his wife, the young woman both Ty and Johnny had claimed to be a near miracle worker, had not also taken over the running of the entire estate? It seemed impossible, and fairly damning of his brothers. Surely they could have eased the burden Sarah Jane was carrying, and they *should* have done so if they were as fond of her as they claimed to be. Why, he had found her in the chapel, wielding a cleaning cloth! Even during her advancing pregnancy, the Muir men had not seen fit to take charge, to ease the worries and the responsibilities that could easily bring low a spirit more indomitable than that of the gentle creature who was his wife.

"Useless, selfish, and quite possibly depraved." That was how Audrey had described his father and brothers to him, and Dante was beginning to suspect that she had been close to the mark. If, as Johnny had said, Sarah Jane had wrought a miracle at Cliff Walk, was it only because she had made it possible for the Muirs to continue on in their usual pursuits while at the same time making their lives more comfortable?

Were his father and brothers all rotters of the first water? And what did that make him—the man who had married the young, eager-to-please Miss Moneybags in the first place?

As Dante closed the ledgers and replaced them in the drawer, he noticed a paper that had slid partway out of a slim leather portfolio bearing the initials D.E.M. Realizing that the page bore the same distinctive handwriting he'd seen in the journals and on the small mountain of notes, he sat back in the chair and began reading, planning simply to scan it, then place it with the scribblings about drainage and livestock estimates.

His nonchalance was short-lived, ending almost as soon as it began, for it became almost immediately apparent that this damning paper contained reminders of a late November communication directed to a London solicitor. The notes concerned the possibility of obtaining a discrete bill of divorcement for "two persons joined in matrimony for monetary consideration and subsequently found to be universally incompatible. Blame for the dissolution will most certainly be shouldered, willingly, by the husband in consideration of his wife's reputation."

Dante read the page twice, then rifled through the desk until he had found a clean sheet of paper. He took up a pen from the holder on the desktop and began copying the note, writing quickly, then compared his handwriting with that on the other paper. It was the same. Not fairly similar, but exactly the same. He had written in the ledgers. He had made all the neat notations concerning drainage and other such matters. And *he* had written the letter to the London solicitor, only shortly after his marriage to Sarah Jane Trowbridge.

The knowledge served to make him slightly sick to his stomach.

"There you are, you silly thing, hiding yourself away in this depressing room when we could have taken a drive to the village or gone strolling down near the pond. Ah, the fond memories I have of those days when we slipped away to the pond and hid behind the bushes, giggling like small, naughty children, even though we knew Ty could not follow after us. Dante? Whatever could be wrong that you should be frowning so? Is your poor head aching again?"

Dante watched silently as Audrey swept into the library, her sunshine yellow gown and golden hair making her an artist's vision of English beauty. He rose until she seated herself on the blue couch, leaning against one arm of it, her legs tucked up on the seat, rather like a kitten curling up for a nap. "We were lovers here? At Cliff Walk?" he asked, hating himself for the man he had been. "Not in London?"

"London? As if I could tear you away from your dreary fascination with this estate. Of course you did send me away occasionally, to our town house in Mayfair, fearing that Ty would one day discover us. You *will* persist in thinking of others, although they wish nothing more of you than that you sacrifice yourself so that they can live high. As I was sacrificed to Ty almost seven years ago."

"Somehow, Audrey, your description of me as the sort who thinks of others is fairly damning, don't you think?"

"Hardly, darling, considering the circumstances. Your bride, if you recall, is about to present you with your brother's child. Dante, I don't know how long I can stay here under such conditions. Not with your memory gone. Not when you had promised me so much."

"And exactly what did I promise you, Audrey?" he asked, folding his hands on the desktop, carefully covering the notes of the letter to the London solicitor. "As you said, my memory is gone."

Audrey snuggled more deeply against the pillows of the couch, smiling artlessly. "Why, to be my own true love, silly, precisely as I've already told you. You've seen Ty now, seen how thin and crippled he is. He has been in a steady decline since the accident. It won't be long before he is underground, poor creature. And then, once you are shed of the little mouse, we can be married, travelling the world with all her lovely money. But if you disappoint me now, I do not believe I can stay here, watching you but never having you, never touching you. How you loved me once, Dante! To think that I had to listen to you recount the bedding of that encroaching creature, even though you swore to me that you did not enjoy the exercise. As she did not, for I was likewise forced to endure a recitation of her horror at the marital act. That she should throw away the man I desire most—and for a looby like Johnny!"

She shuddered and lifted a lace-edged handkerchief to her mouth, sniffling a single time, as if trying not to weep. "Oh, the cruelty, the utter unfairness of it all!"

Dante felt the paper beneath his hands growing hot, as if it were about to burst into flame, like the damning fires of hell come to consume him. "And how was I supposed to rid myself of the *little mouse,* Audrey?"

"Why, a divorce, of course. We did discuss the notion of impregnating her, small as she is, and praying for a tragic childbed death, but we both knew we could not pin all our hopes on any such fortunate chance, even though that crude harridan had promised another fortune upon the birth of an heir. In the end you thought divorce would be best, although I believe such bills are horrendously difficult to procure. We will soon know if one is needed, won't we, as she is due to whelp in six weeks. At least Johnny was finally good for something!"

So small. So tight. Someone was whispering in Dante's ear, saying things that were somehow familiar. *Unsuitable for lovemaking. Dangerous in childbirth.* Bile rose in his throat.

Dante didn't know where to look, how to react, what to say. "Rather coldhearted of us, isn't it, Audrey?" he asked at last, remembering Sarah Jane's soft brown eyes, her low, almost sultry voice, the expression of absolute trust as she looked at him in the chapel. "If I didn't know better, I'd say I was a bastard of the most enormous proportions, even if I were speaking as a man madly in love with his crippled brother's wife, *especially* because of Ty's condition and Sarah Jane's obvious innocence."

Audrey rose from the couch, allowing him a glimpse of her perfect calves as she swung them to the floor. "Why, of course you're a bastard, Dante," she said happily, going over to him and dropping a kiss on his temple. "You are, after all, a Muir. But now I must go, else I won't have time to complete my toilette before the dinner gong is rung. I won't pester you ever again with my agony over our sad dilemma. I shall leave you alone, to sort it all out."

"Are you issuing some sort of ultimatum, Audrey?"

"Heavens no. I await only your decision, and would never force myself upon you. If you wish to break off our association, I shall be devastated but, loving you, I shall have to accept whatever financial settlement you may make upon me. Then I'll go back to Mayfair and pick up the pieces of my life. If you love me, we can begin again where we left off the night of Lady Richmond's ball. Just remember, dearest Dante, that I am the only person in the world who cared enough to come to Brussels, cared enough to be near you as you bravely rode into battle. Surely that must tell you something?"

Dante had just opened his mouth to say something noncommittal when suddenly there was a noise at the door and Lord John burst into the room, his eyes alive with excitement.

"Here you are! And you, too, Audrey. Funny. I didn't know you could read, or would wish to even if you could. Isn't it time you were primping for dinner? You should, you know, for the patriarch has come. Can you believe it, Dante? Our dear father has torn himself away from London long enough to visit his offspring, and with only two fully loaded coaches to hold his new wardrobe."

"Curtis is here?"

"Who did you think I meant, Audrey? The king? I tell you, Dante, I am nearly unmanned by the marquess's concern for us. Either that or it was his waistcoat that brought me to the brink of tears. It's pink, if you can believe that! Or could it be he is home because he is badly dipped and in need of an advance on his allowance? The latter, I suspect. Is it possible that he thought you had perished in battle and the Trowbridge fortune was now his by default? The truth must have given him quite a turn—your survival, that is. But come on, Dante. Don't just sit there staring at me as if *I* were wearing a pink waistcoat. Father's got Ty cornered in the drawing room, and I won't be responsible for either of their heads if I don't get back soon to rescue our brother."

Another Muir. And an equally complicated, equally unlovely one as well. Dante suddenly felt extremely weary and, surprisingly, wishful of having Sarah Jane at his side when he was introduced to his father. He didn't know why, but her calming presence, her sweet confidence, seemed very necessary to him now. And her good opinion of him. He needed to look into her eyes and see himself reflected as a lovable human being and not the heartless, grasping ogre Audrey had portrayed him to be, as the unfeeling bastard the letter on the desk forever condemned him to be.

"There!" Audrey exclaimed, clapping her hands in delight, as if she had accomplished a unique party trick and expected applause. "I *told* you that I had written to the family. How else do you think Curtis could have gotten here

245

so quickly, if it wasn't for my note, urgently begging him to come to Cliff Walk?" She smiled sweetly. "I may be wrong, Dante, but I believe you just might owe me a *tiny* apology. That, and an admission that I am not the sort to tell fibs."

Lord John looked confused. "What's she rambling on about, Dante? Oh, never mind. If I were to attempt to decipher everything she says, I'd be back to drinking again before nightfall. Come on, we mustn't keep our dear father waiting. He might take it into his head to stuff his pockets with some of the pretty little figurines and things with which Sarah has decorated the drawing room. Father was always one to know the value of sentiment on the open market."

"You go on, Johnny, and take Audrey with you, if you please. I want to clean up this mess I've made on the desk. I'll only be a minute."

"All right, Dante. I still have to scare up Sarah Jane anyway. Not that she'll be overjoyed to see her dear father-in-law. I've just remembered how she last saw him nearly nine months ago. Remind me to tell you about that, Dante. It's a dashed funny story! Gad, but I love that girl!"

"Yes, Johnny, *we know*," Audrey said, blowing a kiss to Dante as Lord John turned his back. "Do hurry, Dante. Curtis will be overjoyed to see you."

Once he was alone, Dante took the note concerning his letter to the solicitor and ripped it into very small pieces, wishing he could wipe out his memory of the letter as easily. Then, just to be sure the leather portfolio held no other damning evidence of his base character, he placed it on the desk and opened it, quickly scanning a letter on the top of the small pile.

This letter, also in his own hand, had been written to Tyler, addressing the man as his "dear brother." Certainly not a salutation common to men who disliked each other.

The letter concerned the then coming battle with Napoleon, but this did not interest him. He searched for some sort of personal revelation, some hint of the character of the man who was, had been, Dante Edward Muir.

On the second page he found what he was looking for,

what he had been hoping desperately to see, a mention of his wife, a mention of Sarah Jane.

"I flinch from the thought of leaving her now, with so much between us still to be resolved," he had written. "I believe we could have a good life together, if we are blessed with that opportunity. There are times, many times, when I wish we could erase everything that has passed between us and begin once more at the day we first met, without my bunglings and missteps to stand between us. I could love her, I think, if we were to be granted that precious time. My little pet . . ."

Dante pressed the letter to his chest, silently giving thanks that even with his brains scrambled by a French bullet he had not believed he could be the cad Audrey had painted him to be, giving thanks he had not said anything of Audrey's assertions to Sarah earlier in the chapel.

The man he had once been had done wrong in the past, that was certain. To marry for money, to wed someone as sweet and guileless as Sarah Jane for anything so base as saving a building, an estate, was unforgivable. But he had not acted solely out of greed. The previous Dante Muir *had* felt something for his wife, had cared for her. Now the current Dante Muir, this new being he had become, would do what the old Dante Muir had wished to do. He would begin again.

And he would deal with Audrey, one way or the other. For he was, after all, a Muir.

Sarah made her way toward the family drawing room, wishing for the tenth time in as many minutes that Dante could be with her when she met with the marquess. She had gained a modicum of confidence over these past months, but the memory of her last words to her husband's father was not comforting. He had to believe her to be a brainless twit, incapable of handling the situation fate had now placed her in: being the wife of an injured man, a man who had no memory. The shy, timid, prone-to-hysterics, *drunken* Sarah Jane Muir.

But, she reminded herself, she *had* changed. She had become, admittedly through default, the acknowledged mistress of Cliff Walk. She had refurbished the house and maintained the estate until Mr. Hunsberger arrived to take over the reins, even then overseeing the estate manager's work. She had changed her hair, her clothing, even her *mind,* daring to become, at least in part, the woman she had always wished to be.

But it would be nice if Dante could be with her. Nicer still if he *wanted* to be with her. If, together, they could face down the marquess and send him back to London and his gaming tables and his rich friends. He could even take Audrey with him. That would be very nice indeed.

As nice as the minutes she and Dante had spent together earlier today in the chapel, when she had put her hand on his forearm, when he had smiled at her. And then, when her nerves could take no more and she had made an excuse to leave him, he had said that she must have made a beautiful bride. For a woman who had lately lived for the sound of the dinner gong, she thought she might never be hungry again, for she could feed off that single lovely compliment indefinitely!

She stopped in front of a mirror placed just outside the family drawing room and inspected herself in the glass. Had anyone informed the marquess that he was to become a grandfather in little more than a month? She doubted it, for Audrey had not known. Would the marquess be happy about the coming birth? She rather doubted that as well, for Curtis Muir was a vain man, and the notion of his being a grandfather could be extremely defeating to his sense of consequence, his neck-or-nothing pursuit of youth and gaiety.

Not that he had any choice in the matter. He had known, must have known, that Elizabeth Trowbridge wanted a grandson, had even gone so far as to put a price on the birth. So, in fact, with the promise of more money in the offing, Sarah Jane decided that the marquess might just take one look at her distended stomach and 'fall, weeping, on her neck, overcome by the prospect of more gold finding its way into the Muir coffers.

"You're dillydallying, Sarah Jane," she told her reflection as she put a hand to her short-cropped hair, remembering Audrey's dismay at her persistence in maintaining the style. But she had good reasons for shunning long hair. She was cooler this way, for one thing, and she was no longer forced to endure Mildred's heavy hand with the curling stick. Neither did she have to spend so much of her time bent forward over the tub, doing her best to keep her swollen belly out of the way while Mildred soaped and rinsed her hair.

And Dante had expressed pleasure in the style. That was the biggest, most important reason of all for maintaining it, at least until his return.

"So, Sarah Jane," she said out loud, "square your shoulders, tip up your chin, and go in there and get this uncomfortable reunion over with. You can't leave Dante alone in there with his father."

"Thank you, Sarah," Dante said as his reflection appeared in the mirror just behind hers. "In truth, I wasn't looking forward to this encounter without my wife by my side." He held out his arm to her, smiling in that lovable, one-sided way that still retained the power to curl her toes. "Shall we?"

Renewed hope flared in Sarah Jane's heart, and she felt a flash of courage she knew she should not examine too closely for fear it might disappear. She slipped her arm through his. "I would be delighted, sir," she said, smiling up at him, a smile that remained steadfastly pinned in place as they entered the drawing room and saw the Muir family congregated near the cold fireplace.

"Dante! What's this damned nonsense I'm hearing about you?" the marquess bellowed as he pushed himself away from his studied pose leaning against the mantelpiece.

Sarah Jane realized that she had worried for nothing. She might just as well have been invisible for all the attention her father-in-law was directing toward her. Now her fears centered around her unknowing, unsuspecting husband and how he would react to the unexpected arrival of this nattily clad, broadly smiling man on a scene already overcrowded with unfamiliar faces.

"Hello, sir," Dante said, his voice sounding somewhat strained as Sarah Jane felt herself being pushed to one side so that the marquess could grab his middle son in a bear hug, just as if he felt some real affection for him.

"Hello, sir? *Hello, sir?* By God, it is true! You've never been formal with me. Never been all that civil, either, come to think of it." The marquess stood back, still with his hands on Dante's shoulders, examining his son as if looking for some outward sign of his infirmity, as if the loss of his memory should send Dante to breaking out in spots. "You look fine, Dante," he said nervously, finally releasing his grip. "Just fine! Doesn't he, Audrey? Audrey, boys, tell him he looks just fine. Simply splendid!" That said, he quickly crossed to the drinks table.

"Dante looks as he always has," Audrey answered from her seat on one of the rose striped chairs. "Really, I shouldn't think it healthy to make such a to-do. Do come sit down, Curtis. You're making a cake of yourself."

"Ah, let him bluster, Audrey." Lord John winked in Sarah Jane and Dante's direction. "He's playing the fond papa, though he does it very badly. No wonder he loses so prodigiously at cards, if that's the best he can manage to mask his true self. He's dying inside, Audrey, thinking of all that lovely money possibly going back to Betts Trowbridge by default. So leave him be, please. Allow him his histrionics. I, for one, want to watch."

"Excuse us a moment, please," Dante said, bowing to his family.

Sarah felt Dante's long-fingered hand slipping around her own small one and giving it a squeeze as he steered her back into the hallway. She looked up at him, surprised to see that he was smiling. It seemed an odd reaction. "Are you all right?" she asked.

"I'm more than all right, Sarah," he answered, chuckling

softly. "Didn't you hear the marquess? I'm *splendid*. Is he always like this?"

"I don't know," she answered honestly, looking into the drawing room at her father-in-law. "Mostly, he isn't here. What did Audrey tell you about your father?"

"Nothing much. Just that he is mad for money and periodically sells off a son in order to pay his gambling debts. Johnny's next, according to Audrey, unless I agree to open my purse a lot wider. I also sensed from Ty and Johnny that there isn't much love lost between father and sons. Or perhaps I should correct that. I believe they love him well enough. But there isn't much respect there, if you know what I mean. Is there anything else I should know?"

Sarah Jane considered his question for a moment. "It might help you to know that Curtis is deathly afraid of my grandmother. It was her idea that you hold control of the money she offered upon our marriage. Oh, yes, you and I are both to come into a considerable fortune when a male child is born. Do you think that is important?"

"To the marquess? Yes, I do think it weighs heavily with him. Very well, Sarah, I believe I know enough for the moment. There is nothing left to do but offer you my belated but heartfelt compliments on your fine looks this evening and to thank you for worrying about your poor befuddled husband. Now, shall we rejoin the others?"

Still holding her hand, Dante advanced into the drawing room once more, nodding a greeting to the earl, whose Bath chair was positioned to the left of the cold fireplace, before assisting Sarah Jane to one of the couches and sitting down beside her. She knew it would be difficult to rise again from the soft cushions, but the thought didn't bother her, for she now had her husband here to assist her. Her husband, who thought she was looking "fine." He was "splendid," and she was "fine." Actually, she was better than fine. She was hopeful, for the second time in only a few hours.

"So, sir, you have been made aware of my injury," Dante

said, shifting slightly to address the marquess. "Mrs. Trowbridge, who departed Cliff Walk just prior to your arrival, is most agitated by my loss of memory. Just before sweeping out the door to confer with her solicitor, she accosted me in the hallway to inform me that she believes I should be locked up. For my own good, you understand. Do you think she might ask for the money back as well? That would be a pity, I suppose."

Sarah Jane stiffened on the soft cushions, immediately furious with her grandmother. "How dare she repeat such foolishness in your presence!" she exclaimed, pressing Dante's hand. "It is beyond belief even to consider such nonsense. I shall write to her this evening, reminding her that she has absolutely nothing to say in the matter and that she is forever unwelcome at Cliff Walk."

"That's our sweet angel!" Johnny shouted, leaping to his feet. "She don't say much, but what she says, she means! Dante's not dicked in the nob, he's just been *nicked*. Ain't that right, Ty?"

"True enough," the earl answered evenly. "But Betts does hold all the trumps, doesn't she, Father? The remainder of Dante's money, Sarah Jane's money. Or will you consider Cliff Walk well served as it is, and value your middle son higher than you do your wallet? Please don't answer at once. Take some time to think about it."

Sarah Jane looked quickly at the marquess, suddenly afraid that, between them, Dante's father and her grandmother could carry out the threat of placing her husband in an insane asylum and taking control of all the money.

As Sarah Jane stared at the marquess, the marquess stared at Dante. "You don't remember anything? Not even what you preferred to eat at breakfast? The name of your favorite horse? *Nothing?*"

"Not a single thing, sir," Dante answered in a maddeningly affable tone, lifting Sarah Jane's hand to his lips and kissing the inside of her wrist, making her wonder just what he was about, for he was most certainly up to something. He had never shown affection for her in public, not ever. Why would he do so now? She had a niggling, uncomfortable feeling that she just might be being *used* by her supposedly injured, memory-bereft husband. "This disconcerts you, my lord?"

"No!" the marquess blustered, looking at Audrey. "Not a jot! We'll make do, we'll make do. Somehow. And I'm delighted about the child, by the bye. Ty told me the happy news earlier. Proud of you, son. We Muirs are good studs, excepting Ty here, and that ain't his fault, seeing how he's tied to that damned chair. Audrey, would you care to accompany me on a short stroll around the house before dinner, my dear? I'm already most agreeably surprised at the miracle that has been wrought in the family wing. A tour of the rest of Cliff Walk will doubtless prove equally amazing. My congratulations."

"Sarah did it all," Lord John growled angrily at their departing figures. "If you're thinking Audrey lifted so much as a finger to help, you're more addled in the head than Dante ever could be. Why, I wouldn't be shocked if you both lost your way on your tour, seeing as how neither of you spends more time at Cliff Walk than the chimney sweeps we now bring in twice a year."

"Oh, let it go, Johnny. It's not worth upsetting yourself," the earl said, pushing his chair forward now that his father had gone. "Why don't you open those doors to the patio? The scent of their mingled perfumes has nearly turned my stomach. Good riddance to them both, I say. They'll be heading to Mayfair by dawn tomorrow, the pair of them, if you give them money to fly with. Will you do that, Dante? It would most certainly make our lives easier."

"The marquess, our loving father, can take a dip into the coffers, for I don't believe he is necessary to my recovery at the moment. And I do now feel certain I will recover. But Audrey, my savior in Brussels, will have to accustom herself to remaining at Cliff Walk a while longer. If that is all right with you, *my little pet?*" Dante then smiled at Sarah Jane, who had nearly whimpered aloud upon hearing the offhand endearment.

She could only smile nervously and nod her agreement, remembering that he had questioned her about Audrey earlier, and she silently wondered if she knew as little about her husband as he had led her to believe he could remember about her.

CHAPTER 14

You roll my log, and I will roll yours.

Lucius Annaeus Seneca

The marquess had departed for London the afternoon following his arrival without ever ordering his baggage unpacked, a substantial bank draft tucked up in his pocket and with kind words for all, especially Audrey, who protested that the last thing upon earth she desired was to go with him.

"And *that's* a damned pity, for now *we'll* have to figure out what to do with her," Dante had heard the earl whisper in an aside to Lord John, who had laughed aloud at the remark.

Dante hadn't seen his wife again until the evening meal, having spent the remainder of the afternoon riding the estate with Lord John, finding himself amazed again and again as the estate laborers greeted him with happy waves, tugged forelocks, and wide smiles. *If nothing else,* Dante had concluded, *I must have been a tolerable employer.*

But he had felt no sense of recognition as he toured the farms, as he rode through the village, as he watched the operation of the sawmill. He was still an alien creature in an unfamiliar land.

And so, still with more questions than answers, Dante decided to remain late in the drawing room that night, intent upon speaking privately with his older brother. Audrey, who had retired early to her rooms complaining of a headache, and Sarah Jane, who had likewise excused herself, claiming a general fatigue, were safely out of earshot, and Lord John had been invited to dinner at the Randolphs'.

There was nothing stopping the two gentlemen from indulging in their first real conversation since Dante's rather earthshaking return to Cliff Walk. Nothing save the fact that Dante really didn't have the faintest idea of how he might best broach the subject of his suspicions concerning the countess as he spoke with the woman's crippled husband.

"You always did possess the unnerving ability to stare through a person, Dante," the earl said as he sipped from his glass of port while a small fire slowly died on the hearth and a hard, driving rain pelted the windows.

"Forgive me, Ty. I was thinking, that's all."

"Don't apologize, brother, for you can't help it. It's doubtless something to do with those dark eyes of yours. I've always found it impossible to know what you're thinking. Or have you simply had too much port? Johnny looked much the same when he was half-seas over, as I recall. On the whole, I believe I much prefer him drunk and you sober. At least I am accustomed to that. A man likes to know where he stands or, in my case, where he sits."

"I'm not drunk, Ty," Dante said, putting down his nearly empty glass. "I'm confused," he added honestly, then decided that if he was heading for rough ground, he would simply have to try to get over it as quickly and as painlessly as possible. "Tell me. How well do I like Audrey?"

"Audrey?" The earl rolled his eyes. "Now there's a question! I could have sat here for days and days, speculating on what you might want to know, what information might be of help to you, but I would never, *never* have thought you would ask about my vain, scatterbrained wife. How well do you like her? I don't know, Dante. Truly. You never really said. You knew what I thought of her, what I still think of her. But you were always a closemouthed sort about things personal. It was never like you to go around gossiping or throwing stones. Why do you ask?"

Dante looked past the earl's head, concentrating his gaze on a corner of the chimneypiece. "Because she says the two of us are lovers, and have been for a long time."

"She says *what*? Lovers? You and Audrey? Hell, Audrey and *anybody*! Now, there's a statement to get me up out of this chair beforetimes. Johnny should be here to witness the final miracle, as you've dealt me a stunning stroke, much better than his ridiculous cries of 'fire.' There I'd be, standing on my own for you both to marvel at, just so I could tumble straightaway to the floor, laughing! *Lovers?* Tell me, Dante, dearest war-damaged brother, precisely what in bloody hell are you talking about?"

Dante couldn't decipher everything the earl was saying, but he did know that his suppositions about Audrey had just been confirmed once and for all time. The woman had been lying to him about their relationship. Other than the obvious question of why she had done so, he was now plagued with the thought that, if he could not believe her on this one thing, how could he put any real credence in *anything* she had told him?

"Never mind, Ty," he said, quickly dismissing his brother's half-amused inquiry with a wave of his hand. "Just answer these questions, if you please. One: the child my wife is carrying—is it mine?"

The earl's face turned dark as a thundercloud, his smile reassembling itself into a tight-lipped grimace. "Now I *will* get up out of this chair, Dante—to throttle you! Who else's child would it be?"

"I'm asking the questions, Ty," Dante reminded him tersely, for his temples were beginning to pound and his thoughts were none too clear. He kept seeing Audrey in his mind's eye, Audrey telling him that Sarah was too small, too delicate, to ever enjoy lovemaking. Had she said that to him in the library or at some earlier time? And if so, when? And why would he ever have had such an intimate conversation with his sister-in-law—he who was supposedly a "close-mouthed sort about things personal"?

"All right, Dante. Don't go cutting up stiff on me. Ask your questions."

"Thank you. Two: is Johnny in love with my wife?"

"Johnny? Well, if that isn't above everything stupid! Of course he is, as a brother. They've always got their heads together, talking about elephants and why hens don't have teeth and the possibility that King George has made a pact with the devil and might live on forever, mad as a hatter, leaving Prinny to grow fatter and poorer and duller by the decade. They're like children together, Dante, teasing, laughing, loving *children.* Did Audrey—My God, of course she did! Where else would you have come up with such a wild idea? I always thought she was only vacuous, insulting people by accident, causing trouble by mistake, her tongue hinged at both ends and altogether disconnected to her brain. But she's just plain mean—and spiteful!"

Dante was feeling better by the moment. Better, stronger, more in control, even if he had only his wits to guide him, and not his memories. "You never loved Audrey?"

"When I have always been in love with Emma, even after she ran off and eloped with her late husband, which I have just lately discovered she did only after being warned away by our most beloved greedy father? Hardly."

The earl shook his head, his brow furrowed. "You can't understand any of this, can you, Dante? Look, I know Audrey said, and you said, that the doctor in Brussels didn't want us to go poking at you, trying to make you remember everything you've forgotten. But I think it's time we had a long talk, about Audrey, about Sarah Jane, about our father, about our life here at Cliff Walk, even about these supposedly useless legs of mine. When we're done, if you still have questions, I'll be glad to answer them. Are you agreed?"

Dante picked up his glass and rose, smiling at his brother. "Would you like me to get you another drink? I think we're going to be here a long time, for I have a few things to tell you, too. And then, once we're done with that, I think it might be vaguely amusing to think up some way to repay dearest Audrey for all her *kindnesses* to her injured brother-in-law."

Sarah Jane sat alone in the library, at a loss as to how to occupy herself. Her grandmother was back at Trowbridge Manor, which was just where she belonged after saying such terrible things about Dante and *to* Dante.

Yet Sarah missed her, if only a little, and wished she could be present for the baby's birth. The fact that Mildred had seconded that opinion, admitting her apprehension about being in the same room as a laboring female, had only served to double Sarah Jane's belief that a woman of Elizabeth Trowbridge's forthright, no-nonsense manner might be just what was needed at such a disquieting time.

But she would have Emma, thank goodness. That woman had left strict instructions with Babbitt that she be summoned the moment labor began, and Sarah Jane was relying on her friend, who had firsthand knowledge of childbirth, to be a rock of composure throughout the ordeal. If only she could see more of Emma now, talk to her about Dante, about how he had called her his little pet, just as he had done before he left for the Continent, before he lost his memory.

But that was impossible. She and Emma had only met a single time since Dante's return, since Audrey's return. Until Audrey finally took herself back to London, Emma would not return to Cliff Walk, not even to see Ty.

For the past seven and more months Sarah Jane had kept her mind and hands busy setting Cliff Walk to rights, but now even that was beyond her. Her back ached abominably whenever she attempted to join Cloris and the others in any housework, and her ankles swelled just as abominably in the late July heat, making long walks about the grounds impossible.

Watching the kitchen and house servants go about their daily chores would be insulting to them now that the renovations were complete except for the chapel, a place Sarah Jane felt a compulsion to turn into a more cheerful spot before her son was christened there. She had hired competent staff, and for the most part they did not need her anymore, which was a tribute to her own abilities.

This success, coupled with her grandmother's banishment and Emma's reasonable desertion, did, however, leave Sarah Jane with precious little to do but think about her problems.

Other wives spent time with their husbands. But other wives had husbands who remembered them, who wished to spend time with them. She had only her own memories, not all of them pleasant.

Other wives had children to fuss over. She had only Audrey's dire predictions of a difficult childbirth to repeat themselves in her head, drowning out the reasonable tones of Emma, who had declared Audrey to be a needless worrier.

Other wives had husbands who slept beside them at night, keeping the demon bad dreams away from them. Sarah Jane's husband slept elsewhere, unable to remember that last night, that most wonderful, fateful night when he had loved her, really loved her, and then held her tightly in his arms until dawn.

Perhaps she, like Ty and Emma, should take up watercolor painting, although she had no real desire to do so. She had no desire to read either, or to work on the estate books or even to look through the extensive layette her grandmother had ordered delivered from London. What she wanted, what she needed, was to have Dante call her his pet again, have him hold her again, have him look into her eyes and smile, knowing her, remembering her, dear God, loving her! But he had not sought her out again since they had seen each other at the dinner table last evening.

"My goodness, has this room become the center of Cliff Walk, so that everyone is to be found here, surrounded by dusty books and gloomy dark walls? I can't imagine why. How are you this afternoon, dearest sister? You look rather out of plumb, don't you? Do you think you will ever again have your trim figure back? I don't know many women who have succeeded, poor things. Their gowns hang awkwardly over stomachs stretched past all thought of returning to their former shape; horrid purplish lines mar their sagging breasts! Ah, well, it is a price we women must pay for our husbands' lust, I suppose."

"Hello, Audrey," Sarah Jane said tiredly. She had not been relishing her solitary state, but having her depressingly talkative sister-in-law for company was not a large step up from being alone. "As a matter of fact, I was just thinking I'd return to the family wing and ring for Babbitt to bring me some tea. There's no need for him to carry a heavy tray so far." Wishing she hadn't been raised to be polite, she ended, "Would you care to join me?"

"Aren't you thoughtful! I'd be delighted, Sarah Jane." As Sarah Jane stood up, her expanded figure no longer hidden by the desk, Audrey exclaimed, "You seem to grow by the moment, don't you? Poor baby! At least you will soon have new gowns. I've seen some interesting drawings of nursing gowns in my magazines, although the slits in the bodices seem rather vulgar, not that you'll be going into society. Or is your grandmother considering a wet nurse? I have no real knowledge of these things, you understand, only an abhorrence of them, actually."

"My grandmother has nothing to say in the matter, and I plan to care for the child myself. It must be the plebeian butcher's-granddaughter's blood in me," she added as they made their way down the corridor leading to the family wing, hating herself for using her deceased grandfather to strike back at her sister-in-law. "Why didn't you go to London with Curtis, Audrey?" she asked, quickly changing the subject. "I know how dreadfully boring you find the country."

They entered the family drawing room together, Audrey going to the bellpull as Sarah Jane sat down on a straight-backed chair, her lower back having begun to pain her in just the short time it took to walk from the library.

"And leave Dante in his time of trouble?" Audrey said. "When we have become so *close?* When I am the only one he feels in the least familiar with, his only solid rock to cling to in the storm-tossed sea that has become his existence? Oh, no. I must remain here to be a supporting prop to poor Dante, and to you, dear, as well. It is my duty, my honor! How can you even ask such a question, Sarah Jane? I would never forgive myself. *Never!"*

"And Tyler?" Beginning to wish the woman on the far side of the moon, Sarah Jane pressed on, her hands clenched tightly in her lap. At this rate Emma would not come to Cliff Walk again until Babbitt fetched her to help with the birth. "Are you staying for his own good as well?"

"Hardly." Audrey spread her rose muslin skirts daintily as she sat down on one of the couches and smiled at Sarah Jane. "Let's talk with the gloves off, dear sister, shall we? We both know that Ty's affections lie elsewhere, with that notorious Franklin woman from the village. But scandalous or not, and personally embarrassing as his liaison is to me, I go down on my knees every night and thank the good Lord for sending her back to him. She may make his last days happy, the poor dear. Heaven knows I harbor no burning desire to martyr myself in his lost cause."

The babe moved, delivering a violent kick that Sarah Jane did her best not to acknowledge, for fear of setting off another round of tsk-tsking on Audrey's part about the inconveniences of pregnancy. "Yet you are staying for Dante and, as you said, for me. May I take it, then, that you disagree with Dante's Brussels physician, and you do not believe his failed memory to be a lost cause?"

"All right, Sarah Jane," Audrey said amicably, her usual guileless, vacant smile once more in evidence. "If you wish to see it that way. We must none of us give up hope. Ah, here is Babbitt with the tray. Shall I pour?"

"Babbitt, another cup, if you please."

At the sound of the earl's voice, Sarah Jane turned to see him being wheeled into the drawing room by Farris, and she belatedly but relievedly remembered that it was his custom to take tea every afternoon at about this time. "Hello, Ty," she said, refraining only with a strong application of will from running to his side and begging protection from his wife.

"Hello, ladies," the earl responded when Audrey said

nothing. He waved Farris out of the room. "Lovely day, isn't it? And do you know why it's such a lovely day? No? Then I shall tell you, even daring to put my dear sister-in-law to the blush. I have regained some slight strength in my legs these past weeks, and some *feelings* as well, if you take my meaning. Urges I thought lost forever. I had thought to keep my news as a surprise, but I can no longer hold back my joy. Audrey, my dear wife—my legal, convenient, resident receptacle—I have ordered your woman to move your belongings into my rooms this very afternoon. I can barely wait for nightfall. Perhaps we two shall be the ones to present the next Muir heir after all!"

Audrey's lovely blue eyes widened until they showed white all around them, and her chin dropped nearly to her chest before she ran to the earl's side, kneeling next to the Bath chair. "Oh, dearest Ty, what—what *wonderful* news! That you should be showing signs of recovery after all these years! Sarah Jane, isn't this above everything wonderful? I am all but overcome! Dearest Ty! Did you—did you say *tonight?*"

Sarah Jane nearly laughed out loud at Audrey's obvious dilemma and at her very bad playacting as she once more performed the role of adoring wife. But then she thought of Emma, and suddenly the moment was no longer funny. "Ty . . . ?" she began as Audrey, begging to be excused so that she could compose her overset nerves, pulled herself to her feet and fled the drawing room, daintily weeping into her handkerchief.

"Shhh, little sister," the earl warned, smiling. "No questions, if you please. Unless you wish to know where Dante is waiting most anxiously for his wife to join him. He has something rather important he wishes to tell you."

Sarah Jane didn't know she could still get to her feet so quickly, all thoughts of the suddenly amorous earl and his devastated countess fleeing her mind. "He has regained his memory?"

"Alas, no," the earl told her, still smiling. "But it is very nearly as good. He has found out who he is. *Hmm*. I wonder if Johnny might wish to place a wager on how long it will take my dearest wife to pack in preparation for her flit to Mayfair?''

Dante had not spent a quiet night or a peaceful morning, which had not surprised him. What had caused him more than a modicum of unease had been his reaction to learning the full extent of his sister-in-law's ambitions.

So he and Sarah Jane had not had the best beginning to their marriage. Considering that theirs was a marriage of convenience, he knew he should not concern himself over-much with that particular problem. Not now, not after reading his own words as written to his brother, his own sentiments concerning his growing affection for the woman he'd married and his hope for their happy, shared future.

He was still experiencing significant difficulty forgiving himself for having married Sarah Jane solely for monetary considerations, but the earl had explained in great detail the sorry state of Cliff Walk prior to the large infusion of Trowbridge money, as well as Dante's deep devotion both to his brothers and to the estate. All things considered, and taking into account the almost obscene amount of money involved in Elizabeth Trowbridge's offer, Dante supposed it would have taken either a much stronger man than he or an absolute imbecile to refuse the woman.

He now knew as much as the earl had chosen to tell him about the still absent Emma, Lord John's three-year bout with the bottle, and the shy bride who had wrought such miracles at Cliff Walk, slowly winning everyone's heart along the way. He knew that he had loved his father while cheerfully despising the man's shortcomings. He knew he had paid no or little attention to Audrey Muir, had rarely been in her company, and had valued her opinion only slightly more than he would have that of the village idiot.

He was now convinced, as was the earl, that Audrey, simple but selfish soul that she was, had taken it into her head to use information that was true enough, manipulate and twist it to suit her, turning brother against brother, and then either to extract a larger allowance from an unknowing, unsuspecting Dante or, perish the thought, to connive herself out of a failed marriage and into wedlock with the man she saw as the real power at Cliff Walk, the memory-befuddled "heir" to all the Trowbridge money.

But what had bothered him most, what had kept him from his rest, were the scenes that continued to play within his head at odd moments all night, niggling snippets of memory that made little or no sense yet warned him that, unless he was extremely careful, he could regain his memory only to lose Sarah Jane. If he'd ever had her. If what he thought he saw in her eyes was more than kindness, more than pity from the woman who, his brother vowed, possessed not a single unselfish bone in her small body.

The scenes were confusing, and bittersweet.

. . . A petite, wide-eyed sprite of a child peering down at him through bars—no, balusters—eyeing him as if he were a cross between a knight in shining armor and the most frightening ogre imaginable. . . .

. . . A slight, stiff, unyielding body beneath his, a small voice whimpering. Feelings of shame, self-disgust, abject failure in the midst of great passion, unexpected desire. Feelings of helplessness, even fear. A vow not to injure. . . .

. . . Wounded eyes, pleading with him to understand. Great anger, a feeling of being used, usurped, undermined. A cruel withdrawal, hiding within himself, nursing self-inflicted wounds, burying himself in fatiguing, mind-numbing work, turning his back on what he had begun to believe he might want more than anything in this world. . . .

. . . A soft body, a sweet scent, clinging arms, passion without words, love expressed silently, a reluctant parting . . . long, dark, endless days spent wondering, hoping. . . .

All this and more Dante had sensed since his enlightening conversation with the earl, emotions floating to the surface, memories nipping at the corners of his mind, confusing snippets of dialogue echoing inside his head, tormenting him. His brain ached with them. Ty's voice. His father's. Johnny's. Audrey's. Little Sarah's. Betts Trowbridge's. Even his own. . . .

"Well, there you have it, son. A lovely child. What more could you ask?"

"Here to escort me to the scaffold, are you, Ty?"

"How above everything amazing! First he saves Cliff Walk, and now he thinks he can cure the crippled. What else, dear brother? Please, don't leave me in suspense. Will you raise the dead? Turn water into wine?"

"Your poor little bride, poor little Sarah Jane. That is her name, isn't it? Sarah Jane?"

"Papa spends money, Ty suffers, Dante saves us, and Johnny drinks. All of us Muirs have our roles."

"Just tell me something. Have you ever bedded a virgin?"

"It won't hurt the next time, Sarah Jane. It won't hurt ever again. I promise."
"So you said, Dante. Thank you. I—Would it be possible for me to be alone now?"

"Bungled it, did you, brother?"

"You can't be held responsible, Dante. Audrey explained it to me."

"She is small, isn't she?"
"Yes, Ty, she is. Do you believe she could safely give birth?"
"Bloody hell, Dante, now I see it! If she dies in childbed you'll never get the second half of the money. I misjudged you. You're not falling in love with the chit. You can't. You've already tumbled top over tail in lust with her money."

"Two thousand five hundred? Ten thousand a year? As pin money? Christ, Dante, that's rich! Dearest Sarah Jane, will you marry me? Don't worry about Dante, as I think you've just killed him."

"Can't you sleep?"
"Can you, Dante? Tonight, of all nights?"

"Please, Dante, kiss me. . . . Help me understand why I feel this way whenever you're near."

"Shhh, pet. We have so much to talk about, to learn about each other, but let's not spoil this perfection with words. Let me take this sweet memory of my wife away with me in the morning."

Sweet memory . . . sweet memory . . . sweet memory.

If only he could remember it *all!*

"Dante? Dante, are you all right? I had wanted to come to you directly, but Cloris needed me. Something about the chapel. Dante? Dante, do you hear me?"

He raised his head from his hands and stared blankly across the desk to see Sarah Jane standing there, her beautiful brown eyes clouded with worry. Was it monstrous of him to desire her, most especially in her delicate condition, without fully remembering her? Without fully knowing himself? "I'm well enough, Sarah," he said, quickly escorting her to the blue couch and sitting down beside her. "You've seen Ty?"

She nodded furiously as she settled, somewhat uncomfortably he thought, against the cushions. "I certainly have, and I must tell you something. I have never been so confused in my life! I have spent this last half hour alternately laughing to myself and silently fuming! Should I be ecstatic that Ty has at last regained some hope for his injured legs? Or should I seek him out at once and box his ears for what it appears he is about to do to Emma? To tell Audrey he wishes her to move her belongings to his chamber! The entire scene was most dreadfully embarrassing, as well as upsetting. Dante, stop grinning like a bear. This is *serious!"*

"Never doubt it, pet. Tell me, how did Audrey react to Ty's good news? Badly, I most sincerely hope," Dante said, taking Sarah Jane's small hands in his own, not unaware of the increased beating of his heart now that she was near. Had any woman in her condition been so lovely, so petitely, ethereally beautiful?

Although he kept hold of her hands, she pulled back from him, peering at him cautiously. "Oh, dear. Now I'm *really* worried!" she said. "I've seen that mischievous twinkle before, but only in Johnny's eyes as he was about to pull another prank on Ty meant to rouse him from his chair. I hadn't realized it was a Muir characteristic. What are you and Ty up to, Dante? And what does Ty mean when he says you have not regained your memory but that you know who you are?"

How much should he tell her? Should he tell her about the scenes in his head, the snippets of conversation that had been variously entertaining and condemning him since last night? Would he raise her hopes only to dash them if his full memory never returned?

And how much truth was she able to take in about Audrey's heavy-handed machinations without the shock possibly harming her? He'd have to explain soon, after Audrey came to him begging to be sent to London to escape her amorous husband, after he'd informed his meddling sister-in-law that she was being sent packing to her mother's house instead, and with no increase in her allowance. It had been Ty's idea to give her a small fright first. "Put the fear of God, or at the least of *me*, into her," he'd said. Dante had been more than willing to go along with the joke, however, for he had also suffered under Audrey's massaging of the truth.

"Dante, I'm waiting," Sarah Jane said sternly, so that he nearly laughed at the sight of her solemn face beneath the elfin mop of hair, above the swollen stomach that still looked so incongruous, for she appeared to be little more than a child herself. Yes. He could love this woman. Even without his memory.

"Very well, little pet," he said at last, leaning forward to drop a kiss on the end of her pert nose, secretly pleased that the offhand endearment the old Dante had used still seemed so right. "Sorry. I couldn't resist that," he added when she blushed and blinked rapidly, drawing in her breath in surprise. "Allow me to explain."

He opened his mouth to tell her about Audrey, Audrey's lies, Audrey's malicious misuse of the truth, only to be interrupted by Lord John as the young man bounded into the room, Growler at his heels, and already talking so quickly his words tumbled over themselves.

"Dante! Sarah! You'll never guess what happened. Go on, guess! Oh, never mind. You'd never guess, not in a thousand years! I was at the Randolphs', with Lucy, you understand, looking at her new hunter—it's a bruising mount, truly bruising—and Mr. Randolph took me to one side. I tell you, I was never so astonished in my life! Couldn't open my mouth to spit, I was that shocked! He said he would encourage my suit if I wished to press it. Can you imagine? He wants me to ask for Lucy. *Ask* for her? What would I *do* with her? *Me,* the last penniless Muir. I have nothing to offer her."

He threw himself into a nearby leather chair and flung his long legs out in front of him on the carpet, the picture of dejection. "Should I be happy, Dante? Or should I slice my throat and have done with it?"

"Do you love her, Johnny? No one should ever contemplate marriage without love."

Dante sliced a look at his wife, whom he had married for her grandmother's money, who had married him for his title, his place in society. Or so he had thought. Or so he had believed. Oh, God, if only he could *remember!* He squeezed her hands, so that she turned to gaze up into his eyes. "Sarah? Pet?" he asked, forgetting his brother was still in the room, the universe. "Why did you agree to marry me?"

She averted her eyes, her cheeks burning. "Not now, Dante. Please. Johnny—"

"Will wait," he finished for her, his voice suddenly husky as he once more saw the strangely dressed, oddly coiffed Sarah Jane who could only be a memory, for the woman in front of him bore little resemblance to that shy, awkward, frightened child. "Why did you marry me, Sarah? Did you believe yourself to be in love with me?"

"Is—is that important to you, Dante?" she asked in a small voice, sudden unshed tears flooding her eyes.

"Yes, pet, it is. More than you'll ever know. I believe I could live much more happily with the man who was once

269

Dante Muir if I could believe that you loved him. That the other Dante Muir might have known, might have sensed, that you loved him and wished the marriage to take place. It would make him less the greedy bastard."

A single tear slipped down her cheek, and her full bottom lip trembled, her pain nearly breaking his heart. "Yes," she said at last, when he believed the tension in the room might crush his last breath from him. "I loved Dante Muir from the moment I first saw him, a childish love bordering more on worship and romantic dreams garnered from penny press novels, I suppose."

"You saw me as a romantic figure, pet? I imagine I am flattered."

"Don't tease, Dante, or I won't say any more. You wanted to know how I felt about the Dante Muir I married. Yes, I did see him as a romantic figure, the hero come to rescue me from my gilded tower at Trowbridge Manor. But that was only in the beginning. I loved him even more once I learned to know him, once I saw his gentleness, his concern for his family and the people who depended on the estate for their livelihood, his dedication and loyalty to his country."

She looked fully, almost searchingly into his face. "And now, now that I am about to bear him his child, I love him more fully and deeply than I can ever say. I love *you,* Dante Muir."

"Gad!" Lord John exclaimed in agitation, jumping up from his seat. "Should I be hearing this? I don't think I should be hearing this. I think I'm going to cry! Come on, Growler. Excuse us, won't you? Wouldn't want to go blubbering in front of a female, you understand."

Dante heard Lord John leave, but didn't say anything. He could only continue to stare at Sarah Jane, lifting her chin with the tip of his finger, gazing into her eyes with such wonder, such overwhelming awe at the gift he had been given. "Ah, pet. Little pet. Thank you. I must be the luckiest man in the world," he whispered, slowly lowering his head, more nervous than he could have imagined as he touched his lips to hers.

He slid his arms around her, drawing her even closer,

tasting her sweetness, more flashes of memory—happy memories, exciting memories—exploding behind his closed eyelids. He felt the exultation of happiness undiluted by any shadows of the past as his wife's hands grasped his shoulders and her mouth opened so that he could deepen the kiss.

"There you are! Oh, lud! What am I interrupting? A little billing and cooing? Is that all you Muirs can think of—rutting? Honestly, Dante, you've already done all the damage you could do. There's no need to maul the child again."

Dante pressed Sarah Jane's head against his shoulder, silently wondering if Babbitt might know if there were keys to lock the doors to the library. Johnny had already interrupted, and now Audrey had come strolling in at precisely the wrong moment. Who else might be barging in—a delegation from the village intent upon welcoming him home? And why was Audrey here? Had she already recovered from her expected bout of weeping and begun planning her assault on his purse?

"What do you want, Audrey?" he asked tiredly, looking to the woman who had put her own selfish desires above any concern for Sarah Jane, for her own husband, for any of them. If things had gone as planned, Ty had well and truly spiked her guns, and she had come to beg her brother-in-law to allow her to join the marquess in London.

She pressed her hands to her bosom as she seated herself in the chair recently vacated by Lord John. "Me? I want nothing from you, dear brother, save your full recovery. You have heard the news, haven't you? Already one miracle has occurred, and Ty and I are going to be removing for London within the week. He believes he will soon regain use of his legs. Can you imagine? Parties, routs, *dancing!* Ty was always such a wonderful dancer. And we'll have a child. A son. A son to inherit all this!" she exclaimed, spreading her arms as if to encompass all of Cliff Walk. "Goodness, I believe I might weep happy tears over the wonderfulness of our good fortune!"

"My congratulations, Audrey," Dante said coldly as Sarah Jane pushed herself out of his embrace.

Dante saw at once that something was wrong. Audrey was

too effusive. She wasn't supposed to be ecstatic, weeping "happy tears." She was supposed to be devastated, sobbing copiously and cravenly begging for a draft on Dante's bank and a carriage ride to Mayfair. The featherbrained Audrey was up to something, that was for certain. No one could be so changeable, so mercurial.

"Your endless adaptability is a constant source of amazement," he continued, still not remembering any specific battles in which he had fought, but somehow knowing that his sense of danger would have pricked at the back of his neck in just this way on the eve of each of those battles. "I had thought you and my brother to be hopelessly alienated and that your plans lay, shall we say, elsewhere?"

"With you? Is that what you're trying so delicately to say, Dante, you poor muddled creature?" she responded, laughing. "With the *second* son? Dare I tell the truth at last, and with dear Sarah Jane here to listen? But I must, for now Ty and I are together once more and nothing can be allowed to interfere with our happiness! Ah, dearest Dante, please forgive me for humoring you, telling you what you wished to hear. What you have longed to hear ever since Ty first brought me home as his wife. You ran off to war rather than watch Ty with me, envying your brother to the point of hatred. But the truth, distasteful as it was for me to have to remind you of your ardent devotion to me in an attempt to jog your memory, hasn't helped a jot, has it? I . . . Well, there is no other way to say this, is there? I never loved you, Dante, not even when you threatened me with a marriage of convenience with this poor, unsuspecting child. Ah, well, what's past is past."

"No, Audrey. What's past is prologue, to quote the Bard, for I have not forgotten everything I'd learned before my injury. I need my past to begin again, and you have done your best to muddle that past to your own advantage."

"Whatever you say, Dante. The doctor warned me you might turn on me, your devoted nurse, once you were home." She smiled sweetly, gesturing to Sarah Jane. "Not that you should be too disappointed, considering what I saw when I first came in here and interrupted your most romantic coze. Perhaps we shall all end happily after all! Happy Muirs. Who would have thought it possible!"

Sarah Jane looked from Audrey to Dante, her confusion evident. *"What* is she babbling about?" she asked, placing her hands protectively on her swollen belly. "Were you ever in love with her?"

"I don't know," Dante answered honestly, wishing he could throw Audrey out of the room and explain everything to Sarah Jane, everything Tyler and he had so lately discovered about the beautiful, seemingly flea-witted yet dangerously shrewd, endlessly inventive chameleon that was Audrey.

He shook his head. "I simply *do not* know. Sarah," he began, taking her hands, "we can't think about that now. This is all a big mistake, a harebrained plan Ty and I hatched in order to . . ." His voice trailed off as he realized what he was on the verge of admitting, and he quickly turned to Audrey. The tingle he had been experiencing at the back of his neck now ran through his entire body. "Where is he? Where is my brother?"

"Ty?" Audrey smiled, then sighed dreamily. "We went for a walk, actually, to celebrate our reconciliation privately— something you might have imagined yourself, Dante, considering the embarrassingly intimate scene that greeted me when I arrived in this room. I pushed dearest Ty's chair for him, not without effort, but it was the least I could do, and he won't need it much longer, will he? Such a lovely interlude we had, out by the cliffs, speaking of our future, *our* child. Your money may have saved Cliff Walk, Dante, and your dear wife's talents made it livable, but it is *I* who shall be the mistress of the estate. It was so invigorating, talking about our future. But then I began to sneeze most abominably. Sarah Jane, you remember my telling you how sometimes the summer flowers affect me adversely? I wished to return to the house, but dearest Ty was struck by a sudden inspiration to paint the sea in the afternoon light. Farris is taking his paints to him now."

Sarah Jane was pulling on his sleeve. "Dante? What's wrong?"

Dante looked down at his wife, wondering when he had gotten to his feet. Ty had gone to the cliffs with Audrey? Why had he done that? According to what he had said last night, his brother wouldn't have crossed the street with the woman if the promise of a fortune in gold awaited him on the far side.

"Yes, Dante," Audrey asked, "whatever is wrong? You look as if you've seen a ghost. Sarah Jane, perhaps you should ring for Babbitt. The doctor in Brussels may have been correct, and dearest Dante may be suffering a brain fever. No, no! Allow me to do it. You sit there, and don't cry, dear sister. Everything will be all right. Ty and I will still allow you to live at Cliff Walk. Everything will be fine, I promise!"

Dante pressed his hands to his suddenly pounding head, trying to block out Audrey's voice, her extremely credible, concerned voice. What was wrong with him? Why did he feel such sudden dread, now, in the midst of his newfound happiness?

"I'm fine, Sarah," he announced with what he hoped was believable conviction. "Just fine. A goose walked over my grave, that's all," he added, forcing a smile. "Here, let me help you to your feet. We'll take a leisurely stroll out to the cliffs and tender Ty our congratulations. Audrey, would you care to join us?"

Audrey rolled her eyes. "Join you? Honestly, Dante, I know you've lost your memory, but can't you remember anything? The flowers, Dante, the *flowers.* You two go on. I am suddenly weary, this having been a most delightful, yet tiring day. I believe I'll go to my rooms and pen a note to Curtis. He'll be delighted to hear that Ty is recovering."

Dante didn't try to persuade her, but took Sarah Jane's arm and all but dragged her toward the rear steps of the main building and down the garden path leading to the cliffs.

They were only halfway across the grassy field when Farris appeared, dirty, disheveled, out of breath, his eyes all but bugging out of his head.

The earl's personal servant fell to the grass at their feet, sobbing as he clutched Dante's knees. "I—I did what she said, m'lord. I took out the paints. But he weren't there, where he always is. I looked and I looked. And then I followed the tracks of his wheels, until I lost them near the slope. Oh, m'lord, it's terrible! *Terrible!* I was always so careful about goin' past the slope, what with the trees in some spots and how it's so hard to keep from headin' toward the cliffs. But that's where the earl's chair's gone—off the path, through the scrub, and over the cliffs! I seen it down there, all broken and smashed on the rocks!"

CHAPTER 15

Oh do not die, for I shall hate
All women so, when thou art gone.

John Donne

Sarah Jane wondered why she couldn't cry.

Everyone else had been weeping all of the afternoon and evening—the housemaids, the kitchen help, Farris, and most especially Audrey. Everyone save Dante, who was still out on the cliffs, even now, with a fearsome storm blowing in from the Channel, still calling for Ty through the roar of the wind, still searching for his brother.

Dusk had come unusually early, and with it the first lashings of rain, so that she could no longer stand at her bedchamber window and see the vague outline of her husband's tall, broad-shouldered figure in the distance, his riding cloak blown about his long, lean legs as he stood outlined against the stormy sky at the edge of the incline closest to the house, looking down at the waves as they crashed against the rocks far below him.

Her heart ached for him. For all of them.

Sarah had never considered herself the sort to be a source of strength in a crisis, the one everyone else would turn to for help, for answers. But that role had been thrust upon her today without her applying for the position. Yes, she had often fancied herself to be a heroine, but those were only fanciful childish dreams, and she had long months ago stopped living in dreams. This was reality. This was a terrible reality, without a jot of romantic fancy in it anywhere.

So she could not play the heroine, for this was not a play. She could only react as best she could, shielding those she loved from having to view the rising hysteria inside her, concentrating on the domestic side of the tragedy and keeping on, going on, thinking without really *thinking*, reacting without overreacting, looking at the overall problem without once allowing her mind to conjure up a picture of Ty's broken body lying on the rocks.

It was the only way she could cope. It was the only way she could keep from screaming and screaming and screaming.

People still had to eat. People had to be assigned definite tasks, and she had spent the afternoon and early evening sending servants to the village to gather a party of men to search the rocks and the narrow, stony strip of beach at the bottom of the cliffs. It was Sarah Jane who had calmly instructed Audrey's woman to take the near-to-swooning countess to her chamber and dose her with laudanum. It was Sarah Jane who had ordered food and warmed ale to be served up to the search party in the Cliff Walk kitchens.

And it was she, left almost alone at Cliff Walk, who had met Lord John in the family drawing room just two hours ago and told him about his brother when that laughing, volatile young gentleman had returned after leaving the library, riding pell-mell to the Randolphs', and begging Sir Thomas for his daughter Lucy's hand in marriage.

So now Lord John was out on the cliffs with her husband. Servants were holding lanterns high as they searched through the undergrowth covering much of the area known as the slope, praying to find an injured Tyler, or his body.

The body.

Sarah Jane shivered, drawing her shawl closer around her shoulders as the words echoed in her brain, as she paced the area just inside the French doors overlooking the main path to the cliffs, too numb with fatigue, with sorrow, to pay any

277

but the most fleeting attention to the dull ache that came and went in her lower back.

Poor Emma. How would she react when she heard the news? That she had chosen this day of all days to take Robbie to visit with his paternal grandmother in a village a full six miles from Cliff Walk! Sarah Jane still hadn't decided which would be worse—to post a servant at Emma's door to tell her what had occurred once she returned late this evening, or to wait until tomorrow, when the weather had cleared, and face her personally to impart the sad news.

No matter what she did, Sarah Jane could be certain her news would devastate Emma, and Robbie as well. For Ty was dead. He had to be dead. The Bath chair had been reduced to splinters on the rocks, and the waters of the Channel had swallowed up Tyler Muir forever. If he had attempted to return to Cliff Walk on his own and the Bath chair had proved unwieldy, veering off the path and onto the slope, there could have been no other result. Otherwise, if he had managed to maneuver himself free of the chair before it was irrevocably committed to plunging into the sea, he would have been found by now.

Tyler Muir was dead.

No. *No.* Sarah wrapped her arms about herself and continued to pace the area in front of the French doors. She wouldn't think about that. It did no good to think about that. She wouldn't think about Ty. She would think about other things.

Would Dante and Johnny return soon?

Had their valets laid out dry clothes for them and kept hot water on hand for their baths?

Was there still a pot of stew simmering on the stove? They would both be hungry, having missed their dinner.

Should she have sent for the doctor?

The vicar?

What sort of burial ceremony could there be, without a body?

Why can't I cry?

"Excuse me, ma'am," Babbitt announced from the doorway, his usually rather gruff voice tinged with sadness, but still holding room for a modicum of censure. "Miss Lucy Randolph is without, and *alone,* ma'am. I think she came on horseback. Shall I show her in?"

"Pardon me?" Lucy Randolph was here? Yes, that was plausible. Sarah Jane remembered sending a servant to the Randolphs' to ask them to search the coastline to the rear of their property. Tides could do strange things, and a body once washed away from one shore could very easily—*Stop it, Sarah!* she warned herself silently. *You're not to think. You can't be of any assistance if you begin to think. Just act. Just act.* "Oh . . . oh, yes, of course, Babbitt. Please show her in. And bring us some tea, for Miss Randolph must be chilled straight through to the bone if she rode all this way in the rain."

Lucy Randolph swept into the drawing room a few moments later, her shoulder-length red hair dark with rain, as were the shoulders and hem of her midnight blue riding habit, her long, smooth, manlike strides bringing her quickly across the room so that she could hold her hands close to the fire. Sarah Jane caught a glimpse of the determined look in her green eyes and relaxed slightly, for Lord John's fiancée, a tall woman of the advanced age of five and twenty, was no die-away miss.

"I came the moment I heard, and outran my groom several miles back," Lucy declared without preamble, skewering Sarah Jane with her green gaze. "Where's Johnny? I have to go to him. God only knows what he'll do. I've seen him mad with grief before, after Ty's accident and with Lord Dante off somewhere with Wellington and of no use to us at all. I won't have my Johnny crawling back into a bottle, Lady Dante, I swear it. Not this time. Not while I have breath left in my body! Not that the earl is dead, for he can't be. He simply can't be! Oh, excuse me, Lady Dante. Papa always says I'm too frank by half, and liable to run roughshod over everybody. Goodness, but you're a small one, aren't you, even with that huge belly? I keep forgetting how little you are. Should be dropping that foal any time now, if I'm not mistaken. Are you all right?"

279

"Please, Lucy, as I've asked you before, just call me Sarah," Sarah Jane said, handing Lucy her shawl to drape over her shoulders and ignoring Miss Randolph's offhand comparison of her hostess to a mare. "And I'm much calmer now that you're here, Lucy. If Emma Franklin, my good friend from the village, could be with us I would be even better, as two Boadiceas must certainly be better than one. Johnny and Dante will need us women to be strong. Ty, too, when he's found."

Lucy pushed a hand through her hair, sweeping its dripping heaviness back off her forehead. "It's as cold as a witch's teat out there, at least for July it is. Thank you for the shawl, although it's probably ruined now. Um . . . there hasn't been any news, then, Sarah? Nothing at all?"

"No," Sarah Jane said, her bottom lip beginning to tremble slightly, so that she pressed a hand to her mouth, hoping to physically hold on to her composure. She didn't want to talk about it, think about it. "Not for the last two hours. But certainly that's encouraging? I mean, if they haven't found a body—" Her voice broke and she could say nothing else.

"Oh, come here, you poor scrap!" Lucy exclaimed, gathering Sarah Jane close against her, unknowingly destroying the last of the younger woman's composure with her abrupt offer of sympathy. "You poor, dear, brave little thing!"

Sarah Jane began to cry then, sobbing against the taller woman's thin breast, allowing her grief and her fears the outlet she had been denying herself, not able to control herself until Babbitt had placed a tea tray on a nearby table and withdrawn.

At last, knowing she had to rein in her emotions or else harm the baby and be of no help to Dante when he returned to the house, Sarah Jane pulled herself free of Lucy's embrace, apologizing for her outburst. "Come along, Lucy," she said after wiping her tear-wet cheeks one last time with her sleeve. She took the other woman's hand and gave it a companionable squeeze. "Let's go upstairs and see if Mildred can find you something dry to wear. We're both wet now, and not all of the moisture is from my tears. You can't return home tonight in any case. I'll order a chamber prepared for you."

They had just stepped into the hallway when the French doors opened and Dante and Lord John appeared, the two of them soaked to the skin, their expressions grim. Behind them, rain poured down incessantly and the sky was lit with a sudden streak of lightning, a bone-rattling clap of thunder following almost immediately afterward.

"Dante?" Sarah Jane called out as he turned to push the doors shut against the wind, already knowing that he and Lord John were not the bearers of good news.

She watched as he slipped out of his sodden cloak, dropping it to the floor beside Lord John's without saying anything and then heading for the drinks table behind his brother. She and Lucy exchanged quick glances as Lord John poured out two snifters of brandy.

"Oh, no, you don't, Johnny Muir!" Lucy exclaimed hastily, scampering across the room to preemptively remove the snifter from her beloved's hand. "There's hot tea over there ready to warm you."

"Christ, Lucy, not now," Lord John grumbled, attempting to retrieve the snifter. "I need something more than tea if I'm to go back out there tonight. And what are you doing here in the first place? We've just gotten betrothed, not married, by God. Oh, all *right,*" he exclaimed as Lucy glared at him, so tall that she was nearly on eye level with him as she stared him down. "Damn me if I can figure out how you women do it, and I'm not even bracketed yet. Come on, Lucy, lead me to the teapot."

"Dante?" Sarah Jane reached him only after he had downed his own drink, and he looked at her evenly for a moment before swiftly turning to hurl the snifter into the fireplace, where it exploded into a thousand pieces. "Oh, Dante, don't. Please don't," she begged, taking his arm as he turned to pick up the decanter, obviously intent upon sending it winging after the snifter.

"Don't, Sarah?" he questioned her tightly, wearily rubbing the back of his neck. "Ty's gone, and I helped kill him. My own brother! My brother, whom I was just beginning to remember, to know. And all because I wanted to punish Audrey for lying to me, for trying to feather her own nest because of my loss of memory. It seemed a just and fairly innocent revenge. *Innocent!* Christ, Sarah, that's almost funny!"

Sarah Jane took the decanter from his hand and replaced it on the table. She had begun to tremble at the fierceness in his tone, the near despair, the barely leashed anger.

He turned his eyes upward, as if he could see into the bedchambers above him. "Is she still in her bed, playing the grief-stricken widow? Her hysterics almost convinced me, and would have if I hadn't been in on Ty's joke. God, I know I can't prove it, but this was no accident. She pushed Ty over that cliff and then came back here, so cool, so composed, smiling all the way, regaling us with lies about how happy she and Ty were with their reconciliation. The woman never opens her mouth except to tell lies! I'm going to go up there now and *choke* the truth out of her!"

"Darling, no!" Sarah Jane exclaimed, truly frightened, for she had never before seen Dante, seen anybody, in such a black rage. "We can't be sure. None of us can be sure. And besides, Ty might still be found. There are whole sections of the slope where he could have flung himself free of the chair before it tumbled off the cliff. The path to the spot he and Emma favored for their painting runs along the slope for some distance. When I questioned Farris earlier, he said none of you could tell precisely where Ty disappeared, and the chair had already been washed out to sea by the time you got to the cliffs, so that poor Farris couldn't remember where he had seen it."

"That's true enough, Dante," Lord John said, sitting close beside Lucy, who was pouring him a second cup of tea. "Farris was too overcome to remember where he had seen the chair. We've had to search the entire area. And then the rain started, wiping out whatever tracks we might have hoped to find. Of course, having all those men trampling the area didn't help."

"Exactly!" Sarah Jane exclaimed. "Ty could be lying somewhere, injured but not dead. Why, he could have pulled himself beneath one of the trees and fallen sound asleep waiting for you to find him. Please wait until morning, when the storm is gone. There's nothing more you can do tonight. *Please,* Dante."

"We're looking for a man, pet, not a needle in a haystack. We should have found him by now. Certainly he would have heard us calling for him, at least before this damned storm blew in from the Channel. I can't help but imagine the worst."

"Please, Dante," Sarah Jane repeated, unashamedly pleading with him.

"For God's sake, man," Lord John agreed, holding on to Lucy's hand and unceremoniously pulling her to her feet. "Listen to your wife. Throttling Audrey won't serve any purpose, although the notion does hold a certain appeal. Come on, Lucy, my little love. You look as if you've been ridden hard and put away wet. We all do. I'll take you to Babbitt. He'll find you someplace to sleep."

At last Dante reached out and cupped Sarah Jane's tear-wet cheek with his large hand, so that she turned her head and pressed a kiss into his palm. "All right, little pet," he said at last, gifting her with a glimpse of his one-sided smile, "as everyone seems to agree with you. It's already nearing midnight. I'll wait, and then choke Audrey in the morning, even if we find Ty sitting under a tree, fine as ninepence. We've told everyone to be back here at dawn for another search, so I won't bother trying to sleep. In the meantime, however, I should probably bathe and change and eat something. Could you have Babbitt or someone arrange that, Sarah, before you take yourself off to bed?"

Blinking back tears and mutely nodding her agreement, Sarah Jane watched as her husband tiredly trudged toward the stairs behind Lord John and Lucy. When another pain began low in her back and wrapped itself around her lower abdomen, she told herself to treat it the same way she had dealt with any thought that Ty wouldn't be found alive.

She would ignore it.

* * *

Dante had bathed, dressed, and eaten a few bites of the rabbit stew Sarah Jane had sent up from the kitchens, and it was still only two o'clock. Dawn wouldn't arrive for several more hours, but at least the storm had abated, leaving a cloud-scudded sky devoid of moon or stars, so that he couldn't, even in his nearly overwhelming desire to be out and about, see that a return to the cliffs before dawn would serve any real purpose.

That did not mean, however, that he could stay in his rooms, a prisoner of the night and the unsettling thoughts that persisted in playing inside his head. With most of Cliff Walk shrouded in darkness, he went downstairs and prowled the hallways, unable to settle himself, settle his mind.

How had he allowed himself to believe that revenging himself against Audrey was even remotely important? How had he let himself be amused by Ty's suggestion that he tease her with hints that he wished to resume the intimate side of their marriage? Both he and Ty had behaved badly, immaturely, acting like young boys out for a lark when they should have been rejoicing that the truth had been discovered at last, that Ty was indeed slowly regaining the use of his legs, and that Dante had begun to recall snippets of his past, his memories of Sarah Jane.

Running a rig on Audrey should have been the last, the very last, thing on their minds!

But Ty had told him the story of the trick he and Dante had played on their father one Christmas, lacing the marquess's famous punch with oil of cloves so that all his guests had bolted to the kitchens in a quest for cool water.

That story had triggered a memory in Dante's brain of another prank he and Ty had engineered, an elaborate scheme that ended with the marquess paying five hundred pounds to an unscrupulous agent for an Irish-born breeding stallion that turned out to be a gelding. Dante and Ty had spent a lovely few weeks in London with their share of the money.

The feeling of camaraderie, of kinship, of *belonging,* that had accompanied these memories had served to make the planned revenge against Audrey seem like old times revisited, a union and reunion of brothers separated not only by one's lack of recollection but also by years and circumstances that had dimmed their memories of their happy shared youth.

But now Ty was missing, and most probably dead. It was one thing to reassure Sarah—dear, dear Sarah—with words of hope, but it was another to try to make himself believe that Ty was out there somewhere, injured, soaking wet from the rain, but alive, playing another prank on Audrey without first letting his brother in on the joke.

Did he really believe that Audrey had cold-bloodedly pushed her husband to his death, then returned to Cliff Walk, not a hair out of place, smiling and chattering as if nothing had occurred? Could he believe her show of grief, when he knew she didn't love her husband, had never loved her husband, even before his accident had made him, in her eyes, no more than an encumbrance to her determination to shine in London Society?

"Who's there?"

Dante looked up to see Sarah Jane standing on the stairs, clutching the edges of her long white wrapper against her breasts, a small branch of candles held just above her head.

"What are you doing up and about, pet?" he asked, going to the foot of the stairs to help her descend without tripping over her hem. "I should have thought you'd be sound asleep."

She avoided his eyes as she answered. "I would have thought so too, but I could not help worrying that you might be sneaking back out to the cliffs without waiting for Johnny and the rest of them. One Muir lost on the slope is enough, don't you think? The third step from the top creaks, you know, despite all our efforts to correct the problem, so when I heard it a few moments ago I thought I'd investigate. Are—are you hungry?"

He could feel her trembling as he took hold of her hand, and knew that, like him, she was remembering their interlude in the library before Audrey had come in and, within minutes, their world had turned to tragedy. It wasn't fair that this had happened just as they had begun to know each other, just as he had begun to remember her, as he had begun to believe that there still was such a thing as "happily ever after."

Not really hungry, but sensing that Sarah Jane needed something to occupy her mind, he nodded and allowed her to lead him down the hallway to the kitchens. He took up the chair she motioned for him to occupy and watched, his chin in his hands, as she moved about the kitchens, gathering meat, cheese, and a crusty loaf of bread.

There was something very homely, extremely comforting, in observing her economy of movement as she went about such common domestic chores, a feeling of reality within the unreal world he had occupied since his wound, since his introduction to Cliff Walk.

She placed a knife and two earthenware plates on the table before supplying them with a pitcher of milk and two mugs, then sat down across the table from him, smiling, he thought, rather secretively.

"And now I shall prepare our clandestine meal," she continued as she carved two thick slices from the loaf and began layering them with slabs of cheese and ham. "The bread is to be folded just so," she said, smiling at him, "and then eaten with the hands, like children biting into cookies." She handed him one of the concoctions he remembered as the sort created by the Earl of Sandwich—why he remembered that, he could not know—then sat back to watch him eat.

"We've done this before, haven't we?" he asked quietly, looking at her curiously, seeing her not as she looked now but as she must have looked long months ago, her hair drawn back into a thick braid, her soft mouth vulnerable, almost frightened. He closed his eyes and pinched the bridge of his nose. "I can feel it, feel the two of us here. See us." He gazed across the table at her once more. "But that's crazy. What would we have been doing in the kitchens?"

"Becoming friends," Sarah Jane answered quietly, her smile so beautiful he felt himself close to tears.

And then he remembered. The bits and pieces of memory,

the flotsam and jetsam of his past life that had floated in and out of his consciousness these past days suddenly jelled, coalesced, and became whole.

He remembered.

"And then I made you cry," he said, reaching across the table to take her hand. "More than once," he added, remembering how he had turned his back on her, on her grandmother's money, and for nearly two months behaved like a consummate ass, until the missive from Wellington had arrived and Sarah Jane had come to him, met him more than halfway, and given him the greatest gift he could ever hope to receive.

"Dante, it's all right," she told him fervently. "Everything will be all right."

His breathing was becoming labored, and he squeezed Sarah Jane's hand as memory after memory crashed in on him like the waves against the rocks at the bottom of the cliffs, culminating in the recollection of himself on the eve of the battle with Bonaparte, how he had sat off by himself at Lady Richmond's party, a decanter of brandy at his elbow, penning a long, rambling love letter to his wife. He had told her at last what he should have told her that final night— how much he had grown to appreciate her, rely upon her, care for her, *love* her. What had happened to that letter? Had Audrey found it tucked into the jacket of his uniform and destroyed it?

And what did that matter now, now that he was home again, now that his Sarah Jane, his own sweet pet, was sitting in the Cliff Walk kitchens with him? His most beautiful wife. His most beautiful Cliff Walk. Dear God, the transformation she had made! The miracle she had wrought! No wonder he hadn't remembered his childhood home. Cliff Walk had *never* looked like this!

"I remember, Sarah," he said, squeezing her hand even tighter, holding on fiercely to the single person in this world who could make everything right, even when so much was wrong. "Ah, Sarah, I remember how very much I love you!"

He dropped from the chair and onto his knees in front of her, still holding tight to her hand, his other hand going to the rounded mound of her belly, the evidence of their lovemaking. "I can barely believe this. I know now that we'll find Ty in the morning. This is a day of miracles!"

He looked up into her face, seeing the tears that slid slowly down her cheeks, noticing that she was biting on her bottom lip, biting so hard that a small red pearl of blood was visible at one corner of her mouth. He could feel the rigid contour of her belly growing even harder beneath his hand, becoming a live thing, a huge granitelike fist of contracting muscle. "Dear God, Sarah! What's happening?"

She shook her head slowly, as if any movement at all sent her into new agonies of pain. "I—I don't know, Dante. The babe isn't due to arrive for nearly four weeks, but the pains have grown so much worse in this past hour. I had decided to come downstairs, to seek out Babbitt so that he could send someone for Emma, but I found you instead. I could bear the pains before, Dante, but suddenly they are coming much more frequently, nearly one on top of the other, and I'm afraid—*Oh!* Oh, Lord, something's happening to me. I think I must be bleeding. Dante, I need Emma. *Please, Dante, send for Emma!*"

He caught her as she fainted, then scooped her up into his arms and ran out of the kitchens, calling for Babbitt, for Johnny, for anyone who would help him.

Dante stood beside the bed, his bed, his and Sarah Jane's marriage bed, holding his wife's hand, helping her ride the crest of another wrenching contraction. "That's it, darling, relax now. Relax and regain your strength," he said when he could sense that the contraction was easing.

"I—I'll try, Dante," she answered, looking so small, so fragile, so lost in the middle of the large bed even as her belly seemed to grow with each new pain, rising, nearly coming to a point at times, as if the baby was trying to rip his way out of his mother's body. "Have—have they found Emma?"

"Not yet, pet," he answered truthfully, wishing he could soothe her with a fib. Lord John had personally ridden to the Franklin cottage, only to find it dark. "She must have decided to spend the night with her husband's relatives because of the storm. Babbitt has sent a man to bring her back."

"And the doctor, m'lord?" Mildred asked as she wiped at Sarah Jane's forehead with a dampened cloth. "Where would that gentleman be? It's been three hours, m'lord. This baby shoulda been birthed by now, what with missy's water breakin' and all. Cook says so."

Dante didn't answer at once, for Sarah Jane was writhing in pain once more, her back arching as she fought to escape the agony of yet another contraction until he believed her spine might snap. "It's all right, pet," he soothed her as she gripped his hand with a fierceness he would have thought impossible in such a small woman. "Don't fight your body, pet. We don't have to wait for Emma or the good doctor. We can do this ourselves. Can't we, darling?"

"Emma!" Sarah Jane cried out as the pain finally began to ease and she fell back against the mattress once more. "I need her. I need her to tell me. I need to hear her say it again! It's too soon! The baby is coming too soon! I . . ." Her voice trailed off as yet another contraction racked her body.

"She's mighty scared, missy is, m'lord. She's been scared all along, exceptin' when Mrs. Franklin was about, promising her everything would be all right. Will she be here soon, m'lord? Missy needs her somethin' awful."

Dante had a sudden flash of memory, and his blood ran cold.

"Women like poor Sarah Jane, lud, Dante, you wouldn't wish to put me to the blush, would you?"

"Yes, Audrey, I believe I would."

"Some of us, sadly, are not constituted for—oh, Dante, how can I say this?—for ever enjoying that sort of pleasure. From what Sarah Jane confided to me yesterday and from what I'd already guessed on my own, I fear that she is just such a woman."

"Dear God, you didn't say any of this to Sarah, did you?"

"Say anything? How you wound me, Dante! Of course I didn't say anything. Sarah Jane is so small, Dante, so very

delicately constructed, that lovemaking is impossible for her without pain, ever. I suppose it is nature's way of protecting such women from a potentially deadly encounter with childbirth. I can only pray you have gotten her with child, so that you don't have to go to her again. Then we will all have to live with the fear of seeing her in childbed."

"That bitch!"

Mildred looked at him uncomprehendingly. "Mrs. Franklin, m'lord? Oh, no, sir. She's a good lady."

"Not Emma, Mildred," Dante said, taking Sarah Jane's hand in both of his and leaning closer to her, his voice hoarse, determined. "Sarah, listen to me. Come back from the pain and listen to me. She was lying. Audrey was *lying*. She just wanted to frighten you, frighten both of us. She didn't want you to produce a child who could inherit if anything happened to Ty. Sarah, do you hear me?"

She opened her eyes and looked up at him, her pain and fear plain to see deep in their brown depths. "Dante?" She pulled him even closer, holding his hands against her breasts. "Yes, yes. Tell me Audrey lied. Say it again. Please tell me Audrey lied."

"Oh, God. Oh, good *Christ!*" Dante was trembling, trying to remember everything Audrey had told him, knowing she had told his wife all of it and more as well. And no matter how hard Emma must have tried to convince her to the contrary, the pain now racking Sarah Jane's body was putting the lie to any assurances that all would be well. The baby was coming too soon; perhaps the baby wouldn't come at all. Everything was going wrong.

"Sarah," he whispered close beside her ear, "remember all of Audrey's lies. Remember how she told you that lovemaking was painful, devoid of pleasure. Then remember how we were that last night, that most wonderful night. There was no pain then, Sarah, no pain. Only pleasure, the most beautiful, perfect pleasure two people can share. Two people who love each other, Sarah, the way we love each other. I was here for you then, and I am here for you now. Let me help you, Sarah. Let me help you through the pain."

Another contraction gripped her, and she sucked in her breath, but this time she kept her eyes open, staring up at Dante as he willed her his strength, as tears dripped from his cheeks onto hers, as he died a thousand deaths, knowing that he couldn't lose her now, he couldn't lose his Sarah, his little pet. "Breathe, Sarah," he told her. "Don't fight the pain. Give in to it. Let your body do its work."

"M'lord? The doctor's here," Mildred said from behind him. "He was away from the village takin' care of Squire Baker's gouty foot and was planning to stay the night 'cause of the storm. Shall I let him in?"

Dante nodded, not taking his eyes off Sarah's small face. "Did you hear that, pet? The doctor's come. See how intelligent a puss you are, knowing enough to wait for him? But now it's time, pet. It's time we meet our child."

"You—you won't leave me, will you, Dante?" Sarah Jane asked, still gripping his hands in both of hers. "I'm sorry to be so frightened. I want to be brave. Just, please, don't leave me."

"You are brave, pet. You're the bravest woman in the world." Dante bent his head in order to wipe his streaming eyes against the back of his hand. How had he forgotten her, even for a moment? How could he have blocked his mind to the small miracle that was Sarah Jane Muir.

His bartered wife.

His only love.

She had come to him a stranger, and she had taken on all their burdens, making everything right for everybody in her own quiet way. Her unselfish, loving way. Cliff Walk could fall into the sea tomorrow, and he wouldn't regret the loss, as long as he had Sarah. She had become his world, his life.

"I won't leave you, pet," he promised as the doctor rushed in, tossing orders over his shoulder to Mildred and two housemaids. "I'll never leave you again."

An hour later Samantha Angelique Muir made her entrance into the world, red-faced and screaming with indignation, but perfectly healthy for all of her small size.

Her mother, before easing away into a well-deserved slumber, appeared to be enormously pleased.

Her extremely grateful father, after kissing his wife and child and receiving the congratulations of his younger brother and the rest of the household, donned his cloak and left the house just as a misty dawn broke over the coastline, once again on his way to the cliffs.

CHAPTER 16

You have delighted us long enough.

Jane Austen

Sarah Jane woke slowly, reluctantly, unwilling to leave behind the golden dream that had brought a smile to her in her sleep. In that dream Dante had been close at her side, telling her he remembered her, telling her how much he loved her, telling her that together they had created the most beautiful child ever to be born.

Her eyes opened wide all at once as she realized that it had not been a dream. It was all true. It was all wonderfully, gloriously, miraculously *true!*

Slowly she raised her hands from the mattress and slid them onto her abdomen, then grinned and turned her head toward the soft sounds emanating from the ornate blue-canopied basket near the windows. Those draperies would surely have to be changed now, she thought, remembering how proud Grandmother Trowbridge had been when the basket was delivered, declaring it a fitting cot for her great-grandson.

Samantha Angelique Muir. Quite a mouthful of names for such a small baby. Samantha Angelique. No one would dare to call her Samantha Angelique the way she had been addressed as Sarah Jane. Nor would they call her Sam or

Sammy, even if Dante had cleverly, laughingly, made sure the baby's initials spelled out SAM. Sarah Jane grinned again. And they most certainly would never call her Samuel. Ah, well. It was more than time that Grandmother Trowbridge learned she could not always have everything her way just by waving her money about!

Although, Sarah Jane realized, her grandmother's money *had* bought her granddaughter love. It was the single thing the woman probably had not thought possible.

Sarah Jane moved tentatively on the mattress, longing to go over to the basket and look down on her new daughter, since all she could remember was an amazing shock of coal black hair and two very large blue-gray eyes. But this slight exertion soon reminded her of the day and night of ever-increasing, paralyzing pain she had endured before Dante had broken through to her in those last long minutes leading up to the birth, assuaging her fears with his gentle persuasion, his comforting presence, his strength.

Tears stung her eyes as she remembered how badly she had behaved. Not like a heroine at all. But then she refused to condemn herself, realizing that some of her fear had been most natural for a young woman rather unprepared for childbirth. Any real blame should be directed at Audrey, who had deliberately set out to frighten her.

Besides, there was no such thing as a heroine, at least not outside of her grandmother's novels. A person just did what she could, that's all. Some people might be born to climb mountains, lead armies, or change the world. But most people could only do the best they could under the circumstances, living their lives as honestly as possible, hoping to make those they loved comfortable, helping those less fortunate, and trying not to hurt anyone else along the way.

Some people, Sarah Jane decided, her throat clogging with happy tears, were born to be wives, born to be mothers, born to transform a house into a *home.* And at the moment, with her body still sore and the memory of Dante's tears for her clear in her mind, she couldn't think of anyone else she'd rather be!

How wonderful that first hour after Samantha's birth had

been, she and Dante taking turns holding their daughter, the two of them marveling over the miracle they had wrought together, and Dante telling her over and over again how very much he loved the two women in his life.

Samantha began to whimper again and Sarah Jane bit her bottom lip—oh! what had she done to her lip?—wondering how loudly Mildred would complain if she left her bed and went to the baby.

She didn't have to wonder for long, for the door opened and Mildred came bustling in, her round face wreathed in smiles, tut-tutting as she went over to the basket and lifted out a small blanket-wrapped bundle. "Hush, child," she scolded gently. "Your sweet mama had more than her share of trouble birthing you and needs her rest."

"Good morning, Mildred," Sarah Jane said, trying to push herself up against the pillows and wincing with the effort. Goodness, she *had* been through a battle. "Bring Samantha to me, please. Is Lord Dante still abed, or is he waiting outside, champing at the bit to hold Samantha again?"

As soon as she uttered the words the memory of Ty's disappearance slammed into her consciousness. How could she have forgotten? She held out her arms to take the baby, barely looking at her as she asked the servant, "Has there been any news, Mildred? Any news at all?"

"Lord John found one of the earl's slippers a little while ago," Mildred answered, tucking the blanket more firmly around Samantha's small feet. "It was quite a ways from the cliff, nearby some trees. Nobody can believe they missed it yesterday. They're searchin' there now, with some hope, Lord John thinks, not as if a soul could believe it iffen they was to see the countess. Decked out head to toe in widow's weeds she is this morning, snifflin' into a black-edged handkerchief she had her woman up all night stitchin'—but still wearin' her diamonds."

Mildred shook her head. "She'd better steer a wide berth around that husband of yours, missy, for gennulman or no, he's bound to plant her ladyship a bruisin' facer iffen he claps eyes on her."

295

Sarah Jane peered across the room at the clock on the mantel, seeing that it had gone ten, which explained why the sun had already risen high enough in the sky to come pouring in her bedchamber windows. "Has anyone thought to go to Mrs. Franklin's cottage?"

"Babbitt put someone to it a few minutes ago. He woulda sent someone sooner, but most of the staff's out walkin' the cliffs, and one of the footmen is on his way to your grandmother's. Seems she paid him a gold piece to fetch her the minute he heard the baby was comin'. He was off to Trowbridge Manor at the crack of dawn. I told Lord John as much when he was in the kitchens, gulpin' down tea and showin' off the earl's slipper, and he warned me to arm the servants with pikestaffs and bolt all the doors. As if that'd keep her out."

Sarah sighed, looking at Samantha, who had once more fallen asleep. "If we're lucky, the footman will tell her that her grandchild is a girl and she'll not bother to come."

"That's true enough, missy, thinkin' as how she was so set on seeing a stem on our sweet little apple. But mayhap she'll surprise us all and be glad for you. His lordship was fair to burstin' with pride over Samantha, and over you, too, missy. Never saw a man cry like that, or thought I'd see one willin' to stay around for a birthin'. My mum always told me men only want to be there for their fun, then run like the devil himself is after them when it comes to the rest of it. You've got yourself a fine gennulman, missy. A fine gennulman."

Sarah Jane employed a corner of Samantha's blanket to wipe at her tears. "Yes, I have, haven't I, Mildred? Now if only everything else could end as happily."

There was a slight commotion at the doorway, and Sarah Jane looked up to see Lord Dante and Emma entering the room. They were smiling, and Sarah Jane began to hope.

"Dear girl!" Emma exclaimed, racing toward the bed. "Can you ever forgive me?"

"Forgive you? Emma, don't be silly," Sarah Jane admonished her friend as Emma began to coo at the baby. "You couldn't know I was to give birth last night. It wasn't as if you deliberately planned to be away from home yesterday."

"But I did!" Emma exclaimed, looking at Dante before scooping up Samantha and backing away from the bed. "Dante, perhaps you'd better explain."

"First things first, Emma," Dante said, seating himself on the side of the bed, taking Sarah Jane's hand, and pressing it to his lips. "Good morning, little pet. You look beautiful this morning. Are you well rested? And how is our small darling? I'd hold her, but I'm not up to prying her from Emma's arms."

Sarah Jane looked from Dante to Emma and then back again, unable to understand why they were so calm. "Has Ty been found?" she asked at last.

"My dear brother was never lost, Sarah," Dante informed her, one side of his mouth lifting in that well-remembered self-deprecating smile. "We only thought he was. However, when he is fully recovered and able to stand more solidly on his two feet, I'm going to knock him down. Several times, I imagine. And then Johnny is going to have at him. Do you mind, Emma?"

"Not in the slightest, Dante," she answered, placing Samantha back in her basket. "But our intentions were of the highest, if that means anything, which I most sincerely doubt," she added, smiling sheepishly.

"Now I'm confused," Sarah Jane protested, taking Dante's hand. "Ty's fine and always was? Then why couldn't you find him?"

"Because he didn't wish to be found, pet," Dante said, motioning for Emma to approach the bed once more. "You may want me to explain, Emma, but I'd rather leave this particular confession to you. If you don't mind, I am going to go over there and watch my beautiful daughter sleep."

"Emma?" Sarah Jane questioned as her friend drew up a chair and sat down beside the bed.

Emma sighed, rolling her eyes. "It was so stupid of us, so infantile and thoughtless. But Ty was *so* angry! I've never seen him so livid. Oh, let me begin at the beginning."

Sarah Jane snuggled into the pillows, looking at Dante as he bent over the basket, grinning at their daughter. "That might be best, Emma. You've put this household through a most trying time."

"Please, Sarah, don't remind me. When I think how upset everyone must have been—everyone except that terrible woman Ty married, that is—I just cringe." She shivered, then shook her head, as if to banish an unlovely thought. "You see, Sarah, I have not been as good as you thought me to be. I haven't been staying away from Cliff Walk since the afternoon of Audrey's return. I've only been keeping clear of the house. I sent Robbie off to his grandparents that same day, so as not to corrupt him with any knowledge of my assignations."

Well, Sarah Jane thought, *I may not be a heroine, but it would appear there are some people whose lives resemble the pages of a novel!* "Assignations? How romantic! Why, Emma, my good friend, I believe you are blushing."

"I may have put myself to the blush, Sarah, but I cannot lie and say I am sorry for what I did, what we did. For months Ty and I have been meeting out at our favorite spot on the cliffs, where we would go to paint and to talk, away from prying eyes. Ty would practice his walking. He has been working secretly with Johnny for some months now and is doing quite well, although he didn't want anyone to know until he could walk into the drawing room unaided. After each practice session we would go off under the trees and we would . . . we would—"

"Never mind that," Sarah Jane said quickly, not wishing to embarrass her friend further. "I understand."

"Well, that's extremely charitable of you, Sarah, for I know I behaved like a fallen woman, sneaking about with a married man, making love out-of-doors like some shameless hoyden." She smiled, looking much younger than her thirty years. "Not that either of us felt particularly guilty at the time, you understand."

"And also explaining my older brother's good humor," Dante said. "It was his cheerfulness that made it so difficult for me to remember him, as he had been like a bear with a

sore paw for these last ten years, since Emma's elopement."
Dante chuckled softly, then quickly returned his attention
to Samantha when Sarah wagged a disapproving finger at
him.

"So you had planned to meet Ty on the cliffs yesterday?"
Sarah Jane asked, caught up in the romance of the thing.

"Yes, just as usual," Emma answered. "Audrey asked Ty if
she could push his chair out toward the cliffs, so that they
could speak in private. And, yes, Sarah, I have learned what
he told her yesterday, and I have torn a strip off his foolish
hide for doing anything so stupid! Anyway, Ty thought it
above everything amusing to have Audrey take him to his
assignation and dismissed Farris once they were only a little
space from the house. Not only did he make Audrey push
him, but he insisted she push him farther along the cliffs
than he had ever been—even past me, so that I had to hide
in the tall grass along the slope. By the time he told her she
could stop, she was nearly exhausted and rather angry with
him for putting her to such exertion, I believe. That was his
first mistake."

Sarah Jane frowned. "What was his second?"

"Now, that's easy!" Dante said. "Telling Audrey that he
had been lying to her and that he was seeking a bill of
divorcement in order to marry Emma. He'd asked me
months ago to write to our solicitor about such a bill, and he
has kept the man's answer in his rooms, which was why I
thought, only for a moment, that Audrey had been telling
the truth when she said you and I didn't love each other."
Dante returned to the bedside. "That wasn't Ty's most
brilliant strategy, informing Audrey she was about to lose
everything—just when she had her hands on the handles of
his Bath chair."

"She didn't take the news well," Emma said, rolling her
eyes. "She began yelling at him, telling him that he had
ruined everything. That he should have died after his
accident, as any 'considerate' man would have done, leaving
her a countess. That she had paid dearly with her father's
money for her title and she wasn't about to let him take it
away from her. That, since she hadn't been able to keep you

nd Dante apart so that you wouldn't produce another
)ossible heir and thereby divide up the Muir money further,
t least she should be compensated with her title and a
,enerous allowance. I don't believe Audrey is very over-
rowded in her brain box, do you, Dante? I mean, did she
eally think we wouldn't eventually see through her lies?"

"So she *did* push him!" Sarah Jane turned to Dante. "But
1ow did he save himself?"

Emma answered. "I saw it all. I don't think Audrey truly
neant for him to go over the cliff, or at least I most sincerely
1ope not. She was just so very angry, so incensed, that she
ave his chair a shove and stormed off, probably thinking it
erved him right to be stranded so far out on the cliffs with a
torm rapidly rolling in from the Channel. But then the
hair began rolling down the slope, straight for the edge. I
an't tell you how frightened I became at that moment, even
.nowing that Ty is able to walk, for he still isn't particularly
trong or steady on his feet. Luckily his arms are quite
nuscular, from his habit of ofttimes pushing the wheels
1imself, you understand."

"He threw himself clear of the chair just as it was picking
1p speed—a magnificent move, or so he has informed
ne—then lay on the ground, watching as the chair went
>ver the cliff." Dante chuckled, shaking his head. "He said
1e had always planned to send the chair crashing onto the
ocks once he was finished with it."

Sarah Jane moved her eyes from left to right, feeling like
an observer at a royal tennis match as Emma and Dante
took turns telling the story. It was Emma's turn to speak
again, so Sarah looked in her direction once more, waiting
to hear the rest of it. "Please, go on. Tell me everything!"

"There's not much more to tell, and I am not particularly
proud of the part I played in the scheme. I was at his side in
only moments, frightened that he had been injured, only to
find him lying on his back, *laughing!* I tell you, Sarah, I
nearly boxed his ears for him! But then, when he told me
what he wanted to do, I began wondering if I had fallen in
love with a particularly devious but extremely brilliant
nan."

"He had decided to turn the tables on Audrey?" Sara asked, beginning to understand. "He wanted her to believ she had killed him? But why? And why didn't he tell u. That really was quite bad of him, Emma. Dante and Johnn were devastated! We all were!"

"I know, Sarah, and I'm so sorry. But Ty did have a goo reason, I assure you. And we always meant to tell you, Emma added, frowning. "But first I had to hide him, whic wasn't an easy job, for he could only walk a short distanc before he was reduced to crawling, then pulling himsel along on his forearms. He had me place one of his slippers i some tall grass a good hundred yards from the cliff, and a: equal distance in the exact opposite direction from where h was. He hoped Dante would find it and realize he hadn' plunged over the edge with the chair. Then I helped him t hide in a fallen log that was hollowed out enough for him t crawl completely inside it. Dante? Please tell her the rest.

Sarah Jane obediently looked to her husband, still tryin to imagine the earl stuffed inside a hollow log. She hope there had been ants sharing his hidey-hole, and big hairy spiders. How dare he upset Dante just to get revenge on hi: wife, who was sure to believe herself a murderess? As soor as she asked herself the question she dismissed it, remem bering Audrey's frightening description of childbirth. Per haps the earl hadn't done anything so awful after all!

"After settling Ty," Dante explained, "Emma went hack to her own house to get him some blankets and cold meat. But when she returned we were all out there on the cliffs searching for Ty. She knew she couldn't risk being seen, sc she returned to the village and hid in her cottage, waiting for dark. Ty said he could hear me calling and wanted to answer, but he was so angry with Audrey that he kept his silence."

Emma sighed audibly. "It began to grow dark," she said sadly, "and then all at once the wind intensified and the skies opened up. Oh, that terrible storm! Even after Dante and Johnny had broken off their search for the night, it was too late for me to do anything more than stumble around among the trees in the rain and the darkness, looking for Ty.

then staying with him, keeping him as dry as possible, and praying for the rain to stop. He has caught himself a most prodigiously nasty cold, which soothes me somewhat, although nothing can possibly make up for the upsetment we've caused you. I sought Dante out early this morning, and he helped me move Ty to my cottage before the searches began again, but I was too late to be of any help to you, Sarah, although you seem no worse for my absence. Samantha's a beautiful child, Sarah, and Dante tells me you were simply splendid!"

Sarah Jane slipped her hand into Dante's. "It was Dante who was splendid, Emma, but thank you. Oh, I'm so happy for you and Ty. Does Johnny know?"

"Everyone knows, pet, except Audrey, who saw me earlier in the hallway and most prettily requested an advance on her allowance with which to buy herself a new wardrobe for her year of mourning, as her beloved Ty would have wanted her to be 'comfortable.' We'll allow her to keep believing herself a murderess for a few more days, until Ty is feeling more the thing and you have regained enough strength to be carried downstairs. I think you might want to watch when Audrey first sees Ty. Sir Thomas Randolph, Lucy's father, has not been let in on the joke either, but for good reason, for Ty is planning a drama. Sir Thomas has already agreed to be present, however, so that there will be a witness willing to testify to any interested persons that my dearest sister-in-law tried to do away with her husband. Once Ty is done with Audrey, she'll be wiser than to demand *anything* from us."

"Dante, you're smiling in a most evil way," Sarah Jane said, cocking her head to one side as she looked up at him. "What are you and Ty planning now?"

"Actually, pet, Ty only wanted some sort of public revenge. The completed plan is mostly Johnny's idea," he told her, dropping a kiss on her forehead. "It seems all of us Muirs have a penchant for mischief. I cannot feel guilty, pet, when I remember how Audrey has nearly destroyed us all with her single-minded selfishness. You rest, darling, and we'll see you later. Emma has to go downstairs, leaning heavily on my arm, happy about Samantha but mourning

Ty. Do you think you are up to that much playacting, Emma?"

"If it will get us shed of Audrey, I am willing to recite Shakespeare's complete works while juggling flaming torches!" Emma declared feelingly as she headed for the door, leaving Dante and Sarah Jane alone.

"I love you, Sarah Muir," Dante said, tenderly kissing her sore lips. "I love you because of how wonderful you are, because of Samantha, because of the way you have come into this house and made everyone in it better for your presence. But right now I love you because you don't think all of us Muirs are as mad as hatters."

"Nonsense, Dante," she told him, already yawning, for she was once again very sleepy. And wonderfully happy. And completely, gloriously content. "That is precisely *why* I love you. All my mad, bad, gigantic Muirs!"

Elizabeth Trowbridge arrived at Cliff Walk on the third afternoon following Samantha's birth, just as Dante had begun to believe the domineering woman was purposely avoiding her granddaughter, who'd had the audacity to disobey her and produce a girl child.

Lord John had caught sight of the shiny black traveling coach from the fields at the edge of the estate and immediately ridden to the mill to warn his brother. Dante didn't spare his mount as he galloped back to Cliff Walk, arriving there at the same time Elizabeth Trowbridge was being helped down the steps of the coach by her paid messenger.

"Good afternoon, ma'am," Dante said, slipping from his horse and bowing in front of the woman.

"Dante," she answered shortly. "I'm told Sarah Jane and the babe are both in fine fettle. A girl child, huh? Well, we don't always get it right the first time out of the stable, or so I'm told. You've still got four years, not that you'd remember that, though you'd better soon, son. I'll not have my sweetie living with a lunatic who can't remember his own name, much less what he's been bought to do. But Curtis is sure to point that out to you."

"I'm sure he will, but thank you for the reminder. And

how pleasant it is to see you again. Isn't that the same brooch you were wearing when first we met at Trowbridge Manor?"

Mrs. Trowbridge eyed him warily for some moments, her thick neck, much to Dante's amusement, flushing a deep red. "Your brains unscrambled themselves, then, son? What a pleasant surprise, not that I didn't expect it, you understand. I was never serious about that madhouse business. Well, not *very* serious." She turned to the Muir footman and delivered a stiff cuff to the back of his head. "Clod! A single fat gold piece don't buy half again as much as it used to, does it?"

"Apparently not," Dante replied, offering the temporarily discommoded woman his arm and escorting her up the short flight of steps leading to the family wing. "And no amount of gold, it appears, has served to purchase you a great-grandson. However, if you have come here harboring a plan to disturb my wife with your chagrin, I suggest you immediately rethink the matter. I'll not have Sarah upset."

"Oh, you won't, won't you?" Mrs. Trowbridge countered, seemingly recovering quickly as she stripped off her gloves and threw them at his face, so that he had no choice but to catch them. "Well, good for you, boy. Good for you! Ha! Now look who's standing there with his eyes all bugged out and his mouth agape! What's the matter, son? Did you think the butcher's wife would be ungraceful in defeat? Have I disappointed you? Were you spoiling for a fight?"

Dante handed the gloves to Babbitt and followed Mrs. Trowbridge into the family drawing room. "The prospect had occurred to me, yes," he admitted, watching as the woman unerringly navigated her way to the chair beside a table holding a full candy dish. "However, even though it appears you have reconciled yourself to Samantha's birth, Sarah and I wish for you to know that, although we chose to name our daughter in her grandfather's memory, we neither expect nor will accept the agreed-upon settlement you had planned to provide upon the birth of a male child. We don't expect it now, and we don't want it when our first son is born, most probably within the five-year limit you imposed, if Sarah has anything to say about it. She has quite taken to motherhood and is excellent in the role, as she is in all areas. Please, madam, feel free to let *your* jaw drop once more."

"Really? You're turning down my money? And you still insist you've regained your memory? You're a *Muir,* son, remember? Give yourself a moment to think. Let your Muir blood course through your brain. Never in history has a Muir worth his borrowed salt ever turned down a penny."

Dante leaned against the edge of a small table, careful not to get any of his dust on Sarah Jane's new furniture, for he had been riding most of the day and knew he should bathe and change before sitting in any of the pale chairs. His new concern made him smile, for he had never worried about saving the original furniture, which had been almost past repair anyway. But Sarah Jane was mistress at Cliff Walk now, and she took pride in a neat house.

"Many things about us Muir men no longer apply, madam," he told her, watching as she shoved three sugar-plums into her mouth, one immediately following after the other.

Mrs. Trowbridge smiled around the confections. "Yes, I can see that," she said, then turned to another subject, although her tone was tentative and not at all eager, as Dante would have supposed. "But why aren't you in mourning? Where's the bunting? The crepe? Or was the earl found alive?"

"He hasn't been found at all, madam," Dante told her, having no difficulty lying to the woman, "but mourning clothes would be premature and a sign of pessimism. Two small search parties are still searching the area around the cliffs. We do, however, plan a small memorial service this evening in the chapel, for our hopes are almost nonexistent at this late stage. Your presence is, of course, welcome."

Mrs. Trowbridge sighed and shook her head. "Poor Easterly. Damned shame, that's what it is. I know I said I wanted you to become the earl, but not this way. Tumbling over a cliff? I always pictured him dying in his bed. You know. Neat, clean, and with no question that he'd cocked up his toes. A memorial service, you say? We'll be wearing black for that at least, won't we? Have you sent for Curtis?"

Dante stood up, wiping his hands on his thighs as if to brush away the sight of Elizabeth Trowbridge trying to walk the tightrope between her hopes and her knowledge that she was being more than a little ghoulish.

"No, madam, we haven't. He'd be of no use in a search, and Johnny and I decided we wouldn't care to have the man about, placing wagers on how long it might take until the tide washed Ty's body to shore. Not that he doesn't love his sons. He does, but it's his greater love of gambling that rules his life. Do you wish to see Sarah and your great-granddaughter, or shall I merely ring for Babbitt to refill the candy dish? Even better, shall I call for your traveling coach? There's still enough light left in the day for you to reach a comfortable inn between here and Trowbridge Manor."

"Now, now, son, don't go cutting up stiff on me. You never said a word when I told Curtis that I didn't think the earl would stay above ground much longer and was willing to put my money on you. I don't want to see Easterly dead. I got to liking him during my visit. Truly. But a woman in my position has to be practical—businesslike, you understand. It seemed so reasonable at the time, before I met the lad."

"I was practical as well, madam, listening to you all but bury my brother, and silently cursing you while I held out my hand in order to save my family. I'm not proud of what I did, but I've learned to live with my failings. Fortunately, Sarah has forgiven me and has even come to love me. And so, madam, while I detest your motives and feel ashamed for the part of me you made visible with your offer of money, I most sincerely thank you. Not for the money but for Sarah. She has given me everything I now hold dear—her love and our daughter. She holds more value for me than any fortune you could name. More value even than Cliff Walk itself, which is something I never believed I would live to say."

Mrs. Trowbridge hauled herself out of the chair, her smile self-satisfied. "You mean that, don't you, son? Well, that decides it! You'll have the agreed-upon settlement as soon as it can be arranged. But it's not for you, so don't go getting your back up. The money will be for Samantha. My little great-granddaughter. My little sweetie's baby girl. It'll make her a tolerable dowry by the time she's grown, if you invest it correctly, which I'll make sure you do. Now, that's enough talk of money and such. Where's Sarah Jane? I didn't ride all this way to look at your pretty face all day!"

The chapel was in near darkness, the only light emanating from a few candles flickering on the altar, casting the hollows of the vicar's thin face into stark relief.

Sarah Jane had taken up a seat in the very first left-hand pew, Dante beside her, while Audrey sat in solitary splendor across the aisle from them, beautiful in her widow's weeds, diamonds glinting in her earlobes and at her throat. Mrs. Trowbridge and Sir Thomas Randolph had been positioned directly behind the countess, and Lord John and Lucy took up their stations behind Sarah Jane and Dante.

The wolf stayed where he was, untouched by Sarah Jane's unfinished refurbishing of the chapel, toothily grinning down upon all of them.

The only sound to be heard in the chapel was that of Audrey's quiet weeping as she occasionally lifted a black-edged handkerchief to her eyes and dabbed at them cautiously, for otherwise her tender skin might redden.

This was Sarah Jane's first sojourn outside her lying-in chamber. Her grandmother had all but forbidden it, but Sarah Jane had been adamant. She wasn't sure exactly what was going to transpire in this chapel, but no lingering soreness, not even her love for her child—temporarily entrusted to the loving and increasingly capable hands of Mildred—would keep her from this moment.

"So you're a widower, Sir Thomas? I'd heard that," Mrs. Trowbridge inquired of the small, slim man who was almost ten years her junior. She spoke in her usual booming voice, causing Sarah Jane to cringe in embarrassment. "My estate's in the opposite direction from yours, but certainly not too distant for us to visit each other from time to time."

307

"Visit?" Sir Thomas squeaked. "Well, no, I suppose not, madam."

"You do know that I'm a widow, don't you? Dear Sam, gone these nearly eighteen months, now, in fact. Lonely, ain't it, without a mate? See this ring? Cost me five hundred pounds. Some might say that's too dear for such a small bauble, but not for a woman left as solidly set up as Sam left me. Nope, not a problem with blunt on this end. You well off, Sir Thomas?"

"She's at it again," Dante whispered in Sarah Jane's ear. "If my father were here he'd lay odds your grandmother will have Sir Thomas proposing before the month is out."

"*Shhh*, Dante," Sarah Jane admonished, trying not to smile, knowing that Sir Thomas very much reminded her of her Lilliputian grandfather. Lucy's mother must have been the giant in the Randolph family. "Besides, if she does half so well for herself as she did for us, we should both be very happy for her."

"I'll be happy for anything that keeps her away from Cliff Walk, pet," Dante said, then turned as Lord John tapped him on the shoulder.

"What's the vicar waiting on, Dante, a sign from the heavens? I've been champing at the bit all day, looking forward to this. Did you get a good look at Audrey? She can barely contain herself, thinking about the allowance you're certain to settle on her—and of her next husband, I wouldn't doubt. Countesses, even those who smell of the shop, are sure to bring a good price on the open market. Heartless bitch! I can hardly wait to tell her those diamonds are nothing but pretty paste!"

Sarah gasped. "Johnny! You must be joking."

Dante pressed a finger to his lip, motioning them all to silence. "No, pet, he's not. We're the pockets-to-let Muirs, remember, or at least we were when those jewels were purchased. Ty always considered Audrey's gullibility a good joke. However, I believe we all did her a disservice, dismissing her as a harmless nuisance who'd gotten all she wanted when she became his countess and tripped off to London with Curtis to spend her father's money."

"Excuse me," Lucy Randolph interrupted in a fierce whisper, "but I believe the vicar is about to begin. It might be prudent, Johnny, if you stopped behaving like a perfect yahoo and stopped smiling as if you were pleased as punch that the earl is toes cocked-up. Goodness, Johnny, it's easier to expect I could single-handedly bridle a wild stallion than to believe I'll ever get you to behave. And the rest of you, for that matter."

Sarah Jane quickly sobered and faced the altar, squeezing Dante's hand as the vicar began to speak and Audrey's weeping hitched up a notch. Was the woman feeling guilty?

"My dear friends, my lords, my ladies, dearest countess," the vicar said in a thin, reedy voice. "We are gathered here this evening for a most sad occasion, to mourn the tragic end of our brother Tyler, Earl of Easterly."

"Poor boy!" Mrs. Trowbridge exclaimed tearfully before loudly blowing her nose. "I'd gladly give a quarter of my fortune to see him home safe and sound."

From somewhere in the chapel, but not nearby, Sarah Jane thought she heard someone gasp.

Almost immediately Lord John began to cough loudly, as if something, most probably his delight in Mrs. Trowbridge's rash statement, had become caught in his throat. "There, there, sweetheart," Lucy admonished, giving him three whacking slaps between his shoulder blades. "You must control your grief."

The vicar looked out over the small congregation, waiting for silence, and then continued: "Lord Easterly was not well known to me, as he did not choose to worship with us on Sunday, but he was nevertheless a Christian, one of God's own, a son, a brother, a husband."

"Oh, my husband! My poor Ty!" Audrey wailed, her shoulders shaking with grief. In truth, Sarah Jane thought, the woman cried to good effect. But then, she cried so often. Perhaps it was a talent one could improve upon with practice. "To die so cruelly," Audrey protested, "when we were just beginning our new life together. It's just too *cruel,* too *terrible!*"

"I've always admired the English stiff upper lip, haven't

you?" Sarah Jane heard Lord John ask Lucy. "A few more tears and we'll all be awash in 'em. How did Noah build that ark, anyway? Wasn't it something about forty *cubits?*"

The vicar cleared his throat and opened his prayer book. "'The Lord giveth and the Lord taketh away. Blessed is the name of the Lord.' The——"

"The Lord didn't take me," a disembodied voice intoned loudly from somewhere in the darkness. "I was *pushed* at him."

"What in blazes was that?" Mrs. Trowbridge asked in real fright, throwing her rather large self at the rather smaller Sir Thomas for protection. "Who said that?"

"He was pushed. He was pushed. He was pushed," said another voice.

Emma. It wasn't one of Macbeth's three witches intoning the ominous pronouncement, but it was good. It was very good, in fact, and extremely effective. Sarah Jane covered her mouth with both hands and looked to Audrey, who was suddenly dry-eyed and extremely pale beneath her heavy black veil.

"Pushed?" Lord John asked, rising as if on cue to recite his line, and Sarah Jane sat back, still not completely sure of what was going on, but more than happy to watch as the events unfolded. It was more than time, in Sarah Jane's opinion, that Audrey Muir learned what it was like to be frightened by someone else's innuendo.

"Puushhed," Emma's spiritlike voice repeated, dragging out the single word in a wail that lasted for the space of several seconds. "An uneasy soul, foully murdered and unable to go to his rest until the guilty one confesses to the sin. Confess. Confess. *Confess."*

"Tell them, tell them, tell them," the first voice chanted in Ty's unmistakable baritone. "Give me peace. Give your own soul peace. You must tell. *You must tell."*

Audrey narrowed her eyes and looked around the dim chamber, gripping the back of the pew with her gloved hands, attempting to locate the source of the voices. "This is preposterous! That's not Ty. Johnny Muir, what monstrous foolishness are you up to?"

"Me!" Lord John exclaimed in a fine impression of horror, pressing his spread fingers to his chest. "What in the devil makes you think *I* had anything to do with this? As if I'd be pulling pranks, with my own brother lying dead somewhere, probably feeding the fishes. Stap me, Audrey, you know what I think? I think it's Ty's ghost! And mayhap that's a banshee with him. Come on, Lucy, let's get out of here!"

"Don't be thick, Johnny," Audrey all but screamed at him. "There's no such thing as ghosts or spirits. There isn't! There can't be!"

"Oh, I don't know about that, Audrey," Dante said as he rose, pointing his finger to indicate the deserted altar. "Our dear recently departed vicar seems to have invested at least some small credence in the possibility. Either that or he suddenly remembered a pressing engagement elsewhere. Have you any idea what our spirits are talking about? You were the last person to see Ty, as I recall. Perhaps you might be able to shed some light on the subject."

A confession? Dante wanted to hear a confession from Audrey? Of course he did! And in front of Sir Thomas and her grandmother, who could serve as witnesses if necessary in case Audrey decided to fight the bill of divorcement Ty planned to pursue. Oh, she had married into a family of devious characters! But rather brilliant as well, she decided, and considerably more fun than any adventure she could ever read about or hope to have on her own.

"Yes, Audrey," Lord John prompted, also rising, and taking three rather threatening steps in his sister-in-law's direction. "Tell us."

"Tell them. Tell them. *Tell them!*" the spirits prompted in unison.

"Tell them what?" Mrs. Trowbridge inquired fearfully from her pew, her nose buried against Sir Thomas's waistcoat. "And whatever it is, for the love of heaven, *tell* them so that they'll go away!"

"Tell them . . . tell them . . . tell them. . . ." the voices chanted, their words echoing again and again in the rafters, resounding eerily from the walls, surrounding everyone in

311

the chapel until even Sarah Jane, who knew it all to be a sham, felt herself shivering.

"Stop it! Stop it!" Audrey clapped her hands over her ears, her sobs more convincing than they had ever been those numerous times throughout the years when she had employed tears to get her own way, cover her real motives, and put forth the impression that she was nothing more than a silly, vaporish female. *"I didn't mean it!"* she blurted out suddenly, then looked quickly at Dante, knowing she had said very little, but too much.

"Didn't mean what, Audrey?" Dante asked, taking hold of Sarah Jane's hand. "You didn't mean it when you attempted to destroy my relationship with my wife before it had begun? You didn't *mean it* when you tried to frighten Sarah Jane about childbirth and when you told me Sarah Jane had to be protected from my touch? You didn't *mean it* when you twisted the truth after Waterloo in order to keep me confused and then extract a large allowance from me in return for leaving Cliff Walk behind for the purgatory that is the social whirl of Mayfair without your own 'true love' beside you? You didn't *mean it* every time you attacked Johnny with your neatly veiled insults or persecuted Ty with your backhanded sympathies? *You didn't mean it when you pushed Ty's chair toward the cliffs?"*

Audrey's hands had slipped from her ears and were now pressed against her ashen cheeks. "I—I . . . That's not how it was! You're twisting everything! I never meant to hurt anybody. I just wanted to stay in London. I wanted to have *fun!* It's not fair that you and Sarah should have everything —the title, the heir, the *money.* Two hundred pounds a quarter? A pittance! My father paid for Ty. Bought him and paid for him. *I* paid for him. That was the agreement, binding me to you barbarians, to your poverty. Curtis is the only one who knows how to live!"

"Tell them . . . tell them . . . tell them. . . ."

"Be quiet!" Audrey cried, shaking her small fists at the rafters. "It wasn't murder and you know it! You *tricked* me. You told me you wanted to resume our marriage, and then you told me you wanted a bill of divorcement. I didn't know

which was worse, but neither of them would give me any of Dante's money. So I decided to pretend you'd never mentioned a divorce, to go on being the Countess of Easterly! That would put a spike in your wheel. So it wasn't me. I had no thoughts of murder. *You* did it, Ty. You *made* me push you! It's *your* fault you went over the cliff!"

The silence following Audrey's blurted confession, her angry accusation, was almost deafening, and Sarah Jane held her breath, wondering what would happen next.

And then there was a rustle of movement from the rear of the chapel, from just beneath the wolf's head.

"Evening, all," Tyler Muir said affably as he slowly walked down the aisle, Emma supporting him as he leaned heavily on the back of each pew as he moved forward, not stopping until he was in front of Audrey.

"*You!*" Audrey backed up a step before catching herself, smiling broadly, and holding out her arms to her husband. "You're alive! Oh, Ty, darling, how wonderful! You know I never meant you any harm. It was an accident, really! And I forgive you for this small charade. You must have been extremely angry. But not now, surely? Not now that you are going to be free to wed your childhood love? Not that I would have fought a divorce in the first place. I would have given it to you, gladly."

"Sure, she would have," Lord John said, earning himself a playful swat on the arm from his beloved Lucy. "Right after she stopped screaming, that is."

Audrey shot her young brother-in-law a particularly nasty look, then concentrated her smile on the earl once more. "We haven't been very happy, Ty, have we? A courtesy title still to be mine after the divorce, an adequate allowance, my own lovely town house in Mayfair, of course, and we shall all be happy. Why, this can only add a certain intriguing cachet to my reputation. I shall be slightly notorious! Isn't that right, Ty? Ty, for pity's sake, don't just stand there. *Say* something!"

"That woman spins around faster than a top, don't she?" Lord John asked of no one in particular. "No wonder she made us all so dizzy we couldn't see her for what she is. *She* doesn't know what she is! Do you think even *she* knows what she's talking about? Dearest Audrey's not a murderess—she's an idiot! Ain't that right, Ty?"

"Not now, Johnny. Did everyone hear my dear wife's confession?" Ty asked, turning to look at Sir Thomas and Mrs. Trowbridge.

"Yes, indeed," Sir Thomas responded, taking out a large white handkerchief and wiping his brow. "Mrs. Trowbridge, you might leave go your grip now, if you don't mind. You're crushing the fabric of my sleeve, and I fear I've quite lost the feeling in my arm."

"So that's really the earl? Didn't recognize him standing up. Tall, ain't he?" Mrs. Trowbridge asked, towering over Sir Thomas now that both of them had vacated the second pew. "And that's that Franklin woman. I suppose the earl is going to marry her now. No wonder no one's in black! Well, I'll be twigged! Sir Thomas, dear man, I think I'd like a drink. Care to join me in the red saloon? It's the only decent spot in the whole house, and ever so intimate." She pushed Sir Thomas toward the aisle, then stopped. "Oh, and you, Tyler Muir. About that business of me gifting you with a quarter of my fortune? You can blow that notion to the four winds."

"Pity," Lord John said, looking to Lucy. "I had already begun thinking up ways to borrow from the man. Dante? Isn't there something you wanted to tell Audrey?"

"Indeed, yes," Dante answered, looking levelly at his sister-in-law. "Audrey, you will please us by seeing that you are packed and ready to leave in the morning, as your continued presence at Cliff Walk is neither wished for nor required," Dante said coldly as Emma helped the weary earl to a nearby pew, upon which time he proceeded to have a rather prodigious sneezing fit. "I've ordered our traveling coach for ten o'clock. I doubt your mother and her new husband are expecting you, but I'm sure you'll explain everything to them."

"My *mother?*" Audrey's face crumpled, her bottom lip quivering, reminding Sarah Jane of Samantha's expression just before she broke into a lusty cry, demanding to be fed. "Not—not London?"

"Not London," Lord John broke in happily. "And not with an allowance, not with *any* allowance at all, as you've already gotten more than your money's worth from us Muirs. Those diamonds alone should bring you a pretty penny, if you was to sell them. Ain't that right, Ty? But you're not to worry, Audrey. When Lucy and I go to London we'll be sure to explain to everybody *exactly* why you aren't there. As you provided me with that service so often in the past, I'd say it's the least I can do."

Audrey ran from the chapel, her handkerchief pressed to her lips, and Sarah Jane looked to her husband, who didn't seem to be as delighted as his brothers. "Dante? What's wrong?"

He dropped a kiss on her forehead. "Nothing, pet. Come on now," he said, lifting her into his arms. "It's time you were back in bed."

"You don't think Audrey is going to allow us to win quite this easily, do you?" she asked, his smile not convincing her that he was entirely happy.

"I don't know, pet," he answered, his honesty frightening her. "But she's too selfish to do anything dangerous. She'll probably limit herself to driving Ty to distraction during the course of the divorce."

Sarah Jane tightened her arm around Dante's shoulder and laid her head against his chest. "Then you don't think we'll ever see her again?"

"Ah, pet," he answered, sighing. "Who's to say? Is it ever possible to know how a mind like Audrey's works?"

CHAPTER 17

Let those love now who never loved before;
Let those who have loved, now love the more.

Thomas Parnell

Sarah Jane turned her back so that Dante could undo the small covered buttons on the back of her primrose gown, wishing she could pretend she wasn't nervous. Feeling his fingers against her skin, she took a deep breath and launched into speech, hoping her chatter would cover her apprehension.

"Thank you. Honestly, Dante, we'll have to seriously consider taking on another maid, for Samantha has captivated Mildred to the point where the woman is no longer available to help me—not that I mind. Oh, it *was* a lovely wedding, wasn't it? And Lucy looked more beautiful than I've ever seen her."

Sarah Jane had reluctantly enlisted Dante's aid with her gown after their return from the nursery, where they had visited with their five-week-old daughter until Mildred threw them out, saying they were disturbing *her* baby. "Um-hmm," he answered vaguely as he wrestled with the last buttons before sliding the gown from his wife's shoulders and placing a kiss on the nape of her neck. "Beautiful."

Sarah Jane closed her eyes for a moment, her knees turning to water, then slipped out from beneath his light embrace and skipped over to the dressing table, already removing the rubies from her ears. "You cannot imagine how long and arduously Emma and I labored to teach Lucy not to gallop down the aisle in her usual manner. I only wish the renovations to the chapel had been completed before the ceremony, but Johnny refused to delay the marriage until the painters had gone. He said he was afraid he might change his mind and then Lucy might push *him* off the cliffs."

She bent forward to look into the oval mirror, frowning as she saw that her short hair had curled somewhat in the late August heat. She knew she was talking too much, chattering on and on, but having Dante so close to her, helping her to undress, was decidedly unnerving.

He had been with her in a most intimate way during the birth of their child, infusing her with his strength, comforting her with his avowals of love. He had been with her for hours each day since that birth, the two of them getting to know each other again and learning all about their daughter. Their relationship had been one of friendship, their exchanges of affection limited to hand-holding and a few stolen kisses. They had slipped away for a lazy picnic beside the pond. They had walked through the gardens, Dante commenting on their loveliness and complimenting her on her fine work. They had talked and laughed and enjoyed each other's company.

In short, Sarah Jane had delighted in a lovely interlude with her husband that could best be described as the courting she had not been privileged to enjoy before their arranged marriage.

And through it all, Dante had slept in his dressing room, the dutiful husband allowing his wife sufficient time to recover from her lying-in.

However, since Samantha's departure down the hallway just five days ago to the small bedchamber that had been converted to a nursery, Sarah Jane had become aware of a growing, never-to-be-forgotten tension between her husband and herself that had not been present for a long time.

Not since that last night, when Dante had been about to leave Cliff Walk to join Wellington.

Not since they had come together in love and passion.

Her love.

His passion.

"Sarah? Is something wrong? It has been a long day, the first full one since Samantha's birth that you've gone through without seeking an afternoon nap. Would you like to go to sleep now?"

Sleep? He had asked that question before, all those months ago. Or had it been she who had asked? It didn't matter. What mattered was that she could remember what he'd said and the haunted look in his eyes as he had said it. "I can lie down," he'd told her. "I can even, by a strong application of will, close my eyes. But I can't find my way to sleep. As a matter of fact, dear Sarah, I am very certain that unless I can hold you once more before I leave tomorrow, I will never sleep again."

She turned, holding on to the bodice of her gown, which was in danger of slipping from her breasts. Mildred had only ten days previously allowed her to remove the tight bindings meant to help dry up her milk, as she had been unable to provide the nearly always ravenous Samantha with enough nourishment and a wet nurse had been hired from the village within a week of the birth. It had been difficult to accept the reality that she would not be able to suckle her own child, but Samantha's needs, she had decided philosophically and after shedding only a few tears, were more important than her own. Her breasts tingled now, but not from the weight of milk.

"Sleep?" she repeated, looking at Dante, so handsome in his dark blue coat and breeches, his starched white linen a startling contrast to his tanned face. The Muirs were a handsome lot, but Dante was more than handsome. He was her dark angel, the realization of her dreams, her knight in shining armor, her hero. And he had told her that he loved her. She loved him, more now than ever. So why was she so nervous? "I suppose I am faintly fatigued, but I'm not particularly sleepy. Are you?"

Dante smiled that intriguing, exasperating, adored one-sided smile and slipped out of his coat, negligently tossing it at a chair. His white waistcoat was molded to him, accentuating his slim, muscular frame. "Not I, pet," he drawled, leaning his hip against a tall bedpost. "Not in the least. However, I wouldn't mind going to bed, unless it's too soon, or you . . ."

His voice trailed away, and he looked toward the opened French doors, all at once appearing as nervous as she—unsure, and nothing like the Dante she had come to know and love.

She stood quietly, once more remembering the night she had gone to him, how she had loosened her dressing gown and let it fall to the floor, offering herself to him, quaking inside with the fear that he might reject her. Was he now feeling that same fear?

"No," she said hastily, shaking her head. "I—I have no objections."

She took two small, hesitating steps toward the bed, toward her husband, slipping out of her low-heeled evening slippers as she did so, then stopped, a mulish expression coming over her features as her nervousness left her all at once. She wasn't that overdressed, hideously coiffed ninny of so many months ago. She wasn't that shy, terrified child anymore. She was Sarah Muir—Lady Dante—a wife, a mother, a *woman* in love! The Sarah Jane Trowbridge who had hidden behind the balusters, looking down at the wonderful man who had somehow strayed into her orbit, had not been a part of her for a long time.

"Oh, Dante, this is above everything stupid! Yes, it has been months since we were together in—in that way. And yes, I have been recovering from Samantha's birth these past weeks. But I'm no longer fragile. I won't break. Dante, we *love* each other! Why are we both acting as if we're frightened to make the first move? Why are we dancing around the subject? Dante Muir, do you want to take your wife to bed or not?"

He pushed himself away from the bedstead, chuckling. "Yes, that's my wife. Shy, retiring, wouldn't say boo to a goose, until she wants something badly enough. And then there's no stopping her. Very well, pet, what would you have me do? Toss you over my shoulder and fling you down on the bed before making mad, impassioned love to you?"

She tipped her head to one side, considering his proposal. "That sounds reasonable, Dante. And rather romantic, to a woman who has decided that romantic dreams should take second place to reality. A healthy dose of romance could be just the thing I need."

"Romance, is it? Very well, pet. But I have a better idea than simply flinging you willy-nilly onto the mattress," he said, stepping behind her and quickly doing up several of the buttons he had so lately released from their moorings. Then, taking up a position in front of her once more, he swept her an elegant leg. "Madam, would you do me the honor of dancing with me?"

Sarah was momentarily nonplussed. "Dancing?"

"Dancing, pet. I suggest a waltz." He slipped his right hand around her waist so that she automatically raised her left hand, placing it just above his elbow. She slipped her right wrist through the small satin loop on her skirt, placed there for that purpose, and allowed her right hand to flutter to rest in his left. Surprisingly, she didn't feel stupid or the slightest bit awkward. She felt magnificent, and ready for any silliness Dante might have in mind.

They stood very still for several heartbeats in time, Sarah Jane in her silk stockings, Dante in his shirtsleeves, the two of them alone in their bedchamber, looking into each other's eyes across the scant foot of space separating them. Sarah Jane could feel sudden tears sting her eyes, tears of happiness, of grateful appreciation to whatever gods had given her this man to love.

And then Dante applied a hint of pressure to her waist and they began to move in unison, responding to the strains of violins playing inside their heads, their eyes never leaving each other's face, their steps surer, growing bolder, their bodies swaying, dipping, spinning in breathless circles. Sarah's primrose skirts swirled around her ankles as she raised herself up on tiptoe, a fairy princess in the arms of her prince.

Dante held her loosely but firmly, leading his wife in graceful circuits around the chairs, across the expanse of Chinese carpet, and onto the small balcony outside the French doors. There, in the moonlight, with the stars shining down on them, he pulled her closer still, his smile boyish and excited, a lock of midnight-dark hair falling forward onto his forehead.

The sweeping circles of the waltz became unhurried, increasingly intimate turns as he gathered her closer, ever closer.

Their feet moved more slowly until, reluctantly, gladly, expectantly, Dante and Sarah Jane ended their dance and merely stood there on the balcony, bathed in moonlight, warmed by their love in the coolness of evening, entranced by the moment, all the moments that had led up to this one magical moment of complete togetherness, total understanding, absolute love.

He raised her right hand to rest against his shoulder, then tipped up her chin, his fingers a caress against her skin, his gaze a prayer, a benediction, a promise. "Ah, my sweet little pet," he whispered, his voice a part of the moonlight, a part of the dream of romance come to life.

"I was so lost without you. So damnably alone without the memory of you. All I knew then was that I had misplaced something precious, some untouchable something that gave life meaning. That thing was love. Not Cliff Walk, not money or position or any of the things I had always thought to be important. The love *you* gave me, Sarah, that's what I was missing, what I had been missing every day of my life until you entered into it. That and my complete, unconditional, and everlasting love for you."

Sarah Jane allowed herself to melt against him, tucking

her head against his broad chest, her fingers clutching his smoothly muscled shoulders, drinking in the solid presence of him in her world, holding fast to him as she held fast to her own life. For he was her life, he and their child and the future they would share.

"I do love you, Dante," she said, her voice breaking as at last she gave in to the happy tears that clogged her throat. "I always have, even when I was attempting to live a dream, even when I was a little afraid of you. But now I love you even more, because now I really know you."

He slipped an arm beneath her knees and lifted her high against his chest as he walked back into the chamber and toward the bed. "And who am I, pet?" he asked, his voice rumbling deep in his chest, against her ear, reminding her of the night he had carried her upstairs from the kitchens.

He gently laid her on the mattress and followed her down, her arms still holding him, entwined around his neck. When his mouth was only inches from hers she said, "Who are you? You're the reality who rescued me from my childish dreams. You're the lover who woke me to new dreams. You're the strength that brought Samantha safely into this world. You're my life, Dante Muir. My life and my love, forever."

When their lips met, the salty taste of their tears mingled, then dried, evaporated in an instant by the sudden heat of passion. Clothing melted away from bodies molten with desire, with longings held in check, with love too long unexpressed in this most extraordinary, most elemental of ways.

He kissed her temples, her eyes, the sculpted curve of her chin just beneath her ear, the hollow at the base of her throat. He worshiped her with his mouth, his hands, suckling at her breasts as she laced her fingers through his hair, pressing him to her, cradling him against her, giving and taking, sharing and accepting, teaching and being taught.

A never-before feeling of freedom urged Sarah Jane on, a new awareness of the power of her woman's body, the sure knowledge that she could satisfy and be satisfied because she was a woman, a woman who loved, and a woman who was loved.

She felt his gentle fierceness, could sense that he was purposely holding back, knew he didn't wish to hurt her so soon after Samantha's birth. But she wasn't afraid. Not of any pain. Not of him. Not of herself. She had been a bud, a promise. But now she was a flower. She had bloomed, she had matured, she had lifted her head to the heavens and known the beauty of life lived in the sun.

"Love me, Dante," she whispered, reaching for him, holding him, urging him on to full possession, showing him with her boldness that she wasn't afraid, that she welcomed his possession. "Love me. *Love me.*"

He entered her slowly, resting his weight on his hands as he watched her expression closely, and she knew he was ready to withdraw at the slightest sign that he might be hurting her. She felt his presence, the growing fullness inside her, the completeness that could be experienced only at this special time, when the two people who separately were Dante and Sarah joined and became one.

Her smile was beautiful, although she couldn't have known that any more than she knew that she was smiling. She could only feel the wonder, the love, the sense of wholeness, the *rightness* of being with this man, at this time, for all time.

"Oh, God, Sarah," he groaned, sliding his arms around her back, pressing his cheek against hers. "Dear Christ, how I love you."

"I know, I know," she said quietly, her heart full, her passion growing. She clasped him to her tightly, running her spread fingers along his back, dipping her fingertips into the slight hollows at the base of his spine, drawing her legs up and around his hips.

And then the gods allowed time to stand still, dreams to flourish, feelings to soar, passions to break free and spin off into a galaxy of emotions unbounded by earthly constraints. All the colors of the rainbow bathed them in their light, and the stars exploded in shiny silver sparkles that accompanied them on their floating, falling journey back to earth, showering them with blessings, with hopes, with visions of tomorrow, of all the tomorrows they would share.

Dante didn't know what woke him just at dawn, unless it was the fact that he had been holding Sarah Jane as they slept and his left arm had gone into a cramp, a rather unromantic cramp, he decided, but then, life could not be all romance. Dropping a kiss on his wife's forehead, he pulled on his discarded breeches and slipped his arms into his shirt before strolling over to the French doors, meaning to close them against the early morning dampness blowing in from the Channel.

His hands stilled on the opened doors as he looked out toward the main section of Cliff Walk, admiring the way the rising sun turned the dome atop the building to a glowing golden globe. Was that mist he saw rising from the rear of the building? Strange that there should be mist there and nowhere else.

Dante's blood ran cold, his senses immediately alert. That was not mist. It was *smoke!*

"Sarah!" he called out, tugging on hose and shoes. "Ring the fire bell in the hall! Rouse the servants! Then take Samantha and go to the family drawing room. Be ready to flee if necessary. The round saloon is on fire!

She bolted upright, heedless of the fact that she was naked. "On fire?" She clapped her hands to her mouth. "Oh, my God! Dante, my grandmother!"

"That's where I'm heading," Dante called back over his shoulder. He ran down the hallway, banging on all the doors as he passed by, then tore down the staircase and headed for the curved corridor leading to the main structure. Betts Trowbridge had taken up residence for John and Lucy's wedding and had of course insisted upon occupying the king's chamber. All the other guests save Sir Thomas Randolph had come only for the wedding ceremony and then returned home, and with Johnny gone off to tour the Lake District with his new bride that left only the marquess, the earl, and Lucy's father to help Dante marshal the servants to battle the fire.

But first he had to rouse Sarah Jane's grandmother and haul the woman to safety.

Sarah Jane must have dressed quickly, for as Dante ran, he could hear the fire bell pealing in its tower above the family wing, calling everyone on the estate to come fight the blaze. His heart pounded in rhythm with the clanging bell as his footfalls echoed against the high ceiling of the hall. He threw open the double doors to the king's chamber, breathlessly calling to Mrs. Trowbridge, the smell of burning wood stinging his nostrils even as thin fingers of smoke drifted toward him from somewhere at the other end of the chamber.

"Mrs. Trowbridge?" he called out, approaching the large, four-poster bed, throwing back the heavy draperies that surrounded it on all sides. "Wake up! The building is on fire!"

"On fire, you say? Thought we might be caught out, but I never figured we'd be twigged by a blaze," Sir Thomas answered with more élan than Dante would have imagined possible, his tasseled nightcap falling forward over one eye as he yawned widely and sat up. "Betts," he urged, nudging the still sleeping form beside him, "looks like there'll be another wedding soon after all, unless we're all burned to death in our beds. Up you get, little love. You, Dante, go douse your fire. We'll be fine."

Dante didn't waste time arguing or allowing his mind to absorb more than the sight of the slightly built Sir Thomas Randolph in bed beside the long, large slumbering form of Elizabeth Trowbridge—a woman, it would appear, of many talents as well as an ironclad determination. He released his hold on the draperies, turned on his heel, and made straight for the round saloon.

A half dozen servants had arrived ahead of him and were already beating at the smoky air with strips of old carpet. He stopped just inside the door, frowning at the scene, realizing that the fire was really rather small and had been built in one of the huge fireplaces.

"Everything's all right now, milord. Someone stuffed up the chimney with rags and closed the damper," Babbitt said when he saw Dante. "All the inside doors were closed and the French doors opened, so that the smoke just dirtied all the walls and then drifted outside. We pulled out the rags and opened the damper. Now, why, sir, would anybody do that?"

Dante looked at the fireplace once more, and then at Babbitt, whose face was streaked with soot. "You've done a good job, Babbitt, an excellent job. Set the maids to cleaning in here once they've breakfasted, and you and the rest of the men go get yourselves something from the cellars. I have to return to the family wing and tell everyone that the fire is out."

If anything, Dante made the return trip to the family wing in less time than he had taken to race to the king's chamber, his mind all but tumbling over itself as he tried to find an answer to the butler's question. Why would anyone set such a fire? His training as a soldier told him the fire could be seen as a diversionary tactic. That made sense. But as a diversion to distract their attention from what?

The marquess met him in the hallway with the answer. "Dante, Audrey's up in the nursery," he said, frantically pulling his son toward the staircase. "Sarah's in there with Audrey and the baby, after warning the rest of us away. Dante, it's unbelievable! Audrey's got Samantha, *and she's holding her out the window.*"

"Sweet Christ! Sweet Mother of *God!*" Dante took the stairs three at a time, his heart in his throat, his dreams poised to become ashes, berating himself for his stupidity. Had he really believed Audrey would allow herself to be humiliated, banished, sent back to her mother, that she would give up her position as wife of the heir to Cliff Walk without a fight?

"Dante!"

Dante stopped at the head of the staircase as the earl called out his name. "Not now, Ty," he warned, tight-lipped, knowing his brother could not climb the stairs, could not help him. "I've got to go to Sarah."

The earl stood at the bottom of the staircase, leaning heavily against the newel post. "I know, brother, I know. This is all my fault. Tell her I won't go through with the bill of divorcement, if that's what she wants. She's got Samantha, Dante! Tell her I'll give her anything she wants!"

Dante nodded shortly and turned to walk down the hall, willing himself to be calm, to think, to *think*. Had they become a family, he and his brothers—a real family, caring about each other the way real families did, willing to sacrifice their own happiness for each other—just to have disaster strike? He brushed past the weeping Mildred and entered the nursery, stopping just inside the door.

"Go away, please, Dante," Sarah Jane said quite calmly, and he saw her standing a good fifteen feet from the open doors to the small balcony where Audrey Muir stood, holding Samantha, holding his sleeping daughter. "We're having a lovely coze, Audrey and I, and we don't need you in the slightest. Do we, Audrey?"

"They were paste," Audrey said, looking out over the same sunny morning Dante had awakened to not ten minutes earlier. "Ty said they were diamonds, but they were paste." She shifted her gaze to Sarah Jane. "Do you have any idea how humiliating it was for me to have to listen to the jeweler tell me my diamonds—the diamonds I have worn these past six Seasons—are *paste*? How demeaning it was for me to have to crawl back to my mother a second time, begging her to take me in after I had left her, telling her I would rather live on the proceeds from my diamonds than spend one more day in her presence?"

"Men are such brutes," Sarah Jane said soothingly, taking a single step toward the balcony, her wide-eyed stare never leaving Audrey's face. "You were so wise when you told me that, Audrey. But you and I are sisters! What do men know of our pain, our suffering?"

Dante didn't move, didn't breathe. He knew what Sarah Jane was trying to do; she was attempting to gain Audrey's confidence. He didn't think the ploy would work. After all, Audrey was a past master at pretending to gain someone's sympathy, and would be the first to see through such a gambit.

"The Muirs treated you badly, Audrey," Sarah Jane went on, stopping where she was, making no quick movements, taking no more steps, keeping her voice low and comforting, almost hypnotic. "They took your father's money and gave you paste diamonds. They allowed you a few Seasons in London and then tossed you aside. It isn't fair, Audrey. Life has been unkind to you, to us both. I, too, was bartered. Remember, Audrey? Remember how we commiserated with each other over our fate? We must help each other now, you and I. Tell me, what can I do to help you? I want to help you."

Audrey's eyes narrowed as she looked at Sarah Jane. "Of course you do, little mouse. Little mouse with the horrid hair. That's why I came here. So you could *help* me. You have it all now. Oh, yes, all you miserable Muirs! Johnny has slipped his way into all the Randolph money. Not that *I* was invited to the ceremony uniting my own brother-in-law with his horsy fortune. Ty has his precious Emma. Even Curtis has deserted me, although I was his hostess all these years, although my father's money supported his disastrous runs at the gaming tables. You've deserted me too, little mouse. You're only pretending to be nice to me, the way I pretended to like you. You only want something from me. Well, I want something from you. I always have, you spineless child. Did you think to toss a few gowns in my direction and then desert me?"

"No, Audrey," Sarah Jane protested quietly. "I haven't deserted you. And I do want to help you. You made a small mistake, that's all. You never meant to hurt Ty. We all know that. I would have written you, honestly, only that I have been so busy—"

"Yes, you have, haven't you?" Audrey bit out, cutting her off. She was holding Samantha very tightly, so that the baby began to cry, sending a knife through Dante's heart.

Please, baby, he pleaded silently. *Please don't cry. Don't remind her of your presence.*

"You've been busy playing at lady of the manor, haven't you? The butcher's granddaughter, so good with a mop. How long before they throw you away, little mouse? They already have all the butcher's money. They don't need you now, for they can use your money to *hire* a housekeeper. For that's all you are, a deadly dull housekeeper. Besides, Ty will sire his own puling brats now."

"That's my problem, isn't it, Audrey? Let's get back to the reason you're in this house. What do you want, Audrey?" Sarah Jane asked, once more moving toward the balcony. "Why have you come here? Surely not to harm an innocent child?"

Audrey looked down at Samantha, her lip curling in disgust as the baby began to cry in earnest. "I never saw the attraction, frankly," she said, shifting Samantha so that she was holding the infant at arm's length away from her, Samantha's head lolling dangerously backwards. "Lud, she has wet me! Stupid brat!"

She turned once more to Sarah Jane, who was standing very still, her hands clenched into fists at her sides as she watched her child being dangled near the stone railing of the balcony. "I set the fire, you know," she said conversationally, still holding Samantha beneath her small arms, the child's blanket slipping to the floor so that Dante could see his daughter's tiny feet dangling below the hem of her gown.

"I set the fire, and then I came up here to visit my niece. I wasn't issued an invitation to see her any more than I was asked to Johnny's wedding." Her bottom lip began to quiver, and tears stood bright in her blue eyes. "I have nothing, little mouse, and you have it all. Do you think that's fair? *Do you?*"

"How much do you want, Audrey?" Sarah Jane asked, finally saying what Dante had all but willed her to say. "That's really why you're here, isn't it? You want something. Let me give it to you. Let me recompense you for all your terrible treatment at the hands of the Muirs. As you said, Audrey, it's only fair."

Audrey smiled, not like a madwoman, but like a child

who'd been offered a treat. And she wasn't mad, Dante decided, only calculating. Sly and clever, shrewd rather than intelligent, and used to getting her own way, even prepared to use a helpless infant to get her own way. She had no plans to throw Samantha over the balcony. She wasn't a murderess. But that didn't mean she wouldn't become careless in her self-pitying anger and drop the child.

"That Trowbridge woman offered fifty thousand pounds for a male child, I believe," Audrey said, cocking her head as she looked at the indignantly howling, red-faced Samantha. "I thought you'd offer me at least half that for a girl child. But first I had to get your attention. Do I have your attention, little mouse?"

"That's all, Audrey?" Sarah Jane was in front of the French doors now, blocking Dante's view of his daughter. "You're selling my daughter much too cheaply, Audrey. I would have offered twice as much, five times as much. But then, you always were stupid, weren't you, dear sister? Stupid and heavy-handed."

"Stupid?" Audrey stopped staring at Samantha and looked questioningly at Sarah Jane.

Don't antagonize her, Sarah! Dante screamed silently. *You were doing so well, winning her confidence. We know what she wants. We're halfway there, halfway to safety. I know you're frightened for Samantha. So am I. But don't let your anger overwhelm you.* But at the same time that he thought these things he realized that Audrey's grip on the child was slipping, and that Samantha was in danger of falling. He wasn't close enough to lunge for the infant. Only Sarah, his Sarah, could rescue Samantha now.

"I feel sorry for you, Audrey," Sarah Jane went on over the sound of Samantha's cries, her voice gaining in strength with each small step she took. Dante began moving forward as well, careful to keep out of Audrey's line of sight. "Do you know why I feel sorry for you, Audrey? I'll tell you. Because you'll never know how to love anyone save yourself. You'll never find joy in anything more than diamonds and silks and racing about in Society, endlessly searching for the happiness you wouldn't recognize if you saw it. You're vain and shallow and two-faced and as worthless as those paste diamonds you put such store by. And you know the value of *nothing!*"

Sarah Jane's voice had risen a notch in volume with every new sentence, so that she was nearly yelling now, which was something neither Dante nor Audrey nor anyone including her grandmother had ever heard her do. She was impassioned, authoritative, powerful in her towering anger, her calculated rage.

Audrey stood on the balcony, blinking, obviously unbelieving of this miniature tigress she was facing. "You don't frighten me, little mouse," she said at last. "I may have played my hand badly these past months, but I still hold all the trumps. Don't come a step closer or I might become nervous and lose my grip on the brat."

Sarah Jane's voice diminished in volume but not in intensity. "And then what, Audrey? What happens then? Do I throw you over the balcony, or do I let Dante strangle you first? Or perhaps we'll let you live long enough for the hangman to have at you. I told you how stupid you are; now you must know it as well. You want money from us? I wouldn't give you a bent penny! And now, Audrey, I want you out of my house. I want you out of our lives once and for all. You have done your best to make mischief and you have failed. You came here to extort money from us, but you have ended up trapped on a balcony, a whining child in your hands and urine staining your gown. I am bored with you, Audrey, bored and totally out of patience. Give me that child, *now,* and get out of my house!"

For an eternity of time that couldn't have been longer than five seconds, Audrey hovered at the edge of the balcony, looking first at the child she held and then at Sarah Jane. Finally, just as Dante was about to leap forward, praying he could snatch the infant, Audrey exploded pettishly, "Oh, very well, little mouse. Here she is!" and all but threw Samantha at Sarah Jane and then stomped back into the nursery.

Relief flooded through Dante as Sarah Jane collapsed onto her knees, hugging Samantha fiercely and showering her with kisses so that the child wailed even harder than before.

"Go to the family drawing room and wait for us there," Dante ordered tightly as Audrey walked past him, chin held high. "Try to leave, Audrey, and I will hunt you down and shoot you as I would a rabid animal."

Audrey rolled her eyes. "So dramatic, the pair of you. I wouldn't have hurt her. I didn't even set a proper fire when I could have burned your beloved Cliff Walk down around all your heads. All I wanted was what is mine. All I wanted was an allowance or, failing that, a settlement. But first, I needed to gain your attention. Is that so difficult to understand?" As Dante took a menacing step in her direction she ended rapidly, "Oh, very well, but don't keep me waiting above a few minutes, Dante. I don't wish to remain overlong in the same house with Ty and his whore."

The door crashed shut loudly behind Audrey's departing back.

"Dante?" Sarah Jane's voice was quiet and uncertain, a faint echo of the clear, determined tones she had employed to wrest her baby from danger.

He went to his knees beside her, gathering her and Samantha into his arms, feeling his wife's body trembling.

"I was so frightened, Dante," she told him as he took Samantha from her arms and pressed the infant against his chest. "I've never been so terrified in my life, or so very angry. How dare Audrey touch Samantha? How dare she!"

"Shhh, pet," Dante warned as Mildred raced into the nursery, calling for her baby, and snatched Samantha from her father's embrace. "It's over now," he said, helping Sarah Jane to her feet. "It's over, and you were absolutely magnificent. A real heroine. I don't know how you summoned up the courage to confront Audrey that way."

Sarah Jane allowed him to put his arm around her as she retied the sash of her dressing gown with badly shaking hands, although her expression was once again more mulish than pleased. "I'm not a heroine, Dante," she told him matter-of-factly as they made for the staircase. "I don't even *want* to be a heroine, and can't imagine how I could ever have been so foolish as to believe that heroines were a species to be envied. I was frightened out of my wits a moment ago and was merely doing anything I could to protect my child."

"All right, pet, I won't call you a heroine if you don't like the word. Nevertheless, I'm proud of you," he said, dropping a kiss on her sleep-mussed hair. "I'm only sorry the round saloon is such a shambles, after all your hard work."

Sarah Jane halted on the second step from the bottom of the staircase and looked toward the drawing room. "I forgot about the fire," she said from between clenched teeth. "That miserable, selfish, flea-witted twit!"

She broke free of Dante and stomped toward the family drawing room, and for a petite barefoot woman in a dressing gown she stomped rather well, Dante decided, trotting after her. She entered the room, which was already clogged with people: the marquess sipping brandy at the mantel, Ty with his back turned to his wife in disgust, Betts Trowbridge and Sir Thomas looking bewildered and not a little embarrassed as they sat close together on one of the couches, Audrey standing in the middle of the room, wiping at the front of her gown with a handkerchief and appearing to be fatigued with the whole business.

"You!" Sarah Jane called out, pointing at Audrey as she advanced into the room.

"Now what, Sarah Jane?" Audrey asked wearily, raising her eyes from the stain on her gown. "You've got everything you're so silly as to want. I'll be off just as soon as your brute of a husband allows me license to leave. I'm penniless, in disgrace, soon to be divorced, and condemned to live on the charity of my shrewish mother while her idiot of a husband pinches me in dark corners. Haven't I suffered enough? What else could you possibly want from me?"

"Just this," Sarah Jane said, advancing until she was standing directly in front of the taller woman. And then, rising up on tiptoe, the better to reach her target, she clenched her right hand into a fist and punched her sister-in-law square in the face.

As Audrey collapsed, stunned, rump down on the carpet, the skin around her left eye rapidly swelling and changing color, Sarah Jane turned to her husband. *"Now,"* she told him calmly as she brushed past him on her way back upstairs, wiping her hands as if to signify that her job was finally done, "you have my permission to call me a heroine. Settle with the woman, Dante," she then ordered shortly, hesitating for a moment at the foot of the staircase. "I want her out of my house."

"Well, I'll be damned!" the marquess exclaimed, taking another deep drink of his brandy.

"I think we all will be, Father," Tyler Muir said, "if we dare to cross the mistress of Cliff Walk. She may be little, but as I've heard it said about Gentleman Jackson, she packs a powerful wallop!"

"What did you all expect?" Mrs. Trowbridge asked, chuckling as she pushed herself to her feet and pulled Sir Thomas up with her. "She's *my* granddaughter, isn't she? Now, come along, Thomas, we have us a wedding to discuss."

"Of course, my little pudding," Sir Thomas answered dutifully, the ground rules of their relationship seemingly already set, with Sir Thomas cast in the subservient role, not that he seemed to mind.

"Dante?" the earl asked, gesturing toward his wife. "You want me to sweep up this rubbish?"

Dante looked toward the weeping Audrey and then toward the stairs. He smiled. "You do the honors, Ty. Give her an allowance, whatever amount you wish, and make her sign something legal, some paper that will tie that allowance to her agreement to both the bill of divorcement and her vow to permanently remove herself from England. Perhaps to someplace warm, where her constant tears will dry more easily."

And then he turned, still smiling, and headed for the stairs, and his bedchamber, where his wife—his dear, sweet, wonderful, heroic wife—was sure to be waiting.

EPILOGUE

REFLECTIONS
1821

What is love?
Ask him who lives, what is life?
Ask him who adores, what is God?

Percy Bysshe Shelley

*If thou follow thy star, thou canst not fail of a
glorious haven.*

Dante Alighieri

An unmarked grave on foreign soil, guarded by English
soldiers. He would have preferred to fall in battle," Dante
said sadly, putting aside the newspaper bearing the story of
the death of Napoleon Bonaparte. "I'll never forget the look
in his eyes as he rode past me, the way he almost begged me
to deliver the merciful bullet that would have granted him
the status of legend and not the wasted death of a defeated
emperor."

Sarah Jane took one last stitch in the small shirt she was
embroidering for their son Jeremy's birthday, then knotted
and bit off the thread. "You're a good man, Dante, to have
such compassion for an enemy. Do you think our government will ever allow his body to be returned to France?"

Dante lifted John Tyler onto his knee, clucking the
chubby blond year-old toddler under his double chin so that
the child dissolved into giggles. "If we do, it won't be for a
very long time. Even dead, Napoleon can inspire fear in the
hearts of those who would sit on a throne. But before you

believe me to be seditious, pet, allow me to say that I believe our dear King George deserves his throne. God knows he waited long enough to get it. Did you say you've had another letter from Emma? Where has my vagabond brother dragged her and Robbie off to now?"

Sarah Jane smiled as she watched her husband with her youngest child, their heads close together, one Muir as dark as his oldest son, the other as fair as his uncles. "They've gone to Venice, and from there will travel to Capri. Ty has expressed a wish to visit something called the Blue Grotto, a place he fears is destined to soon be reclaimed by the sea. Emma says Ty won't rest until they have seen and painted every sight from Paris to Athens."

They were both silent for some moments, lost in their own thoughts. It had been five years since Ty had officially renounced his title in favor of his brother, and two since he and his wife and stepson had visited Cliff Walk. Dante had fought his brother, not wishing him to give up his rights as the firstborn in exchange for a generous allowance, but Ty had been adamant. He had spent six years in a loveless marriage, more than two of them confined to a Bath chair, and he fully intended to live the remainder of his life as he wished. And he wished to travel with his wife, seeing all the places he had thought impossible to visit when he believed he would never walk again. He was happy, Emma and Robbie were happy, and Dante's only regret was that his brother did not visit more often.

So now Dante, who loved Cliff Walk, but who no longer valued it above anything and anyone else in life, would someday pass the estate on to his oldest son, his beloved Jeremy, who showed all the signs of ambitions in line with his advanced age of nearly three, declaring that he wanted nothing more than to be a knight and slay fire-breathing dragons.

"Where are Jeremy and Samantha?" Dante asked after a moment, realizing that he, Sarah Jane, and John Tyler were alone in the family drawing room.

"Jeremy is with Johnny and Lucy at the stables, remember? Lucy insists nothing is more important than that he master that pony she and your brother gave him for his birthday. His birthday! It's more than a week away, for pity's sake. Lucy just couldn't wait to seat him on his first pony."

"And Sam?" Dante inquired as Mildred entered the room and scooped up John Tyler, saying he was needed in the nursery for his tea. It was getting to be all Dante could do to keep track of his family on Sundays, the only day he did not ride the fields of Cliff Walk, alternately working on and admiring what had grown to be the finest estate in all of southeast England—at least in his modest opinion.

Sarah Jane sighed audibly, letting him know his pet name for their daughter had had its desired effect, and went to sit beside her husband on the couch. "*Samantha* is out driving with Grandmother Trowbridge and Sir Thomas in their new carriage. I think Grandmother plans to go to London for the spring Season and is practicing looking haughty as she rides in the Promenade. Not that she'll be able to outdo our daughter in that department. And, please, Dante, don't call her Sam."

He decided a small confession was in order. "I only do it so I can delight in watching you roll those lovely brown eyes in exasperation."

She gave him a quick kiss on the cheek. "Yes, I know, darling. That's why I roll them—because pleasing you is enjoyable to *me*."

Dante put his arm around Sarah Jane's shoulders and pulled her against him, kissing her hair. He thought himself to be very clever, discovering the whereabouts of all his children and all the people who seemed to visit Cliff Walk much more often than he would like, at least when he was of a mood to be alone with his wife. "So, our children are being amused. That means we're alone, doesn't it, pet?" he asked, beginning to play with the velvety lobe of her ear.

She snuggled closer against him. "That it does," she agreed, smiling. "The children are occupied, your brothers are with their wives, Curtis is still in Scotland, Grandmother and Sir Thomas are out parading, and Audrey, Lord help her, is still in Jamaica, married to her ancient planter. That leaves just us two old married people, resting our weary bones on a Sunday afternoon."

"I rest better in bed," he drawled, one side of his mouth lifting in a mischievous smile.

"Now, why doesn't that surprise me?" Sarah Jane countered, laughing, as he pulled her to her feet and swung her slim frame up into his arms. She had borne him three children, and she was still as light as a feather in his arms. His petite goddess. His little pet.

Giggling and holding on tight as he carried her to the staircase, Sarah Jane buried her head against his chest as Babbitt walked into the hallway.

"We're not to be disturbed, Babbitt," Dante informed the butler amicably as he brushed past the man and began mounting the staircase.

"Yes, milord," Babbitt answered evenly, although there was the hint of private amusement in his voice. "As is the case *every* Sunday afternoon, milord."

"Oh, Lord, pet," Dante asked his wife in mock astonishment, "have I become predictable?"

"Never predictable, my darling," Sarah Jane assured him as he kicked closed the door of their bedchamber, shutting out the rest of the world. "Merely domesticated."

THE ENTRANCING NEW NOVEL FROM THE
NEW YORK TIMES BESTSELLING
AUTHOR OF *PERFECT*

Until You

by

Judith McNaught

AVAILABLE IN HARDCOVER FROM
POCKET BOOKS

POCKET
BOOKS

JULIE GARWOOD

PRINCE CHARMING

Time and again, Julie Garwood
has delighted critics —and millions of
readers—with her exquisitely romantic love
stories. Her bestselling novels have inspired
such outpourings of praise as "destined to be a
classic...a treasure" (_Romantic Times_), "belongs on
my 'hands off or die!' shelf" (_Rendezvous_), and, simply,
"another gem from Julie Garwood" (_Affaire de Coeur_).
Her hardcover debut, SAVING GRACE, hailed by
Rendezvous as "a wonderfully romantic and memorable
story," was an instant _New York Times_ bestseller.
Now she brings us a very special new love story...

Pocket Books
Proudly Presents

THE SEDUCTION OF THE PEACOCK

Kasey Michaels

Coming from Pocket Books
Winter 1995

The following is a preview of
The Seduction of the Peacock . . .

England in 1819 had become a hotbed of resentment between the government, land and mill owners, and the loyal peasantry who had so lately won a great victory over Napoleon.

Corn Laws that controlled the price of English-grown wheat had beggared many a small farmer and sent whole families into the cities to find any work they could. The introduction of new industrial machines cut into the occupations of the mill workers and those who labored independently in their homes—weavers and the like—causing more unrest, more hunger, more desperation. The poorer classes were rapidly becoming desperate as a generation of poor English children were growing up without ever once tasting meat, subsisting on adulterated brown bread and butter, potatoes, and strong tea.

But then, just as all was dark, something new was added to the mix—the appearance of a hero for the people, a daring, anonymous avenger they called the Peacock.

I vow, I love the game, for this is the finest sport I have yet encountered. Hair-breadth escapes . . . the devil's own risks! Tally ho — and away we go!

Baroness Orczy,
The Scarlet Pimpernel

The outlawed, loosely organized Volunteers for Justice— a motley collection of displaced small landowners, down-at-the-heels veterans, bleary-eyed mill workers, and a few out-and-out ruffians willing to swear allegiance to any cause if there was to be a goodly supply of cheap gin passed around during the speeches—had been meeting for several hours in the back room of the Bull and Cock Inn, just at the fringe of the village of Lower Pillington. Just as the men were preparing to leave, the door was pushed open a mere crack and a small, ragged man, his shoulders slumped from too many hours in the mills, slipped into the room.

"Yer late, O'Dell," one of the men grumbled. "Never wuz a Mick could tell time with anythin' save his stummick."

"Never mind that, and set yerselves down agin,

gennulmen," O'Dell commanded with a quick wave of his hand. "It's news I'm bringin'. All of ye, listen close. He's here, or close ta hand at least."

"Who's here, O'Dell?" Jackey, the acknowledged head of the group, asked, roughly pulling the Irishman about to face him, his tone anxious. "A government man? Did he bring troops? Are we all ta be twigged?"

O'Dell rolled his eyes. "Shakin' in yer boots, are ye, Jackey? All bluster and no backbone, that's our leader, boyos, don't ye know. Ain't no troops. Ain't nobody here exceptin' us straw heroes—and *him.*"

Not a government man? No troops? Then it had to be, it must be *him!* An excited rumble of voices threatened to erupt into shouts until Jackey quickly silenced them all with a wave of his hand. *"He's* here, O'Dell? In Lower Pillington? I know he wuz in Spitalfields last month. A rare ruckus he caused there, him and his men, and a world o'good for the likes of us as well. But he's *here?* How do you know?"

"A fuckin' birdie told me!" O'Dell exclaimed angrily, then stepped back a pace, importantly straightened the greasy rags that wore once his Sunday suit, and finally reached into his pocket and brought out proof to show to the admiring group.

"My littlest kiddie, Sean, found this sittin' atop a cart what showed up in the square no more'an a minute ago," O'Dell said proudly, "the whole thing piled high with God's own fresh bread. He's done it again, boyos, and this time fer us. And that ain't the half of it, don't ye know. Now he's here, there's no tellin' what all he'll do afore the night is over. Look wot he done in Spitalfields. We're saved, boyos —saved! Ah, what a glory!"

Just after ten of the clock that same evening, Herbert Symington bade his host and hostess a pleasant good night and rather drunkenly tripped down the stairs toward the impressively designed, if a tad overly ornate, coach and four that was his latest acquisition and one of which he was enormously proud.

As well he should be, for Herbert Symington had risen from humble origins, scrabbling and clawing all the way, until he had reached the pinnacle of success: ownership of no fewer than three prosperous weaving mills located in Lower Pillington.

"Take me home, Coachie," Symington commanded, giving a sweeping wave to his driver and a drunken kick to the groom, who hadn't moved fast enough in lowering the steps to the coach to suit his master. "Lazy jackanapes, I ought to sack you," he muttered under his liquor-soured breath, pulling himself into the coach and collapsing heavily against the velvet squabs as the coachman prematurely gave the horses their office to start.

"Stupid oafs, the lot of them," Symington grumbled into his gravy-stained cravat as he adjusted his considerable girth more comfortably. And then he blinked—twice, just to be certain—and peered inquiringly into the semidarkness. "Who's there?" he asked, leaning forward to address the vague shape he believed he saw sitting cross-legged on the facing seat. "God's eyebrows, am I in the wrong coach? That'll teach me to steer clear of the daffy. Speak up, man—say something!"

The click and scrape of a small tinderbox answered him, followed by the sight of a growing, disembodied glow from the business end of a cheroot. "Good evening, Herbert. You're looking well," a low, cultured, well-modulated voice answered him at last. "And how charitable of you to share your coach with me. Well sprung, I must say, and doubtless cost you a pretty penny. Enjoy yourself at the trough tonight?"

Symington swallowed down hard at the sudden lump of fear that had lodged in his throat. "What the devil? Who are you? *Coachie!*" he bellowed. "Stop at once!"

"Please, good sir, lower your voice," the unknown intruder pleaded as the coach raced on through the night, bypassing the turn to the right that would lead to Symington's house and rapidly leaving the dark streets of Lower Pillington behind. "The confines of this coach preclude such full-throated volume. Besides, as your coachman and groom have seen fit to leave your employ and join mine—no loyalty in today's topsy-turvy times, is there, Herbert?—I fear I must point out the fruitlessness of further protest. And, to be sporting, I should also advise you that I am armed, my pistol cocked and aimed directly at your ample stomach. Therefore, as any sudden movement might cause the nasty thing to go off, you most probably would be well advised to remain quietly in your seat."

"The devil, you say!" Symington's gin-bleared eyes were fairly popping from his head now as a fragrant, blue-tinged cloud of cigar smoke wreathed the shadowy figure from chest to curly brimmed beaver. "Y-Your coachie, you say? Am I being kidnapped, then?"

A deep-throated chuckle emanated from the shadowy figure. "Hardly, Herbert. Kidnapping you would indicate that I believed you had some sort of intrinsic worth. I am merely here this evening to request a boon of you."

"A—a boon?" Symington repeated, automatically holding out his hand to take the neatly rolled and tied sheet of paper the stranger was now offering him. "And what is this?" he asked, holding the paper gingerly, as if it might somehow turn on him and bite his fingers.

Another blue cloud of smoke issued from between the stranger's lips, blowing across the coach to accost Symington's nostrils. "Yes, it is dark in here for reading, isn't it? You do read, don't you, Herbert? Very well, I shall attempt to recall the salient points. Let's see. Firstly, you are to immediately cease and desist employing persons under the age of ten in your mills. Secondly, you will oblige me in setting up schools for these children, keeping them occupied while their mothers are at work. You will also feed these children one meal a day—even on Sunday, when henceforth no one will work the Symington mills—with meat served to the children twice weekly."

Symington's ample belly shook as he began to laugh. He laughed so heartily, and with such enjoyment, that soon tears streamed from his eyes. "Are you daft?" he choked out between bouts of mirth. "Why would I do that?"

"I do not believe I had finished, Herbert," the stranger said quietly once Symington's hilarity subsided, which it did when he remembered the cocked pistol. "You will roll back the laborers' shifts from fifteen to fourteen hours and present every worker with a mug of beer at the end of each shift. You will employ a doctor for your workers. You will increase wages by ten percent, beginning tomorrow. I think that's it—for now."

The cocked pistol was no longer of any importance, for this man, this arrogant stranger, was talking of dipping into Herbert Symington's pockets, the depth of which were more important to him than his own soul, let alone his corpulent, corporeal body. "The devil I will! Coddle the bastards? Fill their bellies? *And* cut their hours? How am I supposed to make a profit?"

"Ah, Herbert, but you do make a profit. A tidy profit. Enough profit to afford this coach, and that most lovely new domicile you have been building for yourself this past year. You're to move into it early next month, I believe, and have even gone so far as to invite a few of the *ton* to join you in a party to celebrate your skewed belief that fortune and breeding are synonymous. I'm delighted for you, truly. Although I would not have chosen to use so much gilt in the foyer. Such ostentation smacks of the climbing cit which, alas, you are. You know, Herbert, I believe I detest you more for your mistreatment of your workers because you were one of them not so long ago."

"Who are you to judge me?" Symington bellowed, uncaring that his voice echoed inside the coach. This man had seen his house, been *inside* his house? How? But if he had been, then he should know how far Herbert Symington had come since his long-ago years in the Midlands. "Yes, I was one of them—never so bad as the worst of them, better than the best of them. Smarter. More willing to take what I needed!"

"Yes, Herbert. You did. But you chose to make that steep climb on the broken backs of your fellow workers, screwing down their wages, damning them to damp hovels, disease, and crippling injuries," his accuser broke in neatly. "And now you call them the swinish multitude and keep your heel on their throats so that no one else might have the opportunity for betterment that you had. Do you have any idea of the hatred you are fomenting with your tactics? You, and all those like you, are creating a separate society, a generation of brutalized workers turned savage in their fear, their hunger, their . . . But enough of sermonizing. We are nearly at our destination, Herbert, as your monument to your greed lies just around this corner, I believe. Observe. Soon you will be toasting your toes by your own fireside."

As the stranger used the barrel of the pistol to push back the ornate lace curtain covering the off window of the now-slowing coach, Herbert Symington looked out to see his nearly completed house, his pride, his proof of affluence, engulfed in flames from portico to rooftop.

"No," he whispered, shaking his head, unable to believe the horror he saw. His house. His beautiful house! *"No!"*

"The paper, Herbert," the stranger said, coldly interrupting Symington's anguish. "Don't crush it so or you might not be able to read my demands, for shock has a way of erasing recently learned specifics from one's mind. What I have offered you tonight is in the way of a small exercise in consequences. In addition to the home you still inhabit in Lower Pillington, I believe you have recently acquired a townhouse in London. Not in Mayfair, of course, but amid its increasingly fashionable fringes. And we must not forget those three lovely mills. So many possessions. So much to lose. Tonight's lesson would prove enough for an intelligent man. Are you an intelligent man, Herbert? Or are you willing to risk disobeying me?"

"You bastard!" Symington growled, clenching his hamlike hands into impotent fists as the glow from the fire glinted on the barrel of the pistol. "I know who you are now! I've heard the stories. I know what you've done to other mill owners. So now you're after me, are you? Well, I won't bow down to you like the others have. You'll hang for this, you miserable scoundrel—and I'll be there to watch you dance!"

"That's the spirit, Herbert. Down but not out!" the man said encouragingly as the door to the coach opened and the groom reached in to let down the steps. "You take that thought with you. Take it and hold it close to your heart, along with my list of demands. And, oh yes, thank you for the coach. It will bring a considerable sum, I'm convinced, proceeds of which will doubtless fill many a stomach these next months. Once again, Herbert, good evening to you. I sincerely wish I will not find it necessary we should meet again."

"Oh, I'll see you again, you heartless bastard. See you and more!" Symington tried desperately to make out the facial features of his tormenter in the glow from the fire, but it was useless. He felt himself being pulled unceremoniously from his beloved coach before a well-placed kick from his former employee nearly sent him sprawling onto the gravel drive in front of the inferno that was once his house.

The coach drove away, the sound of delighted laughter floating back to mock him, and Symington angrily yanked off the ribbon holding the list of demands, bent on ripping the paper into a thousand pieces.

As he unrolled the single sheet something long and soft

fluttered to the ground and he picked it up, holding it to the light from the blaze before cursing roundly, flinging the thing from him, and turning to slowly walk back toward Lower Pillington.

Behind him, lying abandoned on the drive, a single peacock feather, a twin to the one now resting beneath O'Dell's straw-filled pillow, winked blue and green in the light from the blazing fire.

Lady Undercliff had been sadly out of sorts for a month, or so she informed anyone who applied to her for the reason behind her perpetual pout.

She was incensed because her thoroughly thoughtless husband had adamantly refused to return from his hunting box in Scotland until the second week of the Season, thus delaying the annual Undercliff Ball which, as everyone was aware, had been held the *first* week of the Season these past sixteen years.

"This is entirely your fault, Charles," she sniped at her husband as the hall clock struck twelve and her spirits dipped another notch. "He isn't coming."

"Who? Prinny?" Lord Undercliff asked, frowning. "Who wants him here anyway, Lizzie? We'd have the servants scraping rotted eggs from the windows for a week if the populace caught sight of him rolling his carcass in here. Ain't the least in good odor with the masses, you know, or you would, if you weren't always worrying about all the wrong things."

"Not his royal highness, Charles," Lady Undercliff gritted out quietly from between clenched teeth, *"St. Clair."*

Lord Undercliff looked at his wife down the length of his considerable nose. "St. Clair? That pranked out mummer? We're standing here like statues waiting for St. Clair? Thunder an' turf, now you've gone and slipped your moorings, Lizzie. What do you need with him? He's amusing enough, I'll grant you that, but I can't say I like what he's done to our young men. Everything poor Beau has taught them about proper dress seems to have flown out the window thanks to St. Clair and his colored satins. Soon he'll have us all powdering up our heads, Lizzie, and if he does that I just might have to call him out myself. Demmed nuisance, that powder, not to mention the tax. Besides, didn't we turn the powder closet into a water closet just a few years past?"

"Charles, I don't care a fig if St. Clair has all you gentlemen shaving your heads and painting your pates purple. No party is a success unless he attends. No hostess worth her salt would dare show her face in public again if Christian St. Clair deigned to ignore her invitation. *Now* do you understand, Charles? And it's all your fault—you and your stupid hunting box. I'll never forgive you for this, Charles. Never!"

"Females!" Lord Undercliff exploded, slapping his thigh in exasperation at his wife's outburst. The single life was much preferable, he had often been heard to remark, if only there existed some way of setting up one's nursery without having to shackle oneself with a bride who was never the sweet young beauty you thought she'd be but only a female like any other, with contrary ways no man could ever fathom, a shrewish voice, and feathers for brains.

He peered past his wife and into the ballroom. "You've got Lord Buxley, Lizzie. He's popular enough. And that Tredway chit as well. Wasn't she the toast of London last Season?"

"Yes, Charles—*last* Season," Lady Undercliff informed her husband tersely. "Lady Ariana Tredway lends the party some cachet, as does Lord Buxley, but my primary coup for this evening seems to be the presence of Gabrielle Laurence, although I cannot for the life of me understand the attraction. *Red* hair, Charles. I mean, really! It's not at all *à la mode.*"

Peering around his wife once more, Lord Undercliff

caught sight of a slim, tallish girl waltzing by in the arms of the Duke of Glynnon. He could not help but remember the chit, for he had bowed so long over her small white hand during his introduction to her in the receiving line that his wife had brought the heel of her evening slipper down hard on his instep to bring him back to attention.

Miss Laurence's lovely face, he saw now, was wreathed in an animated smile as she spoke to the duke, her smooth white complexion framed by a mass of lovely curls the color of fire that blazed almost golden as the movements of the dance brought her beneath one of the brightly lit chandeliers. He grinned, remembering her dark, winglike brows, her shining green eyes and, most especially, the small round mole he'd noticed sitting just to the left of her upper lip. Ah, what a fetching piece!

"Your judgment doesn't seem to be bothering the duke overmuch, Lizzie," Lord Undercliff remarked in an unwise attack of frankness, sparing a moment to catch a glimpse of Miss Laurence's remarkably perfect bosom that was modestly yet enticingly covered by an ivory silk bodice. "As a matter of fact, I believe old Harry is drooling."

"Oh, go back to Scotland, Charles, until you can learn to control yourself," Lady Undercliff spat out, then broke into her first genuine smile in a month. "He's here! Charles, darling, he's here! Stand up straight, and for goodness' sake don't say anything stupid."

Lord Undercliff, once a military man and used to taking orders, obeyed his wife's command instinctively, squaring his shoulders and pulling in his stomach as he turned to greet their tardy guest, a welcoming smile pasted on his lordship's face.

"Lady Undercliff! Look at you! *Voyons!* This is too much! Your beauty never ceases to astound me! I vow I cannot bear it!" Lord Christian St. Clair exclaimed a moment later, having successfully navigated the long, curving marble staircase to halt in front of the woman and execute an exquisitely elegant leg while gifting her hand with a fleeting touch of his lips.

Lord Undercliff's own lips curled in distaste as he watched this ridiculous display, taking in the baron's outrageous costume of robin's egg blue satin swallowtail coat and knee breeches, the elaborate lace-edged cuffs of his shirt, the foaming jabot at his tanned throat. The man was a menace, that's what he was, bringing back into fashion a fashion that hadn't been *fashionable* in years. And the young males of Society were following him like stunned sheep, more and more of them each day sauntering down Bond Street in clocked stockings, huge buckles on their shoes, and wearing enough lace to curtain a cathedral.

"I throw myself at your feet, beseeching mercy. A thousand pardons for my unforgivable tardiness, dear lady, please, I beg you," Lord St. Clair pleaded, rising to his full six-foot-odd-three of sartorial splendor to gaze adoringly into Lady Undercliff's rapidly widening eyes. "I had been dressed and ready beforetimes, eager to mount these heavenly stairs to your presence, but then my man observantly pointed out that the lace on my handkerchief"—he brandished an oversize, ornately lace handkerchief as proof— "did not in the slightest complement that of my jabot. Imagine my dismay! There was nothing else for it but that I strip to the buff and begin again." He sighed eloquently, looking to Lord Undercliff as if for understanding.

He didn't receive any. "Could have just changed handkerchiefs, St. Clair," his lordship countered, he believed, reasonably. "Or left off altogether trailing one around with you everywhere like some paper-skulled die-away miss with a perpetual fit of the vapors."

St. Clair's broad shoulders shook slightly as he gave a small gulp of laughter that soon grew to an appreciative, if somewhat high-pitched, giggle. *"Sans doute.* Ah, Undercliff, what I would not give to find life so simple. But I remember now. My affections lay more deeply with the handkerchief than the remainder of my costume. Ah, well, no two hours spent in dressing is ever wasted."

"Only two hours—for evening clothes?" Lord Undercliff spluttered, giving the baron's rig-out another look, this time appreciating the cut of the coat, which was not quite that of the past century, but more modern, with less buckram padding, flattering St. Clair's slim frame that boasted surprisingly wide shoulders and a trim waist. And the man's long, straight legs were nearly obscene in their beauty, the thighs muscular, the calves obviously not aided by the careful stuffing of sawdust to make up for any lack in that area.

"Used to take Brummell a whole morning just to do up his cravat," his lordship continued consideringly. "Just pin that lace thing-o-ma-bob around your neck and be done with it, don't you? And the ladies seem to like it. Maybe you have something here, St. Clair. Thought satins would take longer, but if they don't—well, mayhap I'll give them a try m'self. Rather weary of Brummell's midnight blue and black, you know."

"You gratify me no end, my lord," Baron St. Clair said, preening, his bright smile showing him to be in his element. He turned back to Lady Undercliff and offered her his arm, telling her without words that it was no longer necessary for her to stand at the top of the stairs now that the premier guest had arrived.

And if the Prince Regent did dare venture out of Carleton House under cover of darkness to attend, he could just find his own way into the ballroom.

With her ladyship at his side, the baron entered the ballroom, stopping just inside the archway to gift the other occupants of the room with a long, appreciative look at the magnificence, the splendor, that was Baron Christian St. Clair before setting off to bedevil Miss Gabrielle Laurence, as was his private delight and deepest frustration.

For the beautiful, fiery Miss Laurence, who had been brought into favor by St. Clair, frankly detested him and his carefully orchestrated foppish ways.

If only he could tell her the truth, tell her that he was the Peacock, the most daring, talked about, and admired mystery of London Society . . . But would it be beneath his high ideals to gain her admiration in such a way? Moreover, would it be fair to let her in on his secret identity, thus exposing her to danger?

Look for

The Seduction of the Peacock

Wherever Paperback Books Are Sold
Winter 1995